A CASTLE IN ITALY

Other books by Caroline Harvey

A Legacy of Love
A Second Legacy

JOANNA TROLLOPE
—— WRITING AS ——
CAROLINE HARVEY
A CASTLE IN ITALY

BCA

LONDON NEW YORK SYDNEY TORONTO

This edition published 1993 by
BCA
by arrangement with Doubleday
a division of Transworld Publishers Ltd

CN 2857

Printed in England by Clays Ltd, St Ives plc

To Di

PART ONE

Chapter One

London – 1905

The room wasn't quite dark. Maudie hadn't pulled the blind down properly, not right down to the windowsill, where Isobel liked it to be, safely anchored with its cord wound round a little brass bracket screwed to the window frame. From where Isobel lay in her narrow bed, in her tucked and frilled white nightgown with her hair tightly plaited for the night – too tightly; another sign, like the carelessly drawn blind, that Maudie was upset – she could see a line of light at the bottom of the blind, the whitish-green light from the gas lamp outside in the street. It was a horrible light, Isobel thought. It was equally horrible to have had Maudie banging about her bedroom, snapping at her because she was upset, commanding her to go to sleep as if it would be a wicked and deliberate defiance not to be able to. It was also horrible – the most horrible really – to hear the carriage wheels out in the street go by with a muffled rumble, because they had put straw down on the cobbles. Isobel opened her eyes and mouth as wide as caves to try and stop the tears starting again. They only put straw down outside a house if someone was ill inside it, really ill. Last year it had been for old Mr Fortescue, two doors down, and Isobel, out for her regular afternoon walks with Maudie, had crept past the house, tiptoeing on the straw, full of a mixture of fear and reverence. Now the straw was outside her house, and her blind wasn't pulled down to shut out the night, and Maudie's eyes were red. The straw meant the

9

thing that Isobel dreaded more than anything else in the world. It meant that Mother was ill, ill enough to die.

Part of Isobel was used to Mother being ill. After all, her whole life, all those odd and solitary ten years of her life, had been dominated by Mother being ill. When Mother was ill she wept a good deal, and had headaches and lay on the sofa in her bedroom, and sometimes – Isobel did not like remembering these sometimes – she stood on the balcony outside her bedroom, overlooking the small, sooty garden, in just her nightclothes in the winter wind and screamed that she wished she could die. After one of these scenes, Grandpapa and Grandmamma Morpeth would be summoned by Doctor Waters from their great, heavy house in Lancashire, and Mother would be bundled up in cashmere shawls and she and Isobel would be sent off to Montreux in Switzerland, to the Hotel Monney, which Grandmamma Morpeth believed to be a place which healed all ills of mind and body. Maudie went with them, and so did Edith, who was Mother's lady's maid, and sometimes, if these expeditions were not in the summer, a French mademoiselle went too to give Isobel lessons. Another thing that always accompanied them, in Edith's pocket, was a letter from Grandpapa Morpeth to the manager of the Hotel Monney, to the effect that Mrs Lindsay should be given fine rooms, with a view of Lake Geneva, but that these rooms should on no account open on to a balcony.

Isobel quite liked these trips to Montreux. If they went in winter, which they usually did because the balcony episodes tended to happen on the coldest nights of the year, there would be a little Russian boy staying at the Hotel Monney, with his mother. He was called Piotr, and he lived in St Petersburg where his father was an extremely important soldier, and his mother brought him to Switzerland for his health every year, from October to March. He made friends with Isobel at once, she didn't have to do a thing about it, she just had to accept him. She was pleased to accept him because he was laughing and mischievous and charming and such people were not usually attracted to Isobel, who was plain and sensible. People were always saying so.

'So odd,' her mother's friends would say, supposing her unable to hear them merely because she was a child, 'when Ida's so lovely. But perhaps she'll blossom. She has pretty teeth, after all, and she is so very sensible.'

Piotr didn't know what sensible meant, in any language. He spoke French and English and Russian and liked singing and going

10

too fast in sledges across the new-fallen snow, and jokes. Isobel loved him, with a kind of excited passion. Isobel's mother loved him too. She said he was better than any medicine. Some days, when Piotr's own mother, who was very devout, was occupied in celebrating some obscure saint's day, Ida would take Isobel and Piotr down the lakeside to the Castle of Chillon, and read to them Lord Byron's poem about the poor prisoner who once lived in the dungeons there, chained to the wall for twenty years. They would peer into the dungeons afterwards and Piotr would squeal. Then he would do a handstand and sing several verses of a Russian song his father's coachman had taught him about a flea and a peasant girl, which he wasn't supposed to sing because some of the words were improper. Ida would laugh and laugh when he did this, and kiss him and say he was impossible. She never said that to Isobel, laughing and loving, but then Isobel was never impossible.

'If you don't find charm in your cradle,' Maudie had once said to her, braiding her hair, 'you'll never find it, and that's all there is to it.'

They hadn't been to Montreux now for nearly a year. That should have been a good sign, of course, a sign that Mother hadn't recently rushed on to her balcony sobbing for death in the January cold, but in fact the reason had been more serious. Mother had begun to be ill in a different way, a way that meant more staying in bed and less weeping, more visits from Doctor Waters, more coughing and a creeping weakness that filled Isobel with something close to panic. It was like, she thought, watching a drawing being very slowly rubbed out, a pencil drawing on white paper quietly vanishing under silent, soft strokes from an eraser. Grandmamma Morpeth wanted Ida to go back to Montreux at once or, if the journey would be too much, to come to Lancashire and bracing northern air. Doctor Waters, thinking of the smoking mills nearby that had made Grandpapa Morpeth's fortune, and thinking also that not even Swiss mountain air could affect Mrs Lindsay's lungs now, gently and firmly resisted all such suggestions.

Then Grandmamma Morpeth tried something different. She said a sickroom was no place for a child, and that Isobel must go to school, away to school. She said that she and Grandpapa would pay the fees and lodging costs for Isobel to go to the Sacred Heart Convent in Paris. She said Isobel would learn strict deportment from the nuns there. Isobel, accustomed to compliance, was struck dumb with terror at this suggestion and spent several sleepless nights promising God ludicrous sacrifices if only He would guard her against the nuns of the Sacred Heart. He complied.

Ida said, in her gently fading voice, 'You shan't go because I couldn't spare you, you see.'

It was perhaps the most loving thing Ida had ever said to Isobel, and Isobel treasured it. 'She can't spare me,' she said proudly to her reflection in the looking glass in her wardrobe door. 'She can't do without me. She *needs* me.' She saw herself as a kind of Angel of Mercy at her mother's bedside, like the engraving on the schoolroom wall of Florence Nightingale moving among the wounded soldiers at Scutari, carrying a Turkish lamp, a symbol of beautiful comfort. But Ida didn't want Isobel to be an Angel of Mercy, she wanted her to be pretty and delightful and to distract Ida from her terrors. It is one thing, after all, to wish for death; it is quite another to come to believe that your wish will shortly be granted. Isobel, standing gravely by her mother's bed, waiting to be asked to be useful, or sitting by the fire in her mother's bedroom obediently reading aloud from a newspaper in which Ida had immediately lost interest, could not have been further from a delightful distraction.

'Oh,' Ida cried one day in exasperation, 'I wish at least you could sing! Why can't you sing, why aren't you musical?'

'I don't know,' Isobel said. She bowed her head in real regret at her own inadequacy.

'Oh,' shrieked Ida, flouncing about in her bed in billows of lace and lawn, 'what is the use of you? Where have you come from? At least Papa could *sing!*'

The room fell as suddenly silent as if Ida and Isobel had been turned to stone, as if they had been at the court of the Sleeping Beauty the second she fatally pricked her finger. Ida had said it, Ida had said the forbidden word, the word she had impressed upon Isobel with quite terrifying vehemence must never be uttered again in her hearing, the word that meant all the wickedness and injury and betrayal and heartbreak in the entire world. Ida had said 'Papa'.

Isobel felt sweat prickling out all over her, under the layers of white cotton and cream flannel and dark blue wool that protected her from the outside world. She dared not look up, she certainly dared not speak. She gazed downwards at the point where her black wool-clad legs disappeared into her brown kid boots, laced up round little bright black studs. Her Sunday boots, she thought irrelevantly, were pale kid, with black glacé inserts, and had nine buttons up the sides, made of jet. Grandpapa Morpeth had bought the buttons in Whitby, which he said had a ruined abbey where a nun called Hilda . . .

'Please leave me,' Ida said. Her voice shook.

Isobel looked up, very slowly. Ida had turned to the wall, her head almost buried in the great mound of pillows she required, her body obscured by heaped quilts and the flounces of her negligée.

'Please—' Ida said again. She was crying. 'Send Edith—'

'Yes, Mother.'

'Quickly!'

'Yes, Mother.'

Ida began to cough. Isobel shot from the room and found Edith, pushing the nose of a goffering iron into yet more frills, more ruffles, more miles and miles of white lawn and linen and muslin.

'Mother's coughing!'

Edith put the iron down with a clatter.

'What brought this on? What did you do?'

'I said—' Isobel stopped, clutched at by love and honesty. 'She said – by mistake – she said . . .'

'Go upstairs,' Edith said. 'Go up to the schoolroom. I'll see to her.'

'I couldn't sing, you see, I—'

'Sing?' Edith said. 'Whyever should you sing? Nobody's ever sung here since—'

'No!' shrieked Isobel and put her hands over her ears. She ran out of the room, along the landing with its moss green carpet patterned with tiny fleurs-de-lys in golden yellow and clattered up the bare stairs to the schoolroom. 'No!' Isobel gasped, falling through the door into the empty room. 'No! Not that, I didn't hear it, I didn't say it, I didn't, I didn't!'

The room was terribly cold. Miss Pargeter, who came for four discouraging hours on weekday mornings, to give Isobel her lessons and then to eat with her a meagre lunch of a small chop and a modest helping of semolina pudding, had a throat infection and had been instructed by Doctor Waters to stay away from the house until she was quite recovered. If Miss Pargeter did not come, the schoolroom fire was not lit. Isobel, it was thought, being young and strong, could perfectly well memorize her set lists of French vocabulary and European capital cities without a fire. She took her hands away from her ears and stopped shouting as if brought to her senses by the cold bleakness of the room. Her books lay on the table in neat formation. Over the back of an upright chair hung the mustard-coloured shawl with bugle bead trimming in which

13

Miss Pargeter wrapped herself after an hour in this room, even with the fire. Miss Pargeter was thin and shabby. She refused to teach Isobel literature because she said it would inflame her imagination. Miss Pargeter thought the imagination was to be feared, like a mortal illness.

Isobel went round the edge of the schoolroom, avoiding Miss Pargeter's shawl. There was no comfort in this room, none of the cushioning and curtaining that made the lower rooms, the rooms her mother used, so comfortable. The schoolroom had brown oilcloth on the floor, and brown holland blinds, and brown unpadded furniture, and the walls were cream, but grimy from the London air, and were hung with black and white prints of General Gordon and Florence Nightingale and a dreadful small girl with fat curls giving pennies to some ragged children with bare feet, entitled 'Little Lady Bountiful'. Isobel hesitated in front of 'Little Lady Bountiful'. Grandmamma Morpeth had given her the picture when she was five, with a homily about the obligations of the rich towards the poor which Isobel had not understood. She disliked the picture, but more for the girl's glaring complacency than for its dubious moral message. Slowly, and with a sense of sin, Isobel reached up, unhooked the engraving from the wall, and turned it over.

There was an envelope on the back, pasted to the picture on three sides with strips of brown paper. It was not very evenly pasted, but it was the best that Isobel, who was clumsy as well as plain and sensible, could do. She laid the picture upside down on the cold brown oilcloth on the floor, and slid two fingers inside the open edge of the envelope, drawing out a newspaper cutting. She smoothed the cutting out on the floor with shaking fingers. It was so wicked to look at the cutting, it was so wicked and cruel even to own it. But something in Isobel couldn't help herself, something in her needed to possess the cutting even at the risk of the eternal damnation of her soul.

She looked down at the printing between her fingers. There was a photograph above the printing, and below a heading which read 'The Season's Scrapbook'. The photograph showed a man's face, rather blurred, with smooth dark hair and a finely kept moustache which curled up at the edges. The man was smiling out of the photograph, and his teeth were perfect. Beside him, and smiling at him rather than out at Isobel, was a lady. She wore a hat tilted forward over a curled fringe, adorned with several feathers sticking up straight, like the exclamation marks that Isobel always thought

14

looked more excited in French than in English. The lady wore pearl earrings and although her teeth were far from perfect, her face looked quite lit up, even in a newspaper photograph, as if she had been caught right in the middle of laughing. Underneath the photograph it said, 'Mr Edward Lindsay and his companion, Mrs Muriel Bond. Will His Majesty condone a scandal?'

Isobel had looked up both 'condone' and 'scandal' in the dictionary. It had told her that 'condone' meant 'forgive' and that a scandal was a disgraceful fact, thing or person. Isobel wasn't a fool, however inexperienced. It was perfectly plain to her that Mrs Muriel Bond was all three aspects of a scandal combined into one, yet she couldn't help looking at her. She had thought of blacking her out of the photograph, but she knew she would always be there, even under the blacking, smiling away at Mr Edward Lindsay in that happy, owning, unworried kind of way. Mr Edward Lindsay. Papa.

'Please,' Isobel had sometimes cried to the photograph in the past, 'please, oh *please*—' She could hardly remember the flesh, so long ago had he gone. One of the reasons, Maudie told her, that it had never been suggested that she go to school in England, was the trouble it would have been to explain about Papa. And the disgrace. Maudie said it was very disgraceful to have an absent father who wasn't dead; she made it sound as if it was almost Isobel's fault. Isobel didn't plead to the cutting on this occasion, she simply folded it up again and returned it to its hiding place. It was so odd, she thought, hooking the picture back on to the wall, that doing something as sinful as looking at Papa should somehow make her feel better, not worse. Or perhaps it wasn't odd at all, it just bore out what Grandmamma Morpeth always said about Satan, that he had the softest voice and said the sweetest things in order to trap you into sinning.

Is it, Isobel wondered now, lying with damp cheeks in her not wholly darkened room, because I have sinned that Mother is dying? If I had never cut that piece of newspaper out, if I had never even picked up the newspaper, even though Mother asked me to, and I saw the picture and cut it out so that she shouldn't see it, if I had thrown it away, would she now be well? And if this is a punishment, how will I know, and how will I know when I've got to the end of it and I don't need to be punished any more? Is everything you *want* to do a sin?

A sound caught her ear. Isobel sat up in bed, tense, gripping the sheet. A carriage had come along the street a little faster than was

15

customary, and seemed to have stopped. Isobel thought she could hear voices. She slid out of bed, and pattered to the window, peering out through the narrow space below the blind. Down in the street, lit by the garish glare of the lamps, was the unmistakable figure of Doctor Waters, being ushered into the house by Samuels. A terrible trembling seized Isobel. She sank down on the floor, pressing her face to the wall below the window, dragging her hands down into clenched fists.

'Oh please,' Isobel cried out in anguish to whoever might be listening, 'Oh please, oh please—'

Chapter Two

'He's waiting,' Maudie said.

She stood just inside the doorway of Isobel's bedroom, her hands folded against her apron, her features pinched with disapproval. 'You'll do.'

Isobel looked back at her. She wanted to say she couldn't go through with it, but she knew it would be useless. Maudie might be on her side, but Maudie knew what was right and proper and she also knew that when the inevitable happened, you – or, in this case, Isobel – had to bow to it.

'Turn around,' Maudie commanded.

Slowly, reluctantly, Isobel turned. The smock-like folds of her new black crape mourning dress hardly moved, so heavy were they. Isobel felt bowed down by the dress, crushed by the sombre weight of it, sodden with despair. Her hair, brushed by Maudie until her scalp tingled, was caught up under a huge, despondent, flat black bow. She hadn't been near the looking-glass for fear of what she might see.

Maudie sighed. 'You'll do,' she said again. 'Keep your head up.'

'It won't stay up,' Isobel said truthfully.

'Will power,' Maudie said. 'Will power. If want won't get you through, will power has to. Down you go.'

Isobel swallowed. She looked up at Maudie with eyes as beseeching as those of a spaniel.

'Please—'

'Down you go,' Maudie said inexorably.

She stood aside in the doorway, to let Isobel pass. There was nothing for it. Putting one newly black-shod foot in front of the other like a mechanical doll, Isobel passed out of her bedroom and along the echoing landing, and down the schoolroom stairs, to the fleurs-de-lys carpet of the first floor. Ida's bedroom door was shut. It had been shut for ten days now even though there was nothing to keep inside it any more except the agonizingly reminiscent smell of Ida's tuberose. Isobel did not look at the door. She was training herself not to because if she didn't acknowledge the door's existence, then she didn't also have to acknowledge that there had ever been anything behind it. Neither the door nor Ida's room had ever been, so there. To Isobel's mind this was, so far, the only way of coping with the terrible possibilities of where Ida might now have gone. Grandmamma Morpeth talked a lot about Heaven and Sweet Jesus, but Isobel, her conscience burdened with guilt and grief, could only think of Hell.

At the top of the main stairs, the fleurs-de-lys carpet stopped and gave way to a much grander carpet of deep ruby red, that ran down under glittering brass stair rods, to the hall. Isobel paused with her foot on the top step. Below her, the hall looked as it always did, the round table for calling cards shining above the marble squares of the floor, the solemn carved chairs with their velvet cushioned seats, the ponderously ticking clock with a brass face, the little statue of a blackamoor boy holding up a lamp, the maiden-hair ferns in their matching pots. It frightened Isobel that nothing should have changed, when everything had. She held the polished mahogany handrail tightly. Fifteen steps down, as there had always been, fifteen stairs and then the cold black and white floor and then . . .

Samuels emerged from the door at the back of the hall and looked up, seeing Isobel. His face didn't change, but then it never did. He had one expression only, and he wore it all the time. He came to the bottom of the stairs and merely waited, looking upwards, but his presence was authoritative. Isobel started down the stairs, step after step, holding the handrail as if she were a small, unsteady child, and gazing steadily at the blackamoor boy.

When she reached the bottom, Samuels gave the smallest of nods and preceded her across the hall to the closed door opposite. Isobel, almost in a trance, followed him. Samuels opened the door, and stood against it, like a sentinel.

'Miss Isobel, sir,' Samuels said.

'Hello,' someone said, 'hello, my dear. Thank you, Samuels.'

Isobel stood just inside the door, staring at nothing.

18

'Isobel,' her father said. His voice was gentle. 'Isobel, my poor child, I am so very, very sorry.'

Isobel turned her head a fraction of an inch. He was standing in front of the fire. He wore black, too, as she did. He was not as tall as she had expected him to be.

'I would so like to comfort you,' Edward Lindsay said, 'but I do not expect you will let me.'

Isobel said nothing. She was too preoccupied with two violent longings that had suddenly arisen within her; one was to rush upstairs to the schoolroom and tear the newspaper cutting from its hiding place and rip it into shreds, and the other was to hurl herself into his arms and sob until she could sob no more.

'Isobel?'

She roused herself. 'No, thank you,' she said, politely.

He gave an odd little barking laugh, as if he were trying to cover up impatience with humour.

'I'm afraid you have been taught to regard me as an ogre.'

'Yes,' Isobel said, truthfully, 'but—' She stopped.

'But what?'

Isobel couldn't say that the teaching hadn't been entirely successful. To say that would have been disloyal to Mother. She put her hands together in front of the bulky pleats of crape, and twisted her fingers round and round.

'I will take courage from that "but",' Edward said, watching her fingers. 'Will you come and sit by the fire?'

Isobel moved, stiff and obedient, and sat on the edge of a chair with golden arms and legs, upholstered in dark green damask.

'Tell me what you do here,' Edward said. 'Tell me about your day.'

He sat down opposite Isobel, leaning back, watching her.

'Maudie wakes me at seven,' Isobel said, 'and I wash and she helps me to dress and I have breakfast in the schoolroom and then I go down—' she stopped again and after a pause, went on a little unsteadily, 'I *went* down to Mother's room and stayed there until Miss Pargeter came – I mean comes – and we have lessons and then we have luncheon in the schoolroom and then Miss Pargeter goes home and Maudie and I go for a walk for an hour and then we come back and if there are – were – are – visitors, I go to the schoolroom, and if there aren't – weren't, then sometimes I can – could – oh!' cried Isobel, breaking down despite all her good intentions, 'I did things for Mother then, I did all the things she

19

wanted, but it wasn't enough, was it, I didn't do enough, or else she wouldn't, would she, she wouldn't—'

'Sh,' said Edward, leaning forward, 'sh. You were a wonderful daughter, a most loving daughter.' He took a huge white handkerchief out of his pocket and gave it to her. 'Isobel,' he said, 'is that the kind of day you would like to go on having?'

Isobel stared at him over the folds of the handkerchief. She was amazed. He seemed to have asked her, actually *asked* her, what she would like.

She said, in a whisper, 'But won't it – go on?'

'What, Maudie and Miss Pargeter and meals in the schoolroom? Well, it can, if you would like it to. Your mother has left plenty of money for that.'

'If I don't live here,' Isobel said, still in a whisper, still struggling to grasp the possibility of choice, 'where would I live?'

Edward looked away, into the fire. In profile, Isobel saw that his face was not so handsome but softer and weaker.

'I'm afraid you can't live with me.' After a pause he added, in a slightly more forced voice, 'Much as I would like it.'

'You!' Isobel squeaked.

'It was your mother's express wish that you should not live with me after her death. You see, I shall very likely be marrying again.'

Isobel blurted out, 'Mrs Muriel Bond?'

It was Edward's turn to be amazed. He turned rapidly from the fire, gaping. 'How—?'

'I saw it,' Isobel said, 'I saw you in a newspaper.'

'Did your mother—?'

'No,' Isobel said, 'I cut it out and hid it.'

A smile broke out across Edward's face and he held a hand out to Isobel.

'My dear—'

'No,' said Isobel, shrinking from the hand, 'I wanted to black her out.'

Edward withdrew his hand.

'I may well be marrying again,' he repeated a little more loudly, as if to drown what Isobel was saying.

Mrs Bond would have welcomed Isobel. Mrs Bond wanted children herself and had a cheerful, accommodating personality but Ida had set her face against even the notion of Isobel having a stepmother with a ferocity that Edward wasn't even going to think about confronting. He looked at Isobel. Poor Isobel. Poor Ida. He had loved Ida once, he knew he had. That was when her possessiveness had charmed him and flattered him, and had not exhausted and bored him as it was later to do. After three years with Ida, Edward could not breathe. He was stifled by her and repelled by her hysteria. He looked again at Isobel. At least she showed not the smallest symptom of hysteria.

'Grandmamma and Grandpapa Morpeth very much wish you to go and live with them,' Edward said. He waited, watching Isobel's face. Wishes were not, actually, what had been expressed in a most violent recent interview with his father-in-law, but demands and insistences. Arthur Morpeth had denounced Edward to his face as a reprobate and a blackguard and had told him he was unfit to have charge of any child, particularly a girl child. In his heart of hearts, Edward rather thought he might not be cut out for steady fatherhood, but he was not without sympathy and affection for Isobel, and he also believed that in its way, the great, heavy house in Lancashire steeped in Morpeth money and Morpeth morality would be more injurious to Isobel than he could ever be, even at his most feckless.

'You cannot claim Isobel,' Edward had said to Grandpapa Morpeth. 'The only wish we shall all abide by, as if it were carved in stone, is Ida's wish that Isobel does not live with me. Beyond that, it is for Isobel to choose. She may choose to have a proper governess companion and live on her own. She may choose to come to you. But choose she must.'

'If she doesn't come to us,' Arthur Morpeth had bellowed, 'she'll never see a penny of my fortune! And if she's taken after you in that respect, that'll change her mind if nothing else does!'

Edward had been very angry. It could not possibly be denied that Ida's money had once been for him an added burnish on Ida's charms and Ida's adoring love. The Morpeth fortune, when its extent was made known to Edward by his friends, was going to repair the romantic but decaying glories of Lindsay Castle, retrieve the fleeing tenants, re-stock the river, help Edward towards parliament, appease those clamorous holders of signed bills and notes of promise that plagued him weekly, provide enough for considerable future pleasures and comforts and even, perhaps, for those little speculations he could never resist. When it came to it, of course, Arthur Morpeth had tied up a substantial sum for the sole use of his daughter and any children she might bear, but there was still enough to encourage Edward for a year or two, the solid thousands that both sides knew to be, though it was never articulated, the decent price for marrying out of trade and into the gentry. The non-utterance of this bargain was of extreme importance and Edward's anger had flared up, during this latest – and he hoped last – interview with his father-in-law, because Arthur had broken the rules of propriety. Edward had stormed out. He had forgotten his manners entirely and had flung out of the room swearing he would rather see Isobel starve than eat one crust at the Morpeth table.

He had calmed down a little since, but he still could not bring himself to believe that the best place for Isobel was Lancashire. Watching her, he struggled to be fair.

'You know the house, of course—'

Isobel nodded. It was the darkest house she had ever been in, the thick, bobble-edged curtains never more than half drawn back, tables muffled in plush cloths, beds and chairs shrouded in dust covers, oil lamps always turned down to nothing more than a faint glow.

'And you know and love your grandparents.'

Isobel hesitated. She knew them, certainly, but could love struggle its way out through so much apprehension? Grandpapa had always wished that she were a boy. Grandmamma had always wished that she were good.

'Would Maudie come?'

'If you wished her to, of course she would be asked.'

'Maudie likes London, though,' Isobel said.

'Then—'

'I don't want to stay here with – without – I can't . . .'

'No,' Edward said gently.

'And I don't—' Isobel began, and then stopped, alarmed by the wickedness of actually saying out loud that she did not want to go to Lancashire.

'No,' Edward said, understanding.

A new fear began to rise in Isobel. If she didn't stay in London, and she didn't go to Lancashire, then perhaps the idea of the nuns at the Sacred Heart Convent would be raised again . . .

'May I make a suggestion?' Edward said.

Isobel nodded.

'There are your aunts, you see.'

Isobel said, sadly but firmly, 'I have no aunts.'

'Yes, my dear, you do. You have two aunts. You have two aunts who are my sisters, my older sisters.'

'Mother never—'

'No. I don't expect she did. I don't think your mother and my sisters were very good at making friends with one another.'

22

'Ida Morpeth!' Edward's sister Sybil had shrieked, twelve years before. 'Ida Morpeth! You must be mad! She's ten years older than you and desperate for a husband. Nobody's finances can be so bad that marrying Ida Morpeth is the answer!'

Isobel began to twist her fingers again.

'I – I don't know my aunts.'

'No,' Edward said, 'but they know about you. I wrote to them, when your mother first fell seriously ill, and told them about you. They are both widows. Aunt Jean married a scholar and a traveller who died during an adventure in Asia Minor. Aunt Sybil married a painter, who had a weak heart when she married him, and who died two years after their wedding. So they decided to live together. They have lived together for fifteen years.'

'Oh,' said Isobel.

'They would like you to live with them,' Edward said, 'if that is what you would like.'

'Would they?' Isobel said doubtfully.

'Yes. They would. They said so.'

'What a lark! Parcel her up and send her out at once,' was what Sybil had actually said. Jean had simply sent a note: 'The poor child will be welcome.'

'Do they have a big house?' Isobel said.

'I believe so. Would you like that?'

'Not especially,' Isobel said. 'I would like – I would like – a real house.'

'Real?'

'Yes,' Isobel said. She was worried at the prospect of her aunts being widows. The widows who had come to see Mother had worn black or mauve and had talked about their dead husbands in such a way as to make Isobel feel that they had no proper lives now, that they were only half alive. They used to complain how quiet, how unnaturally quiet, their houses were. Isobel didn't want to live in a quiet black and mauve house full of regretful shadows.

'Perhaps it will help you to make up your mind if I tell you that Aunt Jean and Aunt Sybil live in Italy.'

'Italy!' Isobel was astonished.

'Yes. You know where Italy is, surely.'

Isobel hesitated. She knew *what* Italy was, a long thin country shaped like a boot with Rome for its capital, and a strange sounding place somewhere else in it, called Venice, where the streets were full of water.

'It's next to Switzerland, Isobel. South of Montreux, where you used to go. There are long sunny summers in Italy, sunny enough for grapes to grow there out of doors, and peaches and lemons.'

'I know,' Isobel said severely, 'Miss Pargeter told me.'

'The Aunts live near Florence, among the hills—'

'So,' Isobel said suddenly, interrupting, 'Italy is abroad? Like Switzerland?'

'Of course—'

Isobel clasped her hands together. Something had burst into her mind, something happy and laughing, something associated with abroad, an image, as clear as if he were before her, of Piotr standing on his head and singing his silly song to stop them being too sad about the poor prisoner in the Castle of Chillon.

'I think,' said Isobel, smiling shyly at her father, 'that I should like to go to Italy. If I may.'

Chapter Three

Miss Pargeter began to be seasick even before the boat train left Victoria Station. It had been decided that Miss Pargeter should accompany Isobel to Florence, where a manservant from the aunts' villa would meet them at the station, and relieve Miss Pargeter of her charge. Isobel was ashamed of Miss Pargeter as a travelling companion, and ashamed of being ashamed. It wasn't Miss Pargeter's appearance that shamed her, not even the mustard shawl, but it was her manners. Miss Pargeter spoke in loud, rude, Anglicized French to the railway porters and the restaurant-car attendants, and complained ceaselessly about continental germs. Isobel, used to crossing Europe in Ida's practised, cosseted company, prayed fervently that not even the merest ticket office clerk should suppose that she and Miss Pargeter were in any way related.

Miss Pargeter was terrified not only of germs and seasickness, but also of the money with which she had been entrusted. Grandpapa Morpeth had bought first class tickets for them, all the way to Florence, and had arranged for them to stay in solid, respectable hotels in Marseilles and Leghorn. He then gave Miss Pargeter money for emergencies. Being responsible for this money gave Miss Pargeter headaches and sleepless nights, and because of it, she snapped at Isobel. It did not cross her mind that Isobel, wakeful in her first class berth through the train compartment's partition wall, was equally burdened by worries. The moment she had agreed to go to Italy, the worries had begun. She was horrified at what she had done, but she was Isobel, good, obedient Isobel, and it would never have crossed her mind to take her decision back. When you had given your word, she knew, you kept it, and this word must especially be kept to because it had been pledged after she had been given the luxury of choice. Isobel still marvelled at that; that her father had allowed her to choose.

He had, of course, gone away soon after that. She allowed him to kiss her – not without some qualms of conscience – and even now she could remember the dry brush of his moustache against her cheek and an odd mixed smell of citrus and tobacco. He wrote to her once, a jaunty letter about nothing, in which he called her his dearest daughter and told her that if she didn't like Italy, she could try Timbuctoo next. He said he was enclosing photographs of the aunts, but he must have forgotten, because they weren't in the envelope, and they didn't come by any subsequent post. He wrote, 'Aunt Jean has a heart of gold, and Aunt Sybil is a tease.'

Whatever they had, or were, Isobel thought, lying in her rocking bed, they were still strangers, utter strangers. And in choosing to go and live with them, she had made Grandmamma and Grandpapa Morpeth very angry, and badly upset Miss Pargeter and Maudie and Edith and Samuels who now had to look for new situations, and caused Doctor Waters to say, in her hearing, that it had been madness to ask her to choose since no child of ten could possibly be expected to know her own mind. Edward had asked that the house should not begin to be dismantled until Isobel had gone, but Grandmamma had said that as Isobel was turning her back upon her loving family, then everything that had belonged to beloved, departed Ida should go at once to Lancashire where it would be cherished as ungrateful Isobel might have been, had she so chosen. So Isobel watched, dumb with misery, while men in white aprons packed away all the things that she had known all her life, all the pictures and ornaments and pieces of furniture, the rugs and clocks and lamps. When she left, on an April morning, even the blackamoor boy had been parcelled up in sacking, and stood forlornly among the packing cases in the hall with only his lamp showing. The only comfort – the *only* comfort – Isobel could derive was from knowing that the night before, she had crept out of bed and gone into the schoolroom and unhooked 'Little Lady Bountiful' from the wall, and had then stood on her, rocking slightly, until her glass had cracked.

At the last moment, Isobel would have sold her soul to have changed her mind. There stood Maudie and Edith, sobbing – but more out of reproach, Isobel felt, than anything else – and Samuels with his single expression turned to granite, and the poor house full of boxes and empty spaces, and worst of all, the rooms where Mother had lived and where her memory might, for all Isobel knew, go on living, and refuse to reappear in Italy. It was raining too, cold, thin spring rain, and the streets were muddy and dark, and Victoria Station was huge and echoing and there was a fuss finding their seats, and then Miss Pargeter began to say she felt unwell.

She really was unwell while they crossed the Channel, and Isobel tried to feel sorry for her but couldn't because she was so disagreeable and made Isobel feel that the journey, and the consequent seasickness, were all Isobel's fault. In the train in France, a high, hissing train quite unlike the English ones, Miss Pargeter said she simply could not eat a morsel, so Isobel, with a calm daring that amazed her, went to the dining car alone, and ate slices of peculiar French meat and a helping of interesting French potatoes and a very delicious French pudding that tasted mildly of toffee. The waiters in the restaurant car treated her as if she were grown up. She declined wine and coffee and cognac, spent a long time staring fixedly at some women who were smoking cigarettes, and went back to her compartment feeling very grown-up. The moment the door had closed upon her, however, the grown-up-ness fell from her like a cloak, and she lay down on her berth and cried and cried for Ida and England and home.

It rained most of the way down through France. When they got to Marseilles, the sun came out and stayed out while they picked their way along the quayside to find the Italian boat on which Grandpapa Morpeth had booked them a cabin. Miss Pargeter was a shade more cheerful, having discovered the medical efficacy of adding brandy to her tea. As she always drank a lot of tea, this ensured, Isobel noticed, better spirits altogether, except first thing in the morning when Miss Pargeter was as sour as a lemon. The Italian boat was a steamer, with a short, thick, dirty funnel out of which coal smoke poured in a dense black stream. The crew spoke no English and Isobel spoke hardly any Italian, but they were kind to Isobel, helping her up and down companion-ways. They would have been equally kind to Miss Pargeter if she had allowed them to be.

Halfway across to Italy, the bright French sun went in and dark clouds came racing across the sea, bringing wind and squalls of rain. Miss Pargeter went back to her cabin. Isobel stayed on the open deck and got wet and filthy, and subsequently scolded. It went on raining, even when they reached Leghorn, and the funny old

fiacre which took them, for one franc, the sum specified as
appropriate by Grandpapa Morpeth, from the steamer to their hotel
in the old quarter of Nuova Venezia, leaked and allowed Miss
Pargeter's guide book to become splashed with rain. The hotel was
dark and cold, and Isobel's room looked into a narrow street that
seemed to be all walls, with neither doors nor windows. Miss
Pargeter said that Grandpapa Morpeth – whose first Italian landfall
had been made at Leghorn in 1874, and who therefore believed
that it was the only place from which to embark upon the rest of
the country – had instructed her to show some of the charms of
Leghorn to Isobel, so even though she, Miss Pargeter, was unwell,
bone weary and crippled by anxious responsibilities, they must go
out to see the sights.

'We don't have to,' Isobel said, trying to be helpful.

'We do,' said Miss Pargeter.

The streets of Leghorn were running with rain, and the canals
of the Nuova Venezia quarter had little waves on them, as well as
bits of orange peel and vegetable flotsam. They peered through the
thick air at the red-brick ruins of the old fortress, looked quickly
round the cathedral and hurried past the statue of Ferdinando I,
which Miss Pargeter did not want Isobel to look at, because the
statue's pedestal rested, most interestingly, on the backs of four
chained negroes whom Miss Pargeter considered to be insufficiently
clothed. On the way back through the Piazza Grande, Isobel asked
for an ice cream.

'Not in this weather,' Miss Pargeter said, 'and in any case, it is
bound to be full of germs.'

They ate a sad supper in the hotel dining room, starting with a
thin soup that reminded Isobel of nothing so much as rain. Her
bed felt damp, the sheets had not been ironed very smoothly and
Isobel lay awake for hours, heavy with misgiving. What about this
Italy her father had described, this Italy where the sun shone warmly
and long enough to ripen grapes? Perhaps it would be there in the
morning.

It wasn't. The rain was still raining. Miss Pargeter, however,
fortified by three cups of tea at breakfast, and by the prospect of
being released from the responsibility of Isobel by nightfall, was
almost cheerful. There was a brief bad moment when she hiccuped
inadvertently while paying the bill, but Isobel, worn out by her
anxious night, hardly noticed. They took another leaking fiacre to
the station and, after an embarrassing tussle over the fare – Miss
Pargeter made a mistake in her Italian counting and refused to

28

acknowledge it – climbed onto the train that would take them first to Pisa, where they were to catch another train to Florence.

They had an hour to wait in Pisa. Isobel wished very much to see the leaning tower, but Miss Pargeter refused to leave the station. She said she had had quite enough of Italian rain. Isobel said they could take a fiacre, and perhaps the fiacres in Pisa wouldn't leak.

'Don't argue,' Miss Pargeter said.

When the train came and they finally climbed on board, it turned out to be a train of incredible slowness. For hour upon hour, it crept through the wet landscape, where strange yellow buildings crouched round churches under the dark, pouring sky. Miss Pargeter had bought several dusty, sweetish, dry rolls at Pisa station which she said were quite sufficient for their journey. Isobel, hungry but full of foreboding, could hardly swallow hers. Miss Pargeter suddenly decided she should give Isobel an Italian lesson, and became quite animated reading out lots of incomprehensible vocabulary from a book with a red cloth cover. Isobel, her eyes on the crawling landscape and her mind in a daze, mumbled away in her wake.

'There!' said Miss Pargeter abruptly and almost vivaciously. 'Florence!'

Isobel turned her head as slowly as a tortoise. It was almost dark, and through the rain-speckled windows of the train she could see huge buildings and nothing more. She could have been anywhere.

'Your new life, Isobel my dear!' cried Miss Pargeter, springing up.

Isobel followed her dutifully out of the train and plodded down the platform in her wake. A man stood by the engine in a funny sort of uniform, dark trousers and brass-buttoned short jacket, holding a board on which someone had pinned a piece of paper. On the paper was written in capital letters in black ink: 'Miss Isobel Lindsay.'

'This is Miss Lindsay,' Miss Pargeter said, propelling Isobel forward.

'My name is Luca,' the man said, speaking to Isobel, in heavily accented English. 'I come from the Villa Calvina.'

'Yes,' Isobel said and then, hurriedly, 'thank you.'

'This is Miss Lindsay's luggage,' Miss Pargeter said loudly and slowly, as if speaking to a deaf half-wit. 'She has five pieces. Do you understand me? Five pieces.'

'Yes, Signorina,' Luca said. He looked at Isobel. 'I am to take you to the Villa Calvina. The signoras are waiting for you.'

29

Isobel wondered if he had winked at her. She hoped he hadn't. When soldiers in the park used to wink at Maudie, Maudie made a terrible fuss and said it was a shocking insult, even though she was always flushed and bright-eyed afterwards.

'I would be grateful,' Miss Pargeter said, 'if you would send word, Isobel, when you are safely installed at the Villa Calvina. I shall be at the Pensione Cipoletti in the Via Cavour—'

'I have these instructions, Signorina,' Luca said gently.

'Oh,' said Miss Pargeter disagreeably. Then she brightened and turned to Isobel. 'In that case, we must say goodbye.'

'Yes,' said Isobel. She put out her hand.

'No more meals in the schoolroom, Isobel! No more German verbs! No more rivers and mountain ranges!'

'No,' said Isobel. She pulled herself together. 'Thank you for looking after me.'

'Not at all,' said Miss Pargeter, 'not at all.' There was a dreadful moment when Isobel thought Miss Pargeter was going to stoop and kiss her, but in the end, all she did was take her hand.

'Goodbye, my dear,' said Miss Pargeter.

'Goodbye,' said Isobel.

'Come,' said Luca, 'I must take you away now. The signoras will be anxious.'

He motioned the porter to follow him with Isobel's luggage, and with a touch upon her elbow that was so light she could hardly feel it, guided her away from the platform and Miss Pargeter, and her memories of England.

He shut her into a small, dry carriage with seats upholstered in green leather. There were green curtains at the windows too, and brass footwarmers on the floor. The carriage smelled faintly of lavender, as well as of leather. It went swaying off through the wet streets, and Isobel watched in a kind of trance as lamps went by and people in shawls, or with umbrellas, Italian people. After a while, the carriage left the streets and began to climb quite steeply up hilly roads past walls that might have been the walls of gardens. It was quite dark by now, and the rain had stopped and the smell of lavender and leather in the carriage became mixed with other smells, smells of earth and countryside and wet spring air. Isobel felt she had been travelling all her life and that she might never be allowed to stop. She also felt dirty, and crumpled, and quite incapable of facing the imminent prospect of two strange aunts at the Villa Calvina.

The carriage stopped suddenly, and someone shouted. Isobel

peered out. By the light of the carriage lamps she could see a stout stone gatepost with a metal plaque on it, bearing the words 'Villa Calvina' above crossed keys. Then she saw a man, in shirtsleeves and a waistcoat, come forward and open the iron gates that hung from the stone gateposts, and the carriage went rolling through, up what sounded like a steep gravelled walk, along something flat, and then stopped.

Isobel, stupefied with tiredness and apprehension, waited. She heard Luca jump down, and more shouting, and then the carriage door was opened.

'Come, Signorina,' Luca said, 'we have arrived.'

Stiffly, Isobel climbed down onto a terrace of smooth stone slabs. There was a house in front of her, which she could hardly make out except that several of the windows – big windows – let out a golden pinkish glow.

'This way, Signorina,' Luca said, touching her elbow again.

He led her across the stone slabs to a flight of steps, leading up to a huge door, like a church door, under an arch from which hung a great glass lantern on a curly iron hook. The door opened. Behind it, seeming to go on for ever, was a huge white vaulted space in which more lanterns hung, and against this space, two figures were silhouetted, one short and stout, one tall and thin.

'My dear!' someone said. 'My poor, dear, benighted child! Welcome to Italy!'

Chapter Four

Somewhere, mixed up in Isobel's dreams, someone said crossly, *'Porca Madonna!'*

Isobel's eyes flew open. Her gaze was first caught by the ceiling above her which appeared to be covered with birds and flowers, and then by bright bars of light, yellow light, shining between the cracks in the shutters.

'Porca Madonna!' someone said again.

Isobel sat up. The light coming in round the shutters was so bright it was brilliant, and the long white muslin curtains that hung either side of the window were swishing softly in a little breeze. Isobel looked upwards. There were indeed painted birds and flowers on the ceiling, and the birds held ribbons in their beaks. Below the ceiling, the walls were plain white, hung with dark pictures in golden frames, and the floor was covered with tiles, Isobel thought, the same colour as the flower pots in the greenhouse in her grandparents' garden. She pushed back the bedclothes, swung her feet out and put them down cautiously in a thin line of sunlight lying on the floor. It was warm.

She stood up. She felt unexpectedly free and lightheaded and, putting her hands to her head, found that her hair was unbraided because there had been no Maudie last night to do it for her, nor Miss Pargeter to remind her to do it for herself. She shook her head pleasedly. Then she padded down the line of sunlight on the floor to the window, reached up to the metal bar that held the shutters closed, released it, and pushed them open.

'Oh!' said Isobel, gazing.

32

'*Buon giorno, Padroncina,*' said a voice below her.

She looked down. An old man in blue trousers and a straw hat with a frayed brim was standing below her with a garden trug full of weeds. Perhaps he was the person who had – Isobel's Italian was very rudimentary and she wasn't at all sure she had heard what she thought she had heard – called the Madonna, most shockingly, a pig.

'Good morning,' Isobel said stiffly.

The old man smiled, showing his two remaining teeth. He doffed his hat. He then made a long complicated remark.

'I am afraid,' Isobel said, 'that I don't understand you. And, in any case, if you don't object, I want to look at the view, rather than talk.'

The old man gave a little bow, and creaked down on to his knees again, to his task on the terrace. Isobel lifted her eyes. She had seen views in Switzerland, of course, and in the Lake District in England, during a touring holiday with her mother and grandparents, but she had never seen a view quite like this one. She had never seen so much light in a view, or this kind of loveliness. It made her feel a little dizzy for some reason, and she held the edge of the window frame tightly to stop herself falling out.

Just below her was the broad terrace where the old man was weeding again – weeding and muttering – and along which the carriage had brought her the night before. There were stiff little shiny-leaved trees in pots along the edge of the terrace, and then a balustrade of stone with statues here and there along its length, and wonderful swathes of mauve wisteria wound in and out of the stone banisters and draped themselves round the statues' feet. Beyond the terrace, the land went tumbling down the hill, rough grass and cascades of little pink roses and russet tiled roofs here and there, punctuated by tall, slim dark trees that reminded Isobel of paintbrushes. Then the view became extraordinary, running away down into an immense valley in which a magical city seemed to nestle, a city of domes and towers, and then, beyond the city, the land rose again in folds of hills, blue and green and purple rising up to the clear spring sky, so clear it looked as if it had been polished. Isobel took her hands away from the windowsill and held them out into the air, to feel the sunshine.

Someone knocked at her door. Isobel said 'Oh!' in a frightened voice, uncertain of whether she should have got out of bed, let alone opened the windows, without being told to. The door opened, and Aunt Sybil came in, her last night's dress of black lace exchanged for a pink striped blouse with a lace jabot, and a long cream skirt with whorls of cream silk braid appliqued round the hem.

'Isobel!' said Aunt Sybil, holding out her arms. 'Am I not to get a morning kiss?'

Isobel advanced shyly across the tiled floor. Aunt Sybil had been so extraordinary last night, so kind but saying such terrible things about Grandpapa and Grandmamma Morpeth – and then shrieking with laughter – that Isobel didn't know what to think of her. She put her face up obediently for a kiss. Aunt Sybil swept her into a tightly corseted hug.

'What a stiff little dear little goose you are,' Aunt Sybil said. 'Did you sleep well?'

'Oh yes, thank you,' Isobel said.

'Aunt Jean is down in the *podere* already, of course,' Aunt Sybil said, releasing her. 'She is a ferocious farmer, you know. Her vines are her passion. Can you dress yourself, funny little Isobel?'

'Of course,' Isobel said.

'Well, I shall send you Moody all the same. Moody has been with me since I was a girl. Without Moody and my medicine chest, I should have been in my grave long ago. I am a *martyr* to my health.'

'So was Miss Pargeter,' Isobel said, 'except that she was a martyr to her nerves too.'

'Oh?' said Aunt Sybil, drawing herself up, wrinkling her aquiline nose. Isobel felt it had not been tactful to associate her elegant aunt with a dyspeptic governess in a mustard-coloured shawl. She bit her lip.

'You shall eat an egg for breakfast,' Aunt Sybil said, recovering herself and moving with her graceful, dancing step towards the door. 'And new bread – now don't say Grandmamma Morpeth would say it was indigestible because nothing can be as indigestible as she – and honey from Aunt Jean's hives and *café au lait*. And you shall eat it on the loggia and while you eat it, I shall describe your new life to you, a life,' said Aunt Sybil, swaying out of the door, 'of beauty, sunshine, culture and *plenty* of jokes.'

Isobel stood in the middle of her room and waited for Moody. While she waited, she took in the amazing fact that the headboard of her bed was made of painted and gilded wood, and carved with cherubs. This, for a person who had never slept in anything but a black, cast-iron bed! And the chests where she supposed her sad black clothes would live were painted too, pale yellowish green with wreaths of flowers on the doors and drawers and little curly brass handles and knobs. And the paintings that had looked so dark when the shutters were closed turned out to be rich and glowing, and to be pictures of children with dogs and wooded landscapes with sunlit distances and, best of all, Isobel thought, a girl in a straw hat with a cherry-coloured ribbon round it, reading a book by an open window so that the light reflected from the page was flung back up into her face.

'Good morning, Miss Isobel.'

Isobel jumped. A small, square person stood in the doorway, dressed in black, holding something draped across her arms.

'I am Moody,' Moody said. 'I am from Edinburgh. My name is spelled Mudie. I wasn't able to greet you last night because I was attending one of the young wives on the farm, who was having a baby.'

Isobel's eyes grew wide. She opened her mouth to say something but nothing came.

'I have brought you this, on Miss Sybil's instructions,' Moody said. 'Of course, she is Miss Sybil no longer, but Mrs Carruthers, but to me she will always be Miss Sybil.'

Isobel stared. In Moody's arms lay a soft, full, duck-egg blue dress, apparently the right size for Isobel.

'But—'

'Miss Sybil thinks,' Moody said, 'that it is not good for the health of your mind to go about in black. You shall wear this, with a black ribbon around your arm, as a mark of respect. The dress was made by Miss Sybil's own dressmaker in the Via Strozzi, but we think it will fit.'

Isobel stepped forward and touched the dress. She had never seen anything so pretty.

'In London,' she said, 'the maid who – helped me sometimes, was called Maudie.' She paused and then added hesitantly, 'Maudie – Moody—'

'Then,' said Moody briskly, already mentally going to work upon Isobel's hair and deportment, 'we shall find ourselves quite at home with one another, shan't we?'

The loggia turned out to be a sort of outside room, roofed and with a back wall, but with the other three walls open to the view through huge arches up which various winding green things climbed. A table had been laid for Isobel with a white cloth and white china painted with birds, and beside the table was a long cane chair, a garden chaise longue, filled with cushions in which Aunt Sybil lay, wrapped

35

in a cashmere shawl of green and cream and pink, and wearing huge grey spectacles which she said were imperative to protect her eyes from sunlight.

'When I go into Florence,' Aunt Sybil said, 'I always wear a blue veil, for the same reason. Now, darling child, let me see you in that frock.'

Isobel stood lumpishly, but full of inward delight, in front of her.

'It needs taking in across the shoulders and you shall have shoes, not those terrible boots, and Moody must wash your hair with an infusion of camomile to lighten it. Otherwise, I think you much improved and nicely on the road to being un-Morpeth'd.'

Isobel quivered a little. She was ready to kneel down and worship this fascinating aunt, but her conscience flinched at such a scandalous attitude towards her grandparents, grandparents whom she had been brought up to respect and fear.

'Now sit down, and Maria will bring your eggs and coffee. Aunt Jean will join us when she has finished her morning's scolding of the peasants. If you look down there you will see a camphor tree, whose blossom smells quite ambrosial, and those beds either side of it are full of tree peonies, which are a passion of mine, and roses, another passion, and beyond those are magnolias for the spring and persimmons for the autumn, when they turn gold and crimson, like flames. Try and look at it all. Try and drink it in. Poor child, so starved of beauty, coming as you do from the terrible world of Morpeth where the only object considered lovely is a bank note.'

Isobel opened her mouth to say that Ida's rooms had been much admired by her friends, and that Ida's clothes, to Isobel's reverent eye, had been perfectly beautiful, but she was prevented by the arrival of breakfast. Coddled eggs, white rolls wrapped in a napkin, a pat of butter in a little glass dish and a blue bowl of honey were set on the table in front of her, beside a huge shallow cup filled with pale, milky coffee.

'Thank you,' Isobel whispered, overcome by the beauty of the things before her.

'Good appetite, *Padroncina*,' Maria said. She looked, with an examining eye, at Isobel's skin and hair. Poor child. She had come from England, of course, where the rain poured all year and the sun never shone, and she was motherless, *la poverina*.

'Good appetite,' she said again, urging Isobel to eat.

For some reason, Isobel's eyes filled with tears. She blinked hard. Was she a wicked, dreadful sinner to sit in this beautiful place and be given this beautiful breakfast, and be pleased to be here

36

and thankful not to be in Lancashire? If she was a really good girl, with a pure heart, shouldn't she refuse to live in a house with this irresistible aunt who grew trees like flames and spoke so disrespectfully of her grandparents?

'One of the first things I'm going to do for you, darling child,' said Aunt Sybil, missing nothing from behind her grey spectacles, 'is to take away your sense of sin and drown it in the Arno.'

Isobel gasped, torn between horror and delight.

'Eat your breakfast, or you will offend Maria. I think I've got you just in time, my dear Isobel, just in time before all the spirit was choked out of you for ever.'

Isobel ate. It was delicious, every mouthful, and she was desperately hungry. Aunt Sybil watched her as she ate.

'I am so angry,' she had said to her sister the night before after Isobel, almost speechless with fatigue, had gone to bed. 'I am furiously angry! How typically, stubbornly, cruelly Morpeth it was to send that poor bereaved child by the longest route to Florence known to man, when the new trains would have brought her across the Continent in not much more than a night and a day! To dress up his so-called kindness with first class tickets and dreadful stuffy hotels to make the poor child feel riven with obligation and disloyalty! And then this letter!' She had brandished a long envelope at Jean. 'This disgusting, wicked letter!'

'You should never have opened it,' Jean had said.

'Quite right! I should never have opened it, I should have burned it unopened!'

'We have to show it to the child—'

'Tomorrow, at once, we must get it over with so that she can begin on this new life of sunshine and—'

'You must not show it to her without me,' Aunt Jean said, 'I must be there too. She was taught to love and respect the Morpeths and heaven knows, poor child, she had few enough people to love.'

Poor child she truly was, Aunt Sybil thought, watching her eat now, ravenously hungry but afraid to appear greedy. She could well imagine Isobel's schoolroom diet, the boiled fish and boiled puddings, cold on cold plates. Isobel even looked as if that was what she had eaten.

'Is it good?' Aunt Sybil said.

Isobel hesitated. Was it wrong to feel so excited about food? But would it also be wrong to tell a lie and say it wasn't delicious when it was? She compromised, and nodded violently.

A voice came coo-eeing up the steps from below the terrace,

followed by the top of Aunt Jean's white felt hat, then by her face and then by her stout body clad in a cream cashmere dress of her own design (practical and with not even a nod to fashion) under the calico wrapper she used when down in the *podere*.

'Dears!' cried Aunt Jean, clapping her hands. 'Such a morning! And dear Isobel!'

She came across the loggia, took Isobel's face in both her hands and kissed her resoundingly on the forehead.

'The rain has done wonders for the vines and the wheat, such a blessing! And there are new piglets. When you have finished your breakfast, Isobel, I shall take you to see the piglets.'

'Oh!' cried Isobel.

'And she must meet the families in the *poderi*, and see my new dairy – Beppe has whitewashed it, it looks like a palace—'

'And I must take her to Florence,' Aunt Sybil said, interrupting, 'I must take her to see the pictures and the churches and to meet Professor Vaccari—'

'But not until she has eaten every crumb of her breakfast—'

'And not,' said Aunt Sybil, rearing up out of her cushions, 'until we have disposed of that terrible Morpeth letter.'

Isobel's knife, sticky with honey, clattered on to her plate.

'Oh, Sybil,' Aunt Jean said in sad reproach.

'She has to see it, poor darling!' Aunt Sybil cried. 'She has to see it and then we can tear it up and forget it and think about piglets and Botticelli instead!'

Isobel stood up. She suddenly felt extremely full, almost sick. 'What letter, please?' she said, her voice quavering.

Aunt Jean took her hand. 'Sit down again, my dear. I will sit by you.'

Isobel shook her head. Aunt Sybil drew the long envelope, now a little crumpled, out of her pocket and handed it to Isobel.

'I'm afraid I opened it, darling child,' Aunt Sybil said, 'because I feared it would be nasty and unimportant, and we could then burn it and you would never have needed to be troubled by it. But it turned out to be nasty, nasty as only Morpeths can be nasty, but important.'

Isobel nodded, swallowing. She took the letter out of its envelope and opened it slowly, conscious of Aunt Jean's anxious eyes and Aunt Sybil's grey spectacles fixed upon her face.

My dear Isobel, *the letter ran,*
For so you were once to me and to your grandmother before

38

this wilful and wicked disobedience was instilled in you by your father. I hoped, from the moment of your beloved mother's death, until the second of your departure from England, that your heart would turn back to God and to your loving family. I hoped, by providing, as I saw to be my duty, the greatest care and comfort in your journey to Florence, that I might in turn remind you of your duty to those who have ever had your best interests at heart. No word has come. In vain we have watched and waited for that telegram that would lighten the grief that now hangs, and will ever hang over the lives of your grandparents. I am writing this letter out of the desire to give you one last chance to repent of your bitter unkindness to your grandmother and myself, and to redeem your own life which is, my dear Isobel, doomed if you stay among your father's family. Come back to us here, repent, and all shall be forgiven. Remain at Florence, and I have no choice but, for the sake of your grandmother's health and your beloved mother's memory, to decline to acknowledge you ever again as my flesh and blood. Remain at Florence, and you are a Morpeth no longer, and every obligation I have towards you is at an irrevocable end.

If this is your decision, it will be a fate sealed by your own hand.

> Your loving grandfather,
> Arthur Morpeth.

Isobel dropped the letter. She was trembling violently.

'Oh dear,' Aunt Jean said, stepping forward. 'Oh my dear, we should never—'

Aunt Sybil shot out an arm and seized her sister's skirts as she passed the reclining chair.

'Wait—'

The two sisters, Aunt Jean frozen with anxiety and Aunt Sybil in excited anticipation, watched Isobel. She stood quite still, her face quite expressionless, giving no sign of any emotion beyond the fact that the hands hanging down at her sides, half hidden in the blue folds of her dress, were clenched into fists.

But something was happening inside Isobel, a feeling she only remembered having had once before when she had put the picture of 'Little Lady Bountiful' on the floor, and stood on it until the glass cracked. As if it had a life of its own, her right foot rose suddenly up off the loggia and kicked Grandpapa Morpeth's letter under Aunt Sybil's chaise longue. Then Isobel turned to Aunt Jean. There was a faint spot of colour in both her cheeks.

'I would like, please,' said Isobel, 'to go now and see the piglets.'

PART TWO

Chapter Five

Florence – 1914

The streets of Florence were as hot as ovens, even though it was only early July. Isobel, in a drop-waisted, drape-skirted dress of cream and blue striped cotton, with a straw hat adorned with blue cornflowers from the garden of the Villa Calvina, pushed her way through the crowds in the Via Tornabuoni on her way to Maquay's Bank. She was, as she always was when she came down into Florence, on an errand for Aunt Sybil. Most of the English in Florence banked at Whitby, Maquay & Co and went to the English church in the Via La Marmona and shopped at the Anglo-American stores in the Via Cavour, and Aunt Sybil was no exception. It had taken Isobel no time at all to realize, nine years before when she had come to Italy, that Aunt Sybil was the undisputed social queen of the English community in Florence.

Aunt Jean, who had no time for social life, called the English community 'villadom'. It was true that most of them lived in the villas scattered about the lovely hills to the north-east of the city, and true also that their social lives were very important to them. Ladies with a great knowledge of roses and hats and each other's marital histories, and a rather smaller knowledge of the Italian art treasures over which they went into such raptures, were frequent visitors at the Villa Calvina. Carriages rolled up and down the gravelled drive most afternoons, while Aunt Sybil held court in the loggia if it was cool enough and in the *sala degli uccelli*, a wonderful room papered with Chinese birds and flowers in marvellous colours, if the outdoor heat was too great. If Isobel was at home, it was her duty to hand round the buttered scones, check the teapot – 'No Italian can ever be taught to warm the pot, too maddening!' – and take the duller visitors on a tour of the garden, in order to leave Aunt Sybil with the more fascinating ones, the ones with the gossip.

'Of course, my dear Sybil, this must go no further, but Lady Scott was seen in the Via Strozzi with . . .'

'I can hardly believe it, but that dear little Signor Placci offered me a pair of lovebirds – lovebirds, my dear! – which he said . . .'

'Oh, it's gambling debts, you may be sure of it, and something to do with the Queen of Spain . . .'

Isobel adored her Aunt Sybil and hated these afternoons. Even when Aunt Sybil's more artistic friends, poets and painters and even the odd philosopher wishing to argue about the nature of the Beautiful and the Good, came, Isobel was no happier. And when Aunt Sybil insisted that Isobel accompany her on return visits to the inhabitants of villadom, it was even worse. The villas were, in themselves, lovely, but their inhabitants had transformed their interiors into South Kensington drawing rooms, with chintz curtains and cushions, watercolours on the walls and heavy silver rose bowls, not to mention piles of books from Vieusseux's Lending Library, where everyone fought over John Galsworthy's novels.

'Too silly, this imitation England,' said Aunt Sybil, but she went on going.

Isobel could, she knew, have spent more afternoons than she did down among the vines and the olive groves with Aunt Jean, or helping her with the farm accounts. After all, she dearly loved Aunt Jean, who had been such a rock-like, fond presence all these last years, and she loved the *podere* and its families and the satisfying agricultural work that went on there. But both she and Aunt Jean understood, without saying so, that this would have badly upset Aunt Sybil who had made it plain, years ago, that as her sister was so busy with practical matters at the Villa Calvina, she, Sybil, should take on the greater burden of Isobel's upbringing. Of course, this so-called burden was essentially only of a kind preferred by Aunt Sybil, the instruction in music, painting, literature and conversation; the duller burden of Isobel's winter underclothes, dental appointments, regular bedtimes and diet fell to Aunt Jean and Moody. Aunt Sybil took all the credit for Isobel. As she grew taller, and slimmer, and her sad, indoor London childhood complexion improved, and she turned out to have a talent for languages, and an eye for art, Aunt Sybil was full of self-congratulation. Isobel loved her aunts equally, but knew herself to be Aunt Sybil's slave.

A slave, however, with a mind of her own, and, increasingly, a tongue in her head. There was a lot she would do for Aunt Sybil, and did, but regular attendance at the afternoon tea parties was ceasing to be one of them. With no attempt at deception, Isobel asked Professor Vaccari, who had been her tutor since she was eleven, if she might move her morning lessons to the afternoon. Professor Vaccari, who was scarcely conscious of time in any case, was happy to agree.

'But you simply cannot go down to Florence in the afternoon heat. It's unthinkable!' Aunt Sybil cried.

'No, it isn't.'

'It's perfectly perverse. And how can you do my errands in the afternoon? Everything will be closed until four.'

'Later, after lessons, I can do whatever you want. And then I can go after tea and play tennis at the club at the Cascine.'

'But the bank will be closed all the afternoon.'

'Then I will go down in the late morning, in time to go to the bank.'

'Isobel, you are impossible.'

'And so,' said Isobel, stooping to kiss her forehead, 'are you.'

She pushed open the doors of the bank, and went gratefully out of the glare into the cool dimness of the banking hall. Aunt Sybil had a standing order for ready money at Maquay's – Aunt Jean, as taught by her late husband, had another one, next door, at French, Lemon & Co – which Isobel used to collect for her each week and take back to the Villa Calvina in a small, strong linen bag, tied with tapes. The clerk she usually dealt with was English too, a solid young man with greased-back hair and a celluloid collar whose eyes, just recently, had been filled with admiration when requesting Isobel to sign the receipt slip and handing her the linen roll. Isobel never took any notice of his admiration. She was not in the least interested in Englishmen; the inhabitants of villadom with their insularity and their gossip had seen to that. When Isobel became interested in any man – and this was definitely not going to be for years and years because she had in no way finished her studies – he would without question be an Italian.

The clerk, as usual, put the receipt slip and pen and ink down on a small table, and held a chair respectfully for Isobel to seat herself and sign.

'Warm today, Miss Lindsay.'

'Hot,' said Isobel, signing.

'I shall soon,' said the clerk, clearing his throat, 'be returning to England.'

'Shall you?' said Isobel, without interest.

'My mother wishes it, you see, what with all the trouble brewing in Europe.'

Isobel stood up, holding out her hand for the roll of money. 'What trouble?'

'Relations between France and Germany aren't good, Miss Lindsay. And the Balkan unrest—'

'What,' said Isobel imperiously, interrupting him, 'has that got to do with Italy?'

'Nothing as yet, Miss Lindsay, but—'

'Then I don't know what you are talking about,' Isobel said, 'but I wish you a safe journey.'

'Yes,' the clerk said unhappily. Oh, these young English ladies with their pretty faces and their stuck-up airs, what heartbreakers they were! 'Thank you, Miss Lindsay.'

Isobel swept out on to the street. She couldn't think what he had been talking about, or why he should have wished to engage her in conversation in the first place. Of course she knew about the Balkan wars. She knew about them from Aunt Sybil's newspaper, and from letters from her father. Edward Lindsay didn't write often, being preoccupied, as Aunt Sybil pointed out, with keeping rain out of Lindsay Castle and food in the mouths of himself, his wife and the growing brood of children. Mrs Muriel Bond, now Mrs Edward Lindsay, had proved to be a steady breeder. 'Serve him right,' Aunt Sybil said heartlessly, 'such a hopeless chooser of women.' Yet she and Aunt Jean, to Isobel's certain knowledge, sent regular cheques to Lindsay Castle, especially in the winter. And Edward wrote gratefully back to them, enclosing notes for Isobel which were always, oddly, about the state of affairs in England and Europe.

'He thinks if he wrote to you about affairs at Lindsay Castle,' Aunt Sybil said, 'you would tear up the letter.'

So he wrote instead, Isobel thought, the kind of letters you might have written to a boy, letters about the Serbian invasion of Albania, and the sinking of the *Titanic* with the loss of fifteen hundred lives, and the founding of a magazine called the *New Statesman*, based on something Isobel had to ask Professor Vaccari about, called socialist principles. Professor Vaccari was the fount of most of Isobel's knowledge. He might never know the time, and be forgetful about brushing his clothes or trimming his nails, but in Isobel's eyes he was a hero, both for what he knew, and for what he had imparted to her.

His very first words to her, eight years ago, when as a painfully anxious eleven-year-old she had pushed open the door of his astonishingly cluttered room, had been, 'Please, do not tread on those books, Signorina. They are intended to be read, not trodden upon.'

Isobel had stared at the floor. It was, literally, covered with books, tottering piles of texts and lexicons, leaving only the narrowest path winding through them to the cheap deal desk where Professor Vaccari sat, peering at her through thick spectacles.

'Then why,' Isobel had said, forgetting her fright at the impracticality of his remark, 'are they on the floor?'

'Hah!' said Professor Vaccari. He got up and sidled down the book-lined path to Isobel. He was short, very short, and solid. He peered at her again.

'Do you know Latin?'

'No,' said Isobel.

'Nor Greek?'

'No—'

'And you have not yet read Dante?'

'No,' whispered Isobel. Who was Dante, for goodness' sake?

'Then,' cried Professor Vaccari, seizing her hand and bestowing upon her a smile of extraordinary sweetness, 'we have a long way to travel together, my dear Signorina, and we shall pick a great many beautiful flowers on the way!'

He had been as good as his word. He had taught Isobel Greek and Latin as if they were living languages, simply plunging into the *Iliad* without any Pargeter-like grammar lessons to precede it.

'Do not trouble about language,' Professor Vaccari would cry, 'but *feel* the poetry! Feel it!'

Sometimes, after reading a passage aloud, he would say to Isobel, 'Now, Signorina, please do not try to make an intelligent comment. I see from your face you understood it.' Then he would send her home to wrestle with the rules of language alone. 'We must not waste our time together on such matters! I am here to teach you that poetry is not separated from life, but interwoven in it! Go out

47

into the hills and you will still see what Virgil saw, the same plodding oxen, the same girl cutting grass with a sickle, the same olive trees, the same vines!'

Isobel owed Professor Vaccari to Aunt Sybil. Aunt Sybil had discovered him and appreciated his greatness and had toyed, in an Aunt Sybil-ish way, with the notion of studying with him herself. But it would have been too fatiguing, those hours in that dusty little room with Professor Vaccari excitedly bounding about snatching down books from his crammed shelves and declaiming aloud from them. It was better, in every way, to send Isobel, and remain on her breezy hillside, imbibing little delectable drops of Isobel's new knowledge when she felt like it.

Professor Vaccari had two dusty rooms above an antiquarian bookseller on the Lungarno Acciaioli, with a view, if he had ever troubled to look at it, of the Arno. Stowing Aunt Sybil's money carefully away in her leather bookbag, Isobel went quickly down the Via Tornabuoni, across the Piazza Santa Trinita and out into the sparkling light by the river. She breathed deeply and gratefully. There was never enough air in the streets of Florence during the summer.

She rang the bell at the foot of Professor Vaccari's staircase, as she always did, to warn him of her arrival, and went up the steep wooden stairs to the second floor. Even the Professor had noticed the heat, and had propped his door open with a huge history of the Peloponnesian Wars. He was sitting, as he always sat, in his shabby black suit, immersed in some volume, and he merely grunted when Isobel came in. She was perfectly used to this. She set down her bookbag and opened it.

'I have brought you a rose from the Villa Calvina,' Isobel said, 'and Aunt Jean has sent some eggs for Signora Vaccari.'

'Shall I ever get them home without breaking them?'

'You must try,' Isobel said. The room was very stuffy, despite the open door, and full of the smoke of Professor Vaccari's ceaseless cigars. Isobel went past her tutor's desk, weaving among the books, and after a struggle, wrenched a window open. Professor Vaccari did not appear to notice.

'May I ask you something, Professor?'

'Anything, my dear.'

Isobel perched herself on the stool where she always sat during lessons. 'Is there trouble in Europe?'

Professor Vaccari looked up and regarded Isobel through his thick spectacles. 'There is.'

'What kind of trouble?'

'Last week,' said Professor Vaccari calmly, 'the Archduke Ferdinand, heir to the Monarchy of the Hapsburgs, and to the Austro-Hungarian Empire, was assassinated in Sarajevo, by a schoolboy named Gavrilo Princip, using a revolver of astonishing crudity.'

'What?' cried Isobel.

'It was more than a crime,' Professor Vaccari said, 'it was a challenge to Austria-Hungary as the ruler of Bosnia, and a challenge also to her prestige as one of the five Great Powers. It was extremely serious. There will be repercussions.'

'What repercussions?'

'Military ones, no doubt.'

'War?' said Isobel, leaning forward.

Professor Vaccari's eyes strayed longingly back to the volume of Pascoli on his desk. 'It may even come to that.'

'Will England – I mean, will Italy—?'

'In theory,' Professor Vaccari said, 'Italy is an ally of Austria-Hungary. As she is of Germany. We must wait and see. Now, Signorina Lindsay, enough of this. We have today the last voyage of Ulysses. Please pick up your book and follow me while I read.'

Isobel, for once, couldn't concentrate. She knew nothing about European affairs, had no conception of what war was, but there was something both about what Professor Vaccari had said and about the notion of a solid English clerk going home because of the atmosphere in Europe that unnerved her. It was the first time since Ida died that she had felt her settled safe universe not to be as unassailable as she had always assumed it was, and she could not imagine why. She hardly *knew* the clerk in Maquay's, after all! And he was probably going home simply to comfort an over-anxious widowed mother, and using the reason of bother in Europe as an excuse, in order to seem more manly . . .

'Please concentrate,' Professor Vaccari said, and then added with that perceptiveness which sat so oddly with the rest of his absorbed, absent-minded, scholarly self, 'Do not trouble yourself, my dear. Italy, much as I regret it, is not one of the five Great Powers and the Italian people will be quite indifferent to this argument and will only ask to be left alone.'

'Yes,' said Isobel.

'Then,' said Professor Vaccari, 'apply your mind.'

*　　*　　*

After her lesson, Isobel bought some hairpins and a length of black silk ribbon for Aunt Jean, a tin of homeopathic throat lozenges for Moody, paid Aunt Sybil's weekly subscription of one franc to Vieusseux's library, and collected a new Edith Wharton novel, and then thankfully caught the steam tram home up into the airy hills. She loved the trams, the various people who used them, from English people like herself living outside the city, through professional Italians in rusty black suits like Professor Vaccari's, to ordinary Italian people with salami sausages and huge globe artichokes and newspapers stuffed into string bags, chattering away to one another with the vivacity of people who apparently haven't seen one another for at least five years.

It was a ten-minute walk from the tram stop to the Villa Calvina. It was beautiful now, the light golden, and the air seemed full of butterflies and bees. Isobel walked slowly. Her bag was heavy and her head was full of Ulysses and the schoolboy who had shot and killed the man who would have become Emperor of Austria, King of Hungary. It seemed impossible, on this white dust road on this herb-scented hillside under a sky as blue as delphiniums, that anything so violent and horrible should happen. Why had the boy killed the Archduke? Professor Vaccari said he was one of a romantic group of young men who resented his country being under Hapsburg rule. But all the same, to *kill* someone for that, and his wife, too . . .

Beppe was in the gateway, pulling up weeds around the gateposts. He stood up, beaming, as Isobel came dawdling up. She was the *Padroncina*, the little mistress, the same age as his Chiara, and he always tried to find himself some job down by the gate while the late afternoon trams came up from the city.

'I hope you have studied hard, *Padroncina*!'

'Not today, Beppe, I was very idle and naughty. It was too hot.'

He grinned at her. 'The signoras have visitors!'

Isobel's face fell. 'Oh, haven't they gone? I hoped, by now, that everyone would have gone away—'

'Italian visitors,' Beppe said with pride.

'Italian! But we almost never—'

Beppe pointed. 'Over there. In the Villa Celoni. A new family have taken it and they are calling upon the signoras.'

'Beppe,' Isobel said, leaning forward, 'do you think that if I just slipped down to your house for an hour to see Chiara, I might contrive somehow to miss the visitors?'

Beppe's grin broke into laughter. 'No hope, *Padroncina*! No hope at all! I was sent here with the exact instructions to tell you to go up to the house, as fast as you can!'

'Oh, Beppe—'

Beppe's laughter faded. He drew himself up proudly. 'These are Italian visitors, remember, *Padroncina*. Italian. Very charming.'

Chapter Six

There were three people in the *sala degli uccelli*, besides Aunt Sybil, in rose-coloured lawn, and poor Aunt Jean, fidgeting to be away but chained by her own courteous sense that the Italians, in whose country she was, after all, living, must be made especially welcome. Opposite Aunt Sybil, who lay back in her chair with her feet comfortably on a footstool, sat a ferociously handsome woman in black, with magnificent dark hair piled up under her hat in gleaming coils. Beside her, and wearing an expression of submission, was a girl of about sixteen, dressed with nun-like demureness in grey and white, with no ornaments. Over by the window, and exuding an air of impatience even though Isobel couldn't see him clearly against the light, stood a man.

'Dear child!' cried Aunt Jean, leaping up from her seat in relief.

Isobel stood in the doorway, clutching her bookbag, almost mulish in her desire not to be involved in the tea party.

'Come in, Isobel darling,' Aunt Sybil said, sensing this at once. 'Put down that bag and come in and meet the Marchesa Fosco.'

The Marchesa turned her fierce, handsome head, and the plumes in her hat waved like those Isobel had seen waving on the heads of horses at Italian funerals, stately and slightly terrifying.

'Marchesa, this is my niece, Isobel. Isobel, I may say, is more than a niece to my sister and myself, she is almost a daughter. She has lived with us since she was a child.'

Isobel came forward. The Marchesa held out a long white hand heavy with rings. She said nothing. Isobel took the hand reluctantly, and made an even more reluctant kind of curtsey.

'And my daughter, Donatella,' the Marchesa said in a voice as deep as a man's.

Isobel tried to smile at Donatella, but Donatella did not raise her eyes from her grey lap, and merely gave a little nod.

'And the Marchese,' Aunt Sybil said, inflecting her voice just a little, as she always did when addressing a man. 'Isobel, go and shake hands with the Marchese Fosco.'

Isobel went obediently over to the window to meet Donatella's father. He turned from the view to smile at her, and revealed that he could not in any way be Donatella's father. He could not, in fact, have been so very much older than Isobel herself. He bowed, theatrically.

'Giovanni Fosco, Signorina!'

'Oh!' said Isobel.

He was very handsome.

'Your aunt tells me that you are studying in Florence?'

'Yes, I—'

'With Professor Vaccari?'

'Yes,' said Isobel, looking at his mouth and then at his eyelashes.

'You are most fortunate, Signorina. My mother and I have just come from Rome to Florence, and in Rome my last tutor advised me, if I wished to continue my studies, to seek the assistance of Professor Vaccari.'

Isobel clasped her hands. 'He is wonderful, I admire him so much—'

'Of course,' called out the Marchesa, 'if his father had lived, Giovanni would now be in Switzerland, studying to be a businessman!'

The young man gave his mother a quick glance. Really, his eyelashes were astonishing, almost blue-black and as thick as fur . . .

'But I did – do not wish to be a businessman,' Giovanni said quietly and then, to Isobel, 'Of all the things that you have learned from Professor Vaccari, what has pleased you most, Signorina?'

'Oh, Virgil,' Isobel said, eagerly.

Giovanni Fosco gave another, smaller bow. 'You charm me by your reply.'

'Do I?'

'Indeed you do. I have such a strong feeling for the land, it is very Italian to feel as I do about the land. I believe it is the feeling Virgil had himself.'

'Yes,' Isobel said, half-mesmerized. 'Aunt Jean—'

53

'I was looking down at the *podere*,' Giovanni said. 'I was admiring your aunt's work.'

Isobel beamed at him. So few people admired Aunt Jean sufficiently, they were too dazzled by Aunt Sybil.

'It pleases you that I should say this?'

'Yes,' said Isobel, 'it does.'

'And it pleases *me*,' said Giovanni, 'that you share my feeling for the countryside.'

'But I—'

'If you love Virgil, Signorina, then we are of one mind.'

Isobel swallowed. Giovanni Fosco put out a hand and took her elbow gently.

'Perhaps you would come and talk to my sister now? She is very shy.'

'She is a pious child,' said her mother.

'She is a pretty child,' said Aunt Sybil.

Donatella blushed.

'I think you should dress her in colours,' Aunt Sybil said to the Marchesa. 'You should dress her in pink, and soft blues—'

Isobel sat down next to Donatella. 'Do you like your new house, Signorina?'

'Pretty well,' Donatella whispered.

'She misses Rome,' her mother said. 'We all do. We are Romans—'

'I am a countryman,' her son interrupted.

'We are Romans,' his mother went on, 'but it became impossible to stay after the death of my husband.'

'Why?' asked Aunt Sybil, who was afraid of nobody.

The Marchesa drew herself up. 'My husband's family turned their backs upon us.'

Giovanni Fosco looked frankly at Aunt Sybil. 'I'm afraid my father left a lot of debts—'

'Giovanni!'

'It's true, Mamma. Why pretend? Why else should we, with a family palace in Rome, be living in a rented villa outside Florence?'

Aunt Sybil was laughing. Isobel shot a glance at Donatella. Something in Donatella's downcast expression stirred something powerful in Isobel, a long forgotten something, the bewildered shame of having a father who had done something disgraceful. She reached out and took Donatella's hand. Donatella looked amazed.

'It doesn't matter,' Isobel whispered, 'it has nothing to do with you.'

'I must apologize, Marchesa, for my sister,' Aunt Jean said, pink with confusion. 'I am afraid she is an incorrigible tease.'

'And my Mamma,' said Giovanni, watching Isobel and his sister, 'does not know the meaning of the word to tease.'

'My husband,' the Marchesa said, addressing Aunt Jean as the only sensible person in the room, 'was a Roman by birth, of a Russian mother. He was a brilliant young man, a cavalry officer who became devoted to the arts. He had the highest standards. He always sent his shirts to be laundered in London.'

'If he had had them laundered in Rome,' Giovanni said mercilessly, 'we might not now be living in the Villa Celoni.'

Aunt Sybil regarded the young man with delight. 'I am sure,' she said in mock reproof, 'that your mother has made it very charming.'

'I shall be happy, Signorina,' said the Marchesa, rising to her feet and shaking out her majestic skirts, 'to see you at the Villa Celoni.'

'I shall bring Isobel,' Aunt Sybil said, making no attempt to rise.

'Aunt Sybil, I have lessons in the afternoons—'

'Not every afternoon!'

'Almost every afternoon,' Isobel said, determined not to let Aunt Sybil out-manoeuvre her in public.

'Isobel is a most conscientious student,' said Aunt Sybil to the Marchesa.

The Marchesa nodded. 'Donatella is too delicate to study.'

'Nobody is too delicate to study,' cried Giovanni.

They all rose to their feet as if driven by a physical instinct to prevent an argument.

'We must all study different things,' Aunt Jean said firmly. She was desperate for the visitors to go, so that she might go down and supervise the evening watering. 'Isobel turns out to have a gift for languages. Perhaps Donatella—'

'I want to paint,' Donatella said unexpectedly, looking at Isobel.

'Nonsense,' her mother said, 'music is your gift.'

Giovanni began to laugh. He threw back his handsome head and laughed and laughed. Then he turned to Isobel and spread out his hands.

'You see, Signorina? You see how my life is? No wonder I turn for solace to Virgil!'

'Why doesn't he leave home?' Isobel said later, helping Aunt Jean tie up some exuberant fronds of a climbing rose she was training, for Aunt Sybil's pleasure, over a broken pillar. 'Why does he put up with that mother?'

'Oh, my dear,' Aunt Jean said, 'you know the Italians, you know how family-minded they are. I expect he thinks he must stay and protect his mother and his sister now that his father isn't there to do it any more.'

Isobel cut off a length of soft twine.

'His father didn't sound much of a protector. Aunt Sybil said he kept mistresses and bought expensive horses from Ireland and even more expensive paintings and statues from all over the place.'

Aunt Sybil also said that if she had been married to the Marchesa Fosco, she too would have kept mistresses, but Isobel did not repeat this because Aunt Jean disapproved of that kind of talk.

'He was said to be a little extravagant—'

'But will Giovanni just stay at home for ever?'

'I expect until he marries.'

A thought struck Isobel. She put down the scissors she was holding on the plinth of the stone pillar, and looked at Aunt Jean. 'Exactly like me.'

'Of course,' Aunt Jean said comfortably. 'Now, hold this branch here, would you, just there, so you don't get pricked, while I tie it up.'

Isobel looked about her, at the lovely, lavish terraced garden, full of scents in the declining sun, at the solid, handsome house above her, with its dark ilex wood behind and then the hillside climbing up to meet the smiling blue sky. She then looked down, over the wall that divided the lower edge of the garden from the olive grove, the vineyard, the patches of wheat and vegetables that fell away from her gaze down towards the valley floor. The smells of summer rose up from the warm earth as heady as wine, and except for the tolling of some small far-off bell, and the sound of one of the peasants singing, it was silent and sweet. Then Isobel thought of Professor Vaccari and the clerk in Maquay's bank and the murdered Archduke in Sarajevo.

'Is it right to live like this?' Isobel asked.

'Dear child!' exclaimed Aunt Jean. 'What can you mean?'

'It's all so safe here, and so beautiful, and so happy. But it isn't like that everywhere else. I just suddenly feel that if I go from living like this with you and Aunt Sybil to living like this with a husband, that I shall have – have—' she stopped, unable to explain herself.

Aunt Jean waited.

'That I shall not have lived – properly,' said Isobel.

'My dear,' said Aunt Jean, much shocked, 'what can you have lacked here that you should think like this?'

'Oh!' cried Isobel, rushing to put her arms around her aunt. 'I never meant to sound ungrateful, nobody could have been more loved and cherished than I have been, it's just, it's just—'

'What, my dear?'

'I don't know what it is,' Isobel said sadly. 'I feel it but I can't say it. I don't know what to call it.'

'Perhaps you need more friends of your own age, Isobel. Perhaps it will be good for you to have two young friends now at the Villa Celoni.'

Isobel thought of Giovanni Fosco. Could one possibly consider such a glamorous creature as a friend? And poor little Donatella, so under her mother's thumb that she was more like twelve than sixteen and consequently too childlike to be a friend. If Ida had lived, and Isobel had continued with that London life of Maudie and Miss Pargeter, with occasional little bouts of Montreux or Lancashire thrown in, might she, too, have become like Donatella, a poor mouselike thing at her mother's command? Had Aunt Sybil and Aunt Jean, even with their cosseting ways and their sheltered life, given her a kind of freedom? And if they had, should she not use that freedom . . .

'Isobel,' said Aunt Jean, 'I think you have been studying too hard.'

'No,' said Isobel, 'I think I haven't studied enough.' She paused and then said earnestly, 'I think, you see, that I have only just started to *think*.'

At dinner that night, Aunt Sybil did an excellent imitation of the Marchesa Fosco. Because of the family's reputation in Rome, the Marchesa had brought her children to Florence, to find a wife for Giovanni, and, in time, a husband for Donatella. Aunt Sybil, because of her friends in villadom, knew all the gossip.

'Giovanni is twenty-five. He is reputed to be clever and is certainly amusing. His father wanted him to make money by becoming a businessman, but Cecilia Clavering, who met him at Lady Scott's, told me that he is interested in progressive agriculture. So all he needs now, you see, is an English heiress, who is in love with Italy. I don't see, darling Isobel, why you shouldn't do nicely.'

Isobel, laughing and trying to eat her chicken, said, 'But I'm not an heiress.'

'Well, you will be, darling, in a very modest way, when you are twenty-five, which isn't six years away.'

'Sybil!' Aunt Jean said reprovingly. In Aunt Jean's book, it was never to be contemplated that one should not have enough money, but on the other hand, discussing how much one had was very vulgar.

'Don't be silly, Jean. Ida left Isobel a nice little sum and if she hadn't so annoyed the dreadful Morpeths by preferring you and me, she would have had a sum so nice it hardly bears thinking about. Why should she not know of it?'

'Because it isn't suitable,' Aunt Jean said, 'it isn't proper.'

Isobel leaned forward. 'I never think about it—'

'Well, you should,' said Aunt Sybil, 'money ought to be respected. The Marchesa Fosco has a very proper respect for money. I think she was adding up, in her mind, the value of the drawing room furniture. What a good thing I wasn't wearing my best pearls, or I should have given a very wrong impression of our circumstances. Should you like to marry the beautiful Giovanni Fosco, Isobel?'

Isobel, still laughing, protested she didn't even know him.

'But you have so much in common! Think of Virgil—'

'Sybil, stop it,' said Aunt Jean.

'Why should I? It's a charming game. And we can marry poor little Donatella off to Lady Scott's jolly Harry in a year or two, and he can bear her off to England and teach her to ride to hounds. Donatella reminded me of someone. Who can Donatella possibly have reminded me of?'

'Me,' said Isobel.

Aunt Sybil was delighted. 'Darling child! Of course! Except that Ida had none of the majesty of the Marchesa—'

'I don't know,' Isobel said slowly, 'what Mother was really like at all.'

Aunt Jean shot Aunt Sybil a warning glance.

'I am afraid,' Aunt Sybil said, 'that she was never happy. It is difficult to be charming when you are never happy.'

'Papa made her unhappy—'

'And her temperament did.'

'Do you think,' Isobel said seriously, laying her knife and fork down neatly together on her plate, 'that it's very important whom one marries?'

Aunt Jean gave a little gasp. 'Oh, my dear—'

'Desperately,' said Aunt Sybil, suddenly serious.

'It's the most important thing, dear child,' Aunt Jean said, clasping her hands, 'that you will ever decide, in your whole life. You see, it *is* a woman's life. Marriage must be taken very seriously.' She looked directly at Isobel with her firm, fond gaze. 'When it comes to your marriage, Isobel, that is when your Aunt Sybil and I will be your guardians and your advisers. The right marriage for you will be the matter closest to both our hearts.' She gave a little beat of emphasis on the table with her clasped hands. 'The *right* marriage.'

Love, Isobel thought later, leaning out of her bedroom window to breathe in the lovely night, oh love. What is it and why am I so ignorant that I even have to ask? Is feeling dizzy smelling a rose or reading some lines of poetry something to do with it, and also all these dreams and desires I have that I can't explain so that I feel a perfect fool, and dreadfully frustrated? Is it worse because it's the summer? Or is it worse because if I were a girl of nineteen in London now I should be going to parties and balls whereas here, however much I love it, I have Professor Vaccari and games of tennis with the Dawson girls and dinner with Aunt Sybil and Aunt Jean instead? And if all this bother isn't love, then what is it? Moody would say it was indigestion. Perhaps, Isobel thought, drawing the shutters gently to and padding across to her bed where the gilded cherubs waited, Moody is right. But oh, if she is, then how I hope and pray that love comes along, very quickly, instead!

Chapter Seven

Aunt Sybil took up the family at the Villa Celoni. She declared that it amused her to tease the Marchesa and to try and draw out poor Donatella and encourage her to defy her mother. She was also, plainly, captivated by the young Marchese, who turned out to be not simply amusing, but well-read too, and a sympathetic conversationalist. Aunt Sybil said that it was such a delightful change to have a young man about who appeared as eager as she was to discuss the possible purchase of a small bronze statue for a fountain in the garden or exactly the right spot for a newly acquired lacquer cabinet for the *sala degli uccelli*.

'It's no use asking you and Aunt Jean, you see, darling, because you are far too sensible and would simply say you thought the fountain was perfectly nice as it was.'

'I would,' said Isobel, who associated Aunt Sybil's endless fascination with *objets d'art* with deep tedium. The house was so pretty, what was the point of tinkering on with it in this obsessive way? Yet the tinkering seemed to bring Giovanni Fosco up the white dust road from the Villa Celoni very often, and this Isobel was far too honest even to pretend she didn't like. He brought a kind of excitement to the house, an extra charge to the air, and he was so perfectly at ease with everyone there, from Maria and Luca to the aunts and – well, to Isobel herself. In spite of this – or, perhaps, because of it – Isobel kept faithfully to her timetable with Professor Vaccari, even if she was giving up the chance to go on some charming little expedition with Aunt Sybil and the young Marchese. Aunt Sybil was enjoying these jaunts so much –

to neighbouring villas, or to local village churches where a lovely fragment of a fresco or mosaic was to be found, or to a pretty place on a hillside where Luca laid out a picnic tea in the shade – that she was thinking of buying a motor car. Giovanni, she said, recommended a Lancia, and Luca could learn to drive. Giovanni was also talking about the installation of electric light, which would involve a generator being set up behind the house. Aunt Jean objected to this violently, on the grounds of noise and the smells of the necessary chemicals. Aunt Sybil said she would get used to both, and just think of the joy of being able to read all evening as if by daylight. Aunt Sybil was in the highest spirits.

So, in a rather different way, was Isobel. Even Professor Vaccari, darting his odd, all-seeing glances at her through his thick spectacles, noticed it.

'Hah!' he said one day, 'the sleeping princess awakens at last!'

Isobel had not mentioned Giovanni Fosco to Professor Vaccari. She did not ever speak much of her home life, and Professor Vaccari, who had his own views of the English community in Florence which he kept politely to himself, never asked her about it either. To him, born a Victorian, it was perfectly natural and proper for a young woman like Isobel to live in the care of two widowed aunts, and to pursue her studies until a suitable husband was found for her into whose subsequent care she could then be handed over. Professor Vaccari made no distinction between the sexes in the matter of education; in his view, a good head, male or female, should be as well furnished as it was possible to make it. Isobel unquestionably had a good head, and in his mind's eye, Professor Vaccari saw her taking the fruits of her education with him to enrich both her marriage and her consequent motherhood. It was not necessary, after all, for an education to provide anything more practical for such a one as Isobel; she would not ever be expected to earn her living. And yet . . . There was something in Isobel that made Professor Vaccari feel that she might surprise them all, a quality of sturdy independence, a dawning appetite for a way of life less sheltered than the one she had previously known. Hardly a lesson went by when she did not demand to know what was happening in Europe, and what the increasingly alarming events might signify.

'What was it you said about the Russians, Professor?'

'That they have intervened against Austria-Hungary to defend Serbia.'

'Is that a bluff?' Isobel said seriously.

'I sincerely hope,' said Professor Vaccari, 'that that is all it is. We do not want war between Russia and Germany. And now to work. Now to poetry.'

Professor Vaccari had grown fond of Isobel. He and his wife had not been blessed with children but he had satisfied a good deal of natural fatherly feelings in his affection for some of his young pupils. He looked now at Isobel, as she sat reading aloud from 'Sicelides Musae' – 'We will indulge ourselves this afternoon,' Professor Vaccari had said, 'with something quite easy from the Golden Age' – and thought that the plain, solid English child had matured into something interesting and even pretty. There was a glow about her, too, an inner glow. Could this possibly have anything to do with the personable young man who had presented himself two days ago enquiring at what hour Miss Lindsay finished her lessons?

'That will do,' Professor Vaccari said, gently interrupting.

'Was I reading so badly?'

'No. You were reading well, but your mind was elsewhere.'

'Oh,' said Isobel, growing pink.

'I think, don't you, that that is enough for today?'

'Perhaps,' Isobel said, 'it's so hot—'

'And so distracting,' said Professor Vaccari, twinkling a little.

She stooped hurriedly, tumbling her books into her bag.

'I shall see you tomorrow, Signorina.'

'Yes—'

'Go home, my dear, and read the "Ode to Aphrodite".'

Isobel stared at him. He merely smiled back. She nodded, swallowed, and stumbled out of the room between the tottering piles of books.

'*If now she loves thee not*,' Professor Vaccari quoted gently to her wake, '*she soon will love . . .*'

Isobel fled down the stairs and out into the hot, bright street.

'Signorina Lindsay—'

She spun round. There stood Giovanni Fosco in a cream linen suit, with a straw hat in his hand. He bowed to her.

'Forgive me for startling you—'

'You did!'

'I'm afraid it was a plot. To see you on your own, to offer to escort you home. I had asked the good Professor when your lesson would be over.'

'But I'm early, I wasn't concentrating—'

'And I was waiting early, to make quite sure. Will you come with me to Doney's for a water ice?'

'Oh yes,' Isobel said gratefully.

'You have no sunshade—'

'I forgot it. I always forget it. But I've a perfectly good hat, you see.'

She blinked up at him in the brilliant riverside light. He looked astonishingly handsome in his cream suit. She suddenly remembered Professor Vaccari's parting words and went pink again.

'Can we walk?' she said quickly, turning away so that he shouldn't see her face. 'I must get into the shade.'

He walked beside her as gracefully as a panther, putting himself between her and the sun until they were both safely on the shady side of the street.

'Virgil again today, Signorina?'

'Oh, yes.'

'And do you read Homer too?'

'A little. The words are easier because his vocabulary is quite limited but—'

'But what, Miss Lindsay?'

'I prefer Virgil's vision,' Isobel said. 'I like his countryside being a working countryside.'

She heard Giovanni Fosco give a little intake of breath. At Doney's doorway, he took her elbow to guide her up the stairs to the first floor restaurant.

'My feelings exactly,' he said.

He chose a window table so that she might have a view down into the Via Tornabuoni. Isobel glanced worriedly at the menu. She knew that the Foscos had lost almost all their money, and she should not have allowed Giovanni to suggest somewhere as expensive as Doney's, even though he had done it to compliment her. Giovanni took the menu out of her hands.

'Please do not look so anxiously at the prices, Miss Lindsay. I may be an impoverished aristocrat, but I am not penniless. And I must,' he said, grinning at her, 'be allowed to choose how I spend such money as I do have.'

'I am so sorry. I only meant—'

'To be kind,' said Giovanni. 'I know that. But to allow me to spend five francs on you without objection would be even kinder.'

He summoned a waiter, ordered tea, iced water and lemon water ices, and then said to Isobel, without preamble, 'If I still had a fortune, you see, I should have liked to squander it on you.'

Isobel looked down at the tablecloth, her ears burning. She rearranged the spoons and forks without noticing what she was doing, utterly charmed and confused.

'Do I offend you?'

'Oh no—'

'I had such preconceptions, prejudices even, about the English, and you have destroyed them all. I can see you now, coming into your aunts' salon, such a picture of charm and reluctance! I was standing by the window, remember, watching you before you noticed me and I saw you forcing yourself to be obedient. Am I right?'

'Yes,' Isobel said, at last looking up, 'quite right.'

He leaned forward. 'Are you happy with your aunts, Isobel?'

'Oh yes!' she cried at once. 'They have done everything for me, everything—'

A waiter appeared with a tray and set out the teapot and cups, the glasses, the dishes of water ice and a plate of biscuits shaped like fans.

When he had gone, Giovanni said, 'But however happy our childhoods were, we outgrow them. The things that satisfied us when we were very young don't always continue to satisfy us.'

'No,' said Isobel doubtfully, pouring tea.

'For example, it won't satisfy me to live much longer with my mother who, however absurd she may sometimes seem, has borne great troubles with even greater fortitude. But I want to strike out now, I want to make my mark upon the world!'

'What kind of mark?' Isobel asked, handing him his cup.

'I will tell you,' he said leaning forward. 'I want to get away from the city and city life, I want to find some land that is still undeveloped agriculturally and make my life there, farming by the new methods, bringing neglected land to life again.'

Isobel took a spoonful of her ice. 'Where will this land be?'

'Oh, here, here in Tuscany! I want to find some difficult land, land that has not been tilled for centuries and make it yield. I don't want to live like so many Tuscan landowners, simply handing all the hard work over to my *fattore* while I sit on the loggia with white hands and gaze at my property from afar. I want a lifetime's work, you see.' He looked penetratingly at Isobel. 'And you?'

'Me—'

'Yes, you. Do you want to live your English young lady life all your days?'

'No,' said Isobel decidedly.

64

'Then?'

'I hadn't thought of an alternative really, I just know—' She stopped.

'What do you just know, *bellissima* Isobel?'

'I would like to be useful,' Isobel said.

'But your *Zia* Jean is useful! Why don't you remain like her, looking after the olives and the vines and the peasants?'

'Are you teasing me?'

'No,' Giovanni said, 'I am challenging you.'

'Then—'

'Then?'

'Then I would like my usefulness to be on a bigger scale than Aunt Jean's, less safe, less domesticated. Marchese—'

'Please call me Giovanni.'

'Giovanni,' said Isobel, trying not to be distracted by the elegance of his pale brown hand lying on the white tablecloth, 'I am afraid my ideas are very unformed but I do know that I am not cut out for drawing rooms, and I should like my world to be a bit – a bit—'

'A bit what?'

'Bigger,' said Isobel.

He said nothing, but, without warning, lifted her hand from where it lay, ready to pick up her tea cup, and kissed it. She did not, she discovered, want him to put it down again.

'I shall remember this afternoon always,' he said, 'and now I must take you home.'

On the way to the tram, he did not take her arm again, but he walked so closely beside her that he made her feel breathless. She glanced at him once or twice, so urbane and immaculate in his city suit, and tried to imagine him in the rough shirt and trousers he would have to wear in the pastoral, Virgilian life he planned for himself. Oddly enough, it wasn't difficult. For all his elegance, he was strongly made with broad shoulders and long limbs. Isobel decided she would not try any more to picture him in an open-necked shirt because, for some reason, the attempt made her feel quite faint.

In the tram, he sat beside her and talked easily of his childhood. He said that he and Donatella had been like only children because of the great distance between them in age, and that he and his father had been at odds with one another from his earliest recollection. His father had been a city lover, a man whose only pleasures were sophisticated ones, and who was shrewdly planning to have his son restore some of the family fortune that he had squandered. Giovanni had known since he was a boy that his father was publicly unfaithful to his mother, but that, he said, was so common in the circles in which his parents moved that it was a long time before he understood how much his mother was hurt.

'She made the mistake, you see, of loving my father.'

Isobel said nothing. For the first time in her life, she felt a strong and disconcerting urge to talk about her own childhood, her own father's infidelity, her own mother's broken heart. She wondered if this was in any way disloyal, and, if so, to whom?

'Do you think one should marry for love?' Giovanni asked.

Isobel looked out of the tram window, at an old brick wall they were passing, over which yellow banksia roses were tumbling in a glowing cascade.

'Yes, I do.'

'So do I. I believe my mother married for love, and my father for blood and money. My mother's family were better born even than my father's, and they were wealthy too.'

Isobel said, in a tiny voice, 'My father married for money.'

Giovanni turned to look at her. 'Did he?'

'Yes. My grandfather had made a fortune – in trade, you see. But my mother married for love.'

He seized her hand. 'But we are the same!'

'It killed my mother in the end, I think,' Isobel said, feeling a great releasing rush of candour. 'I think she wasn't very stable or very stoical, but he was the centre of her world and when he went away, she didn't want to live any more. She used to stand out on the balcony of her bedroom in winter in her nightclothes and call for death. She did die of it, of her love for him, in the end. She got pneumonia, they said, but she wouldn't have got it if she'd been happy. And if she had gone on living—' She stopped.

Giovanni bent his head so that their cheeks were almost touching. 'Yes?'

'I wouldn't have been able to be happy,' said Isobel in a guilty whisper.

'I know,' he said, 'I am like that. I must break away to breathe.' He squeezed her hand slightly. 'Have you a faithful nature?'

'I think so.'

'I have too. I am not like my father. I am not like my mother either. Nor is Donatella. Poor Donatella, my mother is crushing the life out of her.'

'I know. I saw it. I – recognized it.'

66

Giovanni moved his hand slightly so that it rested with its palm against Isobel's. Then he slipped his fingers between hers.

'We are so much the same—'

'Yes,' she said. She thought he must be able to see her heart thudding away under the green, satin-striped cotton of her dress. 'But I am English and you are Italian.'

'Is that bad?'

'No, it's good,' Isobel said. 'I don't like the English here, I don't like the way they talk or behave. I don't like the way they talk about European politics just now as if they knew all about it but that nothing was going to affect them. The only things I know worth knowing, I learn from Professor Vaccari.'

The tram hissed to a halt, and Isobel and Giovanni rose and made their way out of it and into the hot, still, late afternoon.

'Will you take my arm? And give me your books to carry. How I admire your studies, how I—' he stopped and then said, after a pause, 'I must restrain myself,' and laughed.

They set off up the road to the Villa Calvina together, kicking up little puffs of white dust that settled thickly on the weeds and the thyme bushes that grew at the edges. Below them, the heat shimmered and danced on the domes and towers of Florence, and the Arno caught the sun like a golden snake.

'It's so beautiful!' Isobel cried, pausing to look down on it.

'And I,' Giovanni said, pausing too, very close to her, 'would like to make somewhere abandoned as beautiful as this. As beautiful as you,' and then without warning, he dropped Isobel's bookbag in the dust, took her in his arms, and kissed her firmly on the mouth.

Chapter Eight

On 4 August, it was known throughout the English community in Florence that Great Britain had declared war on Germany, after the latter's invasion of Belgium. The carriages from all the villas went flying out along the white dust roads bearing the news and even more, the reactions.

'Oh, my dear, *brave* little Belgium—'

'Do you know, Sybil, I really feel we should *do* something, though heaven knows what—'

'I wonder if we should go back to England? But then, I wonder if we *can* get back if the Germans and the French are going to be fighting all over France . . .'

'My dear, you may depend upon it, it will be over in a moment. My brother-in-law, Tommy, knows several people in the Cabinet and they have been saying all summer that there really isn't anything in it—'

'Will there be refugees? I suppose if there were refugees from Belgium they would go to England, surely?'

'Oh, *brave* little Belgium!'

'Isn't it odd, I've lived in Italy now for nearly eleven years, but all this makes me feel frightfully patriotic . . .'

'Eddie is quite sure it will be over by Christmas. Do have another sandwich—'

Isobel listened in incredulity and rage. Professor Vaccari, lifting his eyes reluctantly from the 'Ode to Aphrodite', had said sadly and gently to her, 'Ah, Signorina, this will be so very terrible. There has been no war between the Great Powers since 1871, so it is only old men like me who remember it. The people of Europe are all leaping so eagerly into war, and they all think they are defending their own existence, even though their method of defence is to invade someone else's territory. Six million men are being mobilized! Six million—'

'And Italy?' Isobel said.

'Ah,' said Professor Vaccari, taking off his spectacles and tiredly rubbing his eyes, 'Italy has withdrawn into neutrality. Both sides will compete for her favour, but she is asking just to be left alone.'

'Is that so?' Isobel demanded of Giovanni Fosco on one of the late afternoon walks that had now become a habit with them.

'So the politicians say—'

'And you? What do you say?'

'I say, Isobel, that it is ignoble that Italy, who rightly claims to be a Great Power, should remain neutral in such a conflict as this. War would invigorate us!'

'Would it?' Isobel said, doubtfully. She was full of conviction that England had done right in coming to Belgium's rescue, but she was full of doubt about this war too. She looked at Giovanni, leaning against the parapet of the Santa Trinita bridge, his beautiful profile shaded by the brim of his hat, and felt an awful tremor. If young men all over Europe were rushing to defend their nations, what was to stop Giovanni rushing too, if Italy were to join the war? It was, of course, glorious to fight for your country, but was it – well, worth it? Isobel swallowed and looked away. That was her sensible side thinking, the sensible side that only Aunt Jean had ever seemed to appreciate and value.

'Isobel?'

'Yes—'

'Don't look so sad. Nothing will happen quickly and it may be all over before anything happens at all.' He came away from the parapet and drew her hand through his arm. 'Smile for me—'

She obliged. He led her across the bridge towards the Oltr'arno.

'Come, we will walk in the Boboli Gardens. Isobel—'

'Yes?'

'Do your aunts know how often we meet?'

'No,' Isobel said.

'Shall you not tell them? Why don't you tell them?'

'I like it being secret.'

'Do you? I would like it better if it were open. Why don't you tell your aunts? *Zia* Sybil would be pleased, she likes me.'

'I know she does,' Isobel said, 'it's just—'

69

He bent to look into her face. 'Just what?'

'It's just that I was waiting to be sure, quite sure, of my own mind, you see.'

He said nothing, but simply lifted the hand that lay on his arm to his lips. For over three weeks now they had met after Isobel's lessons, and had walked through hot, drowsy late afternoon Florence, sometimes sitting in the cool, incense-scented darkness of churches, talking about their pasts and the hopes they had for their futures. They had been enchanted afternoons, idling, talking, stopping occasionally in a quiet shady corner to kiss, dreaming the time away in a golden world of their own.

Now, on a secluded seat by an oak hedge on one of the higher terraces of the Boboli Gardens, Giovanni took both Isobel's hands in his and said, 'Are you, *carissima* Isobel, now sure of your own mind?'

'Oh yes,' Isobel said candidly.

'Even though we have known each other so short a time?'

'Why should that matter?'

'It doesn't matter anything to me. But I want to be sure that I am not hurrying you faster than you would wish to go.'

'No,' said Isobel, 'you aren't.'

He leaned forward. 'I love you, you see.'

She looked steadily at him. 'And I love you.'

'Do you?'

'Yes,' she said.

'Even though I have nothing to offer you except my name and my hopes? Isobel, I have no money.'

'I know,' she said, 'but that doesn't matter, because I have. Some, at least, when I am twenty-five. Enough,' she said, her face lighting up, 'to buy our farm, I should think.'

He gave a cry of pleasure and flung his arms around her. 'I adore you!'

'Dreadful behaviour,' a passing English voice said to its companion. 'Italian, of course—'

'Oh, of course—'

'Will you be my wife? Will you be the Marchesa Fosco?'

Isobel could hardly speak for joy. The thought that she would have someone of her very own almost choked her, let alone the fact that that someone should be the almost godlike Giovanni! She held his face in her hands. She loved him so much – indeed, at that moment she loved all Italy so much – that she thought she could easily die of it.

70

'I am so happy!'

There were tears in his eyes. 'I can hardly believe this—'

'But it's true—'

'Yes, it's true, and we will make our dreams happen.'

'Yes,' she said.

'I am so lucky!' he cried, leaping up and pulling her to him. 'What have I done to be so lucky?'

'Careful,' she said, clutching at her hat, laughing.

'I adore you. Do you understand me? I adore you. There is no-one else like you in the world.'

'Stop it,' said Isobel.

'No,' he said, tremendously excited, 'why should I? Why may I not tell the whole of Florence how wonderful you are and how lucky I am?'

'Because it would embarrass me,' Isobel said, laughing and delighted.

'Come, we must celebrate. We must find champagne and music, we must—'

'Giovanni—'

'Yes? I love to hear you say my name. Say it again, say "Giovanni"—'

'Giovanni,' Isobel said, 'I think perhaps now that I ought to go home and tell my aunts.'

They looked at one another, suddenly sober.

'Now?'

'Yes. Then we can celebrate, when we have their blessing. And – your mother's.'

'But my mother loves you!'

Isobel smiled. 'Your mother wants a good match for you. I may not be good enough.'

'Dearest, don't talk like this!'

'I have to.'

He looked at her face for a long moment, at the clear hazel eyes, the short nose and the wide mouth with its perfect teeth. She was adorable and in some ways formidable. He sighed, and took her hand.

'Then we must tell the aunts—'

'I must.'

'Not together?'

'No,' said Isobel, 'I must tell them on my own.'

*   *   *

71

'My darling!' Aunt Sybil cried. She was on the loggia, reclining in her cane chair with a fan in one hand and a novel in the other. 'The heat! The heat down in Florence must have been truly terrible. I drove all the warmongers off this afternoon, I simply could not bear one more word about Moltke and Joffre and Grand Duke Nicholas or whether modern armies can or can't move faster than the Romans. Take your hat off, darling, and sit next to me, at least there's some air here. Maria shall bring you some lemonade.'

Isobel took off her hat and sank gratefully into a cushioned chair. The air was full of aromatic, late-summer herby smells and down in the valley, a lone bell sounded a single thin metallic note.

'Where is Aunt Jean?'

'Need you ask? Supervising the haymaking. I wish she wouldn't, in heat like this, but what is the use of protesting? She is going to send for wool so that we can all knit socks for the soldiers.'

'Good.'

'I knew you would like that. Isobel, why are you looking so buttoned up?'

'I'm not—'

'You are, darling child, you are all tight with secretiveness. What did you learn in Florence today that we shouldn't know?'

'Nothing—'

Maria came out onto the loggia with a glass jug of lemonade and a tumbler on a tray. She smiled at Isobel. She adored Isobel, the *Padroncina* who had grown up so graceful, so pretty, a credit to the Villa Calvina.

'Thank you,' Isobel said gratefully.

'Now,' Aunt Sybil said, as soon as Maria had gone, taking with her Isobel's discarded hat to hang up in its proper place, 'tell me what you have to tell me.'

'Not until Aunt Jean comes—'

'Oh! You are as bad as she is, such sticklers for propriety! I shall send Luca down to the hayfield for her—'

'Please don't.'

'You are so provoking, Isobel, so stubborn. How can we beguile the time? I know – there's a letter from your father. He wants you to go to Castle Lindsay for some of this autumn.'

'But I—'

'Quite. He wrote this letter before the war began. There's no question of your going now. Should you, however, have liked to have gone?'

Isobel hesitated.

'Would you go if it were not for your stepmother?'

'Perhaps—'

'Why should you still bear her a grudge? By all accounts she's a perfectly nice creature and has made your father happy.'

Isobel drank her lemonade slowly. 'I left all that behind, you see—'

'But if it hadn't been for your father's kind interference, you would have been Morpethed to death instead of living here. And if he hadn't married again, you might have lived with him, so you see, you owe something to her as well.'

Isobel nodded, and reached over to squeeze her aunt's hand.

'I know. Perhaps I was – am – afraid I might like my step-mother—'

'Hah!' Aunt Sybil exclaimed. 'There we have it! Now look, there's a note for you.'

'From him?'

'Yes,' said Aunt Sybil, opening her fan and picking up her novel again. 'On the table by the tray. From your father.'

Dearest Isobel, *the note ran,*

I so hope you will feel able to accept the invitation to Lindsay this autumn. It is, after all, your family home and perhaps you will feel able to recognize by now both the presence here of your stepmother and your step brothers and sister. You would have the warmest of welcomes. I confess I long to see you – Then why, thought Isobel, have you never come to Italy? – and enjoy for myself the great charms your aunts so fondly testify to.

       Your loving father,
       E.L.

Isobel folded the note up and put it in her pocket. She could not, of course – oh bless the war – go to Castle Lindsay, but she must write to her father and tell him, too, of her engagement. He at least would be pleased, as pleased as he always seemed to be, to have arrangements made for Isobel in which he could rejoice without troubling himself . . .

'Isobel?'

'Yes?'

'Here comes Aunt Jean,' Aunt Sybil said. 'I can see her hat.'

The familiar white hat – straw now that it was so hot – was coming bobbing up the terraces.

73

'Coo-ee!' called Aunt Jean, as she came, 'coo-ee!'

She emerged into the loggia pink with heat and exertion.

'Oh, my dears, how cool you look! And lemonade! What a blessing! We have stooked the whole of the small meadow and half the larger one and Beppe says the wheat is the best he has seen it in years. Isobel, you look quite pale, dear.'

'It's the heat—'

'And the studying, perhaps. Shouldn't you give up Professor Vaccari just during these hot months?'

'It isn't the heat,' Aunt Sybil said crisply, 'or the studying. It's because she has a secret she is not looking forward to telling us.'

Isobel pressed her lips together. Aunt Sybil was unfair, but then Aunt Sybil was often unfair. She poured a glass of lemonade for Aunt Jean and took it over to her.

'What secret, dear?' Aunt Jean said gently.

Isobel looked at her gratefully. At least she would understand, she would see Isobel's need to have someone of her own, someone to build a practical as well as a romantic future with. Aunt Jean would not object to a three-week courtship and a penniless suitor. Isobel went back to her chair and sat down, deliberately upright, her hands folded in her lap.

'These last few weeks,' Isobel said, 'I have been seeing the Marchese Fosco, after my lessons with Professor Vaccari.'

She stopped. Nobody said anything. Both aunts were quite motionless, watching her.

'We have been for walks, all around Florence, talking. We have sometimes been to churches, and once to the Uffizi Gallery, and occasionally to Doney's, for an ice, but mostly we have just walked and – and talked. We have talked about everything. He is the first person with whom I could talk about my childhood because his, in a way, wasn't so very different. And we have talked about the future. His dream is to rescue an abandoned estate and to bring the land back to prosperity by all the new agricultural methods. My dream – my dream is – to help him.' Isobel paused, drew a breath, and then said, a little more rapidly, 'This afternoon, in the Boboli Gardens, he asked me to be his wife and I accepted him.'

Then there was silence. It went on, it seemed to Isobel, for a very long time indeed and then Aunt Sybil rose gracefully out of her chair and said, 'Darling child, what perfectly charming news!'

Isobel stared at her. 'You don't mind?'

Aunt Sybil stooped and enveloped Isobel in her scented embrace.

74

'Mind? Why should I mind? He is an accomplished, good-natured young man of excellent family. How perfectly lovely to have a love affair happening under our very noses!'

Isobel, too bewildered at this unexpected reaction to be openly delighted, turned to Aunt Jean. She sat there, in her grey cashmere dress, as immovable as a little rock.

'Aunt Jean?'

'Impossible,' Aunt Jean said.

'But—'

'Jean! Dear!'

'It's unthinkable,' Aunt Jean said, 'it's absolutely unthinkable! And it is absurd of you, Sybil, to rejoice as if this was just a pretty little matter of no consequence, absurd!'

'Jean!'

'Listen to me!' Aunt Jean cried, almost shouting. 'Giovanni Fosco may be a perfectly nice young man but young men like him are two a penny! He may be charmed by Isobel, it's hardly surprising if he is, but he is doubtless charmed by her money too!'

'Aunt Jean—'

'Don't interrupt me!' Aunt Jean exclaimed, stamping her foot on the loggia floor. 'Isobel's marriage is the most important decision we have to take, the right marriage is what all these happy years have been leading up to, but this is *not* the right marriage! Your head has been turned by a handsome face, Isobel, and because this is the first time you have been in love, you suppose it is the only time. You shall *not* marry young Fosco, Isobel, you shall not. You are wholly unfitted to be the wife of a poor man, there has been nothing in your upbringing to train you to live in discomfort or with hard physical work, *nothing*. Let him fulfil his dream if he wishes, and when he has a prosperous home to take you to, then let him come back for you. But this scheme is preposterous, it is the play dreams of silly children!'

Isobel burst into tears.

'Jean,' Aunt Sybil cried, 'how harsh you are! Can't you remember being in love?'

'When I accepted Arthur Fanshawe,' she said stoutly, 'I was accepting protection and companionship as well as love.'

'And mightn't Isobel—'

'He has no money!' Aunt Jean repeated. 'He has no money and he wishes to get his hands on some!'

'He loves me,' Isobel said, between sobs.

'He is too young to know. And so are you.'

'But Isobel loves Italy, loves the Italians, and of all Italians Giovanni does seem one of the most delightful—'

'Delightful!' spat Aunt Jean. She was quivering with fury. 'And when did delightfulness ever put food in your mouth and clothes on your back?'

'He is serious about the farm,' Isobel said shakily. 'He is really idealistic.'

Aunt Jean glanced at her. There was nothing soft in her glance.

'Where is your good sense, Isobel? If you had used but an atom of it, you would have realized that you are in any case in no position to marry a penniless man, and you won't be, for five years. I am going in now, to change, and perhaps you will reflect a little on your foolishness while I am gone. And you, Sybil, will come with me.'

Aunt Sybil hesitated. She was the imperious one, the one around whose will and whims life at the Villa Calvina ran, and Jean never attempted to contradict or overrule her. But then, Jean never lost her temper, never made a stand about anything, so that there was never occasion for conflict between them. She looked at her sister. Jean was regarding her with a steady and imperious eye. And perhaps, charming though young Fosco was, and fascinating though it was to have a love affair – how terribly long ago, Sybil often thought, her own and only one was! – happening all around them, darling Isobel must be encouraged at least to wait a little . . .

'Coming, Jean,' Aunt Sybil said docilely and followed her sister, her skirts swishing silkily on the tiles, into the house, leaving Isobel alone and desolate on the loggia.

Chapter Nine

Italy – 1915

Aunt Jean was adamant. She had been adamant for months. As far as she could effect it, all communication with the Villa Celoni ceased, and when Isobel went down into Florence for her lessons, Moody was despatched on a later tram to escort her home. The only way for Isobel and Giovanni to meet, throughout the winter, was for him to catch an early tram to the city, wait there for Isobel's arrival, and walk with her to Professor Vaccari's. He was there, every weekday, without fail, and also, without fail, told Isobel that she was his love and his life and that her constancy meant all the world to him.

Isobel had no trouble in being constant. It was in her nature both to be loyal and to endure, and whatever fury and unhappiness was caused her by Aunt Jean's obduracy was more than compensated for by finding Giovanni waiting for her daily at the tram stop, his face lighting up like a beacon at the sight of her. He said his life was a desert but for those twenty-minute walks between the tram and Professor Vaccari's. He said he could only bear the remaining twenty-three hours and forty minutes of each day because of knowing he would see Isobel again, and because he was planning for their future.

'Of course, we shall have our future.'

'Of course,' Isobel said. She might be outwardly complying with Aunt Jean, but inwardly, she was doing nothing of the sort. An excited infatuation for Giovanni Fosco was growing, day by day, into a profound desire to share her future with nobody but him. They were like two pieces of a jigsaw, carefully cut to interlock with one another, sympathetic in everything. The only difference between them that Isobel could see was that he had more beauty, and she had more patience. Indeed, Giovanni, day by day, was losing his grip on what little patience he had been born with.

'How long must this go on, this farce, this outrageous situation? Even my mother has given her consent! My mother! You will not come and see her because you say you will not disobey your aunt. How long will that be, this refusal? How long must poor Donatella wait for her sister? How long must I go on seeing you for twenty minutes, how long?'

'For as long as it takes,' Isobel said.

'What nonsense, what terrible nonsense! What can you mean?'

'I mean, we must wait until Aunt Jean comes to see how serious we are. You know we can't marry without her blessing because we have no money, you *know* that. She has to learn to trust in you, to see how happy you will make me.'

'I will, I will!' he cried, adjusting his umbrella over her against the February rain. 'I will make you so happy, you will think yourself in paradise! But why should *Zia* Jean ever change?'

'Time will change her,' Isobel said.

'Who says so?'

'I do. And Aunt Sybil.'

Aunt Sybil rustled with secrecy. She adored the drama of it all. She would not openly defy her sister, but she would not discourage Isobel either. She thought the spectacle of Isobel in love was both charming and exciting, and she believed it good for Isobel to feel so strongly, so passionately. And she had a great weakness for Giovanni Fosco. He was not only a joy to look at, and eloquent and amusing, but he wasn't hearty like most young Englishmen, nor childishly frivolous like most young Italians. He even had a purpose, with his visionary agricultural plans, even if it was a purpose Sybil could hardly bear to contemplate on account of the uncomfortableness that must accompany it. When they were married – and Sybil was sure they ultimately would be – how could she possibly go and stay with them in their peasant simplicity? Moody would have to go on ahead, days in advance, to make things tolerable. But even Sybil knew that such objections were trivial. The essential things, like a good heart and a good mind and good family,

78

were all there in Giovanni Fosco. And in rather under five years' time, when Isobel came into her little inheritance, nobody could stop them in any case. She had tried to say all that, over and over again, to Jean, but Jean would have none of it. To Jean, the young man was an adventurer and his agricultural notions were piffle. Nothing but progressive – how Jean hated anything progressive, bless her – piffle.

'He will leave her destitute!'

'No, he won't—'

'He will. He will squander her money on his silly schemes, and leave her destitute.'

'Then she can come back here.'

'Sybil!' Aunt Jean cried, again and again, 'Isobel should not just be *married*, she should be properly married, well married!'

'We can't marry her off against her will—'

'I'm not suggesting that, I don't wish for that, I just will not consent to her marrying the first young man that comes along.'

'But he is more than that—'

'Piffle,' said Aunt Jean, and then, more grimly, 'waiting will cool her ardour. You'll see.'

Edward had been written to. Isobel had written stating – not asking – that she was to marry a young Italian Marchese, and was to reclaim a decayed Tuscan estate with him when she was twenty-five, in possession of her fortune from her mother, and they were able to find a suitable property. She said she considered herself engaged to the young man, and she didn't ask for Edward's permission or even approval. Aunt Sybil had written a long but ultimately evasive letter about Isobel's happiness and Giovanni's attractions, which skated rapidly over her sister's objections. She said airily, at the end of her letter, that as everyone in question was so young, and because of the money and the war, nothing could happen in any kind of hurry. Aunt Jean wrote demanding that her brother should come out to Italy at once, war or no war, and prevent his daughter even contemplating such a terrible mistake, by taking her back to England with him if necessary. Edward read all three letters, reflected upon the complexities and pressures of his own family life at Lindsay Castle, and elected to believe Sybil's letter, as the one comfortably suggesting he did nothing about the situation, but wait. He did exert himself sufficiently to write to Isobel.

'I rejoice to hear of your great happiness, dearest Isobel, but with your youth and present financial dependency, and the world so preoccupied and disturbed as it is just now, I would counsel you to wait.'

I am waiting, Isobel thought in exasperation, reading the letter. What else can I do? She threw the letter into the wastepaper basket.

'As long as I don't bother him,' Isobel said to Giovanni, 'he wouldn't much mind who I married.'

'I mind desperately who you marry,' Giovanni said. 'If you marry anyone but me, I shall kill you both and then shoot myself.'

'How messy,' Isobel said, but she was delighted. She loved the way he talked, these exaggerated sentences emerging from his perfectly turned out exterior, the contrast between the control of his appearance and the passion of his speech.

'What did your father say to you in his letter?' Aunt Jean demanded, having scrutinized the post, as she always did these days in case there was a note from the Villa Celoni.

'He asked me to wait.'

'What? He isn't coming?'

'No. He says the war is creating problems with manning the estate. He says it's impossible for him to leave, and that he trusts to my good sense.'

'You must regard his request that you should wait as a promise,' Aunt Jean demanded.

'But I am waiting,' Isobel said patiently. 'Promise or no promise, I'm waiting. I haven't a choice.'

Aunt Jean glared at Isobel. Isobel reflected that if she had had a quarrel with Aunt Sybil, Aunt Sybil would have declared that Isobel's attitude was making her ill. But Aunt Jean was no blackmailer. Aunt Jean was a woman of unswerving honesty and old-fashioned principle, who would rather break her heart over her adored Isobel than let wrong become right. Looking at her now, inexorable in her grey cashmere dress and her winter *podere* hat, Isobel felt a great conflict of emotion, a resentment that Aunt Jean's attitude was casting such a bitter blight on some of the best years that Giovanni and Isobel might ever know, happily planning their future, and an admiring affection for the disinterest of Aunt Jean's love for her. How sordid that it should all come down to money! Yet it had to and Isobel knew it. In love and alight with hope, Isobel still knew that it would never be romantic to starve. She leaned forward and kissed Aunt Jean's cheek.

'I will obey you,' Isobel said, 'as I always have. I will wait. We will wait. For now, at least.'

*   *   *

The winter seemed interminable. The elements of their old, happy life at the Villa Calvina were still there, the house and the garden, the farm and the peasants, the afternoon callers, the lessons with Professor Vaccari, the view and the flowers and the books and the conversation, but the heart of it had shrivelled and gone sour. Isobel's outward dutifulness but inward disobedience was felt throughout the household like a small, cold draught, and affected everyone. Aunt Sybil refused to knit socks for soldiers out of the rough, greasy khaki wool Aunt Jean had obtained for the purpose, and spent the evenings yawning and complaining how dull her afternoon company had become, with all its endless talk of war. Aunt Jean, grimly knitting for two, was mostly silent, and when she did speak, only talked of the farm. Even Luca, friendly, competent, obliging Luca, stopped being fascinated by the newly installed electric generator, declared it to be the invention of the devil and refused to have anything more to do with it. The great containers of chemicals that were supposed to be the lifeblood of the apparatus sat about in ugly piles, rusting in the long winter rains, and the household reverted, with loud complaints from Aunt Sybil, to lamps and candles.

'I *wish* you would speak to Luca, Jean!'

'Certainly not.'

'But you must! You can persuade him to anything!'

'I have no wish to persuade him. I had no wish for this absurd generator.'

Brief silence, during which Aunt Jean gave Isobel a small but telling glare, since the generator had been Giovanni's suggestion.

'But Jean, it was glorious to have the light—'

'It was *not* glorious to have the noise and the smells.'

'We should get used to those—'

'I should never get used to them.'

'Jean' – pleadingly – 'speak to Luca. Just for me. Just for your Sybil.'

'No,' said Aunt Jean.

Then there were the newspapers. These had long been the source of delightful diversion at the Villa Calvina, not just for the social and cultural pages – devoured by Aunt Sybil – but also because all the less pleasant events of the world, read about on that beautiful Tuscan hillside, were interesting but in no way threatening. The disputes of nations had been inaudible from such a safe distance. Now, however, they could be heard all too clearly, and, in the clamour of warring voices, were increasingly loud ones demanding that Italy make up her mind.

'She is being courted,' Professor Vaccari said, 'like an heiress. The Germans have offered her Trieste and the Tyrol if she will stay neutral. The Allies have offered her Trieste, the Tyrol and much more besides, if she will enter the war on their side.'

'What will happen?' Isobel said. She was thinking of Giovanni. These days, she thought of little but Giovanni.

Professor Vaccari sighed. 'She will give in to the Allies.'

'But the Italian people don't want to enter the war!'

'My dear,' Professor Vaccari said, 'the Italian people are not being asked. The politicians want war, so do the journalists and the influential writers. They believe it will inspire the nation.'

'Do you believe that?' Isobel said, leaning forward.

'I believe,' Professor Vaccari said tiredly, 'that the notion of war is often inspiring but that the reality of it is quite the reverse. You are worrying about your young man.'

Isobel nodded.

'He is impatient?'

'Yes—'

'All young men are impatient. Impatience is as natural to them as breathing. Many of these agitators who want war are young.'

'I don't mind waiting,' Isobel said, 'I don't like it, but I can put up with it. There's so much to learn about farming for one thing and, for another—'

'Yes?'

'I wouldn't feel right to defy Aunt Jean so absolutely. I've only defied two people in my life before, and they were my maternal grandparents whom I feared but didn't love. But I do love Aunt Jean.'

Professor Vaccari looked keenly at Isobel, but he did not speak. He had seen her, in her late teens, ready for love like a ripe fruit hanging on a tree, and he had also seen the young man who had been the first to spot the fruit and reach up and pluck it. Professor Vaccari had no opinion of Giovanni Fosco, beyond thinking that his agricultural aspirations were interesting and imaginative, but he could see that the young man had thrown Isobel abruptly into adulthood. The cherished treasure of that pampered English household in the hills was deep in her first moral and emotional dilemma.

'Whatever we do,' Professor Vaccari said, 'we must mingle reason with instinct. We must listen to the heart as well as the head.' He twinkled a little at Isobel. 'And now we shall return to epic verse.'

*　*　*

To say Giovanni was now impatient was an understatement. He was in a fever of restlessness. At first, when they were newly engaged, he had said that he could wait for ever, as long as he could have Isobel as his final reward; months would be nothing to him, years, decades, he would wait as long as he was required to and the time would speed by on the wings of his happiness. Now, in the spring of 1915, he talked rather differently. He was bored, he said, cooped up with his mother and sister at the Villa Celoni, he was frustrated, he saw his life, or at least the best years of it, pouring themselves uselessly like water into sand. He began to tell Isobel that she was responsible.

'How can I be?'

'Because you still obey this aunt. Because you will not think of our marriage before nearly five more years.'

'But—'

'Don't talk to me of money!'

'But I have to. I want to buy a farm as much as you do, but how can we do that with no money?'

'We cannot!' Giovanni cried, striking the wall of a palace they were passing with a clenched fist. 'We cannot! You are right and sensible and I am going mad!'

'But what else can we do?' Isobel enquired anxiously. 'If you can think of it, I'll do anything you like to help—'

'There is nothing!' Giovanni shouted. 'I am trapped, like a bird in a net!'

'Then do you—' Isobel stopped, her heart almost bursting.

'Do I what?'

'Do – you want to be free of me?'

'Do you want to kill me?' Giovanni cried. He seized her, in full view of passers-by in the Via dei Leone. 'What a wicked suggestion! How cruel you are!'

'I'm *not* cruel!' Isobel said indignantly, 'I meant only to please you, to help you—'

'Then never suggest such a thing again!'

'I don't know what to suggest—' she said, close to tears.

'Nor I,' he said, suddenly calmer.

They looked at one another.

'I love you. I adore you.'

'And I you.'

'What are we to do?'

'You *know* what we have to do,' Isobel said despairingly, 'we have to wait.'

He took her hand and kissed it. 'I can't do it any more. I must take some action.'

She thought of her conversations with Professor Vaccari and her mouth dried. 'What action?'

Giovanni took her arm, and steered her between the carriages crossing the Via dei Neri.

'I know some students here. Two of them are friends of mine from my university days in Rome. They are going to Rome next month, in April, to help organize mass demonstrations.'

Isobel stopped walking and a man carrying a picture done up roughly in sacking almost cannoned into her.

'Demonstrations? What for?'

'For war. Italy must enter the war. I have told you this before and I will tell you again. Italy must prove herself equal to England and France, she must show herself to be a great power, greater than the little powers of Sweden and Switzerland.'

'Professor Vaccari,' Isobel said stoutly, 'says Italy can't afford a war.'

Giovanni threw up his arms. 'Why do you listen to this dusty old scholar?'

'Because he knows a great deal and he talks sense.'

'And me? I do not know anything and I talk rubbish?'

'Giovanni, I don't want to quarrel—'

'Don't you? Then listen to me. I am an Italian. I adore my country. You have grown up here and you are planning to spend your life here with me. You must adore it too.'

'I do—'

'Then you too must wish for Italy's greatness!'

'I do,' Isobel said, 'but I am so afraid of your being in danger.'

'Danger? What danger could there be in Rome?'

'Demonstrations are dangerous—'

'These ones will not be. These ones will be organized by intellectuals.'

'And – and if they succeed? If Italy goes to war?'

He looked at her penetratingly. Then he touched her cheek.

'*Cara* Isobel, *carissima* Isobel, if Italy goes to war, then of course I must go with her.'

Chapter Ten

'The Florentine irises are out,' Aunt Sybil said. She was sitting at the breakfast table in a morning dress of lilac lawn, its two-tiered skirt cut fashionably above her ankles, an innovation of which Aunt Jean disapproved. 'And those lovely new parrot tulips I ordered. I shall try auriculas next year and Maud Scott said she had seen purple tulips in the garden at Forte dei Reggio so dark they were almost black. I crave them. Think of black tulips among pale irises! Rapture. Isobel, are you listening?'

Isobel, deep in a newspaper, shook her head.

'What paper are you reading?' Aunt Sybil demanded.

Isobel sighed. She lowered the newspaper six inches and said, '*Popolo d'Italia.*'

'Darling!' Aunt Sybil said with mock outrage. 'Wicked child! You'll break your Aunt Jean's heart, if you haven't successfully done so already. Wasn't it started by disgraceful young Mussolini? Darling, he's a *socialist*.'

'Not any more,' Isobel said, 'they've expelled him.'

'Why?' Aunt Sybil said, scenting gossip and leaning forward.

'For ceasing to be an opponent of war and starting this paper in favour of it. With French money.'

'French! How very naughty. What has changed his mind, I wonder?'

'I expect he wants power,' Isobel said, quoting Professor Vaccari. 'He now says that blood makes the wheels of history go round. I'm only reading it because it reports all the demonstrations in Rome more fully than any other.'

'And?'

'And what?'

'And what does it say about the demonstrations?'

Isobel picked up the paper again, to find her interrupted place. There were circles under her eyes. Sleep, always such a pleasure and refuge for Isobel, had become elusive since Giovanni had left for Rome. He had said he would only be away a few weeks, and that she was to think of nothing but him in his absence. That was an instruction she hardly needed.

'Our national poet,' Isobel translated obediently, 'Gabriele del Annunzio, has returned from France to use his golden gifts of oratory to rouse his countrymen to war. He is filling the Italian nation with impassioned patriotism as he tours the cities. Ten thousand men yesterday filled the streets of Rome—' Isobel stopped suddenly. Ten thousand! How could ten thousand men filled with impassioned patriotism be anything other than dangerous?

'You don't know Giovanni was among them, darling,' Aunt Sybil said quickly, seeing her stricken face.

'He will be,' Isobel said, 'it's what he went for, to be part of it. He is ripe for impassioned patriotism.'

'Not very sensible—'

'I don't love him because he's sensible!' Isobel flashed at her. 'I love him because he is idealistic and I'm sensible. I hate being sensible. It buries you in the earth, being sensible.'

Aunt Sybil said nothing. She finished the coffee in her cup – one of those fine white cups painted with birds that Isobel had been given to drink out of on her first morning at the Villa Calvina – gathered up her book, spectacles and letters, and rose gracefully from the table. For some moments then, she stood looking at Isobel, pale and frowning, and pretending to be deeply reabsorbed in her newspaper.

'I think you shouldn't cross bridges before you come to them, darling,' Aunt Sybil said. 'All this warmongering noise may well come to nothing. The supporters of neutrality are very powerful, after all; all the bankers and businessmen who have grown so stout on lovely German advice and money. I expect all these young men will expend their energy rampaging harmlessly all over Rome shouting, "Down with the barbarians," and then parliament will vote in favour of neutrality and they'll all come home very satisfied, feeling they've had a good day's hunting.'

Isobel looked up. Aunt Sybil was smiling at her, that slightly ironic smile she had always used to indicate she thought that Isobel was being, just now, very dear but also the smallest bit silly. Isobel nodded, and tried a smile in return.

'I shall be on the loggia,' Aunt Sybil said, 'if you want me,' and drifted out.

Isobel crumpled the *Popolo d'Italia* onto her lap, propped her elbows on the table and put her head in her hands. It had been a long ten days since Giovanni had left in the middle of May, not just because of his absence and the anxiety of not knowing where he precisely was, or what he was doing, but also because life locally had suddenly and disagreeably changed. It seemed that the Italians, even if still officially unasked for their opinions about the war, were making up their minds in any case, and the central streets of Florence, those havens of security where young English ladies could go about their innocent business unperturbed by any unpleasantness, had abruptly become dangerous.

Professor Vaccari had warned Isobel to be very prudent, even accompanied by the redoubtable Moody, on her walk from his rooms to the tram-stop in the late afternoons. Isobel had listened politely but had not taken him very seriously. When he said that street fights were breaking out among opposing factions who were using crowbars to emphasize their points, Isobel had murmured that it sounded just like medieval Guelphs and Ghibellines, and thought no more of it. Then poor Moody, advancing respectably across the Piazza Santa Trinita, was knocked flying by a group of bellowing men in pursuit of another, and was brought to Professor Vaccari's door much shaken, streaming blood from a cut cheek, and with a broken tooth.

Isobel had been shocked. She had also felt responsible. She and Professor Vaccari had assisted Moody – apparently damaged far more in her dignity than in her flesh – upstairs and laid her carefully on a makeshift couch of books, with Isobel's new spring cape as a pillow. A doctor had been sent for and during the ten minutes he took to come, Isobel sat by Moody and held her hand and said how sorry she was.

'Ruffians,' Moody said indistinctly, her head turned away out of embarrassment about her tooth. She had been born in an alley in the Old Town of Edinburgh, and had seen plenty of ruffianly behaviour as a child. 'A war would be too good for them.'

'I'm so sorry, Moody,' Isobel said, 'I feel so badly—'

'It's no' your fault.'

'It is, it is, because if it wasn't for me, you'd never have been down in the city in the first place.'

'Och,' Moody said impatiently. 'Don't you whinge.' She moved her head slightly. 'Take this cape away, Miss Isobel, or I'll be soiling it and it cost Miss Sybil enough.'

Isobel had taken Moody home in a fiacre. Moody was outraged at this, saying she was perfectly well enough to wait for Luca to be summoned with the carriage and that the extra expense would be a wicked waste, but Isobel hadn't listened. Moody tried to sit upright, as usual, in the fiacre, but she was greenish-white around the plasters on her cheeks, and kept falling backwards against the seat. She kept her mouth tightly closed, so that the fiacre driver shouldn't see the broken tooth, except for opening it sufficiently to hiss to Isobel that the cab fare should not be allowed to exceed two francs at the outside.

The upshot of the Moody episode was twofold. The first change was that Aunt Sybil, horrified at the possibilities of an attack upon Isobel, demanded that her lessons should revert to the mornings, when the streets were full of people going about their ordinary marketing business. She also declared that, for the moment, the lessons should be reduced to three a week. But the second change was more crucial to Isobel. Aunt Jean, seizing her chance, decreed that Luca should accompany Isobel both to and fro on her journeys to Professor Vaccari, armed with a stout stick and instructions not to leave Isobel's side for a moment.

Isobel had now had a week of this regime. While Giovanni was away, it was of no consequence to her whether she was accompanied by Luca or the entire household of the Villa Calvina, but when he returned, how could she possibly snatch even a second alone with him, impeded as she now was by Luca and the stout stick? And then there was another consideration which also gnawed at her mind. With a few deft strokes, the aunts seemed to have wrapped her up, like clever spiders with an unwitting fly, in exactly the stifling, unbreakable silken bonds that she had so painstakingly, over the last year or so, struggled to escape from. She seemed to herself, particularly during those interminable nights on the cherub bed, beneath her painted ceiling where the birds still flew so carelessly, to be back exactly where she had once been, having lessons when it suited Aunt Sybil, handing round sandwiches in the afternoons to people saying, 'My dear, too awful, but the Army seems completely bogged down in Flanders,' and, 'Oh, Sybil, what a wicked hat!' with the one thing that mattered to her – Giovanni – receding from her like a beautiful fleeting dream.

Sitting there at the breakfast table, with the warm May sun

filtering in through the bright new wisteria leaves that framed the window, Isobel succumbed to unhappiness and with it, such were the habits so deeply instilled in her by her childhood, to guilt. She had, by any standards in the world, a wonderful life, a safe, happy, lovely life in which she knew both stimulus and affection – and yet she thought she could not bear it another moment. She could not bear not to have Giovanni and she could bear no longer just being a thing, a well-dressed, well-educated, well-spoken, well-fed useless *thing*. She raised her head. Maria was standing in the doorway, politely waiting to clear the table. *La poverina*, Maria thought, with the young Marchese away and all this spring weather, so perfect for love, so beautiful.

'I'm so sorry,' Isobel said, getting up, 'I'm so sorry to delay you.'

'It's no matter,' Maria said. She clicked her tongue gently. '*Padroncina*, you should go out into the air.'

Isobel looked at her. There was something in Maria's expression that made her feel she might burst into tears if she wasn't careful. She swallowed and nodded.

'Yes,' she said.

'Too much thinking,' Maria said later to Luca, in the kitchen. 'All these lessons! Bah! What use are they to a girl?'

Isobel found her hat, told Aunt Sybil she was going out for a walk, and went down the steep, gravelled drive to the gates of the Villa Calvina. It was a clear, bright morning, except for a slight blue mist of heat that already lay over the domes and towers of Florence and gave the city the appearance of floating. It was odd not to be going down there every day now, and Isobel had been worried by the loss of income that her reduced lessons would mean to Professor Vaccari. Aunt Sybil said that she had offered to pay him the same sum for three lessons as he had charged for five each week, on account of the enormous benefit he had been to Isobel, but he had declined. He had said that his wants and those of Signora Vaccari were both few and modest. Isobel could only hope that this was true, and that poor Signora Vaccari had not, in fact, been both disappointed and vexed. She vowed now that she would never go to a lesson empty-handed, that the Vaccaris should benefit from the oil and wheat and eggs and fruit of the farm at the Villa Calvina as long as it was in her power to effect it.

The verges of the road were already pale with dust. Isobel turned away from the view of Florence, and started slowly uphill, past a clump of umbrella pines and the walls of the gardens of other villas, including the Villa Celoni, which Isobel, in obedience to Aunt Jean, had not passed in nine months. However, with Giovanni in Rome, it seemed perfectly all right to do so now. The villa gates were shut, and a chain had been slipped around the bars, and padlocked. The drive, curving away between more umbrella pines, was unweeded and empty, and the house wasn't visible. It was a decent house, Giovanni said, but not – here he laughed – a gentleman's house, although his mother had tried to make it so with stately family possessions, and the conversion of an upper room into a chapel.

'Donatella is required to pray there night and morning. I have escaped. Mamma's piety has a more lenient category for men, thank heavens.'

Isobel peered through the bars of the gate. She imagined poor, pale Donatella praying dutifully away in there, or practising equally dutifully on some instrument while her fingers fidgeted to paint. Guilt flooded Isobel again. How dare she feel even slightly constrained when there were girls like Donatella about, girls with their own tastes and talents forced to be prisoners of someone else's, quite different, ideas for them? Giovanni said his mother was brave but also stupid and overbearing.

'Donatella is afraid of her.'

'What will happen to Donatella?' Isobel had asked.

'She will marry as instructed by Mamma, and then she will be afraid of her husband too.'

'How heartless you sound!' Isobel had cried.

'I'm not heartless. But I can do nothing for Donatella now. I can do nothing for her until we are married.'

Isobel gripped the bars, and stared through them as if she could will Donatella to appear. Nothing stirred; no-one came. Isobel let go of the gate, and began to walk, with more purposefulness, up the white dust road towards the little shrine where Moody had brought her, as a child, to lay wilting bunches of wild flowers in front of the statue of the Virgin. Moody disapproved of the statue. She said it was popish, but she felt it right to encourage some kind of religious instinct in a child brought up in a household where one guardian (Sybil) thought God was a lovely idea but rather a trouble to do anything about and the other (Jean) thought He was superstitious nonsense.

The shrine, like a flattened whitewashed pillar with a pediment above it and a tiny stream trickling out of the bank at its foot, stood on a curve of the road so that the Virgin, gazing out of her niche with her bright blue glass eyes, could see all the way down the hillsides to Florence. Local men had built a curving wall of loose stones behind the shrine to shelter it from the winter winds, and it was perhaps the same men who gave it an annual coat of spring whitewash. Isobel could, on account of its dazzling and newly renewed whiteness, see it from a long way off, and she could also see that there was someone beside it, either kneeling in the road or sitting on the bank. As she drew nearer she saw that it was, in fact both, for a person, white-haired and caped, was kneeling before the shrine, and beside the person, on the bank, was a bundle.

A few steps away, Isobel hesitated, and then stopped. The person in the road turned a little, and revealed herself to be an elderly woman, weather-beaten and bright-eyed, with the cockle-shell of the pilgrim pinned to her cape.

'*Pellegrina!*' Isobel said, charmed. 'Where have you come from?'

'I have travelled nine years,' the woman said. She stood up. She was very small, but upright. 'Nine years of wandering prayer. I pray for the souls of the living and, in these Holy Places, for the souls of the dead.'

Isobel came closer. The old pilgrim's eyes were deep as well as bright and they looked at Isobel in a way that made her feel they were not quite human.

'Can you,' Isobel said shyly, 'can you tell me something?'

'Ask me.'

Isobel leaned forward slightly. The Virgin seemed suddenly to be watching, her glass eyes alert.

'Tell me, please,' Isobel said, 'what do you think of this war? Will – will Italy fight?'

The woman eyed her penetratingly. 'Italy is fighting,' she said.

'No, *pellegrina*,' Isobel said politely, 'not yet. We haven't yet had any news from Rome.'

'*Ma sì*,' the woman said emphatically, '*che c'e la guerra.* War is come. Italy fights. God has sent the war to punish us for our sins, we are proud and must be humbled.' She turned from Isobel, picked up her bundle of clothes and blankets and settled it easily on her head. 'I will pray for you,' she said, 'and I will pray for your English wounded. It were better for you English, for your souls, were you Catholic, but God be thanked that at the least you are not pagan.'

Then she turned away and began to walk, steady and unhurried, up the white road towards the pinewoods. Isobel watched her, with a kind of longing, until the hillside, curving out over the road with its creamy bushes of broom, hid her from view.

*   *   *

She almost ran back down the road, and arrived back at the gates of the Villa Calvina out of breath and with the hem of her skirt floury with dust. Beppe's invalid son, born with a hunch-back and poor eyesight, had been set to paint the wrought iron gates with their yearly coat of glossy black, and at the sight of Isobel, he paused, gave her his wide, sweet, toothy smile and said, 'Visitors, *Padroncina*.'

Isobel panting still, shook her head. 'No, Cecco. Not until this afternoon.'

He waved his paintbrush towards the house. He said, more emphatically, 'Visitors. La Marchesa!'

Isobel stared. The Marchesa Fosco? At the Villa Calvina? What had happened? She picked up her dusty skirts in both hands and hurried up the steep drive and along the terrace to the front door. Even as she approached the steps, she could hear a raised and ranting voice.

In the *sala degli uccelli* was an astonishing sight. Both the aunts were standing in front of the awesome figure of the Marchesa Fosco, who in majestic funerary plumage was making them a stirring speech about their all now being united against the foe, striving together for the same glorious freedom and thus obliged, by the nobility of their shared and splendid purpose, to bury all past differences and difficulties and throw themselves, as sisters, into one another's arms.

'Poor woman,' Aunt Sybil was murmuring, her eyes glinting with amusement.

'Some lemonade?' Aunt Jean said at intervals, in an attempt at reducing the situation to normality. 'Some mineral water? Some tea?'

In the window embrasure, half hidden by the curtain, Donatella lurked in an agony of miserable embarrassment. Isobel caught her eye and, for a fleeting second, considered winking at her, as those long ago soldiers of Isobel's childhood had winked at Maudie in the London parks. But a wink might well have shocked Donatella, so Isobel contented herself with a smile, and by clearing her throat loudly to attract attention.

'Darling!' the aunts cried, bright with relief.

The Marchesa swung round. She looked magnificent, her eyes glowing with fervour. 'Signorina Isobel!'

Isobel sketched a stiff bob of a curtsey. 'Marchesa.'

'Signorina, the Chamber of Deputies has decided for the glory of Italy! Yesterday a crowd of patriots broke the windows of the

92

Parliament House in Rome to demonstrate the strength of their enthusiasm' – here there was a small snort from Aunt Sybil – 'and the Chamber has obeyed the call of the people. We shall no longer groan beneath the yoke of Austria! Italy will be free! Italy, Signorina Isobel, will be great! I have come to tell your aunts this great news from Rome. Italy is at war!'

Isobel looked at her with a mixture of contempt and horror. How could she speak like that? How could the mother of a son, suitably aged for military service, speak so, of war? She put her chin up. She had not run all the way home to have her own news upstaged in this manner.

'I know,' Isobel said coldly. 'I already know.'

Chapter Eleven

The night before Giovanni left to join his father's old regiment, Aunt Jean relented and allowed him and Isobel an hour together on the loggia. Isobel, expecting to find Giovanni in the state of almost ridiculous exultation – ridiculous, at least, to part of her mind – that had gripped him before he went down to Rome, found instead that he was, though determined, much more sober at the prospect of going to war, than merely on a demonstration.

'I have looked at the map,' he said. 'It is not promising. We will have to fight our way up from the plains because the Austrians hold the mountains, and if we try and advance into Istria, we shall be threatened from the rear, by the Austrians in Southern Tyrol.'

Isobel longed to ask him if, in that case, he might not change his mind and stay at home. But she knew she couldn't do that. She couldn't ask him not to do what all his friends and contemporaries were doing; she couldn't ask him to stay and endure the chafing tedium of waiting with her for her twenty-fifth birthday; she couldn't ask him to allow himself to look, in the world's eyes, as if he lacked the courage to fight.

So she said, instead, 'The men from the farm here will have to go.'

'Yes.'

'Luca, Beppe, all the boys from the Zanichelli family and Poppi—'

'Who will run the farm?'

'The women and the old men. Cecco can do little things. Aunt

94

Jean and I can cut fodder—' She stopped, gave a little laugh and said, 'It will be good practice.'

He leaned forward in the dusk and took both her hands. 'This isn't what we meant.'

'No.'

'But if we must wait – and you say we must wait – then isn't it better to be busy while we wait, to have occupation?'

'War,' Isobel said, 'isn't exactly an occupation.'

He dropped her hands. 'It doesn't help me if you talk like this.'

'What would help you?'

'If you believed in me.'

'I do believe in you,' Isobel said, stoutly, 'but I don't have to believe in your going to war.'

'You do! I am an Italian, I am going to fight for Italy!'

She stood up and went to the edge of the loggia, leaning against one of its pillars which was cushioned with clematis, a mass of white, double-petalled flowers. Far below her, in the deep hyacinth blue evening, the lights of Florence shone, disembodied in the dusk.

'I don't want to quarrel,' Isobel said.

'Nor I!' cried Giovanni, springing up. 'I want to spend this evening in a way I can treasure in my memory while I am away, I want—'

'It's always easier for men,' Isobel said, interrupting, staring down at Florence. 'It's always easier to go away and *do* things. Men never get left behind to worry and wait.'

'But that is how things are, how they have always been—'

'That's no reason.'

'Isobel!' Giovanni cried. He was much shocked. He moved quickly beside her and put his arms around her. 'Isobel, are you crying?'

'Of course I'm crying,' she wailed, turning into his embrace. 'Of course I'm crying! You'd cry if you were me!'

He held her, kissing her hair. He thought how he would write to her while he was away, wonderful letters full of love and hope. She was so sweet like this, sobbing and pliant. He lifted her face and kissed her mouth.

'I shall be on leave soon,' he said, 'and in the meantime, I think the most dangerous thing I shall be doing will be a bit of mountaineering—'

'Oh, Giovanni—'

'Isobel,' he said, 'we have all our lives before us.'

'Yes.'

'And much to learn.'

'Those are my lines,' she said, 'those are the things *I* say.'

He kissed her again. 'Then take comfort, *cara*, from knowing how hard I listen to you!'

Three days after he left, news came of the fate of British and Australian forces in the Dardanelles. Both English and Italian newspapers began to suggest that the plan to distract the Germans by an attack from the east was not going well. The Turks seemed very well prepared and no headway was being made. British soldiers were reported exhausted and discouraged.

'Jean dear,' Aunt Sybil said, 'we must have some here. To convalesce.'

Aunt Jean, anxiously preoccupied with plans for the farm now that all the able-bodied men were to be called up into the army, said absently, 'Soldiers?'

Aunt Sybil's mouth twitched slightly. 'Well, officers, darling. Shall I write to the Red Cross?'

Isobel looked at them both. 'What would they do here?'

'Do, darling?'

'Yes. Do. Wouldn't they rather go home?'

'Nonsense,' Aunt Sybil said, 'this is the best place on earth to recover. You should know that. You are our prize example.'

'But young men—'

Aunt Jean eyed her thoughtfully. 'I think, don't you, that we are a match for a few sick, tired young men.'

Isobel said indignantly, 'They won't be that! Think of the pictures in the newspapers! They'll be – they'll be—'

'What?' said Aunt Sybil, twinkling. 'Young gods? Jason and the Argonauts?'

Isobel gave a little cry and fled from the room.

'I'm a horrid tease,' Aunt Sybil said without remorse.

'Sybil—'

'Yes, dear?'

'Sybil,' Aunt Jean said slowly, 'I think your idea is an excellent one.'

'Oh, good. You seldom think that. I suppose you think we shall receive a selection of upstanding young Englishmen, one of whom will do nicely to take Isobel's mind off Giovanni Fosco.'

'Exactly,' said Aunt Jean.

'I fear you underestimate her constancy and her nose for a quiet deception.'

'We could use the rooms in the east wing, you see. And as they recovered, I could use them in the *podere*.'

'Aha—'

'And Isobel could—'

'Fall in love?'

'Show them the sights of Florence,' Aunt Jean said crossly.

'Jean,' Sybil said, suddenly serious, 'this is all very tiresome, the war and the upheaval and the changes.'

'But we must do something—'

'Of course. And at least you must be pleased that the danger to Isobel has taken himself off to the mountains.'

'Sybil,' Aunt Jean said seriously, 'I am thankful.'

A small silence fell, during which the sisters regarded one another with a quiet sympathy. Then light footsteps were heard in the corridor and Isobel appeared again in the doorway.

'Sorry,' she said, 'for rushing out.'

'There's nothing to be sorry for,' Aunt Jean said kindly.

'I want – I want to ask you something—'

'Certainly, dear.'

'Now that – that Giovanni is away, and we shall have so much more to do with the farm and the soldiers, might I try and make a friend of Donatella and have her here with me?'

Aunt Sybil said languidly, 'Poor little scrap—'

'Is this the thin end of the wedge?'

'No, Aunt Jean.'

'Let her go, Jean. Let her go and tourney with the dragon Marchesa to set the princess free—'

'Don't be silly, Sybil. Why do you wish to do this, Isobel?'

'Because she's lonely and crushed and might be more happy and useful here.'

'Useful—'

'Yes, Aunt Jean.'

They waited. Aunt Jean looked down at her lists. She was to lose seven men from the house and farm, seven able-bodied men. She said, without looking up again, 'Well, go to the Villa Celoni then and see what you can do. She might at least help with the grapes later. Any fool, if light-handed enough, can pick grapes.'

Isobel, dressed in pale grey and white linen, went slowly down the unkempt drive of the Villa Celoni. Since Italy had entered the war, the Marchesa, for some reason, had ordered the chain to be taken off the gates, which now stood open, as if signalling that the Fosco family, despite past disgraces, was now condescending to rejoin the outside world. Isobel, though pleased to be allowed to attempt to make a friend of Donatella, was downcast. There had been no word from Giovanni for two weeks, and that morning she had had a long and saddening conversation with Beppe who, with the other men from the farm, and Luca, was due to assemble at Fiesole for military service in a few days. Tears had coursed down Beppe's face, running unchecked into the stuff of his worn blue work shirt.

'What am I to do, *Padroncina*? I can neither read nor write, so who is to tell my family news of me? And how shall I have news of them? And who will gather the grapes and olives? Who will sow for next year's harvest?'

Isobel had held his hand. The palm was as hard and grainy as cowhide.

'Perhaps it won't be long—'

'Even a few months now, *Padroncina*, is very bad. The harvest will be soon. And my poor Cecco cannot help his mother!'

'We will help,' Isobel said.

Beppe looked in despair at the hand that held his, and shook his head. 'It is a calamity.'

It is too, Isobel thought now. All these grandiose notions of the glory of Italy and the greatness of freedom only meant, in the end, that thousands of good, simple countrymen like Beppe were being wrenched away from everything they knew and held dear to risk their lives for something they hardly understood. For Beppe, who were the Austrians, let alone the Germans? Beppe just wanted to live as his ancestors had lived for centuries, following those ancient, matchless rhythms of time and season, those rhythms Virgil had described and that she and Giovanni were going to bring again, by new methods, to some ruined estate benefiting both it and all the Beppes who would work there. It was a wonderful prospect and it was terrible that something like a war should stand in its way.

The Villa Celoni, though set higher than the Villa Calvina, had an inferior view, being hemmed in by pines and by an inconvenient spur of hillside. It was, in consequence, a gloomier house, and the Marchesa Fosco, wherever she directed her formidable energies, clearly did not direct them at the outward appearance of her house. The urns of the terrace were unplanted, the box hedges needed trimming, and the number of closed shutters along the south façade made the house look unwelcoming.

Isobel paused before she rang the bell, to smooth her gloves and shake out the pleats of her skirt. She wished to give the Marchesa no cause for complaint as to her suitability as a friend for Donatella, at least as far as appearances went.

'Oh, perfect,' Aunt Sybil had said at the sight of the grey linen. 'Nun-like and irreproachable. Do try and keep your temper, darling.'

A manservant in livery came to the door. Isobel thought she might have guessed he would wear it, a fine display of what Aunt Sybil called 'all that Fosco fol-de-rol'. He led Isobel through a dark, echoing hall, up a staircase whose walls were painted with the busts of frowning Roman emperors, and, after an announcing flourish, opened the door of a room on the first floor and bowed her in.

The room was not dark, but it was certainly dim. It was also almost empty of furniture. A square of carpet lay in the centre of a marble floor and on it was a heavy table, marble-topped on golden lion legs and feet, and two chairs. On the two chairs sat the Marchesa Fosco and Donatella. The Marchesa was reading aloud.

'Signorina Isobel!'

Isobel, to ingratiate herself, dropped a proper curtsey. 'Marchesa. I hope you will forgive my coming unannounced.'

The Marchesa rose and held out her hand. Donatella rose too.

'We are delighted. I was reading to Donatella the life of St Catherine of Siena.'

'Oh—'

'Donatella can never have enough of the lives of our martyred saints.'

Out of the corner of her eye, Isobel saw Donatella give the smallest shake of her head. She said, 'I'm afraid I've never read them—'

'But then you are not a Catholic,' the Marchesa said, with infinite condescending pity.

The footman now appeared with a third chair, which he placed on the island of carpet, on the opposite side of the marble table to the Marchesa and Donatella. The Marchesa graciously waved Isobel to sit down. Donatella, Isobel observed, was watching her like a hawk. She too was in grey, her habitual grey, and her thin face was as pale as the moon. The Marchesa ordered wine to be brought, and *panettone*.

'Please go to no trouble—'

'Entertaining charming visitors – of whom we see too few – is that not so, Donatella? – is never a trouble. Do you admire the bust of my grandfather, Signorina?'

Isobel turned as directed. Behind her, the immense and self-satisfied head of a man, carved in black marble and crowned with a wreath of gilded olive leaves, sat on a matching black pillar.

'Most impressive, Marchesa.'

'He was a scholar and a statesman, Signorina. Neither of my children have inherited his gifts.'

'Marchesa—'

The Marchesa bent her stately gaze upon Isobel.

'Marchesa, it was about one of your children that I wished to speak to you—'

'*Cara* Signorina!' cried the Marchesa, clasping her hands, 'We may not speak of that! We may not speak of that until the most excellent *Zia* Jean—'

'Not Giovanni,' Isobel said steadily, 'but Donatella.'

The Marchesa was amazed. 'Donatella!'

She looked at her daughter as if it were beyond credulity that anyone should have thought sufficiently of her to wish to speak about her.

'Donatella?' she exclaimed again.

'Yes,' Isobel said. She took a breath. 'We are full of activity at the Villa Calvina, you see, everything is changing because of the war.'

'Ah, the war!' cried the Marchesa, scenting a chance for oratory.

'Because of the war,' said Isobel steadily, taking no notice, 'we are going to be very short-handed on the farm. Aunt Sybil has also written to the British Red Cross, offering to take, at a time, ten convalescent officers from the Dardanelles campaign, at the Villa Calvina. We shall need all the help we can get, all the willing pairs of hands we can persuade to assist us.'

The Marchesa stared.

'Farming?' she said incredulously. She looked at Donatella, who was gazing at Isobel with an expression as beseeching as a dog's. '*Nursing?*'

'There is a war on,' Isobel said. 'Aunt Jean and I are both becoming adept with the sickle. I don't think there will be much nursing, it's more a matter of amusement and conversation.'

'English officers?'

'Yes.'

A tiny, pleading breath escaped Donatella.

'In any case,' Isobel said, almost carelessly, 'I should be so grateful for Donatella's companionship myself.'

'My dear Signorina, you may avail yourself of Donatella's company under my roof at any time you please.'

'That,' said Isobel, 'would be very pleasant, but it would not help the war.'

'Please,' Donatella whispered.

'But your studies!' the Marchesa said. 'Your music! Our times of quiet reflection and prayer!'

'I'm not suggesting all of every day,' Isobel said, leaning forward, 'but just an hour or two. At first—'

'Look at her hands!' the Marchesa demanded. Donatella immediately hid them under the table. Her mother reached over, snatched them out and laid them on the marble surface as exhibits for Isobel's inspection.

'Those are lady's hands!'

'*Please*, Mamma—'

'It doesn't mean they might not be useful.'

'Useful!'

'Marchesa,' Isobel said, 'do you not believe in this war?'

'With my whole heart!'

'Then may not Donatella do something as – as—' Isobel searched for a word to impress her listener – '—as magnificent as Giovanni? May she not use her hands to help Italy?'

The Marchesa looked at her. Then she looked at Donatella. Donatella's dark eyes were now glowing like coals. The footman entered with a silver tray bearing a bottle of amber-coloured wine, three beautiful Venetian glasses and a dish of *panettone*. He paused by the table, waiting for his next instruction. The Marchesa looked back at Isobel. She drew herself up.

'For one hour only, each day,' she said, in ringing tones. 'For one hour, only.'

Chapter Twelve

Everybody, Aunt Jean declared, must be kept busy. This was not just because there was so much to be done, but also because everyone's mind needed distracting from the infinitely distressing parting from the men on the farm. Everybody had wept bitterly that day, men, women and children, and when the little procession had finally straggled away along the road to Fiesole, a terrible melancholy had settled over the Villa Calvina and the farm, despite the heartless blue sky and shining sun. Aunt Jean had become very businesslike. She stood on the lowest terrace of the garden, above the first little wheatfield, and read out a list of tasks, leaving not even the smallest child – Luca's little son of scarcely three – with idle hands. Isobel, watching her small, determined, authoritative figure, was filled with admiration. Aunt Jean was dispensing the best sort of kindness, the sort that she, Isobel, was going to have to learn. If you were too sympathetic, too soft, Aunt Jean said, then everyone simply gave up trying and lay about wailing, and in consequence their depression deepened. Occupation was the cure for sadness, practical occupation.

And also, Isobel thought privately, the luxury of a little hope. Her own private hoard of hope lay in her pocket, a letter from Giovanni, in an envelope so smudged with official stamps and military marks that it was impossible to tell where it had been posted. It was dated ten days earlier, and, for an address, Giovanni had written at the top, 'The back door of Austria.' He said there had been little fighting so far, but that everyone's spirits were high and there was general optimism. He was, Isobel thought, maddeningly brief about the details of his days, the smallest of which she was hungry for, but this was because he had something exciting to tell her. A fellow soldier had an estate to sell, an estate he had inherited from a distant cousin, in southern Tuscany, an estate he did not, himself, intend to farm. It had about three thousand acres, a villa, several farmhouses and a history that went back to the Etruscans. It had been very neglected for well over thirty years but wasn't that, Giovanni wrote, his sentences exploding with exclamation and question marks, exactly what they wanted? On his first leave, they would go and look at it. It was not far south of Siena, below a great mountain that was, in fact, an extinct volcano. He loved her, he wrote, he missed her, he dreamed of her at nights. Would she please, he added in a postscript, give his dutiful love to his mother and sister, and tell them that his health was good and his heart was high?

'I have heard from Giovanni,' Isobel said to Donatella.

Donatella had now been coming to the Villa Calvina for three weeks, and each day contrived to extend her allotted hour by yet another ten minutes. Aunt Sybil had found among her cupboards and trunks an enormous rose-pink apron which Donatella tied over her grey frocks, and which illuminated her face. Together, she and Isobel had been set to sweep out the rooms of the east wing, and clean the windows. At first she said nothing. Isobel complained, out of disappointment, that it was like spending an hour in the company of a large moth; fluttering, pale grey, and mute. Then one day, Donatella said out of the blue, 'That corner is still dusty.'

'Sweep it, then,' Isobel said briskly. She was polishing a window. Maria had told her to add vinegar to the water when cleaning windows and the results were very satisfactory.

'I did not mean,' Donatella said, in her new whisper of a voice, 'that you should sweep. I was simply pointing it out.'

'Why?'

'Because I never noticed dust before,' Donatella said patiently, 'because dust was not my concern.'

'Well, it is now,' Isobel said heartlessly, polishing like a dervish.

'I know,' Donatella said mildly. 'I like it that way.'

Isobel stopped polishing and looked at her. She was sweeping the neglected corner, still a little clumsily, as if the broom had more control of the situation than she did. Aunt Sybil had made her tie up her hair in a piece of flowered lawn, and she looked, Isobel thought, not exactly pretty but certainly far less like a gaunt little medieval saint in the middle of martyrdom.

103

'When you're sweeping,' Isobel demanded, 'what are you thinking about?'

'Sweeping,' Donatella said.

'Not painting and religion and music and the glory of Italy?'

'No. I am tired of all those. I prefer to think of sweeping.'

'I think of the future,' Isobel said grandly.

Donatella said nothing. She stooped and swept the little heap of grit and feathers into a dustpan.

'I have heard from Giovanni,' Isobel said.

Donatella straightened up and looked at her.

'Is he well? Is he safe?'

'Yes. Very well and there has been little fighting so far. He sends you and your mother his love.'

'My mother will be pleased.'

'Was she anxious?' Isobel enquired, trying to imagine the Marchesa Fosco feeling an emotion as commonplace as anxiety.

'Giovanni is my mother's only son,' Donatella said reprovingly. She put her hands up to untie the flowered scarf. 'I should go home now. I have been one hour and a half, more, perhaps.'

'Tomorrow, we make beds. Ten beds for ten men. Ten young Englishmen,' Isobel said deliberately, her eyes on Donatella's expresionless face.

'Yes.'

'Have you ever seen ten young men together before, Donatella?'

'No,' Donatella said composedly, and then, in a slightly louder voice, 'and I do not imagine that you have, Signorina, either.'

Isobel grinned. '*Touché!*'

'*Buon giorno*, Signorina.'

'*Buon giorno*, Donatella. *A domani.*'

The door closed quietly behind her, and Isobel heard her steps going away down the long stone-floored passage of the east wing, light, quick steps. What a mysterious girl, as withdrawn as her brother was extrovert, as plain as he was beautiful, as elusive as he was open. My sister-in-law, Isobel thought, going back to her window, and gazing out of it at the kitchen courtyard where Maria's pots of basil and oregano stood, and then at the sunny hills beyond. My future sister-in-law. I must make her call me Isobel, I must make her smile more. I must persuade her to talk about herself. She reached up, with a clean duster, towards the very top of the window, and the letter in her pocket gave out a small, reminding, reassuring crackle.

'I think about the future,' she'd said to Donatella.
She smiled to herself. It was true. She did.

The young officers came up from Florence railway station in three
cabs. Moody met them at the front steps in order to ensure they
weren't overcharged by the cab drivers, and also to make sure that
the three old men Aunt Jean had directed to carry the luggage did
as they had been bidden. Behind Moody, as a sort of welcoming
committee, Aunt Jean and Aunt Sybil waited on the top step as they
had waited to greet Isobel all those years before. Isobel was with
them and so, without her becoming pink apron, was Donatella.

The young men got stiffly out of the cabs, and stood about on
the gravel. It should, if there was any justice in heaven or upon
earth, as Aunt Sybil had pointed out, have been a perfect day, to
welcome these weary heroes to their brief Italian paradise. Instead,
it was overcast and a small, damp wind was blowing along the
hillsides, and Florence, down there in its valley, managed to look
deeply ordinary, and not in the least magical.

If she had been expecting young argonauts, Isobel was not only
disappointed but also rather shocked. The young men standing
awkwardly on the gravel below the steps could hardly have been
further from golden heroes. They were thin, and grey-faced, and a
miasma of low spirits hung about them like a fog. Aunt Jean had
said some of them still had dysentery, and that all of them, after
months on that harsh Turkish shore, had some lingering infection
or gastric trouble. The aunts' own doctor was coming up from
Florence to examine them.

'Poor things—' Aunt Sybil said.

'Poor boys—'

Isobel glanced at Donatella. She was looking at the young men
with an amazed interest.

'So thin!'

'So gloomy,' Aunt Sybil said.

The four of them advanced slowly down the steps.

'Mrs Carruthers?' one of the young men said. He had a pleasant
face and blue, unmistakably English eyes. 'Mrs Fanshawe? We are
– all – so very grateful—'

'Dear boys,' Aunt Sybil said, sweeping forward, 'dear boys, don't
start being grateful. You haven't the energy. You can save being
grateful for later. Now, come in, all of you, and see your quarters.'

They gazed at her. One man, taller than the others, and with a
strange, craggy face exaggeratedly hollowed by fatigue, leaned back

against the cab that had brought him as if the sight of Aunt Sybil, all effusion and charm and lawn and lace, was altogether too much for him.

'This is Miss Lindsay and Miss Fosco' – obediently, like a class of schoolboys, the young men bowed in the girls' direction – 'and this is my invaluable Moody.'

'And you,' said Aunt Jean, anxious to get her charges indoors before at least half of them fainted on the gravel, 'are six lieutenants and four captains, and we shall learn your names when you have rested.'

'Will you follow me?' Isobel said, a little hesitantly. They turned towards her. The blue-eyed one said, 'Jolly kind, Miss Lindsay.' He smiled. 'We'll be better company shortly—'

'Antonio will see to your luggage.'

Slowly, the group began to climb the steps behind Isobel into the house. She heard murmurs of gratification at the sight of the long, polished hall, the pictures and rugs, the great bowls of roses.

She turned back, smiling. 'It's a lovely place.'

'Certainly is, Miss Lindsay—'

'Jolly lucky—'

'Awfully grateful—'

At the back of the group, the tallest of them was staring ahead as if he saw nothing of the charm of his surroundings. He looked, Isobel thought, both worn out and exasperated, as if convalescence in an Italian villa was the very last thing he wanted. By his side, Donatella, of all people, was hovering with a solicitude Isobel had never seen her display before, gazing up into his haggard face as if she sympathized completely with whatever it was he was feeling.

'We are accommodating you in the east wing,' Isobel said, feeling suddenly rather silly, and began to lead the way up the stairs.

The blue-eyed one was called George Mason, Captain George Mason. He said, over and over again during the first few days, that they all felt they were jolly lucky and they were certainly awfully grateful. At this point the tall, gaunt soldier said in a low voice, but one that was perfectly audible, that he was not particularly grateful and that his chief feeling was one of disappointment at not being invalided home.

George Mason coloured. 'Awfully sorry. You must forgive him. Splendid fellow, but he lost his brother a month ago in the Dardanelles and he's had dysentery worse than any of us. Capital fellow, though.'

Isobel had looked coolly at the capital fellow. He might have suffered worse than anyone, she considered, but he also might now have the grace to acknowledge the hospitality of the Villa Calvina. Aunt Sybil had even devised special diets for those who'd had gastritis or dysentery, and the east wing, if not exactly luxurious, must seem so by contrast with a tent on a Gallipoli beach to anyone who wasn't a monster of ingratitude.

'Lieutenant Fleming, Miss Lindsay. Patrick Fleming. First-rate soldier, Miss Lindsay, but just a bit knocked about.'

'But you're all knocked about,' Isobel said, implying that *their* physical condition didn't seem to have affected their manners. They had all slept for almost twenty-four hours after arrival, and had then emerged from the east wing onto the terrace, anxious to be good guests and equally anxious, it soon appeared, to find a way of getting down into Florence and obtaining some whisky.

'Champagne is better for you,' Aunt Sybil said. The tom-toms of gossip beating along the Florentine hills said that a group of young Australians convalescing in a villa kindly lent to them by the eminent art historian, Bernard Berenson, were each drinking a bottle of whisky a day. Aunt Jean had been horrifed. To one of her generation, growing up in Scotland in the previous century, whisky spelled only the senseless degradation of the gutter.

'We shan't become inebriated, Mrs Fanshawe,' George Mason said, 'we shall only become more cheerful.'

'In that case,' Isobel said tartly, looking at the unhelpful figure of Patrick Fleming staring crossly down at the incomparable view of Florence, 'the sooner you can get some down Lieutenant Fleming, the better.'

'He is sick,' Donatella said.

She was proving an admirable nurse, patient and sweet and quiet. She was, as everyone acknowledged either openly or covertly, a far better nurse than Isobel. Watching her tucking in sheets, speaking softly, smiling with such natural ease, Isobel was reminded by contrast of her solid ten-year-old self, longing to be of service to her sick and fretful mother, and not having the faintest idea of how to go about it. She didn't seem to have improved in any way. She found herself wanting these jaded young fellows to be rapidly well enough again to respond to her aunts' charms and kindness properly, and to be employable on the farm. She despised them for only wanting to go down to Florence to find whisky and pretty girls. Where was their vision, for heaven's sake?

'You expect too much,' Donatella said.

'And you don't?' Isobel said unkindly.

'No,' Donatella said. 'I cannot be more than myself, so why should they?'

After ten days, a party of the convalescents did indeed find their way down into the city and returned much elated by the triumphant welcome they had received in the streets of Florence, as heroes of the Dardanelles.

'I do wish, though,' George Mason said to Isobel, 'that people wouldn't keep asking for the honour of shaking my hand. Makes a fellow feel such a fool.'

Lieutenant Fleming, Isobel noticed, made no attempt to go down to Florence. Neither did he join the party who had offered their services to Aunt Jean, on the farm, partly no doubt because they wanted to and partly, unquestionably, because Beppe's daughter, Chiara, and her sister, Silvia, were both prettier than either Isobel or Donatella, and certainly more approachable. Lieutenant Fleming, however, didn't seem susceptible to the lures of either whisky or prettiness. By far the slowest of the party to recover, he spent most days on the terrace, in the farthest corner away from the sociable loggia, either sketching, sleeping or staring into space. Though not exactly rude, he was making little social effort, and such as he did make was directed almost solely at Donatella.

'You are taming our bear,' Aunt Sybil said to her.

'He explains to me about drawing. His father is an artist. His father paints the lords and ladies in London but he will not paint them, he says, he will paint the countryside.'

'I see,' said Aunt Sybil, watching her. This was possibly the longest speech Donatella had ever made, a speech drawn out of her by the briefest of contacts with one of the crossest young men Aunt Sybil had ever encountered.

'So good of you, Lieutenant Fleming,' she said, later in the day, finding him lying along the terrace balustrade with a hat over his eyes, 'to take such trouble with our little Marchesa. Such a sheltered life, you see, such a particularly fearsome mother.'

Lieutenant Fleming tumbled off the balustrade and on to his feet. 'It isn't good of me, Mrs Carruthers,' he said, 'it isn't good of me at all. I don't do it to be kind, I do it because I like it.'

'Then perhaps,' Aunt Sybil said briskly, 'we must simply be grateful that your selfishness happens by chance to be a benefit.'

He stared at her. She was as sharp-tongued as her niece and, by the look of things, as critical. Then he smiled, the first smile he had given to anyone but Donatella.

'Yes,' he said.

'An odd young man,' Aunt Sybil said later to her sister.

'Who, dear?'

'Lieutenant Fleming. He appears to think good manners are a form of hypocrisy.'

'I fear,' Aunt Jean said, seriously raising her head from her account book, 'I fear he won't do for Isobel.'

'Oh Jean!' Aunt Sybil cried, laughing, 'of course he won't do for Isobel! Of course he won't!'

Chapter Thirteen

By the autumn, nothing seemed to be going well. The Dardanelles campaign had finally ended with the tragic disaster of Gallipoli, and the Italians had made repeated but hopeless attempts to dislodge the Austrian army from its mountain stronghold. The only bright spot on the horizon, for Isobel at least, was that Giovanni was granted ten days' leave.

He arrived back at the Villa Celoni on a dark October day, with low skies and lashing rain. Isobel, secretly on watch since the early morning, saw the fiacre go by with its hood up, splashing through the pale mud of the road. It was misery to see the cab and not be able to stop it, and spring in, and throw herself into Giovanni's arms after all those months of waiting, months which had seemed to Isobel, for all her busyness, the longest of her life.

It wasn't simply the work that needed doing at the Villa Calvina, and on the farm throughout the summer, nor the lessons with Professor Vaccari – now reduced to two a week – that had kept Isobel busy, but the schemes Aunt Jean had devised for Isobel to show the convalescent officers the splendours of Florence. Patiently, Isobel did as she was told, marshalling her charges through the squares and churches and galleries and, with every instructive word she uttered, reminding herself horribly of Miss Pargeter, reeling off lists of facts and names and dates from the cocoon of the mustard-coloured shawl. Oddly, and painfully, it was on these unrelaxed afternoons in the company of Botticelli, Brunelleschi and various young English soldiers, their eyes glazed with politeness and the longing to slope off somewhere and smoke, that Isobel missed Giovanni most. It wasn't just that these amiable, mildly philistine fellow-countrymen of hers seemed so alien to her, so excellent and hearty and empty, but that she had no idea how to handle them, she couldn't even, it seemed, talk to them. After Giovanni, they seemed both dull and incomprehensible, there was no ease and no fun in their company, or at least none of the right kind of fun. It was, Isobel said to Aunt Sybil, like taking large, jolly dogs for a walk, cheerful but hardly rewarding. Aunt Sybil said, with mock reproof, that she was sorry to see Isobel had turned into such an intellectual snob.

'But it isn't that!'

'Isn't it? What is it then?'

'It's just that – after Giovanni, they seem so – so unfinished, so crude, and I – I don't know what on earth to do with them.'

'I know you don't,' Aunt Sybil said, 'and that is a great disappointment to Aunt Jean.'

Aunt Jean knew that Giovanni Fosco was coming on leave. She had asked both Isobel and Donatella, and had been informed by the Marchesa.

'It is a tragedy!' the Marchesa had cried, clasping her hands. 'These battles of the Isonzo! Battle after battle. England is to blame, cara Signora Fanshawe, for enticing our brave people in!'

'Untrue,' said Aunt Jean.

'My poor boy is so tired, exhausted! A nature as noble as his must suffer more than most. He is coming on leave shortly, and we shall cherish him and revive his spirit. Ah, if only he had done as his father wished and become a businessman!'

'Then I expect,' Aunt Sybil said wickedly, 'he would be making a great deal of money, selling arms to the Germans.'

The Marchesa had taken no notice. She was working up a new tragic grievance that both her children had – or shortly would have – sacrificed themselves to a cause that had appeared pure and splendid, but had turned out to be only some self-interested English scheme. Her duty was to nurse Giovanni and his crushed ideals back to some kind of health. She attempted to prevent Donatella continuing at the Villa Calvina, in order to assist at the bedside of her brother. But Donatella, in a few months, had learned the beginnings of a small independence. She had seen, however court-eously expressed, Isobel's defiance of Aunt Jean, Aunt Sybil's scarcely concealed mockery of her mother, and that strange in-teresting young officer's contempt for many of the social con-ventions she had been brought up to regard as almost as sacred as

111

religion. Donatella was never going to join in any teasing of her mother but then neither was she going back into complete slavery. Isobel could have shaken her. Who could possibly even think of giving up the chance to nurse Giovanni, if offered it?

But Giovanni did not need nursing. News came from the Villa Celoni only hours after the cab had splashed past Isobel in her hiding place to say that he was well, in excellent spirits, and only waited for a word from her to be at her side. Isobel, made reckless by her longing to see him, did something she had never done before. She sent a note to Professor Vaccari to say she was unwell, and would not be attending her lesson in the morning, and another to the Villa Celoni, asking Giovanni to meet her on the road, by the shrine below the pinewoods.

She was there long before the time she had suggested, holding the bookbag with which she had, with such duplicity, set off from the house. The rain of the day before had cleared, leaving the sky damp and uncertain-looking, and a mist shrouding Florence and almost obscuring it from view. Isobel, in a dress Giovanni had always admired, of fine cream wool braided in green, waited by the shrine, her gaze fixed on the road below her up which he had come and with, seemingly, the Virgin's blue glass gaze once more fastened upon her. It seemed an agony of time before she saw his unmistakable figure coming up the road almost at a run, lithe and easy.

'Oh heavens,' Isobel said to the Virgin, dropping her bookbag, 'I think I'm going to faint—'

She was in his arms almost before she could think further, being kissed and exclaimed over as a miracle, as a beautiful, brave, wonderful miracle that had kept him going all those months in the mountains.

'Was it terrible? Was it dangerous? Were you in danger?'

'Hardly ever, my darling. It wasn't dangerous, but just boring, deeply, desperately boring. Never again do I want to climb another mountain, you cannot imagine how it is, all those hours and hours struggling up among the boulders and the snow and then, boum, boum, the Austrian guns and down we must go again.'

He looked, Isobel thought, quite magnificent. He seemed to have broadened and thickened, and his face was tanned and his hair lay on his head as dark and smooth and precise as the wing of a bird. She felt dizzy with relief and adoration.

'I should be in Florence, you know, with Professor Vaccari—'

'You are playing truant for me?'

Isobel nodded.

Giovanni smiled delightedly. 'This is excellent! And the *Zia* Jean?'

'As before.'

'Cara—'

'We mustn't think of that. We mustn't waste time talking of that. I have made friends with Donatella.'

He held her away from him for a little, gazing at her.

'You are superb! You are so good-hearted!'

'Don't—'

'When we are married, Donatella shall live with us!'

'Of course.'

'I have missed you so! Every day, I looked at all these men round me, and missed you so. The married ones wished to talk of their children, and the unmarried ones of their horses and their mistresses, and I wished to be alone and think of you.'

Isobel leaned her cheek against his shoulder. 'What happened to the glory of Italy?'

'Don't tease me—'

'I didn't mean to. I want to know.'

'War is not glorious,' Giovanni said gravely, and then, with a kind of anger, 'I saw men die for no reason.'

Isobel thought, with a sudden clutch of fear, of the men from the farm. Giovanni said, as if reading her mind, 'Our peasants make such good soldiers. They are simple, but properly led, they will go anywhere. But I saw some die by accident, out of carelessness.'

She raised her face to look at him.

'All the time,' Giovanni said, 'when I did not think of you, I thought of our farm. I thought of the lives we would give our peasants.'

She nodded. 'I've thought of that too.'

'I have something to show you.'

He dropped his arms, smiling down at her, and put his hand in his pocket.

'Have you? What?'

'This,' he said, drawing out of his pocket a long folded paper. 'A map!'

'Our map? Our place?'

'Our place, maybe,' Giovanni said, and turned to unfold the paper and lay it along the top of the wall that curved round the shrine.

'Lorenzo drew it for me one day when there was a ceasefire. It

113

was a beautiful day, and we spread this paper out on a rock and he drew. Of course it is very rough.'

Soft black pencil lines were scrawled across the paper, interspersed with rectangles of various sizes, scribbled names, hatched areas and, in the top left corner, an explosion of small marks, like exclamations.

'That is the mountain. That is the old volcano, Monte Alba. And there is the villa, and these smaller boxes are the farms, and these lines are tracks and those darker places are woods, mostly oakwoods. And this place is an Etruscan burial ground and all over here is hills. Is it not wonderful?'

'Yes,' Isobel said, bending over the map, eyes alight.

'The villa is set on a ledge above the valley. Lorenzo says it is a most beautiful place.'

'Is the villa beautiful?'

'It is not,' Giovanni said carefully, 'medieval, but it is in a beautiful place.'

'Could I make a garden?' Isobel said eagerly, fired with a sudden vision of her own camphor tree, her own irises and roses, her own lemon trees, shiny leaved and precise, standing in pots along her own terrace.

'Of course.'

'And there are peasants there already?'

'Indeed so, but Lorenzo says they need someone to inspire and discipline them.'

Isobel straightened up. 'What would such a place cost to buy?'

Giovanni hesitated. 'Many – thousands of francs. Many.'

'Oh.'

'Yes.'

'So – we come back to waiting.'

He took her hands in his. 'Unless we have a miracle.'

'There are no miracles,' Isobel said determinedly.

Giovanni glanced at the Madonna. She was looking past them, away down at her view.

'What a place to say such a thing!'

'We will only get what we want by waiting. Will Lorenzo wait for us?'

'I should think so. I hope so.'

'Giovanni—'

'*Cara?*'

'I don't think,' Isobel said suddenly, 'that I can bear this, the waiting and not seeing you and the atmosphere of the war and the house being full of these men who aren't interested in us—'

Giovanni interrupted. 'I do not like these men at the Villa Calvina.'

'No, nor do I. They are decent young men but it seems to me that all we do for them is virtually wasted, that they think the aunts are comical and don't see how kind they are—'

'I do not mean that.'

She looked up at him. His face had darkened.

'What do you mean, then?'

'I mean that I do not like my betrothed and my sister to have daily contact with all these young Englishmen.'

'Giovanni, don't be ridiculous—'

'I am not ridiculous!'

'There's a war on, Giovanni, these men come to us as invalids. My main involvement with them is trying to show them the treasures of Florence when all they want to do is play tennis and drink whisky and flirt with anybody with a pretty face. Frankly, I bore them and they bore me.'

'I still don't like it!'

'Well, you will have to put up with it, because as long as they are sent to us by the Red Cross, we must take them.'

He glared at her. 'You defy me?'

'In this case, when we are trying to do good, and you are simply being absurd, of course I do!'

'I cannot believe this.'

'Nor me.'

They stood, trembling and furious, face to face.

'We have no choice,' Isobel said.

Giovanni put his hands to his head and let out a wild cry.

'Always you say that! We have no choice, we are not free, we must wait, we can do nothing—'

'Well, it's true,' Isobel said stubbornly. 'I hate it, I hate it more and more being imprisoned in this way, I've just said so, but I can't make things different, I *can't*! Why do you always blame me?'

He flung his arms about her. 'Because I love you.'

She burst into tears.

'Don't cry, *cara*, don't cry, don't cry! I do not mean to make you cry! I thought this war would make the time pass more quickly, I thought it would calm my impatience, but the frustration of these battles with the Austrians is terrible. I try to read because I am a thinking man, but all I want to do is to put my thoughts into practice. Sometimes, I think I must go mad.' He took one arm away

115

from Isobel and banged his hand down on the map. 'I have never seen this place, this estate of La Crocetta, and yet, in the nights, I was walking its woods and hills and planning where we should cut water channels and plant our vines, I was—' He stopped, almost choking. 'Perhaps I am just a fool—'

'No!' Isobel cried, 'no, of course you aren't. You're – you're—'

He looked down at her. 'What am I?'

'Wonderful,' Isobel said. Her face was shining with earnestness. 'Just wonderful.'

'Signorina,' Professor Vaccari said, 'you are not paying attention to me or to Ovid.'

Isobel withdrew her gaze very slowly from the milky November light lying on the Arno.

'I don't much care for Ovid, you see.'

'Ah. Now that, if true, is only part of the reason for your inattention. I would like you to tell me what is on your mind, in order to unburden yourself and then, with your mind cleared, I should like you to concentrate upon Ovid who, although more effusive and, shall we say, occasionally palpitating than many other poets, is not without his merit.'

Isobel looked at Professor Vaccari with gratitude and affection. In all the years she had been coming to him, his appearance had scarcely changed; the same rusty black suit over crumpled white linen, the same tufty hair and untidy beard – both these were now greyer than they had been – the same shrewd bright eyes behind spectacles as thick as the bottoms of bottles.

'They have all gone,' Isobel said, laying down her book and leaning her elbows on her knees.

'All your gallant officers?'

'Yes.'

'Now that this tragic enterprise of the Dardanelles is over?'

'Yes. They have all gone, and Giovanni has gone.'

'I see.'

'And Giovanni's sister has been called home by her mother, now that the soldiers are no longer there, and—' she stopped.

'Signorina?'

'I am quite isolated again,' Isobel said, almost in a whisper.

Softly, Professor Vaccari closed the book that lay in front of him. Poor girl, he would say to his wife later, poor girl; every advantage, and yet so far, no outlet for all her capacities. Signora Vaccari would say that what the young signorina needed was a husband,

116

and a houseful of babies and the professor would agree, to be obliging, and would think to himself that there was something in the young woman that led him to suspect she might manage a husband and babies and a great deal more besides. He also thought and had wondered how to say this to the captivating but headstrong Mrs Carruthers that it was time Isobel's lessons stopped. She was a young woman now, not a schoolgirl. Her education, he wished to say, should be given into her own hands. He sighed a little now, looking at Isobel and thinking of Aunt Sybil. Perhaps it was to Isobel he should speak first, but not this morning, when she was so distracted.

He said gently, 'No more Ovid today, my dear.'

'Oh, but—'

'You have too much on your mind.'

'Thank you,' Isobel said, from a full heart.

She put on her hat, and the swirling coat Aunt Sybil had had made for her out of pale lilac cashmere, picked up her bookbag, and went slowly down the stairs into the street. It was an ordinary Florentine weekday, and yet nothing at the moment could be ordinary, not even for these busy citizens, and probably, Isobel thought, never could be quite the same again. She remembered the clerk in Maquay's Bank, the first person to have given her even an inkling of war, and wondered if he had reached England and, if he had, if he was now wrestling in the mud to help gain possession of some tiny, nameless Belgian copse. And what would become of cheerful, polite George Mason, and uncouth Patrick Fleming and all those other young men whom the Villa Calvina had taken in and nursed back to a state where they were fit enough to be sent back into that closed and terrible soldier's world where you asked no questions and expected no explanations? And what, oh what, of Giovanni?

Isobel set her chin. There must be no giving in, particularly not to self-pity. Tomorrow she would apply herself to Ovid with determination and today she would concentrate on being grateful that the war had at least freed her from being escorted through the streets of Florence like a prisoner. 'True freedom,' Professor Vaccari said, 'exists only within one's own mind, within one's own power.' Even, he had implied, within the oasis from the real world to which the Villa Calvina had now reverted.

Chapter Fourteen

In the summer of 1916, Aunt Sybil took Isobel to the sea, at Viareggio. She said Isobel was looking peaky. They rented a small villa on the edge of the pinewoods, and in the mornings, while Isobel bathed in the sea and lay on the beach wishing ardently for friends and Giovanni, Aunt Sybil and Moody performed the former's long toilette and agreed that Viareggio was very dull and if it wasn't for the child's health, they would never have come.

It was a curious, disembodied two months, the evenings only enlivened by the occasional play at the little theatre by the shore, usually a violently anti-Austrian piece which left the audience sobbing with patriotic emotion, and Isobel sick with renewed anxiety for Giovanni. Once, on the beach, she saw a group of children burning a crude effigy of the Emperor of Austria on a bonfire of pine needles, and jumping round their pyre shouting, 'We want liberty! Death to Austria!' A man called Oberdan had been caught walking into Vienna with a bomb in his pocket that he intended to throw at the Emperor, and in Viareggio he had become a hero. There were puppet shows on the beach, telling his story, full of fervent songs and speeches, while the quiet sea played on the shore and Isobel lay on the sands and wished for the summer to be over.

Yet the following winter and spring were little better. The winter was fiercely cold, the desperate struggles for the Isonzo raged on, Edward Lindsay wrote to say that bread was to be rationed, and that the British Royal Family were renouncing their German names, and the chain was put back on the gates of the Villa Celoni. News came that young Poppi, an orphan boy who had worked on the aunts' estate for five years, had died of gangrene from a wound received in his foot, and Isobel's lessons from Professor Vaccari ceased for several months while he recovered from a bad bout of influenza. It was, Aunt Sybil said, with her passion for ill health, the Spanish influenza. It was a particularly violent kind, and an epidemic was predicted for Europe. The aunts decreed that precautions must be taken. Isobel was forbidden to go and see Professor Vaccari at home until he was quite recovered, and they could both sit by an open window, and, when in trams or other crowded public places, she was instructed to wear a mask of white gauze made especially by Moody and impregnated with coal tar. The coal tar made Isobel's eyes water and after five self-conscious minutes wearing it in the tram, the mask remained in her pocket.

Letters from Giovanni came irregularly and infrequently. He had, not being a professional soldier, obtained leave from his superior officers to drive an ambulance for his regiment, and he said this was a far better solution to his agitation of mind. He said there were several Englishmen, volunteers, driving ambulances also at the Italian Front, most of them Quakers. He said he could not understand Quakerism. What did a man do, if he was a Quaker, with his natural bellicosity? He complained he received no letters from Isobel, despite the fact that she wrote almost every day, letters she feared would hardly amuse him, being full of the endless repetitive details of days that seemed to her to be so like one another that she could hardly distinguish the weeks and months.

'One can, you know,' Professor Vaccari had said smiling, before he was ill, 'grow used to anything.'

'But I don't want to,' Isobel said stubbornly.

She could not believe that life at the Villa Calvina could go on so placidly. Sometimes, in the early morning, she would be woken by the sound of raggedly tramping feet as yet another band of young recruits from the villages in the hills were marched down to Fiesole singing snatches of '*Addio, mia bella, addio*' as they went. Sometimes, too, letters from her father made her realize the suffering and endurance in England as relations and friends left for the front, and Zeppelin raids plagued London. But most of the time, the days went on as they always had; Aunt Jean had found an eager boy, disqualified for military service on account of having flat feet, whom she was training to do some of Luca's work. He had even learned to drive and went into raptures at the sight of the Lancia, gleaming and unused since Luca's departure.

119

'I feel it is so wrong to live in an ivory castle,' Isobel wrote to Giovanni. 'It's a less comfortable castle than it was, of course, and we can't get enough butter or sugar for love or money – the sugar comes in tiny screws of paper – but we are so much better off than most people. Of course, the war is all anyone ever thinks about, and there is talk all day here, most of it that rather detached and superior talk that Aunt Sybil's friends go in for, but nobody seems to do anything *but* talk. Yet, what can they do? What can I do? I cut fodder yesterday for two hours and felt rather better, but it isn't enough. I so envy you, driving your ambulance. When we have our farm, I shall work all day, dawn to dusk, like the peasants do, you see if I don't.'

The summer wore itself away, day by painful day. Aunt Jean persuaded the holy brothers who ran an orphanage high among the precipices round the Madonna della Corona to allow her relays of boys to help with harvesting first the wheat and then the grapes. Isobel went thankfully down to join them while Aunt Sybil lay on the loggia as usual, receiving visitors, planning the garden and reading T. S. Eliot, whom she had just chanced upon and whose poems she said were extremely arresting. Beppe returned from the front amid much rejoicing, invalided out of the army with the loss of an eye, but in a shocking physical state which suggested that the men at the front were looked after no better than cattle, and Isobel's twenty-second birthday came and went with no outward show, but with an inner resolve on her part that not another year should be wasted in this sterile state of young ladyhood. Aunt Jean, as if reading her mind, began to say that as soon as the war was over, they must all consider Isobel's spending some time with her father. Aunt Jean did not spell it out, but a sojourn in Scotland would, of course, be for the purpose of husband hunting. Twenty-two, in Aunt Jean's book, was the perfect age to be a wife, as long as that wife did not belong to Giovanni Fosco. Isobel said nothing to this scheme. It was becoming her only defence, saying nothing, while her mind, like a mouse on a wheel, went round and round, seeking a way of escape.

In October a note came from Professor Vaccari to say that he had been to the sea, for his health, that he was now fully recovered and that he should like very much to see the Signorina Lindsay at his rooms on the Lungarno Acciaioli. Isobel was puzzled.

She said, holding out the note to Aunt Sybil, 'He says nothing about lessons—'

Aunt Sybil was looking at a small bronze she held in her hand, the figure of a boy with a bow in his hand and a quiver of arrows on his back, which one of her pet dealers from the Via dei Fossi had sent up for her inspection.

'I'm sure, darling,' she said absently, 'he *means* lessons.'

'He mightn't,' Isobel said, seized by a sudden idea. 'He mightn't, he might mean that, at twenty-two, I'm far too old for lessons and that I should—'

Aunt Sybil looked up. 'Don't be silly, darling. Nobody is ever too old for lessons. If you were a boy, you would be at the university.'

'But—'

Aunt Sybil crossed the room and placed the little bronze boy carefully on the carved chimneypiece.

'There. He's going to be charming.'

'Aunt Sybil—'

'Go away, darling,' Aunt Sybil said. She put her hands to her temples. 'Go away and see Professor Vaccari. I have a headache, and you are definitely making it worse.'

Isobel went out of the *sala degli uccelli* and into the hall whose floor the new young employee, Roberto, was vigorously polishing. He stopped when he saw Isobel and gave a little clumsy bob of respect. Don't do that, Isobel wanted to say to him, don't do that when I am so useless and you are so useful. She smiled at him.

'Have you seen the *Padrona*?'

'In the *podere*,' Roberto said. 'Two people are ill, Luca's wife and a little one. The *Padrona* fears it is the influenza.'

Isobel looked over her shoulder at the closed door of the *sala degli uccelli*.

'Say nothing of that to the signora, Roberto.'

'No—'

'She must not know of influenza here. Roberto, I am going down into Florence and I think I won't be back for lunch.'

He nodded. No wonder the *Padroncina* was so thin if she would not eat. Maria said it was an aching heart that prevented her from eating and that the *Padrona* was responsible. Roberto did not know about aching hearts; his ambition was to find a wife who would bring a sufficient dowry and prove a tireless worker. When did love, after all, fill anyone's belly?

Isobel went down into Florence, glad at last of an errand. The

121

city was at its most seductive, bathed in soft autumn light, and, war or no war, there were plenty of women on the streets in the new short draped skirts and wide-brimmed hats that Aunt Sybil had declared delicious and Aunt Jean immodest. When she reached the Lungarno, the door at which she had knocked so relentlessly for ten years of her life stood open, to her amazement, and from the top of the staircase that led up to Professor Vaccari's study, came the sound of his voice, raised in evident excitement.

Isobel hurried up the stairs. The door to the professor's study was open and through it she could see both him and the house-keeper of the building.

'But it must be cleared, Signora! This is an emergency! I will help you all I can, but—' he broke off, catching sight of Isobel. 'Signorina Lindsay! I had quite forgotten about you—'

'I'm so sorry, but I got your letter, you said I might—'

Professor Vaccari hurried past the housekeeper and seized Isobel's hands. He was certainly thinner, but otherwise looked exactly the same except for a violent agitation in his face which was certainly not a fever.

'Signorina, I am thankful to see you. Forgive me, but everything was driven from my head by this calamity. I have been up all night with them—'

'Who?' Isobel said. 'What calamity?'

'There has been a terrible attack by the Germans and Austrians at Caporetto, not far from where I was born. My poor people! My poor villages! The Italian Front has collapsed completely, and the Veneto is being evacuated. Train after train comes in of these poor country people, turned out of their homes. They have nowhere to go. I can put a family here, in my study, but not,' he suddenly shouted, whirling round upon the housekeeper, 'unless I have some help in moving all these books!'

'I will help,' Isobel said.

'Signorina, you may do more than help move books. These people need blankets and clothes and boots and food. They have nothing. I have been at the station all night and I must go back as soon as I can. Can you help me?'

'Yes,' Isobel said thankfully. She was ready to embrace him, to kneel down in that funny, familiar, dirty little corridor between the stacks of books and kiss his stubby black boots. He was not, beloved, sympathetic Professor Vaccari, asking her to talk or to think, he was asking her to *do*. 'Oh yes. And so gladly!'

*   *   *

122

She took a cab back to the Villa Calvina, recklessly offering the driver double the fare if he would hurry. The aunts were at luncheon, Aunt Sybil picking at a chicken breast, Aunt Jean dividing her attention between eating and reading an account of the US Senate's rejection of President Wilson's suffrage bill.

'And perfectly right—'

'No, it isn't, Jean. Women haven't got second-class minds.'

'That isn't the point—'

'Of course it's the point. Please don't raise your voice, darling, my head is bursting. Isobel!'

'So sorry,' Isobel said breathlessly from the doorway, 'but it's an emergency—'

'What is?'

'Florence is full of refugees, as a result of a German attack at Caporetto. There's thousands of them, Professor Vaccari says, pouring in by every train and they haven't enough clothes or food or anything. May I borrow Roberto and the car? Can I take all our spare blankets? Can I go round to Lady Scott and the Rennishaws and the Foscos and everybody else to collect things? Can I?'

Aunt Jean put down her newspaper. 'Of course, darling. Get Maria to help you—'

'Do be careful!' Aunt Sybil cried. 'Do please be terribly careful!'

'Of course,' Isobel said, 'and thank you.' Then she whirled from the doorway and they heard her running down the passage to the kitchen, calling loudly for Maria. The aunts looked at one another.

'Extraordinary,' Aunt Sybil said, pushing her chicken away from her, 'quite extraordinary. I don't know when I've seen her look so happy.'

Florence station was so crowded that there was scarcely room to move. The long, low platforms were packed with people, women of all ages, children and old men, wearing the shuttered empty expressions of people who do not even begin to understand the catastrophe that has befallen them, but who fear that there may be yet worse to come. A lot of the children, exhausted and frightened, were crying and their wails rose into the clamour above the hissing of the trains and the muted chattering of the people, pitiful and inconsolable.

Isobel, elbowing her way through the crowd, found Professor Vaccari by a canteen the Red Cross had set up to dispense milk and coffee.

'Signorina!'

'I have a car full of clothes and blankets.'

'I won't thank you,' the professor said, 'but you may make yourself useful, distributing them. The children first, of course—'

Someone tugged at Isobel's sleeve. A peasant women in a black shawl was peering up at her.

'Have you seen my Bartolo?'

'I'm sorry—'

'He was with me! He was with me when we crossed the bridge! Do you have my Bartolo? Have you seen him?'

Isobel said gently, 'I'm so sorry, I know nothing of your Bartolo.'

The woman stared at her for a moment and then let go of her sleeve.

'I had him, you know, I had him with me!'

'Yes—'

'I will ask someone who knows,' the woman said, 'someone else will have seen my Bartolo!'

She drifted off into the crowd.

'They think her son fell into a river, pushed in by the sheer volume of people crossing a bridge.'

Isobel's eyes were full of tears. 'Poor woman—'

'They are all poor,' Professor Vaccari said, 'they are all bewildered, stranded here with their bundles, dazed with fear. The enemy bombed them as they fled, stumbling across the countryside they had farmed for generations, these people who have among them the neighbours of my family.'

'I don't know what to say—'

'There is nothing to say,' Professor Vaccari said, 'there are only things to do. To work, young lady, until there is not a family on this station without a blanket and some clothes.'

It was a sad, confused business. All the while that Isobel was attempting to wrap exhausted children in blankets or persuade a stony-faced old man to accept a scarf, or a whole pair of boots, offers of shelter were pouring in from householders all over Florence. But the refugees would not move. Deprived of everything familiar but one another, they clung to their little groups of families and friends, huddled round their bundles of household things, exhibiting an obstinacy Isobel could only sympathize with. But their condition was pitiable. They had about them the maltreated, fearful, neglected look that poor Beppe had had, returning from the front with his crudely bandaged empty eye socket. Over and over again, Isobel's mind was flooded with fury at the sight of these people who were, as Beppe had been, the victims not just of a defeat, but of other people's decisions and commands. Stooping to wrap a shawl donated by Lady Scott round an old woman, a most unsuitable shawl patterned with oriental birds in violent colours, a vision of La Crocetta rose before Isobel, a vision of this place she had never seen but which she knew would give freedom to her, and, at the same time, security and satisfaction to people like those all around her now, clinging to one another and their pots and pans on a strange and draughty railway station, miles and miles from home.

Dirty and exhausted, Isobel and Roberto did not reach the Villa Calvina until after midnight. Professor Vaccari had said he would welcome her help in the morning and that perhaps the aunts might be persuaded to offer a cottage or two, or even a few rooms, to some of the refugees, at the Villa Calvina.

'There will be a new front line drawn, you see, not far above Venice. All the people from those villages along the River Piave, we haven't seen half of them yet—'

Isobel thought, as the car crept up the drive to the house, that she wouldn't suggest the possibility of housing refugees to the aunts until the morning. She also thought, with a small and startled pride, that she had seemed to be able to do for those poor people on Florence station exactly what she had been unable to do for the convalescent officers; she had been able to touch and comfort. Why that should be, she was too tired to think, but it consoled her to reflect upon the day, upon what had been achieved.

Roberto stopped the car at the front door, and made to get out, and come round to open Isobel's door.

'Don't move,' she said, 'please don't. You have been such a help.'

'They are Italians, *Padroncina*,' Roberto pointed out. 'It is natural to help them.'

Isobel nodded. She climbed out of the car, and went up the steps to the front door. The great hanging lamp was extinguished, but a small one, fuelled by oil, of the kind Aunt Jean insisted was preferable to electricity any day, stood on the hall table.

'Isobel!'

Isobel looked up. On the staircase, small and stout in her blue wool winter dressing gown, with her white hair in its night-time pigtail, stood Aunt Jean, holding a candle.

'Dear, I'm so glad you're back. I was listening out for you.'

Isobel moved to the foot of the stairs.

'You shouldn't have worried, Aunt Jean. I was perfectly safe. It's just that there were so many poor people needing wrapping up and feeding—'

'No, dear,' Aunt Jean said, interrupting. 'It's Sybil. I wanted you to know about Sybil.'

A small fear clutched at Isobel. 'What about Aunt Sybil?'

'She isn't well. Not at all well. Dr Piaggi has been from the Via Nazionale. Sybil insisted upon it because he had treated Professor Vaccari. You see, dear, we think it is the influenza—'

'Oh, no—'

Aunt Jean held out a hand. Isobel went up the stairs, and saw, from a closer distance, that her aunt's face, usually so steady and full of resolve, was pale with distress. Isobel took her hand.

'She is never ill, you see. Is she? All her life, she has fancied herself ill, she did as a child, in the nursery. And it was so sudden, in just a few hours today, she went from having a mild headache, to this terrible fever.'

Isobel squeezed Aunt Jean's hand. 'Is she awake? May I see her?'

'We will look in the door, dear. Moody is sitting with her. It's such a comfort that you are home.'

Hand in hand they tiptoed across the landing to Aunt Sybil's bedroom door. It was pulled close, but not latched. Isobel gave it the smallest push and it swung open, revealing the redoubtable figure of Moody, upright in a chair by a reading lamp, indefatigably mending. She looked up as the door opened and put her finger to her lips, motioning her head towards the bed.

On the bed lay Aunt Sybil, turned away from them with her head almost obscured in a great heap of pillows. Her body was equally concealed and in a way that made Isobel's mouth dry with a sudden remembered terror. There lay Aunt Sybil beneath exactly such a billow of lawn and lace and carefully goffered frills as Ida had lain beneath, all those years ago, in the darkened, over-furnished London bedroom.

'Oh no,' Isobel said involuntarily, and far too loudly, 'oh no, please not, oh please, oh please—'

Chapter Fifteen

Aunt Sybil died six days later, at eight in the evening. Dr Piaggi said it was her heart; the fever, he said, had simply been too high, her heart could not have been strong. They were all with her when she died, Aunt Jean and Isobel and Moody, with Maria in the doorway and Beppe waiting respectfully for news in the kitchen. Everybody was stunned. It was so quick, so brutally sudden.

'It is how this influenza is,' Dr Piaggi said. 'It is one of its characteristics. It falls upon the patient like the blade of a sword.'

He left a sleeping draught for Aunt Jean.

'She won't take it,' Isobel said.

'She had better. Weakness makes people susceptible.'

'I'll do my best.'

Dr Piaggi looked at her. 'Grief is debilitating, Signorina.'

I know! Isobel longed to shout, I know, I know, do you suppose I haven't suffered any? She gave Dr Piaggi a little bow, instead of a smile. How could Dr Piaggi know the nightmarish quality of the last six nights during which Isobel had relived, in every kind of detail, that long ago childhood night in her bleak nursery, while her mother lay dying of pneumonia and a broken heart on the floor below? Her mother, whom she had tried to love and who had tyrannized her. And now it had been Aunt Sybil, who had certainly tyrannized her too, and who had, like Ida, been spoilt and selfish, but whom Isobel had had no trouble in loving. Lying wakeful in her cherub bed beneath the painted birds and ribbons, Isobel could recall with an almost agonizing clarity that other childhood bed, with its iron frame, and the irritation of the

127

imperfectly fastened blind, and Maudie's temper, and the sinister muffled sound of wheels outside in the straw-covered street. Now the menace was being repeated, in this happy place, in this little paradise where she had been loved and cherished for over half her life, and from which she now, so wickedly, she told herself, just longed and longed to escape.

Aunt Jean, devastated by her sister's death, did not believe in showing it. The most emotional thing she said to Isobel was a sudden exclamation, over an almost untouched breakfast, of, 'Do you know, dear, I do rather wish I had some form of religious belief. It must be such a comfort at a time like this.'

Apart from that, she insisted that nothing about their days should be changed. She would go on about the house and farm; Isobel would receive visitors, all Aunt Sybil's friends who came to offer their condolences and weep, gently, into the glasses of wine that Isobel had been instructed to offer them as being, on such an occasion, more fortifying than tea. When she wasn't thus occupied, she was sent to help Moody – an almost silent, red-eyed Moody – in going through Aunt Sybil's possessions. It was an awful task.

A wire was sent to Edward Lindsay in Scotland, informing him of Sybil's death, asking him to see the family lawyer and – this was Isobel's plea – to come out to Italy, if he possibly could. In deference to Aunt Sybil's vague affection for the church, the Reverend Knollys was summoned from the English Church of the Holy Trinity in the Via La Marmora and told to arrange the simplest of services.

'But lots of flowers,' Isobel said.

'No, dear, just severe simplicity—'

'No,' Isobel insisted, 'banks and banks of flowers. I shall go to the Mercato Nuovo and collect them myself. Mountains of flowers.'

The Marchesa Fosco came, and solemnly embraced Isobel and attempted to embrace Aunt Jean as well. Donatella was in tears.

'She was so good to me—'

'I know.'

'She was always laughing. It will be empty here without her.'

'I know that too.'

Donatella gave Isobel a quick look. She whispered, 'What will you do?'

Briefly, Isobel shut her eyes. 'I don't know. I wish I did. I *wish* it. My father is coming next week, if he can get a passage. It's so difficult, with the war. Perhaps I shall go back with him.'

'Do you want to?'

Isobel shook her head violently.

'You must not go,' Donatella said, in a low, fierce voice. 'What will become of Giovanni?'

'I wouldn't go to Scotland for long, just for a little time. But Giovanni isn't here, and while he isn't here, I can't stay, not any longer, not now.'

'Isobel,' Donatella said suddenly.

'Yes?'

'I have a letter – a letter from the young soldier Fleming.' She darted a glance across the room at her mother, wholly engrossed in a critical examination of Aunt Sybil's ornaments on the chimney-piece. 'My mother doesn't know.'

'What does he say? Where is he?'

'The letter is about painting. It is to encourage me, he says. He is in hospital again, in England. He was wounded in France, in the lung. He wishes to be remembered to you.'

'Thank you,' Isobel said stiffly.

'I loved those months,' Donatella said, beginning to sob again, 'I was so happy here. And now—'

Despair seized Isobel. She took Donatella's hand.

'I can't help you. I just can't, not now. I would if I could, but I can't. I don't even know, just now, if I can help myself.'

Later that day, over a supper of veal in Marsala, tenderly cooked by Maria to try and tempt them to eat, Aunt Jean said that now that there was just the two of them, they must learn to be happy and useful together in a new way.

Isobel, cutting her meat into smaller and smaller pieces, but not eating any of it, was silent.

'We owe it to her memory,' Aunt Jean said, drinking mineral water. 'We owe it to Sybil, with all her gaiety and charm and cleverness, not to allow ourselves to become dull and self-pitying. That would be self-indulgent. It would not be worthy of her.'

Isobel waited. Plainly Aunt Jean was working up to something. Isobel put her knife and fork together on her almost untouched plate, and folded her hands in her lap.

'You have been indulged,' Aunt Jean said. 'It was both Sybil's and my delight to indulge you. And where we could not indulge, because it would have been wrong to do so, we tolerated.'

Isobel raised her eyes, and looked steadily at her aunt. Aunt Jean looked steadily back.

'We have tolerated,' Aunt Jean said, with slightly more emphasis in her voice, 'your attachment to young Marchese Fosco. It was unsuitable in every way, but you are young and innocent, and we understood that and made allowances. But now that Sybil is gone, it is time for you to grow up. You must teach yourself, for Sybil's sake, to see this attachment as the youthful folly that it is. There is to be, Isobel dear, no more Giovanni Fosco.'

Isobel could hardly breathe. She found that a tide of hot blood was rushing up her body and face and neck. Her cheeks felt on fire. She gripped the edge of the table.

'No,' she said.

Aunt Jean folded her napkin with deliberate precision.

'There is no "no" to be uttered, dear. You are now my ward for three further years until you gain your little independence, and thus my responsibility. I cannot allow you to squander yourself when I know what is best for you so much better than you know it yourself.'

Isobel made a wild gesture, and her knife and fork went flying across the table, spattering the polished surface with gravy.

'No!' she shouted. 'You can't do this! You can't take advantage of Aunt Sybil's dying like this, you can't!'

Aunt Jean rose to her feet.

'There is no point discussing this further, I see, when you are so overwrought.'

'I'm not overwrought! I'm grief-stricken as you are, but I'm also twenty-two and won't, do you hear me, won't be treated like a child any longer!'

'Then you must not behave like one. We will not speak further tonight. I see there is absolutely no point. We will not speak of this again, Isobel dear, until your father comes.'

Edward Lindsay arrived at the Villa Calvina almost three weeks after his sister's death. He said the journey had been terrible, in unheated, blacked-out trains that had no dining cars and were carrying nothing to drink except bottled water and some vile apology for coffee, made almost entirely of chicory. He sounded aggrieved, as if Sybil had caused him both danger and discomfort by inconsiderately dying in wartime.

Isobel was full of nerves about seeing him. Just as she had loitered anxiously at the top of the staircase in London over ten years before, so she now hung back outside the *sala degli uccelli*, where Aunt Jean had ordered a fire to be lit, out of carefully hoarded wood. She could hear them inside, murmuring together, the oldest sister and the younger brother. If I'd had a brother, Isobel thought irrelevantly, my life would never have been like this.

She turned the door handle quietly and pushed the door open. Aunt Jean, in her grey cashmere with a black silk shawl over it out of respect for Aunt Sybil, was standing on the hearthrug. Beside her, not so very much taller than she and definitely not as tall as he had been ten years ago, stood a slight man with grey hair and a grey moustache.

'Oh!' said Isobel.

Edward Lindsay turned. He held his arms out.

'Isobel!'

She almost had to stoop to be embraced by him.

She said impulsively, quite without intending to, 'I'm so glad you've come!'

'Are you, my dear?'

She nodded violently. He had Aunt Sybil's eyes, she saw, and the same little ironic twist of the mouth. He looked, to her amazement, blessedly familiar.

'I have grown small and grey,' Edward Lindsay said, 'while you have bloomed. You are a splendid advertisement for life in Italy.' He glanced at his sister. 'I'm afraid I was very fretful about coming, but I'm delighted now that I'm here. England and even Scotland to some degree, are very grim. Everyone has someone to grieve for, and there's not enough food or fuel.'

'Will it soon be over?' Isobel asked. She rather wanted to put her hand in her father's.

'We have been asking that since it began.'

'And – and the children?' Isobel said bravely. 'And – my stepmother?'

Edward grinned at her. 'They want me to bring you home with me.'

'Oh—'

'An excellent plan,' Aunt Jean said.

'It's ten years now, you know,' Edward said gently to Isobel. 'Ten years ago. Do you not think perhaps that after ten years you might think of forgiving me and your stepmother? With the children, of course, there is nothing to forgive.'

Isobel said hurriedly, 'It isn't that. Not any more—'

'Then?'

'I shall manage perfectly well on my own,' Aunt Jean said.

Isobel's face was full of dismay. She looked from her aunt to her father.

'Perhaps – perhaps just for a few months—'

'Yes.'

'I'm so sorry, I don't want to sound ungrateful. I do want to come to Scotland—' She stopped, in great confusion, and then added, 'Perhaps, when the war is over—'

'Are you afraid of a little discomfort?' Edward asked teasingly in his sister Sybil's voice.

'Oh no!'

There was a little silence and in it, Isobel could sense Aunt Jean waiting for her to confess, waiting for her to say that she had been headstrong and foolish, and allowed her heart to rule her head. She looked down at the Persian carpet beneath her feet, at its not quite symmetrical pattern of lozenges and flowers. She would talk to her father; she would tell him of Giovanni all over again, of their hopes and plans, just as she had done in her letter to him, but she would not utter one syllable of this in front of Aunt Jean.

Edward watched for a moment. She had grown, certainly, and blossomed unquestionably and become both characterful looking and almost pretty, but somewhere in her lurked still something of that poignant child who had sat opposite him and reluctantly confessed that she had a secret picture of him, hidden in her schoolroom. He put a hand out, and took one of hers.

'Another time,' he said. He smiled across at his sister. 'There's no hurry, and in any case, I am famished for my dinner.'

The following day, Isobel took Edward down to Florence to see Aunt Sybil's grave. She had been buried, naturally, in the English cemetery, a strange, melancholy oval-shaped ground, dotted with marble obelisks and grieving angels, in the middle of the Piazza Donatello. Elizabeth Barrett Browning had been buried there, and the poet Walter Savage Landor, and Aunt Jean had been most insistent in securing for Aunt Sybil a place not far from these illustrious personages, and shaded by a row of cypress trees. The grave was very simple at the moment, simply the turf laid back on the earth within a kind of marble fender, but Aunt Jean had ordered a splendid headstone with a bas-relief of lilies upon it, made of white marble.

'Poor Sybil,' Edward said, gazing down, his hat in his hands.

Isobel, standing opposite Edward the other side of the grave, rather thought it was those left behind without Sybil who were poor, but she said nothing. She had, during the tram ride down into the city, told her father of her abiding love for Giovanni, and

132

it had been his turn, then, to say nothing. He was listening intently, Isobel was sure of it, but he said nothing and only, when she finished speaking, gave a little grunt which might have meant either anything or nothing. They had walked from the tram stop almost to the cemetery without speaking. Isobel hoped that her father, this father whom she scarcely knew but who was curiously familiar, was deep in sympathetic thought.

'Poor Sybil,' Edward said again.

'Was she? She always seemed so happy.'

'Such a waste, marrying Carruthers. Odd, bookish fellow, no fun in him that anyone could see. Wonder why she never married again?'

Isobel said, fired by romantic loyalty, 'Perhaps she didn't want to. Perhaps she loved him. People don't always understand about other people's loves, anyway.'

Edward raised his eyes from the gentle green mound that covered his sister, and regarded his daughter. She was wearing a full, soft, pale lilac-coloured coat, with an exaggerated caped collar and huge pockets. Aunt Sybil had forbidden mourning, so Isobel's only token of respect was a narrow black ribbon, tied around one sleeve. She looked both young and modern among the stately Victorian memorials of the place.

'At least,' Edward said slowly, 'Carruthers left her well provided for.'

'Yes,' Isobel agreed. She supposed he had. Aunt Sybil had never seemed to stint herself of anything and had been enormously generous. Economy, despite Aunt Jean's account books, was not a word much used at the Villa Calvina.

'What has she left you, Isobel?'

'Her books,' Isobel said, 'and two paintings, and her amethysts, and the furniture in my bedroom, because she bought it specially for me, when I came.'

'Is that all?'

'Yes!' Isobel said indignantly, resenting any implication that Aunt Sybil had been other than generous. 'It's not *all*, it's everything, she gave me my clothes and my education and she—'

'You're right,' Edward said, 'it isn't all.'

'What do you mean?'

'Isobel,' Edward said, 'your aunt remembered all of us.'

'What—'

'She has left all her share of the Villa Calvina and the farm and the contents of the house to your Aunt Jean. That is only as it

133

should be, that is right and proper. She has left me ten thousand pounds. It will save me, it will almost save Castle Lindsay—'

'Oh, I'm so glad!' Isobel cried, interrupting.

'And wait, Isobel, wait. She has not forgotten you. She has left you the same sum, my dear, the same sum as myself, ten thousand pounds, with a message that I was instructed, in a note, to pass on to you. The message is this. My sister Sybil said, "Let Isobel have her heart's desire." '

PART THREE

Chapter Sixteen

Tuscany – 1919

The valley lay below Isobel, empty under a blazing September sky. No valley could possibly be more different from the valley she had looked at all her growing years, that fertile, beautiful valley of the Arno, with its cypresses and church towers and the incomparable city lying at its heart. This valley was not only empty, it was bare. It was also, or at least about three thousand acres of it were also, hers; hers and Giovanni's. They had bought it, land, woods, villa, ruined farms and decayed olive orchards, six months before, with part of Isobel's inheritance. They had bought it a month before they were married.

Isobel sat now, fanning herself with her hat, at the very point that she and Giovanni had come to, on New Year's Day, to see this place they had both dreamed of for four years. If either of their hearts sank at the sight of it – and Isobel's had slightly, to her dismay – neither confessed it. A neglected river, choked with boulders and silt, crept across the wide, bleak valley where there were few trees, only tired looking bushes and tufts of broom. The whole place was ringed by hills, harsh bare hills, whose summits looked as if they had been scoured by wind and sun, and which were dominated to the west by the mountain, the immense, rearing slopes of Monte Alba. There were hardly any buildings to be seen, and the woods of scrub-oak and chestnut that clothed the lower slopes of both the mountain and the hills looked dark and secretive.

137

'Imagine!' Giovanni had said. He'd had his arm around her. She leaned against him, partly to be out of the wind, partly for reassurance.

'We shall arrest the erosion of those slopes, we shall rebuild the farms, we shall turn those great wastes and spaces into fields of wheat!'

His voice was full of elation. It was infectious. Isobel looked down again. She half-closed her eyes. She saw, she thought, the river bed cleared and the water running freely and, beside it, the optimistic pale green of new wheat.

'It has to look like this,' Giovanni had said, tightening his arm, 'it has to look like this for us to have the work to do! If it looked any better, it wouldn't need us!'

She had nodded. She had nodded again, later, when he had, driving the new Lancia also bought by Isobel, taken her to see the estate house, the villa of La Crocetta. Isobel had already had a private vision of her hoped for villa, the vision of a medieval house with a deep loggia, and great stone fireplaces and a little, perfect courtyard at its heart, with a well, or, even better, a fountain. But La Crocetta was not like that. La Crocetta was quite old, but it was very plain. Its rooms were dark, and its doors were made of ugly pitch pine. It lacked a bathroom, electricity, and even a garden. But it stood, as Giovanni's fellow soldier, Lorenzo, had promised, on a ledge at the head of the valley, with a view sweeping down the course of the river, past the great mountain, to the setting sun.

'I shall love it,' Isobel said to Giovanni.

She meant it. She meant to love everything, from the people to the pebbles of this uncompromising landscape. The agent for the estate was very discouraging. He pointed out that of the twenty-five tiny farms on the estate, only two had houses in good repair, and that of the three thousand acres, most was unprofitable woodland and the rest lay fallow, except for a fraction planted with vines and olives. Roads must be made, he said, and thousands of trees planted to stop the erosion of the soil, and farm buildings must be repaired, and farm implements bought. Nothing had been spent on La Crocetta since before the turn of the century. Hundreds of thousands of lire must be spent now, if the Marchese seriously meant to restore the estate. The first thing the place needed was capital.

Giovanni did not even glance at Isobel.

'We have it,' he said superbly.

Five days after that first sighting, they had signed the deeds; La

Crocetta, neglected, three-quarters ruined, and full of promise, was theirs. Three weeks after that, at eight in the morning, Isobel and Giovanni Fosco were married at the church of the Santissima Annunziata in Florence, attended by the Marchesa, Donatella and Professor Vaccari and his wife. Aunt Jean did not come, and nor did she send any message. Isobel hardly expected it. After all, shortly after Aunt Sybil's death, Isobel had left the Villa Calvina, and had heard the gates, on Aunt Jean's instructions, shut behind her.

A terrible few weeks had followed Aunt Sybil's death. Aunt Jean had chosen to take Isobel's legacy as a direct insult to herself, as well as a mark of disloyalty from that sister whom she had lived with for so long and cared for so indulgently. It seemed she could hardly bear the sight of Isobel. She busied herself on the farm all the daylight hours – 'Heaven knows what she's doing,' Moody said, 'except getting in everyone's way' – and chose to take her meals alone in the little closet off the hall where she did, so painstakingly and earnestly, the farm accounts. Isobel felt entirely helpless. The only consolation she could give Aunt Jean was the one she refused to give, because it meant all the world to her. After almost a month, Isobel gave up the struggle, and left the Villa Calvina. It was, she saw, almost a kindness to Aunt Jean to do so, because to go of her own accord avoided the deep unpleasantness of having to throw her out.

The Marchesa Fosco implored her to come to the Villa Celoni.

'You cannot live alone, my dearest Isobel. It is not suitable. It is not proper. How will you go on, brought up as you have been, to do nothing for yourself? Here, you will be so comfortable! You shall hire a maid, and she may look after both you and Donatella.'

For a split second, Isobel had wavered. She was indeed apprehensive at her competence to live alone, but she was not as apprehensive as she was excited. She was also, she discovered, with surprising firmness, not going to assist with the household expenses at the Villa Celoni. The money – her money – was for hers and Giovanni's future. She evaded the Marchesa's importunities and, with Professor Vaccari's help, found a small flat in a building looking over the river, three rooms and a kitchen. Signora Vaccari sent her own maid's younger sister to help with the cleaning and cooking.

For the first few weeks in her apartment, Isobel did little but sleep. Worn out by argument and misunderstanding, by the steady resolve needed to reject pressing invitations to go to the Villa Celoni, or to Scotland, she found she was sleeping through the afternoons as well as through the nights. Edward had returned home after only

139

a week saying, with his characteristic distaste of any kind of confrontation, that as neither his sister nor his daughter had the smallest intention of changing their minds, his staying further was pointless. He had begged both to be less adamant; it was a quality, he said, he could not bear in people, it was such an unreasonable way to go on when life, in the end, was always composed of compromises. Writing from Castle Lindsay later to Isobel, he implored her not to let the situation develop into a feud. 'I hate to see these Morpeth traits in you,' Edward wrote, 'I hate to see anyone so unbending.'

But he hadn't bent, Isobel told herself, when he had wished to leave Ida and marry Mrs Bond; he had gone right ahead and done it, just as she was going to do. She had torn his letter up, because it had angered her just when she was beginning, at last, to love him. His letter was a blight upon her happiness, in any case, the happiness that grew each day as she revelled in the freedom of being her own mistress, in her own rooms, leading her own life. The day she was able to go into Maquay's bank and sign for the opening of her account was a day she felt she would never forget. Aunt Sybil had been governed by her own whims and fancies, but she had, in the end, understood Isobel's need for independence.

In two months' time, Isobel thought now, blowing on the insides of her wrists in a vain attempt to cool herself in the heat, all that would be almost two years ago. Two years, the first of which had been spent learning, so pleasurably, to live alone and devoting her days to helping with those poor refugees from the Veneto who were forced to linger in Florence, unsettled and, it often seemed, unsettleable, until the slow peace negotiations of 1918 allowed them to return to their neglected and devastated farms. The second of the two years had, of course, been taken up with Giovanni home at last and on fire with eagerness to marry Isobel and start on their new life. She had taken him to Maquay's Bank and proudly had his name added to hers as a legal signatory on all cheques. They had had a second courtship, that winter of 1918 with peace at last across Europe, an open courtship with the adventure of La Crocetta before them.

I am now, Isobel thought, in the adventure, and it is taking all kinds of forms I never thought of. Its chief aspect, that September day, looking down on the river bed which still only seemed to hold a despondent trickle of water, was the size of it. Almost every day now, for seven months, she and Giovanni had ridden out on mules along tracks too rough for the Lancia, and come home with a fresh list of things to be seen to, leaking roofs and broken windows and fallen bridges and always, eternally, land that must be ploughed but, to be ploughed, must first be cleared of stones. And then there were the people. Encouraged by the relationships she had built up among the refugees, Isobel had imagined that she would find no problem with the people, that they would respond to her desire to help with their health and the education of their children. But the people of La Crocetta did not behave like that. Stubborn, suspicious and deeply resentful of Isobel's Englishness – hadn't the English, after all, embroiled the sons of Italy and these farms in that wicked war? – they showed no desire to have anything to do with her.

'What am I to do?' Isobel said to Giovanni.

'Persevere,' he said.

He had no need to persevere. Every day for him seemed a day to be met with enthusiasm. Every day, he gave new orders, drew up fresh plans and wrote yet more cheques drawing on the account in Maquay's bank.

'Giovanni,' Isobel said to him, hesitantly, 'please be careful. This has to last, this money. We have to live.'

He looked up at her, eyes bright, the pipe he had taken to smoking as a sign of being a true countryman between his teeth.

'But we shall have more! Your next birthday—'

She looked away. She couldn't explain it – didn't want to – but the thought of her next inheritance, from her mother, going into that account at Maquay's and there becoming so – vulnerable, gave her a small cold feeling of dismay in the pit of her stomach. Giovanni was talking of a water pipe, to come down to the house from a mountain spring six miles away . . .

'Six miles!'

'Then we can install a proper bathroom. You can have a garden—'

She longed for a garden. It was exhausting, too, to live with all the household water having to be taken from the well in the courtyard behind the house.

'What will a pipe cost, a six-mile pipe?'

'Oh,' he said carelessly, 'a few thousand lire perhaps. I haven't worked it out.'

He smiled at her. If anything, out there in these wastes of Southern Tuscany, in his rough, countryman's clothing, he looked even more beautiful than he had, tailored in cream linen, in the streets of Florence. He seemed almost untouched by those years away at the front, as if he had been so sustained by the power of his dream of the future that he had been almost oblivious to the life he had led. He would hardly speak of it. He said nothing that had happened then had any bearing now on his life with Isobel.

'I wish—' Isobel had said, and then stopped.

'What do you wish, my darling?'

I wish, she had been going to say, that you would be more practical. But how could she find herself wishing anything of the kind? She loved him for being impractical, for his vision and passion, she always had.

'It doesn't matter,' Isobel said.

She had then said, the next day, that she must have just one afternoon off, one afternoon in which she wasn't patiently inspecting the slow repairs to the *fattoria*, the main farmhouse, or laboriously filling in the interminable forms applying for government subsidies that Giovanni was too impatient to bother himself with.

'What will you do? Do you wish to go shopping in Siena?'

'Oh no,' Isobel said, 'I just want to be alone somewhere—'

'Alone?'

'I want a few hours when I'm not planning things, not working out what things cost, not trying to persuade people that their children will have better lives if they can read and write at this school I want to start which nobody has much interest in but me.'

'*I* have an interest in it,' Giovanni said, putting his arm around her, 'I have an interest in everything!'

'I know you do.'

It was too true. Evidence of Giovanni's interests lay everywhere, planting plans and irrigation plans, drawings for buildings and pumps and wells and roads, catalogues for seeds and trees and various makes of the new mechanical ploughs that would, Giovanni said, till the earth far deeper than it had ever been tilled before. Hardly a flat surface in the house was free of these piles of paper, tottering, scattered piles in no order that Isobel could ever see, not one scrap of which was ever to be thrown away.

'You have your afternoon to dream,' Giovanni said, most lovingly. 'You take a book with you.' He peered at her. 'You are tired, my darling,' he said tenderly, and then he went tearing out into the courtyard behind the house, calling for his mule.

So Isobel had come up here, to this high, lonely spot above the villa, whose russet roof she could see below her, backed by a scruffy wood of scrub-oak which Giovanni wanted to replace with beech. If she looked to her left, along the hillside, she could see the olive

142

groves where Giovanni had gone for the afternoon to supervise the picking, believing, as he always seemed quite effortlessly to believe, that he would be a better judge of ripeness than the slow, impassive men who had been picking olives for generations. In the cellars of the *fattoria*, which was built right next to the villa, was a millstone for crushing the olives, worked by a blindfolded donkey. After the olives were ground, the peasants told Giovanni, the resulting pulp would be put into rope baskets and crushed under great wooden presses which took four strong men at a time to operate. Isobel thought – and said – that this was probably exactly how the oil had been made in the time of Virgil. Giovanni had been horrified.

'It is so primitive! All this darkness and sweat, so unhygienic! We must set apart a special room, a tiled room and I shall investigate the cost of installing electric presses and separators, it will be an investment.'

Everything he wanted to do became an investment. Money, if it was spent with the aim of making La Crocetta into an admired modern estate, could not, by definition, be wasted. Only money that Isobel wished to spend on making the house just a little more comfortable, a little less charmless, was wasted. As long as the roof did not leak, and the windows were glazed, Giovanni saw no cause for complaint, and he reproached Isobel if she pointed out, critically, the broken brick floors or dingy old wallpapers.

'We have left all that behind, my darling, we have left behind in Florence that life of false values and vanities. We are living as we wish to live, by the seasons and the weathers. We mustn't forget that, we mustn't forget what we set out to do.'

Isobel could never answer him. Of course he was right, clinging so tenaciously to their original nobility of purpose, but was he right, too, to expect her to live quite so primitively? She still felt, with great energy, that Aunt Sybil's ceaseless and sole preoccupation with creature comforts and pretty objects was no way to approach life, but was it really necessary to live in a house that was scarcely possible to keep clean, it needed so much doing to it, and where there was hardly a corner where it was pleasant to be?

Isobel looked down at her hands. They must be amazed, she thought, by the things she had asked them to do recently, just as she was amazed at how capable they had proved. They were going to have to prove their capabilities even more in the months ahead, the months that Isobel had wished to think about alone for a few hours, before she said anything to Giovanni. Only Assunta knew, the maid whom Signora Vaccari had sent to her in Florence, and who had asked if she might stay with Isobel after her marriage and come down with her to La Crocetta. Assunta knew, because she had guessed, and, being a direct creature in every way, had asked a straight question.

Stopping suddenly, while they carried in together yet another great pail of water from the well, Assunta had demanded, 'Are you pregnant, Signora?' She would not call Isobel Marchesa, out of socialist principles.

Isobel hesitated. 'Yes. I mean – yes, I think so—'

'Then put this bucket down!' Assunta had shouted. 'Put this bucket down at once!'

Chapter Seventeen

Giovanni burst into tears. He wept quite openly, holding Isobel against him and telling her he adored her and that he would adore her even more when she was the mother of his son.

'We can't be sure—'

'Of course we can be sure!'

She felt so happy and triumphant, standing in his embrace while he wept with an openness of feeling that no Englishman, Isobel thought, would have dared to express. The old doctor in Siena had told her to have a thankful heart at conceiving so easily. There was no need to tell Isobel anything of the sort; she was awash with thankfulness. How simple a process it all seemed, this getting pregnant, after the terrible and long drawn out business of marrying the man you had set your heart on! Isobel blushed against Giovanni's shoulder. The process wasn't just simple, after all, it was also an amazing pleasure, and one that Isobel had hardly looked for. Was one, she wondered, *supposed* to enjoy making love so much? Giovanni said of course she was, she was to enjoy it like all the other good and natural things of life.

'You are so English!' he said laughing at her. 'So Protestant! So puritan!'

She hardly knew what she was any more except, at this moment, happy with a deep and marvellous contentment. It wasn't just that she was going to have a baby, it was also that she and Giovanni would be able to give this baby all the things they had never had themselves, the steadiness and security of a family life where the parents were united in both feelings and purpose. She saw, in her

145

mind's eye, the house with all its doors and windows open to the sun, and children running through them, calling for her and for each other.

'Oh!' Isobel cried, clinging to Giovanni in rapture at her vision.

He mopped at his face with a huge red handkerchief.

'Now I must arrange for the water pipe. You can't have a baby without running water!'

'No—'

'And we must paint rooms for the nursery, and buy furniture, and look about for a girl to help as nursery maid—'

'Assunta and I—'

'Dearest,' Giovanni said, 'you must take care of yourself. We must find more people for the house, the floors must be repaired, you must rest in the afternoons.'

'I want to go on almost exactly as before,' Isobel said.

'No!'

'Yes!'

He took her face in his hands. He was laughing. 'I know you will,' he said, 'I know that look. That is the first look that ever I saw on your face in the *salone* of *Zia* Sybil!'

The next few weeks were filled with hope. Isobel, feeling obscurely that her pregnancy gave her a new authority, inspected a small empty building on the far side of the *fattoria*, which had once been used for a granary, and declared that it was here she would start her nursery school. The roof needed some small repairs, the walls needed whitewashing, a floor must be laid, and the tiny windows, not much more than medieval arrow slits, must be enlarged to let in light and air. Isobel asked Giovanni for three men from the farm to carry out the work, one of whom must be a carpenter capable of making simple desks and chairs. He, as elated as she was, said she could have ten men if she wanted them.

The allotted three arrived with visible reluctance. It wasn't the work they minded so much as working for the Englishwoman. They stood about, wearing expressions of extreme truculence, while Isobel explained, with far too much confusing detail, what she wanted them to do.

'They are stupid,' Assunta said.

'You mustn't say that. It's not their fault that they can't read and write—'

'It's their attitude that's stupid,' Assunta said. 'In this place, it's the same all over! They don't like their lives, but they won't change them.'

'We'll change them, though,' Isobel said, 'the Marchese and I.'

Assunta snorted. She said the countryside was like a grave but, in the same breath, that nothing would induce her to leave Isobel here, alone, among these pig-headed peasants. She was, Isobel thought affectionately, so like Moody, so generously dedicated to being a part of someone else's life and yet so resolutely herself at the same time. Moody had never, in twenty-five years, stopped saying 'Foreigners!' in a disgusted tone, but she would have been outraged to have been taken at her word and sent away from the Villa Calvina.

'They don't know what a school is,' Assunta said scornfully. Her own schooling and her older sister's had been paid for by Professor Vaccari. 'They'd be better off building pigsties. They can't even write their own names.'

They worked, Isobel thought, with a determined slowness that set her teeth on edge. Half a dozen times a day, dressed in old breeches of Giovanni's reefed in round her expanding waist with his old military belt, a coarse blue workshirt bought in a market in Siena and with her hair tied up in a piece of checked cotton, Isobel clambered up the decayed staircase to the first floor of the old granary, to see how the roof was getting on. Two of the men, the older ones, would hardly speak to her, and the younger one would say only as little as possible.

'It's slow work, *Padrona*. This is a difficult job.'

'It isn't,' Isobel would say. 'The roof beams are perfectly sound, it just needs new battens and new tiles in a few places.'

'It is slow work,' the man insisted. He wouldn't look at her. Neither would his workmates. Giovanni said it was because of the breeches, but Isobel knew it was because of her sex and her Englishness. When Giovanni went up to the top floor of the granary, the men doubled their speed.

'Persevere,' Giovanni said again to Isobel.

'I want the school to be running by the time the baby is born!'

'It will be.'

'But they're so slow and so stubborn, they're driving me mad—'

'Do other things. Don't go up there so often.'

The two daughters from the family in the *fattoria* came in to scrub the house. Isobel had often asked for them, but nothing had happened until Giovanni, fired into protectiveness by her pregnancy, had ordered them to go. They were only in their teens,

147

heavy, silent girls, who moved through the house like a pair of reluctant oxen. Both were promised as brides to young men on the farms.

'They'll have a baby a year,' Assunta said, 'and by the time they're twenty they'll look forty, and by forty they'll be dead.'

'You should be sorry for them,' Isobel said, 'not despise them. What else are they supposed to do? What choice do they have?'

'They should copy you,' Assunta said. 'They could copy me. They shouldn't just plod through the days, never thinking, doing just what their ancestors did. If we were all like you,' she said to the older sister, a moon-faced girl called Paolina, 'we would still be living in caves and gibbering like apes.'

Paolina gaped at her.

'There you are!' Assunta said mercilessly, 'if you could only see yourself!'

Slowly, the two sisters scrubbed away at the rooms which Isobel and Giovanni had not yet attempted to use. Giovanni took one of the men off the roof of the granary, and set him to re-laying, and then waxing, the broken bricks of the floors. He didn't like this work, without his two companions, and so, if not watched like a hawk, would work at a snail's pace in the house for an hour, and would then slip out, as silently as a shadow, to rejoin the others in the granary. He had to be endlessly retrieved by Isobel and Assunta since Giovanni was, invariably, miles away across the estate working out which fields should be the first to benefit from the new plough, ordered from a factory in Milan, and due to arrive at La Crocetta by Christmas. One day, the workman simply wasn't in the house at all.

'Where's Pietro?'

'Where do you think?' Assunta said. She was, at furious speed, sewing flowered linen curtains on a treadle machine Isobel had found in Siena.

'I'll go and get him,' Isobel said.

'Is it worth it, Signora? Isn't it better to get in some proper craftsmen from Siena who will do the job quickly and well?'

Isobel said a little hesitantly, 'The Marchese only likes us to use our people here, people from La Crocetta—'

'Even when they are useless?'

'Don't be impudent, Assunta.'

Assunta broke off a thread with a snap. 'Go then, Signora, go and find Pietro and tell him that he will be dismissed from the estate if he doesn't do the job he has been set to do.'

'We can't do that, Assunta, you know we can't. There's this great Tuscan tradition of a landlord's responsibility towards his tenants. If you farm here, you put the land and its people before yourself, you know that.'

'Fetch him, then,' Assunta said carelessly.

Irritated, Isobel went out of the villa through what would one day be a cool and airy kitchen with electric light, and into the *fattoria* courtyard. It was a golden day, one of those autumn days that start and stop with an hour of beautiful misty blue light, and the courtyard, for all its present grim bareness, looked full of possibilities. Isobel stopped to consider it. When all the rubbish – old bits of rusty ironwork – had been cleared out of it, she would plant creepers against two of the buildings that edged it, and have tubs of herbs, as Maria had done at the Villa Calvina, and bring the hens up from the cellar where they presently lived in stinking darkness to peck and mutter about in the sunlight on the cobblestones. It would be a cheerful place, a clean, busy, cared-for looking place, just as her school would be when Pietro and his companions had at last finished what they had been set to do.

She stepped into the old granary. It was quite silent, except for the faint slow chinking of a hammer on stone from far above.

'Pietro!' Isobel called.

The chinking hammer stopped.

'Pietro!'

Complete silence. Isobel, sighing with exasperation, climbed the broken staircase – Giovanni had expressly forbidden her to do this – and emerged into the upper storey to find the three men exactly where she had last seen them, two days earlier, laboriously dressing the stone tiles for the patch of roof on which they seemed to have been working for weeks. They all looked away as she appeared.

'Pietro,' Isobel said, trying extremely hard to sound reasonable and not in the least imperious, 'Pietro, you should be in the house, you know, finishing the floor on the landing.'

Pietro waited, immovable.

'The Marchese will be back at midday. I don't want him to find that not one more brick has been laid since yesterday. Do you?'

Very slowly, Pietro laid down the tool he was holding. Then, still very slowly, he lowered himself through the hole in the roof on to the floor below, and stood there, staring at his feet.

'I am going back to the house now,' Isobel said, sensing approaching victory and not wishing to humiliate the man by insisting that he accompany her, like a captive, in full view of

149

anyone who might be watching from the *fattoria* windows, 'And in five minutes, please, Pietro, you will follow me. Five minutes.'

She turned and put her foot down towards the top step of the staircase. As she did so, one of the older men still outside on the roof said something in a low voice and the others barked with laughter. Stung even though she couldn't hear exactly what they had said, Isobel called out, 'You forget I understand Italian perfectly!'

They laughed again, more loudly, as if it pleased them to see her understand their insult, and Isobel, stepping forward too quickly both to escape them and to salvage the shreds of her dignity, missed her footing and fell, clumsily, down the short rough wooden staircase to the earthen floor below.

Giovanni drove the Lancia like a mad thing into Siena to fetch Dr Roselli. Isobel protested she was only shaken and bruised but Giovanni, summoned from the olive orchard by a visibly shaken Pietro, was taking no chances. He was in a towering rage.

'I shall dismiss them all, they shall go tonight, I will not have my wife shown such disrespect! You are a Fosco now, they have insulted the name of Fosco!'

'Please, Giovanni, don't send anyone away, please don't. I'm sure I shall be fine, I'm sure the whole episode will have cleared the air—'

'No!' Giovanni shouted. 'No!'

He had driven off in clouds of dust, leaving Isobel lying on the cherub bed in the bedroom she was trying so hard to like, with its stern view of Monte Alba and its heavily, darkly beamed ceiling. Assunta had put her to bed and now came in, every ten minutes or so, pale with rage, to see if Isobel was starting to bleed.

'Hanging is too good for men like that.'

'They didn't mean this to happen,' Isobel said tiredly. She was, in a way, appreciative of Giovanni's and Assunta's protective anger, but she couldn't help wishing they could be angry somewhere else where she didn't have to react to it. 'They just went too far, that's all. They thought they could get away with it. I expect they're sorry now.'

'Men like that,' Assunta said, 'don't know how to be sorry. They're brought up by their mothers to think they rule the world.'

Dr Roselli arrived with Giovanni, wearing the kind of rusty black suit that reminded Isobel, with a burst of weird nostalgic longing, of Professor Vaccari. He stooped over her, muttering, smelling of eau de cologne and garlic, applying one huge, hairy ear to a little silver trumpet he inverted over her belly. He said she must rest for two weeks, in bed, and that if there was any sign of bleeding she must not move a muscle until he could get to her once more.

'You must calm your mind, Marchesa.'

'I am calm.'

'Your pulse is too quick. You must quiet yourself. A light diet and no movement that cannot be avoided.' He turned to Assunta. 'Regular infusions of camomile, to soothe the nerves.'

Giovanni bent over Isobel.

'You must do everything the good doctor says, dearest. Everything! You must do nothing to risk the safe arrival of my son!'

'Our son.'

'He will be born here!' Giovanni cried, straightening up and taking no notice. 'He will be born in this room, the first Fosco at the seat of the Foscos!'

Dr Roselli looked down at Isobel. She was a healthy girl, certainly, but no-one brought up as this young English marchesa had been had the physical resilience of a sturdy peasant.

'She should go to a nursing home,' Dr Roselli said. 'There is a first class one in Siena.'

'We shall get a nurse here!' Giovanni said. 'You shall attend her yourself! We shall have everyone here we need!'

Dr Roselli glanced again at Isobel. She had closed her eyes. He put a restraining hand on Giovanni's arm.

'Not now, my dear Marchese. Not now. We must let the patient sleep. There is plenty of time to discuss the birth later.'

'But my son—'

'Please,' Dr Roselli said, propelling him towards the door, 'please, my dear sir, we must leave the Marchesa to be quiet.'

Behind them, on the bed, Isobel felt fatigue begin to lie on her like a leaden blanket. She also felt, with a stab of pain she tried to tell herself was pure self-pity, that her greatest comfort just now would have been to hear Giovanni declare, even for a moment, that his first concern was for her welfare, let alone her wishes.

Isobel did not miscarry. She lay in bed for two weeks as instructed, looked after by Assunta and cooked for by the wife of the *capoccia*, the head farmer. The day after her fall, Pietro had brought six new eggs to the villa in a little rough basket woven of grape vines, and handed it without a word to Assunta. Isobel thought it a most eloquent apology and wanted nothing more said on the matter; she was sure, now, that the granary would be finished by the time she was allowed out of bed. But Giovanni was adamant.

'They insulted you, and because of you, me and my family. They insulted the name of Fosco. La Crocetta is now the home of Fosco and nobody should work here who doesn't understand that.'

'Please,' Isobel had pleaded, 'please don't send them away. I forgive them completely. Why can't you?'

'I've told you why,' Giovanni said. 'They insulted me. They endangered my son's life.'

Unwisely, Isobel had lost her temper.

'You are ridiculous!' Isobel had shouted, sitting up in bed and beating the covers with her hands. 'You are making a fool of yourself! Where are all your wonderful progressive ideas? Where is your sympathy? You sound like some feudal caricature out of a bad pantomime!'

That was fatal. By next morning, the three men who had worked on the granary had been dismissed, along with their families. Isobel, helpless in bed, and consumed with remorse and anxiety, could only send the slow Paolina out after them with a message that the moment she was well enough to get up, she would do everything she could to help them find new positions. But Paolina came back to say she was too late. She said the little procession had left the estate before dawn, as ordered, and that it was thought to be heading for Siena. There was more chance of work there, Paolina said importantly, as if announcing a great truth. Isobel, thwarted and miserable, fell back on her pillows and wept out of sheer frustration. When she tried to open the subject again with Giovanni, he said that there was no more to be said, that the matter was over and that he wouldn't give it another thought. He had, he said, many other things to think of.

One of these things he did not choose to tell her until she was almost well enough to get up again all day, and certainly well enough to come downstairs in the evening to the room which would one day, lined with bookcases and filled with pretty things and good furniture, be the *salone*. As it was, it still looked a good deal better than it had done when they arrived, with rugs on the newly gleaming floor, and Assunta's curtains hanging by the long windows and the first fire of the autumn crackling brightly in the fireplace.

'I have good news,' Giovanni said. He was sitting opposite Isobel in one of the two comfortable chairs they possessed, and looking

152

at her with that particular proud tenderness that had come into his expression since he knew that she was pregnant.

'Good,' Isobel said. She had been reading her old battered copy of Virgil's *Georgics*, with all its schoolgirl pencilled scribblings down the margins, comments and bits of vocabulary. She waited for Giovanni to tell her about the discovery of a big swarm of bees, of the early arrival of the plough or of his latest ideas for enriching the soil. Last week's one had been the planting of acres of clover, and the week before that, the planting of acres of alfalfa. Both, of course, when the plough came.

'I cannot believe,' Giovanni said, smiling at Isobel, 'how settled I feel here. I feel as if we have lived here always, not just you and I, but my family. It's as if my roots were waiting for me here, waiting for me to seize them and grow from them. I feel, Isobel dearest, as if the Foscos have come home.'

Isobel nodded. She was pleased for him, of course, but she could not truthfully say that she too felt a dynastic pull from this strange, harsh, challenging place. Nor did she particularly feel herself to be a Fosco. She felt herself very much to be Giovanni's, but there was a deep reluctance in her, however affectionate she might feel towards Donatella, to be profoundly part of a family that contained anyone full of such pretension and false grandeur as the Marchesa.

'It's sad, in a way, that there is only the two of us here, don't you think?' Giovanni went on. 'Soon there will be three, of course, but we Italians are family people, we have such loyalty to our families, we love to have them about us, and when we have land, we need to share this land.' He glanced again at Isobel, but this time, his look was less tender and more wary. 'My mother has been so worried about you, *carissima*. When she heard of your fall, she was beside herself. I didn't show you her letters because they were so emotional and I thought they might upset you. She has worried me, my mother.'

Isobel put her book aside. 'Worried you?'

'Living as she does, you know, a recluse but for Donatella. And on this miserable pension.'

'But she chooses to be a recluse!'

'Only because she can't hold her head up as she should. Only because my father's debts left her a burden of shame that she can't possibly be blamed for. I know she is sometimes absurd in her behaviour, but she's brave and without self-pity. I've said this before, but I must remind you of it.'

153

Isobel swallowed. She fixed her eyes on Giovanni. 'Why must you?'

'To recall to you what a good and noble woman she can be. A woman who would only, I do believe, have your best interests at heart. And you do need help and companionship. Since your fall, I've seen that so clearly, and you cannot spend your time just with Assunta, particularly not after our son is born. Also, you always said that you wanted so much to do something for Donatella.'

Isobel's voice seemed stuck in her throat. She said, in a strangled whisper, 'What are you saying to me?'

'I'm saying,' Giovanni said, artless and smiling, 'that my mother has suggested that she and Donatella come to live here, to help with running the house, and to keep you company. And I, my dearest Isobel, have agreed to her suggestion.'

Chapter Eighteen

The Marchesa Fosco and her daughter arrived at La Crocetta in a procession that was medieval in its size and timelessness. Across the valley, along the track from the Siena road, a long creaking line of most of the carts from the farms on the estate, drawn by oxen, trundled the Marchesa's beds and tables and chairs and, swathed in blankets and lashed upright with ropes, the black marble bust of her august grandfather. At the head of the procession came the Lancia, driven by Giovanni, with his mother beside him in her black plumes and his sister behind him in her grey clothes. Giovanni drove slowly, in order that the farm workers, who had been ordered to line the track, might be able to pay their respects to the dowager Marchesa as she was carried grandly by.

Isobel thought Giovanni had gone completely mad. She had refused to go into Siena to meet the train and take part in what seemed to her this ridiculous pageant. Her refusal had meant another quarrel. She and Giovanni had quarrelled almost daily since he had announced his mother was coming, quarrels which ended with Isobel in tears of rage and despair and Giovanni rushing out of the house to organize or reorganize yet another project. She had started by refusing point-blank to accept the Marchesa at La Crocetta.

'It is *my* house!' she yelled.

'It is our house,' Giovanni said quietly, shaming her.

She had then declared that she would, of course, as promised, offer a home to Donatella, but never to the mother.

'You cannot leave my mother alone in Florence! You simply

155

cannot! You, who have everything, propose to condemn an old woman who has nothing to live a miserable and lonely life just because she embarrasses you sometimes?'

'It isn't that. It isn't that at all. But I'm afraid she will try to overrule me all the time—'

'I am here,' Giovanni said. 'Do you think I will allow her to dominate our lives?'

'She can't help it!' Isobel cried, forgetting herself. 'She can't help it, she's a domineering woman. You know she is! Look what she's done to Donatella!'

Then Giovanni had lost his temper, accusing Isobel of cruelty, snobbishness and the unwomanly unpleasantness of trying to use her superior financial status as a weapon. They had gone round and round, day after day, and after an especially ugly few days and several wretched nights in which Giovanni had insisted on sleeping apart from Isobel, they had come to an uneasy compromise. The Marchesa and Donatella should come to La Crocetta for a year at first, and Isobel should, in turn, be allowed to give birth to this first child of the Foscos at the nursing home in Siena.

Watching the valley from the space outside the villa which would one day be a terrace, Isobel thought that the Marchesa did not look like someone who was only proposing to stay a year; she looked like someone who intended to stay for ever. Giovanni said his heart rejoiced to think of his family possessions at La Crocetta – 'Home at last!' he had said – but Isobel, remembering the black bust and the massive marble table on golden lion legs, had great misgivings. La Crocetta was not a small house, but it wasn't a grand house, either. It was, above all, a country house. As she watched the procession lumber ever nearer, Isobel felt as if she were the chatelaine of a medieval castle, and she was watching the inexorable advance of the army of a rival baron.

Assunta, standing a little behind her, said nothing. Born and bred a Florentine, she was ready and willing to dismiss the Foscos as Roman upstarts before they uttered one word or performed one deed. She had been prepared, on arrival at La Crocetta, to give Giovanni the benefit of the doubt, on account of his looks and his evident devotion to Isobel. Now she was beginning to wonder about the true direction of that devotion. She was also beginning to wonder how Isobel was going to control the rate at which Giovanni was spending money. For all her misgivings she had, with a good grace, however, prepared bedrooms for the Marchesa and her daughter; one of the two large front ones with a view of Monte

Alba for the one and a smaller one, facing north towards Siena and the olive groves, for the other. Isobel, she noticed, had taken great trouble with the smaller bedroom, covering the bed with a lovely old piece of embroidery and the bricks of the floor with soft white rugs. Perhaps, Assunta thought now, looking at Isobel watching the advancing cavalcade, perhaps the signora will now find herself a friend.

The procession began to wind up the hillside towards the villa, and the sound of the Lancia's engine and the creaking carts grew louder. There was no sun, and no wind, and every murmur carried clearly in the still autumn air. After a while, Isobel could make out her mother-in-law's great hat – she still clung, as Aunt Sybil had loved to point out, to the huge, stagey hats of the era before the war – and Donatella's apologetic figure in the back of the car, plainly, even at this distance, hating being made a spectacle of in front of the people from the estate. The Marchesa, on the other hand, was waving like a queen.

The car breasted the last steep incline of the hill and emerged onto the plateau where the villa stood. Giovanni hooted the horn in triumph and Isobel lifted her arms and waved, forcing herself to smile. The car stopped, and Isobel ran forward, over the rough grass and patches of cobblestone.

'A paradise!' the Marchesa cried, rising out of the Lancia like some vast bird of prey. 'A paradise!' She stood there for a moment, arms outflung, and then she turned and embraced Isobel fervently. 'My dearest Isobel! My daughter! What a day this is! What a place! Ah, my dear child, I am home at last!'

Her possessions were everywhere. She had exclaimed, upon arrival, that she would live like a nun in a single room, private and silent. Within three days, she had emerged from her bedroom, rounded up Paolina, her sister, and two young men from the *fattoria*, and set them to distributing her furniture and pictures and *objets d'art*. The black statue stood at the foot of the stairs, glaring at the front door, and the marble table was placed before him, in the centre of the hall, bearing two enormous gilded lamps and a vast reliquary in a glass case which the Marchesa declared contained a toe bone of St Sebastian. Two huge mahogany console tables, also marble topped, six gilded armchairs and an immense oil painting of the martyrdom of St Catherine upon the wheel invaded the *salone*. The future dining room, empty as yet, was taken possession of by a fleet of grim black chairs, heavily carved, around a table which could,

157

the Marchesa said proudly, seat twenty. Up the stairs marched representations of the Stations of the Cross, bas-relief on brown-coloured marble, and almost every window became shrouded in curtains of velvet and brocade, ruby coloured and damson and dark brown, pulled half across, even in daylight, and looped back with cords and tassels of unbelievable complexity.

Isobel was almost too stunned to protest.

'I cannot, you see, dearest child, leave these treasures of my ancestors to rot in barns!'

'No, but—'

'And Giovanni is so proud to have these things! Do you know, he said to me that he felt every day that this house was more his, that he couldn't believe Foscos had not lived here for ever. He said he never appreciated before what possessions could mean to you, what it was to come from an old and illustrious family.'

'She can't do this!' Isobel had whispered fiercely to Giovanni one night in bed. 'You promised you wouldn't let her, you promised!'

'I know,' he said. He turned on his side and stroked her belly. 'I am so sorry. But I can't make her take them away all at once.'

'Just some things,' Isobel pleaded. 'Just the curtains!'

'What is wrong with the curtains?'

'They are old-fashioned and quite wrong in this house and far too heavy and – and sort of *pompous*.'

Giovanni stopped stroking. 'Pompous?'

'Yes. All her things are. As well as being hideously ugly. I can't live with them, Giovanni. I can't and why should I? This is our house.'

Giovanni whipped over on to his other side. 'You call my family furniture ugly?'

'Yes. I'm afraid it is.'

'Don't talk like that!'

'I must!' Isobel said. 'I must be allowed an opinion! It's heavy, hulking, nineteenth-century furniture. It may look all right – just – in a city, but it certainly doesn't look all right here! Does it? Does it?'

But Giovanni wouldn't reply. He lay in the dark, with his back to her, and she knew that he was sulking. She had, yet again, trespassed on to this new minefield of family feeling, the pride of the Foscos. Where had that been, five years ago? Certainly not in the breast of that amusing young man, the caller at the Villa Calvina who had actually teased his mother in front of English strangers. Where was that Giovanni now?

'War,' Edward had said to her, after Aunt Sybil's death, 'war changes everyone. You have to be a heartless monster to escape it.'

Was that it? Was it the war, and all the things that had happened and which he would never speak of that had changed Giovanni? Tears filled Isobel's eyes, not tears for herself but tears for him and all he had endured, and tears of remorse at her own behaviour. She turned and, as closely as she could manage, laid her cheek against his back.

'I'm sorry,' she whispered.

He didn't even grunt, to acknowledge he had heard her.

At least there was the small comfort of Donatella. She might have been too downtrodden by the habits of years to stand up to her mother in defence of Isobel, but her looks and her manner when they were alone together proved her sympathy. She had been enchanted by her bedroom, turning to Isobel with a face full of gratitude. Yet it wasn't much of a room for a girl of twenty, Isobel thought, remembering her own room at the Villa Calvina with its painted furniture and ceiling and muslin curtains like snowy clouds. And life at La Crocetta wasn't much of a life for a girl of twenty either, with hers and Giovanni's preoccupation with this demanding land, and no society, and no lovely and cultivated city only a tram-ride away. She looked at Donatella's thin face alight with pleasure at the sight of her bedcover. Perhaps even La Crocetta was better than the Villa Celoni, at least her and Giovanni's presence would dilute the overpowering company of the Marchesa.

Assunta thought Donatella a pitiful waif.

'I shouldn't think she even menstruates, poor creature.'

'Assunta!'

'She looks like a child, Signora, yet you tell me she's a young woman. But what do you expect if she has lived all her life with that—'

'Assunta!'

Donatella attached herself to Isobel like a shadow, as if by being constantly in her presence, she could recapture those happy months at the Villa Calvina when, for the first time in her life, she had had just a glimpse of life outside the cage. She also had a secret to share with Isobel.

'You see – I have letters.'

Isobel looked up from her desk in the *salone*, in reality a table covered in a piece of dull rose brocade. It was a November afternoon, cool and sunny, and they had lit a fire. The Marchesa, with many flourishes, had gone up to her room to have what she insisted was a quiet devotional hour. Nobody, passing along the landing during this sacred time, could fail to hear that the devotions were punctuated by rhythmic snoring.

'What letters?' Isobel said, a little abstractedly. She had been concentrating on the road building estimates which Giovanni had ordered. He had declared that the estate needed at least twenty miles of metalled road. Isobel, horrified, had protested that they must start only with the essential roads, from the house to the Siena road and from the house to the nearest farms. Even so, the estimates were alarmingly high and the anxiety this raised in Isobel was compounded by the fact that Giovanni was, so far, refusing to ask his mother to contribute towards her and Donatella's keep. He swore he would do it, when they were all more settled; he insisted it would be both improper and indelicate to do it now.

'What letters?'

Donatella drew out of her pocket a packet of letters written on the kind of square white paper that Edward always used when writing from Castle Lindsay.

'From the *Capitano* Fleming. He is now a *capitano*, you see, after the battles in France.'

Isobel turned round properly in her chair.

'Donatella!' She leaned forward. '*Love* letters?'

'No,' Donatella said, not blushing, 'not love letters. The letters of a friend.' She let the packet fall apart in her lap. 'Look how many! More than fifteen.'

Isobel said, smiling, 'So he has been writing to you ever since he came to the Villa Calvina?'

'Yes,' Donatella said, 'all the time. I don't know why.'

'Perhaps he's lonely. He was a very strange fellow, so rude—'

'His letters aren't rude. Sometimes the language is difficult because he writes a little in English and a little in Italian. I wrote to him a month ago and told him that I should now be living here, with you.'

Isobel got up and crossed the room to sit by Donatella. She looked at the letters in Donatella's grey flannel lap.

'None of them have envelopes—'

'No,' Donatella said, and then in a very matter of fact voice as if trying to conceal any disloyalty to her mother, said, 'They come in typed brown envelopes, you see. At the top he types "Royal Academy of Art, London". They don't look like private letters. And

160

always inside there are reviews of art exhibitions and postcards of paintings that can be shown, you see, quite freely.'

'I do see,' Isobel said with admiration.

'It's not a deception,' Donatella said, 'only – only an omission.' Her thin hands hovered protectively over the pile of letters like wings. The writing on the letters was strong, in sepia ink. Isobel longed to read one. How did they begin?

'What – what does he write to you about?'

'A lot about painting. He wants me to know your English painters, Whistler and Augustus John. And he wants to give me lessons, in these letters. I send him sketches back, and then he criticizes them.'

Isobel thought of the chained gates at the Villa Celoni, only released to allow the servants out for marketing, or for the grand weekly exits of the Marchesa on her way to mass.

'How did you send him letters? How did you get away with it?'

Donatella said, almost complacently, 'Why, Chiara helped me.'

'Chiara? Chiara from the Villa Calvina? My Chiara?'

'Oh yes,' Donatella said. 'I would leave the letter and a little money in a hole in the wall of the garden, and she would collect it and post it for me.'

'But how – why—'

'Because I asked her to. I would have asked you, but you made it plain you didn't like the *Capitano* Fleming.'

'So why are you telling me now?'

Donatella looked up. Her dark eyes were almost shining.

'Because I think you have softened now that you have Giovanni and your heart's desire and the baby is coming. Because now I would like you to post my letters, and, when he asks to come and see me, I want you to invite him here.'

Isobel gazed at Donatella. She remembered another conversation they had had together, sweeping out the rooms for the soldiers at the Villa Celoni, when Donatella had first astonished Isobel by her quiet independence of mind, and composure.

'You absolutely amaze me,' Isobel said.

'Why should I? Why shouldn't I have a friend? You have Giovanni—'

'It isn't that,' Isobel said, 'it's these plans, these quiet little plans of yours. You write secretly to a young Englishman for four years and now you say he will be coming to see you.'

Donatella sifted through her letters, and selected one. She held it up, as if it were proof of evidence.

161

'He says he will be coming. He is a painter all the time now, as he always wanted to do. He is coming to Italy to paint, for months and months, for his own exhibition. He says he doesn't know where he will settle, but he says he'll certainly come to Florence to see me. I've written to say don't come to Florence, come here.'

Isobel nodded, still marvelling.

'Of course—'

'It will be in the spring, I think. Or early summer.'

'Yes—'

'He writes to me of other things, of course, of his feelings for his dead brother and of the war, of his time in France which he says still gives him nightmares.'

'Yes—'

'I like the English,' Donatella said, gathering up the letters, 'I like their self-control, and the way they keep their passions deep inside. I think you could trust an Englishman.'

Isobel stood up. 'And how will you explain your English painter friend to your mother?'

Donatella looked up at her. For a second, Isobel saw in her face just the wilful determination she often now saw in Giovanni's.

'I won't have to, you see. The reason I ask you, as my dear sister and friend, is that when the *capitano* comes, he comes as your guest, your English guest, and not as mine.'

Chapter Nineteen

That winter was long and cold. Giovanni had ordered plans for the installation of central heating to be drawn up – his imagination was fired by advertisements he had seen for a domestic boiler of Swiss design, fuelled by wood, in which the estate abounded – but Isobel had insisted that they remain only plans. The house was certainly uncomfortably chilly to live in, and the sight of the low grey clouds, heavy with winter rain, hanging over Monte Alba was deeply depressing, but Isobel was adamant. There would be the usual wood fires, and nothing else. The hours she spent over accounts at her table in the *salone* (each week, it seemed, having to sit a little further away as her belly expanded) had convinced her that not only was the capital allotted for the improvement of La Crocetta pouring away at a terrifying rate, but also that the budget of a thousand pounds a year they had allowed themselves to live on was being severely stretched by the addition of the Marchesa and Donatella.

Not even Isobel, at her most anxious and therefore cross, could claim that Donatella cost much to keep and, even if she had, the sum would never have been begrudged. But the Marchesa was another matter. She not only insisted on food being of a far more sophisticated kind than Giovanni and Isobel either planned or wished for, and which thus involved expensive shopping trips to Siena, but she also began to order herself comforts and luxuries from Rome: books (which she seldom read), embroidery silks and wools, fine soaps and gloves, bottles of Hungarian Tokay which she said were essential to her health. Giovanni signed the cheques.

163

'Don't do it,' Isobel pleaded. 'She can pay! She can pay out of her pension! Isn't it enough that we feed her and keep her?'

'She is still paying my father's debts, you see. And she is a noblewoman. You should not forget that.'

'I don't. How can I when she reminds me thirty times a day? But why should I pay for her while she pays your father's debts? It means, in the end, that *I* am paying those debts.'

Giovanni said grandly, 'But you are a Fosco now, dearest. We are all one, to rejoice and suffer together.'

'I'm your wife!' Isobel cried despairingly, 'I'm not just a pawn to be used to pay the debts of a man I never knew!'

Then the Marchesa demanded a maid.

'You see, dearest child, that I am a young woman no longer. I cannot do things for myself, as once I could and, to be truthful with you, it's hardly fitting that I should have to. In this rustic place I feel terribly the lack of those more sophisticated comforts I am so naturally accustomed to—'

'No,' said Isobel.

They were seated, eating the over-elaborate dinner the Marchesa demanded at one end of the immense table. Isobel hated the table; it was black and heavy like the chairs around it, and somehow reminded her of death and funerals. She bent her head.

'No.'

Mother and son exchanged glances.

'Dearest child—'

'Dearest Isobel, you should not forget what is due to my mother—'

'I don't forget,' Isobel said stonily. 'She has a home and food here. But it isn't right that she should ask for more.'

'Not right?'

'No!' Isobel flashed, raising her head. 'No. We have our own family to think of, our own future! I am not a bottomless well of money!'

Giovanni laid down his fork and rose and came round the table, and laid his hand on Isobel's forehead.

'You mustn't excite yourself, Isobel. You should go and lie down. Donatella will take you upstairs.'

Isobel rose. She would be thankful to leave the room since, by staying in it, she would doubtless only humiliate herself by bursting into angry tears. She glanced at her mother-in-law.

'No maid, Marchesa,' she said defiantly.

'You won't defeat her,' Donatella said, as they climbed the stairs together.

'I will!'

'You won't, Isobel. She will find a way.'

Isobel stopped and turned tiredly towards her sister-in-law. 'How can you bear it? How have you borne it all these years?'

'She is my mother.'

'All the same—'

'I have plans.'

'What plans?'

'I can't tell you yet—'

They reached the door of Isobel's bedroom. Assunta had lit the lamps, and the pillows on the cherub bed were piled up invitingly.

'I have plans too,' Isobel said.

Donatella, holding Isobel's arm, waited.

'I have plans,' Isobel said again. She moved towards the bed, longing to throw herself on to it and howl into the pillows. 'I will endure – this, until the baby is born. Then things will be different, things will change. You'll see.'

'Oh, Isobel,' Donatella said, squeezing her arm. 'Oh, Isobel!'

Three days later, Paolina was instructed to give up her household duties and present herself, in a clean apron and with washed face and hands, to the dowager Marchesa, to begin a training as a lady's maid. Giovanni and Donatella, unsurprised and apprehensive, waited for Isobel's reaction. But there was none, or at least that they saw. Isobel's jaw was set and she didn't seem much inclined to speak to anyone except to snap at them, but there was no explosion. She allowed the order to go down to the dressmaker in Siena for a black dress for Paolina – knowing the Marchesa, poor Paolina would no doubt end up looking like a parody of a Victorian parlour maid – and merely asked the *capoccia*'s wife if the third of her daughters, known as Nina and only thirteen years old, would come to the villa in Paolina's place. The *capoccia*'s wife accepted at once. Nina, Isobel thought privately, less blank-eyed than her elder sisters, might well prove a possible, and willing, extra pair of hands for the baby.

Christmas came and went. The whole family attended mass on Christmas Eve in Siena, Isobel sitting a little apart in her Protestant state of gracelessness. Even the Marchesa had yet to embark upon the campaign of converting her. There was no card from Aunt Jean, but there was one from Moody in which she had written that life at the Villa Calvina was just the same though very quiet; that the wheat harvest had been better than the grapes this year, that Luca had returned disabled from the war, and was thus unable to resume his old work. Aunt Jean was giving him a pension, of course, and it was doubtful if Roberto, his replacement, would now stay since he had offered marriage to Beppe's Chiara and she had turned him down. He was taking it very hard, Moody wrote, and Aunt Jean was displeased with him for showing it. For herself and her employer, they were a little older and stouter but still had their health, thank God. There was no indication in these lines if Aunt Jean ever spoke of Isobel, or even if Moody considered she thought of her. Isobel certainly thought of Aunt Jean. In fact, since she had known she was pregnant, she had thought of her most days. She sent a Christmas card to Moody and another to Aunt Jean with a letter telling her about the baby. 'Hoping so much that I may see you,' Isobel wrote in the card, 'from your always loving niece, Isobel.'

An uneasy truce prevailed at La Crocetta over the New Year and into February. Giovanni was out most of every day supervising the first new road to the house, constantly wishing it to be wider than the specifications, or to turn this way or that to afford a different and better view of the house. Donatella was busy with paintings of the seasons for the walls of the new nursery school, a project which, to Isobel's amazement, seemed to have the Marchesa's blessing, and Isobel herself spent a large part of each day wrestling with the accounts and the so-called budget, anxious to have the estate within some kind of financial framework before the baby was born.

The weather was raw and bleak, apart from the occasional brilliantly blue day which lit up the bleached winter valley with an almost eerie clarity. The new plough had arrived, ceremoniously escorted onto the land by teams of oxen and crowds of skirmishing children, and was now turning up acres and acres of dark, shining earth, ready for the spring sowing. Isobel had gone down from the villa with the priest from the tiny village nearby to walk behind him with the farm people, while he sprinkled the newly turned earth with holy water and chanted blessings. She had gone not so much because she believed in the ceremony but out of politeness towards the peasants, who believed in it utterly. Giovanni had refused to come, saying it was anachronistic and superstitious, so Isobel had walked by herself, bulky now in her

166

citified lilac cashmere coat, an incongruous, lonely, courageous figure in the Tuscan winter fields. The farm people, ignoring the gesture she was making towards them, and remembering only the dismissal of the three families from La Crocetta, ostracized her completely.

Then, without warning, the Marchesa decided that Paolina was too coarse, intractable and stupid to become a personal maid. She despatched her, aggrieved and muttering, back to the kitchen and sent for Nina.

'A more sensitive girl, you see, more pliable and quicker to learn.'

But Nina refused to go. She stood by the stone sink in the kitchen where she was scouring pans and shook her head at her sister's muttered instructions.

'But you must!' Paolina said.

'No,' said Nina.

Assunta, folding sheets for ironing, looked across at them both. 'I shall fetch the signora,' she said.

Isobel came in from the *salone*, slowly as was now her custom. Nina was still standing by the sink, her head bowed.

'What is it, Nina?'

'The Marchesa has sent for her,' Paolina said. 'She won't go.'

Isobel looked at Nina. Her face – not much older than a child's face – was set and mutinous.

'Nina?'

'I don't want to, Signora,' Nina hissed between clenched teeth.

Isobel stooped closer. 'You would rather wash pans than learn to be a lady's maid?'

Nina gave her a quick, imploring glance which mutely said everything.

'You don't have to do anything you don't want to,' Isobel said. 'In any case, I shall need you, when the baby comes.'

Nina nodded vehemently. Isobel went back out of the kitchen, and slowly up the stairs to the first floor. Outside the Marchesa's bedroom door, she paused, took a break, and knocked.

'Come, Nina!'

Isobel opened the door. The Marchesa, in an elaborate and old-fashioned peignoir of silk and lace, was standing regally in the middle of the room.

'Isobel!'

'I am sorry,' Isobel said, 'but Nina is not coming.'

'Not coming? But I sent for her!'

'She doesn't want to come,' Isobel said, hardly caring if she was

167

rude. 'She wants to work in the house until the baby is born, and then she wants to help with the baby.'

There was a small pause, and then the Marchesa said, in a voice of deep reproach, 'You have told her not to come, Isobel.'

'No. I told her only that she could choose. She has chosen not to come.'

The Marchesa slowly and majestically turned away, revealing her cascade of heavy, magnificent, almost unreal hair.

'Please leave me.'

'Certainly—'

'I shall not be coming down today. Please have my luncheon sent up here to me. A breast of chicken, please, lightly grilled, and a salad dressed only with lemon juice.'

Isobel shut the door and leaned against it for a moment with her eyes closed. Then she went down to the kitchen, to give, without catching Assunta's eye, instructions for the Marchesa's luncheon tray.

'I cannot believe this,' Giovanni said. He stood looking down at Isobel, lying on her bed in an attempt to rest. 'My mother asks for the help of a young girl who can neither read nor write and who is unskilled at everything and who could thus only benefit from daily contact with someone as cultivated as my mother, and you *refuse* her?'

Isobel turned her head away. Out of the window, the afternoon sky was pale and soft.

'I didn't refuse her,' Isobel said. 'Nina didn't want to go and I didn't force her. I went upstairs to tell your mother because she was afraid to. I'd have been afraid to, in her place.'

'It wasn't your choice,' Giovanni said, more loudly. 'When my mother wishes for something, it isn't your choice whether she shall have it or not! Why are you so cold to her, so rude and – and *undutiful*? Why do you have no name for her? "Your mother," you say in your chilly English way! "Your mother!" She is your mother now, too, Isobel, you are a Fosco!'

Isobel withdrew her gaze from the high clouds and looked at Giovanni.

'I'm your wife, Giovanni, but she isn't my mother and never will be. My name is now Fosco because I have chosen to take it, but it doesn't mean I must take responsibility for you all. I've been so patient these last few months, so patient, I've borne so much since your mother came!' She levered herself up and propped herself on

168

her arms. 'Giovanni, who is your priority? Who is? Your mother
– or me?'

He looked back at her. His face seemed to sag, and his shoulders
too. He put his hands on the footboard of the bed and leaned on
them.

'You, of course.'

'You hardly sound as if you mean it!'

'Of course I mean it.'

Isobel knelt up, with difficulty, so that her face was closer to his.
'Then please, Giovanni, please, *please* send her away!'

He said nothing. Isobel rushed on.

'I don't want to send Donatella away, I'm truly fond of her and
I think she is of me, and in any case, she doesn't try and change
our lives all the time and impose her own. But, you see, Nina is
our servant! I pay her as I do all the household servants, and
therefore I'm responsible for her and I won't make her do things
against her will. And this is, Giovanni, only one more incident. If
it isn't Nina, it will be something else, on and on and on until we
all go stark, staring mad. *Please* think of our future! Please think
of our lives together, all those years ahead with our children. Please
send your mother away!'

He drooped over his hands. 'I can't – send her back into the life
she had before, I can't—'

'I'll give her a pension!' Isobel cried, seizing his hands. 'After my
birthday, I'll give her a pension so that she'll be more comfortable—'

'You would turn my mother into – into a *remittance* woman?
You would *pay* her, to stay away? Like the black sheep of the
family? How dare you?' He snatched his hands from her grasp.
'You are a cold woman, Isobel. A cold, hard, selfish woman. Your
money has corrupted you!'

She gave a little scream. '*My* money! The money you use as if
it were your own, the money I – I—' She stopped, unable to
say, 'The money I am so generous with,' but equally unable not
to think it.

'Yes,' he said. 'That money that is ours, now that we are married.
The money that you promised to share with me.'

She lost her temper completely. She lunged forward, seizing the
sleeves of his jacket, furious tears pouring down her face.

'And what have you shared with me? Nothing! Nothing! I don't
want money from you, I don't want any material thing, but I do
want love, I do want consideration, I do want to be acknowledged

169

in both public and private as the first person in your life, to whom you give the respect that I, more fool me, give you!'

He wrenched his arms free. 'Fool? Fool?'

She subsided down onto the bed, sobbing in great gasps, her hair escaping from its pins and straggling over her wet face and neck. Giovanni looked down at her almost as if he could hardly remember who she was.

'Don't do that,' he said, almost coldly, 'you will harm the baby.'

She put her hands over her face, quite unable to speak.

'I shall send Donatella to you. She shall bring you some tea. And perhaps she may be able to calm you into seeing that you owe my mother an apology.'

Isobel heard him turn, and then cross the bedroom floor to the door, which he closed behind him with exaggerated care, as if pointing out the difference between his manners and her madness. Then she heard him calling for Donatella, followed by the unmistakable sound of the Marchesa's bedroom door opening. Isobel sat up and fumbled in her pocket for a handkerchief. She blew her nose, hard. She thought she wouldn't look in the mirror, it would only depress her to see those very ordinary features of hers quite disfigured by the tears of frustration and despair. Instead, she climbed wearily off the bed, found her hairbrush, and took it over to the window, pulling out the few remaining hairpins before she began to brush. She gazed out as she brushed, almost unseeing. Oh, if only this view could at least give her comfort! But it wasn't that sort of view; it was a view to challenge you and never console.

There was a tap at the door. Assunta came in with a tray of tea. Her face was set.

'You should be in bed, Signora.'

'I was—'

Assunta put the tea tray down and then took the brush out of Isobel's hands.

'Come and lie down, Signora.'

'Is Signorina Donatella coming, Assunta?'

'She is with her mother, Signora. She will be with you in a moment. The Marchesa sent for her. Come now, on to the bed.'

Isobel climbed awkwardly back against the pillows. Assunta picked up a rug folded over the back of a chair and spread it over her. Isobel shut her eyes and clenched her fists under the rug in order not to fling her arms around Assunta and burst into tears and tell her how wretched everything was and how she could not, just now, think what she was going to do.

'Your tea, Signora,' Assunta said.

Isobel took her hands out from under the rug. 'Thank you.'

'Signora—'

'Don't speak to me, Assunta. Just don't. Or we'll have the sort of conversation we shouldn't have.' She looked up at Assunta, her dark face almost thunderous in her disapproval of Isobel's position. 'I know what you think, and I'm so grateful, but we mustn't—'

'Isobel?'

Donatella was in the doorway, still in her painting overalls. Assunta gave Isobel one last fierce glance, and slipped out past Donatella, closing the door behind her. Isobel patted the bed beside her.

'Come and sit down.'

Donatella hesitated.

'You're in an impossible position,' Isobel said, 'I know you are. So am I.'

Donatella came forward, very slowly. 'I must not stay—'

'She has told you not to?'

'She sent me to see that you had not injured yourself—'

Isobel gave a snort of disgust. She reached over to the bedside cabinet and put her teacup down.

'*She's* the one who has done me an injury!'

'Oh Isobel—'

'Before she came, Donatella, Giovanni and I had our disagreements like all married people do, I imagine, but we didn't *quarrel*. Now we quarrel every day, and the reason for the quarrels lie always with your mother.'

Donatella said, 'It will be different when the baby comes.'

Isobel sighed. 'Will it?'

'Oh yes, it will. Giovanni will be different. Everything then will be for the baby.'

'And for me?'

'Of course for you. You are the mother of the baby.'

Isobel looked down at her belly. She put her hands round it and held it, for reassurance.

'Am I very weak?'

Donatella was amazed. 'Weak? You? No, never!'

Isobel gave a rueful little laugh. 'I wonder. I was thinking, looking out of the window just now, that I must be weak, otherwise I wouldn't have spent my life being dominated by older women. First my mother, then my aunts, now your mother. It looks like weakness to me.'

Donatella sat suddenly on the edge of the bed and seized one of Isobel's hands. 'You're not weak! You are just loving!'

They looked at one another, almost shyly. Then Isobel gently took her hand away. 'Thank you.'

Donatella leaned forward. 'I have had another letter!'

'Have you?'

Donatella laid her hand on her paint-smeared overall over a pocket. Paper crackled faintly. 'He says he will be in Tuscany in May. He is going to spend April in Venice, for the spring light on the lagoon, and then he will be in Florence and Pisa and Siena. He says he would so much like to come and see me.'

Isobel smiled. 'Then he shall.'

'You will ask him? You will ask him here, as your guest, as a guest once of *Zia* Sybil and *Zia* Jean?'

'Of course.'

'In May, you see, the baby will be almost two months!'

'The baby—'

'Yes!' Donatella cried. She leaned forward so that she could look penetratingly into Isobel's face. 'The baby! Think of him, Isobel, only think of him. Don't think about my mother, or Giovanni or this place, don't think about anything except the baby!'

Chapter Twenty

Giovanni Eduardo Bartolomeo, heir to the house of Fosco, was born on a bright March day in the nursing home in Siena recommended by Dr Roselli. He arrived without fuss, a plump and healthy baby, with his mother's eyes and his father's hair. Lying holding him in her high white bed while the soothing nun nurses glided about in their starched overalls, Isobel thought that not only had she never been so happy, but that she could scarcely remember what anything except this great happiness felt like.

Giovanni was ecstatic. He filled her room with flowers, narcissi and white tulips and bunches of dark and velvety violets. He told her she was adorable and beautiful and wonderful. He carried his son up and down the room, gazing into his tiny face with a kind of possessive rapture.

'My son! I have a son! I knew he would be a son. I am so proud and happy! I want to tell the world about it, I want to shout it from the roof of the cathedral! There has never, ever been a baby like this.'

Even the Marchesa, discarding her customary black for suspiciously new-looking purple silk in honour of the occasion, was mellow and full of praise.

'He is a beautiful baby. Dearest Isobel, dear daughter, you have given me a grandson even more beautiful than my son! He will make us all so proud. I am proud already. What have you given me, Isobel? You have given me a future! You have given me hope!'

She presented Isobel with a necklace of topazes.

'My father gave them to me when Giovanni was born and so I

give them to you for little Gianni. They will bring you luck. Wear them always for me!'

'Not for gardening, perhaps—'

The Marchesa laughed, her gracious, unnatural laugh. She leaned over the bed and kissed Isobel with a heavily-scented, powdery kiss.

'We are friends now, aren't we? Everything is behind us. Little Gianni is our new beginning.'

'I told you so,' Donatella said later, 'I told you everything would be different when he came.'

'Yes,' Isobel said, lying against her pillows, secure in her baby and her success.

She stayed in the nursing home for three weeks. Gianni was as good a baby as his trouble-free arrival had promised. This didn't much surprise Isobel who had had, after all, no previous experience of any baby, good or difficult, but what did surprise her was the strength of her feelings. She had felt love before, unquestionably, love almost to the point of obsession, but no love like this tigerish, devouring, consuming love she felt holding Gianni. She also felt complete, as if this was something she was entirely designed for, as if this empty space had lain within her for twenty-four years, unfulfilled yet yearning for fulfilment. She felt, quite often, so grateful to Gianni for just being there, that she was quite shaken by it.

In the first week of April, Giovanni drove his wife and baby proudly home in the Lancia. It was the most lovely day for months, with new bright spring growth on the trees and the sun shining out of an almost polished sky. The roadmakers were now almost a quarter of the way to the villa, and as the car bowled past, they stopped work and took off their caps and waved and cheered. On the slopes either side of the road, so long so bare and starved looking, there were brilliant patches of new green, the first wheat fields at La Crocetta for over thirty years. Isobel's heart rose and rose.

'We have such surprises for you!' Giovanni said.

'You do?'

'Yes,' he said, 'you will be enchanted. Lovely things.'

There was an arch of lilac branches, mauve and white, at the entrance to the courtyard. That was indeed lovely. Then the servants came pouring out of the house, smiling and laughing in welcome, and that was even lovelier. Giovanni stopped the car, sprang out and hurried round to Isobel, in order that he might lift the precious baby out of her arms and carry him triumphantly into the house.

174

Isobel followed, on Assunta's arm. Everybody was smiling, the sun was shining, the baby was both adorable and a boy. How wonderful, Isobel thought, stepping inside, how wonderful, I am genuinely pleased to be home!

In the *salone*, the Marchesa waited, with Donatella. They both looked exactly the same. The *salone* did not; the *salone* was, apart from the painting of St Catherine and the purple brocade chairs, entirely filled with new furniture. Even the curtains were new, replacing the velvet ones Isobel had learned to endure. These curtains were of pale grey brocade, printed with enormous golden fleurs-de-lys. Isobel, dumbfounded, simply stared.

The Marchesa flung out her arms. 'Are you not delighted?'

Isobel stammered something. She looked round her wildly. The great console tables had been replaced by cabinets inlaid with brass, and porcelain medallions, and the old faded rugs had given way to a vast white carpet patterned with a heraldic design in purple and green and gold.

'Where – where did it all come from?'

'I bought it for you!' the Marchesa cried, 'I sold some of my own things to do this for you, so that this house should become fitting for us, magnificent! Are you not in raptures?'

Isobel licked her lips. Giovanni, holding the baby, was watching her warily.

'It's – very kind of you—'

She stopped. Her brain was reeling. What had it cost, this terrible, vulgar, boastful furniture? And who had, in reality, paid for it? And where were the chairs that she and Giovanni had bought together, in Siena, and sat in during those long ago, and now such happy-seeming months, before the Marchesa came?

'Come and see upstairs,' the Marchesa said beguilingly. She put a hand on Isobel's arm. 'Come, Isobel, such beautiful things.'

She drew Isobel across the hall – at least, mercifully, nothing there had changed and Isobel gave grandfather Fosco a glance of near affection as she passed him – and up the stairs.

'You will be so enchanted. I have made for you a bower, a veritable bower—'

She threw open the door of Isobel's bedroom with a flourish. Isobel gasped.

'There! I knew it would delight you!'

The room was absurd. It might have been too austere before, too dark and forbidding, but now it was ridiculous. It had almost

175

vanished under waterfalls of brilliant rose-pink brocade which cascaded down beside the windows, across the great bed and fell in billows from a huge golden crown suspended from the ceiling above the pillows. The simple country furniture Isobel had bought locally had all gone. In its place was golden curly stuff, all twists and knobs and flourishes, inset with looking glass and upholstered in pink. Looking round, Isobel could see nothing she recognized. She held the nearest chairback.

'Where is my cherub bed?'

'Dearest, in another bedroom. That was a child's bed, not at all suitable for a marchese and a marchesa. We shall bring it back for little Gianni, when he outgrows his crib.'

Isobel subsided onto the chair. She closed her eyes. Looking at this poor travestied bedroom made her feel that she was in her imagined idea of a brothel.

'I think, perhaps, I'll rest a little—'

'Oh, you shall, dear child, you shall! We have bought Irish linen sheets for you, the sheets my husband always insisted on.'

'But we had sheets made locally—'

'Never again!' the Marchesa cried. 'The heir has come home! We can now live once more as we were meant to live!'

Isobel bowed her head. Panic was rising in her like an engulfing tide and there was only one way to stem it. She must take no notice of this terrible woman, and concentrate only on the one thing that mattered.

'Would you be so kind,' Isobel said, fighting for self-control, 'as to ask Giovanni to bring me the baby?'

'She took such trouble,' Giovanni said sorrowfully. 'Her taste may not quite be yours, but she meant so well. She meant to please you.'

Isobel lay exhausted in the pink bed, gazing upwards with revulsion at the golden crown. What would Aunt Sybil have thought of it? Aunt Sybil would have doubled up with laughter; she would have done one of her brilliant imitations of the Marchesa, and said that all the crown needed for perfection was a plume of pink ostrich feathers.

'But it's my house,' Isobel said. 'She had no right to do it, and especially not behind my back.'

'It was to surprise you, to surprise and please you.'

Isobel rolled her head to look at him. He sat on the far side of the bed in silk pyjamas and a dressing gown she didn't remember seeing before. It was very handsome, dark blue, piped with a gleaming cord in claret red. Something had happened to Giovanni's wardrobe recently. It had apparently returned to the urbane elegance of his Florence days. Where, Isobel wondered, was his one-time determination to live, dress and work like a simple countryman?

'Why didn't you stop her? You knew I would hate it! And what happened to your great principles of living the simple life and despising people like Aunt Sybil who fussed about curtains and cabinets? What's *happened* to you since your mother came? You seem as helpless in the face of her will as Donatella is! Really, truly, Giovanni, where do your loyalties lie?'

He looked, as he so often now looked when not full of some righteous indignation, a little hangdog.

'She was so enthusiastic, she so wanted to do something for you—'

'If she really wants to do that, she should go away.'

Giovanni leaned over and tried to take one of her hands. 'She sold the tables from the *salone* to help pay for it and those tables were her grandfather's and you know what he meant to her!'

Isobel moved her hands out of reach. 'Two tables,' she said stonily, 'didn't pay for all this.'

There was a silence and then Giovanni said, 'No. Not quite.'

'I can't believe it,' Isobel said, 'I simply cannot believe the extent to which you and your mother are prepared to exploit me. Even behind my back, when I'm occupied in having a baby!'

Giovanni got up and came round the bed in order to kneel down by Isobel. He laid his head against her. She looked down at his shining dark hair, so close to her hand. She had no desire to touch him.

'I am so sorry, *carissima*. I beg you to forgive me from the bottom of my heart. It was only a misjudgement. It was meant only for love but we were wrong.'

He waited for her reply. She tried to make one, but could hardly summon up the energy, so worn out was she by this unexpected return home and the effort, all those endless hours, of keeping a grip on her temper. Instead, she lifted one hand and gave Giovanni's head the briefest of caresses.

'Come to bed,' Isobel said. 'We must sleep. I'm so tired, I could die. We'll – we'll talk about this in the morning.'

He got up meekly, kissing her hands as he did so.

'Isobel. My beloved wife.'

She made no response. He went round the room, extinguishing

the lamps, and then slid into bed beside her, lying still at some little distance from her as if to emphasize his respectful contrition for having upset her. Isobel lay, wrung out with weariness, staring into the darkness. She found that even more than sleep, she longed and longed to hear Gianni's voice, crying from his crib in the next room, so that she might have the excuse to go to him and hold him while he fed, and remind herself that he was here now, to make life worth living.

In the morning, unrefreshed by a fitful night, Isobel took herself reluctantly to her desk in the *salone*. The table at which she had previously worked had been replaced by a fanciful escritoire, a bad imitation of an eighteenth-century piece, but it bore exactly the same discouraging piles of paper that its humbler, and preferable, predecessor had done. Isobel looked despondently at the correspondence that had accumulated while she was away, all the further estimates and relentless bills which Giovanni, as was his habit, had ripped from their envelopes, given a cursory glance, and flung down. Isobel went methodically through the pile, separating estimates from bills, and those bills that must be paid immediately from those that might wait a few weeks. At the bottom of the pile was a white envelope, an English white envelope of the kind used by Maquay's Bank, in Florence. Isobel saw that it had been opened, and that the letter it contained had been neatly, almost furtively, replaced. She took it out.

The letter was from Mr Matheson. Mr Matheson was the assistant manager of Maquay's Bank, and he had received Isobel that proud day when she had opened her account with the inheritance from Aunt Sybil. He had been very courteous to Isobel, and had said how sorry he was about Aunt Sybil and how much he would miss her. 'One of our most charming and delightful customers, Miss Lindsay.' He now wrote to say that, with infinite regret, the Bank could no longer honour cheques drawn upon the Marchesa Isobel Fosco's account, for the simple reason that the account had run out of funds. He would, of course, be only too happy to restore the Bank's services upon receipt of further funds, which he had no doubt would soon be forthcoming. He was returning, he said, with many apologies, the last three cheques proffered to the Bank, which there had not been sufficient monies to honour. He presented his compliments.

The lines of clerkly writing on the letter danced before Isobel's eyes. She felt burning hot, then icy cold, and then sick. She looked at the three cheques. All, needless to say, had been signed by Giovanni, two to firms in Rome she had never heard of, and one to the road contractor in Siena. She put down the cheques and the letter on the desk, and then covered her face with her hands. There was no more money. Giovanni and his mother, secure in the knowledge that a second inheritance was to come and careless of Isobel's feelings, had simply spent and spent until the well was dry. No wonder Giovanni had been so uncharacteristically contrite last night! No wonder he had hidden the letter at the bottom of the pile! In a flash of pure fury, Isobel wondered that he hadn't burned it before she even saw it! The fury was followed by the horror of realizing what had happened: that ten thousand pounds had been spent in little over a year. Ten thousand pounds! More than most people saw in a lifetime. Ten thousand pounds, with little to show for it beyond the possession of a place she hardly now thought she wanted. Shaking, Isobel put the letter and the cheques back in the envelope, and went in unsteady search of Giovanni.

He wept. Isobel watched him while he wept, and thought how much more moved she had been by the last men she had seen weeping, the peasants leaving the Villa Calvina in 1915 for the Italian front. He said a great many broken things while he sobbed in front of her, but they were all the same old things, the assurance of love and a wish to please and the desire to make somewhere neglected prosperous again as a fitting place in which to bring up this wonderful child of theirs.

When he grew a little calmer, and stopped trying to seize Isobel's hands and cover them with kisses, she said coldly, 'I shall have to go to Florence, now, and take out a mortgage on the estate as security for a loan from the bank.'

He blew his nose. He said, 'There is no shame in that.'

'I'm not remotely interested in shame,' Isobel said. 'Shame is what you and your mother should be feeling. I'm only interested in how we shall live in the future.'

He licked his lips. She could see him first debating whether to mention the approaching, rescuing inheritance due on her twenty-fifth birthday and then deciding against it. Instead, he vowed reform.

'It will never happen again, Isobel. I swear it to you. I will ask you about everything.'

She was amazed to hear herself saying, 'You only talk like this because you are frightened. You are afraid that you have seriously angered your golden goose, aren't you, Giovanni?'

179

'That isn't what you are to me—'

'Well, it's what I *feel* I am to you. If it wasn't for Gianni—' She stopped. They looked at each other for a long moment.

'What?' Giovanni said at last.

'You know,' Isobel said softly. She regarded his handsome, abject face and felt a strange distance from it, as if it had no particular meaning for her. 'You know very well. And now I have to make plans to go to Florence.'

'Yes,' he said. He looked suddenly much happier, as if Isobel's going to Florence was going to dispel the dark clouds presently hanging over him, and bring out the sunshine of prosperity again. The sight of his smile, and all it implied, drove Isobel to sudden fury.

'Yes!' she shouted. 'Yes! I had a baby less than a month ago, and I have to plan to journey to Florence because of *your* greed, *your* extravagance, *your* cowardice in front of your mother!'

His smile vanished and was replaced by a look of deep concern. 'You must take Assunta, dearest.'

'Of course I'll take Assunta! I'll take Assunta and the baby!'

'And will you—' he drooped a little. 'Will you see the *Zia* Jean?'

The suggestion doused Isobel's anger in a trice. 'I might – try.'

'And will you tell her—'

Isobel let out a long, sighing breath. She let her gaze fall on Giovanni again, on that beautiful face and the elegant figure for which she had defied her aunt and her father, secure in the conviction that she had found her true companion in life.

'I don't know what I shall say.'

Giovanni looked back at her. A little bit of fight had returned to his expression. 'You are my wife, Isobel.'

'Yes.'

'Before God and in the eyes of the law, you are my wife.'

She turned away. 'I know,' Isobel said.

Chapter Twenty-one

The train journey from Siena to Florence took three hours. Giovanni had wanted Isobel to take first class tickets, but she had refused, saying that for the same sum, she and Assunta could both travel third class. Giovanni had made a small scene on the station about the public dignity of the Foscos which Isobel had largely managed to ignore. It was a struggle not to remind Giovanni yet again that it was his fault she was having to go to Florence at all, and she only just won it. Clasping Gianni to her and followed by Assunta with his possessions, and a porter with the rest of the luggage, she climbed into the carriage among the baskets and bundles of the other passengers – one of them had a rabbit and a hen shut up together in a wicker cage – and settled herself for the journey.

Assunta arranged Gianni's wraps and bags ostentatiously on the luggage rack, and sat down opposite Isobel. The last week had been one of almost unbroken discord, with Isobel sending for the furniture suppliers from Rome to come and take all the new furniture away, and the Marchesa shut up, offended, in her room and refusing to come down to meals, and the Marchese shouting and his sister creeping about the house with her eyes red with weeping. Assunta looked at Isobel. She was bending over the baby in her arms and talking and smiling to him. For all the smiles, she looked desperately tired. No wonder, Assunta thought; heaven knows, she was tired enough herself, with the rows and the bitter atmosphere making the house so unpleasant, and affecting the servant girls who lurked apprehensively in corners and had to be kicked and goaded into working. Nina had grown so afraid of being in the same house as the Marchesa that she had skulked at home on several days, and Assunta had had to go and haul her out, reminding her that the signora didn't pay her good wages to hide in the dairy, behind the cheese presses. It was a relief, Assunta thought, to be going to Florence. People were civilized in Florence and she'd have a rest from that dreadful stony countryside and the louts and oafs who lived in it; no manners, no brains and no ambition.

Isobel looked across at Assunta, and smiled. However discouraging the errand, it was lovely to be going back to Florence and lovely, too, to be in this carriage full of ordinary Italians, all beaming and cooing at Gianni. They reminded Isobel nostalgically of the tramloads of Italians who had shared her journeys in and out of Florence all the years of her growing up. She looked out of the window. April in Italy was a delicious month, and the little town of San Gimignano, on its hill to the left of the railway track, rose exquisitely out of a froth of spring green. Then there would be Certaldo, where Boccaccio had been born, and Castel Fiorentino, and then the line would run down the side of the Val d'Elsa, bright with young planting, towards Florence and the beloved skyline that still spelled home for Isobel, try as she had tried to transfer her loyalties.

Giovanni had wanted her to stay at the Grand Hotel on the Piazza Manin.

'No, Giovanni, it's too pretentious and too expensive and no place for a baby.'

'Then the Palace. Or the Bristol.'

'I am going to the Pensione Cipoletti in the Via Cavour.'

'Why are you? Why do you deliberately choose to take my son to a pensione—'

'Because,' Isobel said, 'it will be cheap and clean.'

'How do you know? How can you tell?'

'In 1905,' Isobel said, almost dreamily, suddenly seeing in her mind's eye a mustard-coloured shawl with black bugle beads draped round the upright and awkward figure of Miss Pargeter, 'my English governess stayed there, and she was very particular.'

'1905! 1905? It is *1920* now, Isobel, you are mad, quite mad—'

'Yes, I expect so. But I am also very determined.'

He glanced at her. There was no point arguing. There was no point, Giovanni considered, in very much just now. What could he do, to advance his great projects at La Crocetta, if there wasn't so

182

much as a sou forthcoming just now to finance them? He would be on thorns until she returned with more money. He couldn't, in his more buoyant moments, understand her anger or her reproachfulness; if the boot had been upon the other foot, if he, Giovanni Fosco, had had two fortunes to shower upon Isobel Lindsay instead of the other way about, he would have begrudged her nothing! It would have been hers! And he would have been able to order her, then, to stay in a hotel suitable to her station, and not in a shabby pensione in the Via Cavour.

The Pensione Cipoletti was not shabby, but it was the wrong end of the Via Cavour. Miss Pargeter had chosen it, Isobel remembered, because it was near the Botanical Gardens, and Miss Pargeter was interested in botany, or at least, with her mania for facts, in botanical names. Isobel and Assunta were given two rooms at the back, looking into a very dull courtyard but quiet for the baby. They unpacked with an air of excitement at the sheer pleasure, undistinguished pensione or not, of being back in Florence. Assunta asked if she might take little Gianni to show him to her mother. Isobel said of course, and they must see the Vaccaris, and Assunta's sister and she, Isobel, must take a cab up to Fiesole to see her aunt. Her voice faltered a little as she said this. Assunta, remembering the vacant place so conspicuously left by this aunt at Isobel's wedding, remained sympathetically silent.

'But first,' said Isobel, 'first of all, I must go and see Mr Matheson. At the bank.'

Nobody would ever, even after his twenty years' residence in Florence, have mistaken Mr Matheson for an Italian. He was thin and pale grey, and he dressed as a pre-war English bank clerk, in decent black, with a celluloid collar and a bowler hat which he wore in the streets, winter and summer alike. He had joined Maquay's Bank after his mother, who had dominated him, had died, and the girl he had hoped to marry after his mother's death had chosen his younger brother instead. In Mr Matheson's quiet life, coming out to Florence to take a job in an English bank was the equivalent of joining the French Foreign Legion.

He had meant to stay only five years, yet here he was, twenty years later, still uncertain as to whether he liked Italian food or Italian demonstrativeness but, at the same time, very certain that he didn't wish to return home to the terraced house in Hackney which his mother had grudgingly left him, and which was now rented to a fellow bank clerk who had a sickly wife and three pale

183

children. In any case, Mr Matheson was a clerk no longer. He was assistant manager at Maquay's and, as such, in a position to take responsible decisions about the financial affairs of such interesting young women as the Marchesa Isobel Fosco.

Isobel interested Mr Matheson because she had married an Italian, and also because she did not, in many ways, conform to the stereotype of English young ladyhood who lived in the Fiesole villas and came into Florence to flirt and play tennis and gasp, in Mr Matheson's presence, at the way their monthly allowances had vanished, simply vanished, without their having touched a *penny* of it, truly, Mr Matheson, not a penny! But Isobel had received the kind of classical education Mr Matheson had associated previously with well-to-do English boys, and she had chosen to spend her money on land, rundown Italian land. Privately, Mr Matheson thought La Crocetta a very poor investment, but at the same time, he admired her enterprise. He had not, however, admired her choice of husband, and he was not, in consequence, surprised to have had to write to Isobel, nor to find her sitting in his office. He thought she looked tired, and not at all as one expects someone to look who lives in the depths of the countryside, miles from urban dissipations.

'Marchesa.'

'I wish you wouldn't call me that,' Isobel said, 'I wish you would call me Miss Lindsay. Being called Marchesa makes me think of my mother-in-law.'

Mr Matheson gave a small and wintry smile, but said nothing.

'You know why I'm here—'

Mr Matheson bowed.

Isobel looked down at her lap. It was going to be extremely difficult to explain her predicament without disloyalty to Giovanni, and even if she felt anger and resentment towards him, she still didn't want a bank manager to see either emotion.

'The estate, you see, is proving far more expensive than we had imagined. I mean, there was hardly a house fit to live in when we came, and the land was almost entirely fallow and there was no irrigation and no roads.' She looked up at Mr Matheson and tried a kind of silly-little-me smile. 'I'd no idea, you see, what even a yard of road might cost!'

'Quite.'

'And when one takes on an estate like this, one naturally becomes responsible for all the people on it. I'm trying to start a little school, and of course there should be a clinic.'

'Yes,' Mr Matheson said, 'but not in too much of a hurry.'

Isobel glanced up at him. He understood her, it seemed, perfectly.

'In a few months,' she said, in a less bright tone, 'I will of course come into my mother's money.'

Mr Matheson drew a leather folder towards him. 'I have been in touch with the trustees of your late mother's estate. You will receive, on your twenty-fifty birthday, some fifteen thousand pounds.'

'Only that!'

'There has been some speculation, I fear, on Latin American railroads. It was within the trustees' powers to invest as they saw fit and they were advised, on this occasion, by your grandfather.'

'My grandfather,' Isobel said in amazement. She had a rush of rage against Grandpapa Morpeth. Could he – would he have invested some of her inheritance in order to diminish it deliberately, to *punish* her?

'Fifteen thousand pounds,' Mr Matheson said reprovingly, 'is still a very handsome sum.'

Isobel gazed at him, not as if she were seeing him, but as if she were visualizing the great, greedy spaces of La Crocetta, and all the Fosco family just waiting there for her to sustain them. She licked her lips.

'It is, Mr Matheson, but it has to go a very long way.'

Mr Matheson again looked as if he quietly comprehended everything. 'Is the Marchese aware of the size of your inheritance?'

'He – I – we thought it would be more.'

'Is it your intention that the sum should be paid directly into your account here at Maquay's?'

Isobel stared. 'Of course. Where else?'

Mr Matheson leaned forward. 'Think about it, Marchesa.'

'I don't understand—'

'I cannot advise you directly. As a loyal employee of this bank, I cannot do other than suggest obliquely that you think about this money and your own future. You see, I cannot, if there are funds in your account, fail to honour cheques drawn on your husband's signature. And I cannot remove his name as a signatory on your account without his sanction, his written sanction. Once that money is in your account, it is as much at his disposal as it is at yours.'

Isobel nodded. She felt as sick as she had felt on discovery of Mr Matheson's letter. It would be at least ten years, Giovanni had predicted, before La Crocetta was a truly profitable estate and he

185

was notoriously optimistic. Perhaps, Isobel thought now, it never actually would be, and estates like theirs needed a solid private income from some quite unrelated source to keep them going. And if they had managed to spend ten thousand pounds in little over a year, how long, for heaven's sake, would fifteen thousand last them?

'Might I make a suggestion?' Mr Matheson said.

'Oh, please—'

'Will you authorize me to open a reserve account, in your name only, into which the monies received from your trustees in the summer may be put until you have made up your mind as to what you will do?'

'Yes.'

'And I will, of course, allow an overdraft facility of fifteen hundred pounds against this account, a facility that will, I'm afraid, attract interest.'

'Yes,' Isobel said, sinking lower in her chair.

'Prudently managed, a capital sum of fifteen thousand pounds would yield a very satisfactory income.'

Prudently managed! Giovanni had never heard of prudence, and even if he had, would have kicked the notion contemptuously aside.

'I – I had hoped, you see, Mr Matheson, that the bank might allow us to take out a mortgage against the estate, so that not everything we have is tied up in land and houses and—' She stopped.

Mr Matheson cleared his throat. He had despatched a junior, in fact, some two weeks ago, to go down to Siena and take a covert look at La Crocetta. It was as well, he believed, to anticipate most things a client might ask.

'I am sorry, Marchesa,' he said, 'but I'm afraid it isn't the bank's policy to take such a property as security.'

A wretched place, the junior had reported, one decent house but still accessible only by a track, poor earth and much of it too steep to be cultivated by any method except expensive terracing, little or no natural water, stuck out in the middle of nowhere . . .

'I see,' Isobel said. She rose, very slowly.

'A little planning,' Mr Matheson said, 'a little retraction of ambition, and all is not lost.' He was smiling at her.

She tried to smile back. How could he know how utterly hopeless it was, in association with any Fosco, to even contemplate either?

'Thank you,' Isobel said, 'thank you for your help.'

He bowed. 'My pleasure, Marchesa.'

In the early afternoon, Isobel took her courage in both hands, and telephoned the Villa Calvina. Aunt Jean, it seemed, had succumbed to the relentless advance of hated progress, and had had a telephone installed, though she still drew the line at electric light. It was Maria who answered, and who then made Isobel want to cry, being so welcoming and fond and plainly thrilled to hear her.

'Will – will *Zia* Jean speak to me?'

Maria's voice dropped to a conspiratorial whisper. 'Are you alone, *Padroncina*?'

'Alone?'

'Yes. Is the Marchese—'

'No, no. He's at home. I'm here by myself, with the baby.'

'The baby!' Maria cried in rapture. 'The baby! Wait, wait, I will fetch the signora. Do not go, do not leave the telephone.'

Isobel heard her feet hurrying down the echoing length of the hall – she could visualize every step – and then a door being opened, and then silence. After what seemed like an hour, slower, tireder feet came back towards the telephone.

'Yes?'

'Aunt Jean? Aunt Jean, it's Isobel.'

A pause, then, 'Yes?' Aunt Jean said again.

'I'm here in Florence, Aunt Jean. Staying at the Cipoletti. I've got my little boy with me, Gianni. He's four weeks old.'

'Yes?'

'May I – may I bring him up to Fiesole to see you? This afternoon? I would so like to see you. I won't stay long, but may I?'

There was another pause, longer this time and then Aunt Jean said, for the fourth time and with no especial warmth, 'Yes.'

Isobel dressed carefully for the visit. Aunt Jean, if she could possibly help it, shouldn't guess from Isobel's appearance that there was even a cloud on the sunny horizon of her married bliss. She put on the one new dress she had had in a year – at Giovanni's insistence – a drop-waisted, drape-skirted dress of fine pink wool which made her look by contrast, she thought, peering in the tiny looking glass in her pensione bedroom, almost completely colourless. Assunta dressed Gianni in a newly ironed white lawn smock, encrusted with tucks and frills, and rolled him in a cream cashmere shawl. Both she and Isobel considered, when she had finished, that no heart was too flinty to be entirely melted at the sight of him.

They took a cab up to the Villa Calvina. The drive up was almost unbearably familiar to Isobel – the same walls, the same cypresses, the same twists and turns in the road, even the same cascade of yellow banksia roses – and she was full of apprehension. The gates of the villa stood open – no Beppe waiting there, nor Cecco – and when they reached the steps from the terrace to the house, the front door was open too, and Moody was hovering there, unchanged except for a certain tremulousness of manner.

'Oh, Moody!'

'Miss Isobel—'

Isobel kissed her.

'Let's see the baby.'

Isobel took Gianni from Assunta's arms. 'There. Isn't he beautiful?'

Moody had a long look. Then she said, decidedly, 'He is.'

'Is Aunt Jean—?'

'In the *salone*, expecting you.' She looked at Assunta, who was examining the hall with an expression of extreme approval. 'You'll come with me to the kitchen, young woman, and Maria will look after you.' She jerked her head at Isobel, and then at the door of the *sala degli uccelli*. 'In you go.'

Aunt Jean was in a chair by the window, pretending to read a newspaper. She looked, like Moody, exactly the same; white bun, grey cashmere dress, black rimmed spectacles.

'Aunt Jean?'

'Come in,' Aunt Jean said, not looking up. 'Come in and sit down. Moody shall bring us tea.'

Isobel crossed the room between all those pieces of furniture that seemed to her as dear and recognized as old friends, and sat down opposite her aunt.

'I've brought Gianni for you to see, Aunt Jean.'

Aunt Jean took off her spectacles, and folded them, and put them down on top of the newspaper. Then she leaned forward and, like Moody, gave Gianni a long look.

'He's handsome,' she said at last, 'and he looks well.' She glanced up at Isobel. 'Which is more than you do.'

Isobel coloured. 'I'm just a bit tired, that's all. The journey here—'

'Why have you come?' Aunt Jean said. 'Why have you come to Florence? To see me?'

'Yes, of course, but—'

'It wouldn't surprise me,' Aunt Jean said, interrupting, 'if you hadn't come to beg the bank to lend you some money.'

Isobel bent over Gianni.

'And I shouldn't wonder, either,' Aunt Jean went on, 'if you've come to see me for the same purpose!'

Isobel sprang upright. Gianni, jerked awake, began to whimper. 'Never!'

'I told you how it would be,' Aunt Jean said. 'I told you! You think I don't know what's going on but I do. I know about that estate and the way that young man spends your money, just as I predicted he would, and I know that dreadful mother has landed herself on you now. I can't help you. I tried to but you wouldn't listen and now there's nothing I can do. It would only be throwing good money after bad!'

'I'm not asking you for help!' Isobel cried, struggling to control her own distress, and comfort Gianni. 'I'm not asking you for anything! I just came to show you my baby.'

Aunt Jean grunted. 'Then sit down again.'

Isobel, shaking and holding on to Gianni as if he were a lifeline, obeyed her.

'After my sister, Sybil,' Aunt Jean said, softening a little, 'and Arthur, of course, you were the person who meant most to me. I may have started out doing my duty by you, but I came to love you as if you were my own. So no wonder I'm disappointed in you. No wonder! I give you the best upbringing I know how, every advantage, and you throw it in my face!'

'I didn't—'

'You defied me, Isobel,' Aunt Jean said, 'you threw aside everything I had taught you to believe in. I still find it hard to credit. I still wonder where your sense has gone because, even as a little girl, you were always so sensible!'

She was gazing at Isobel, her face pink with indignation.

'I came to see you,' Isobel said, 'to show you my baby and to try and make things up between us. I didn't come to be lectured, all over again.'

'What could you expect!' Aunt Jean cried. 'What else could you possibly do but upset me when I know you are having exactly the problems that I so dreaded for you?'

'Then why did you say I could come?'

Aunt Jean blew her nose fiercely. 'I wanted to see you. I wanted to see your son.' She blew again. 'At least you have him.'

'Yes.'

'I can't do any more for you,' Aunt Jean said, suddenly rushing on, 'you see that, don't you? I can't leave you this house and land because that bounder would get his hands on it. I shall leave it all to Edward's children, I'm quite decided now, quite. I don't know them, but at least they won't squander it!' She looked up at Isobel. Her beloved old face was full of misery. 'Oh Isobel, what have you done to us all? And what, oh what is to become of you?'

Chapter Twenty-two

Isobel left Florence with the deepest reluctance. It hadn't been a happy visit, but it had at least been a kind of respite from the problems at La Crocetta and the dreaded presence of her mother-in-law. She had been to see the Vaccaris, who though far too tactful to mention it, plainly knew of her difficulties and were very tender with her. Professor Vaccari had cataracts growing in both his eyes and was finding reading difficult.

'But I have an excellent memory, luckily. What I can no longer read, I must recite.'

He was thinking of retiring, he said, of giving up his few remaining pupils and going back to his village in the Veneto, on the Piave River, where his brother still farmed.

'I shall have a quiet, agricultural old age, my dear,' he said to Isobel. 'In the end, it's where we all belong, closer and closer to that earth to which we must return.'

Isobel, conscious only at the moment of her own failed dreams, burst out, 'I wish I felt that!'

Professor Vaccari said nothing. He thought about the stout and frowning child who had appeared in his rooms all those years ago, declaring almost defiantly that she'd never heard of Dante. She'd sounded as if she never wanted to, either. So sad that the determination she had always displayed should have landed her, by some bitter irony, in this predicament. Assunta had of course told her sister about the situation at La Crocetta, and the sister had told Signora Vaccari who, while declaring that she could not possibly listen to servants' gossip, couldn't help hearing some of it all the same. That handsome young man, with his interesting ambitions, had turned out, it seemed, to be only another adventurer. The Vaccaris sighed together. Signora Vaccari said that it was at least better to see money spent on ploughs and wells than wasted on women and gambling, but the Professor said he doubted it.

'She has no moral leg to stand upon now, my dear. You see, the place was once their joint dream and he can now, while spending and spending against her wishes, accuse her of losing the faith while he is keeping it!'

When Isobel left, Signora Vaccari gave her a piece of polished branch coral hanging from a silver ring.

'For the *bambino*. When he is teething. It was mine, all those years ago, when I was a baby, and I kept it in hope. Now I want little Gianni to have it.'

Isobel kissed her. She was a small round woman, with the rosy face of the countrywoman she had once been and which she plainly looked forward to being again. All those years, Isobel thought, she had lived and worked in that cramped set of rooms behind the Lungarno, with only the narrowest of balconies for air and a few geraniums, and all because her scholarly husband had wished to come to Florence in pursuit of the intellectual riches the city might give him. Smiling and comfortable, Signora Vaccari had given up her own desires for his. Plainly, she held nothing against him. Then why is it, Isobel thought later, that I find it so hard to give up anything for Giovanni? Why do I struggle against him all the time? Why am I – if I am, as he says often I am – such a reluctant wife?

The train, climbing slowly up the hills to the south of Florence, seemed to echo her reluctance. They had to change trains, this time, at Empoli, and Gianni, as if he sensed that something was the matter, was uncharacteristically fretful and dissatisfied. Even Assunta was very quiet. She was preoccupied by the fact that she had found herself saying to her mother and her sister in Florence that even though she was devoted to Isobel and the baby, she didn't think she could put up with many more months at La Crocetta.

'There's one girl there, Nina, not much more than a child, but at least she isn't as pig-stupid as the others. When I've got her trained a bit and she's some use with the baby, I'll be back looking for a place here in Florence. I can't stand it there, honestly I can't. It's a godforsaken hole in the first place and the old Marchesa's a monster. I'll do my best, but I can't sacrifice myself for ever. I mean, I'd have as much hope of finding a husband there as of flying to the moon.'

She hadn't meant to say any of this, but once she had said it, she knew it to be true. She couldn't put up with much more. Looking at Isobel, who was lying back against the harsh cloth covering of the railway seat with her eyes closed, Assunta thought that she didn't appear like someone who could put up with much more either. Isobel hadn't confided in Assunta, of course, either her conversation at the bank, nor her conversation with the aunt in the beautiful villa (now there was a place, Assunta thought, where she'd be happy to work!) but Assunta didn't need to have it spelled out to know that neither had been satisfactory. Isobel plainly had nowhere now to turn for help. Regarding her, Assunta told herself she couldn't abandon her just yet but nor could she, in her heart of hearts, promise to stay for very much longer.

Giovanni was waiting at Siena station. He wore a cream suit, the jacket edged in matching braid, with a cream rosebud in his buttonhole. He seemed in excellent spirits, so good, Assunta observed, that he hardly seemed to notice that Isobel was greeting him with almost no enthusiasm at all. He hurried round them, organizing porters and luggage, instructing Assunta to take the baby, exclaiming with joy at having them back again, shepherding them out into the sunshine to where the Lancia waited to take them back to La Crocetta.

'I hope there will be no changes this time,' Isobel said faintly, climbing into the car.

Giovanni gave her a look of pained reproof. 'There is nothing. Everything is as you wish it. Nothing has been done that was not of your commanding.'

Isobel nodded, without much conviction. Giovanni slipped into the driving seat, pulling on cream leather gloves – why, Isobel thought miserably, why couldn't she stop noticing every detail of his appearance and wondering if it was new, and if so, what it cost? – and started the engine. Isobel looked out of the window blankly, hardly seeing the old and lovely streets of Siena slide by, the church of San Cristoforo, the Piazza del Campo and then the Botanical Gardens and the Tufi Gate, and the cemetery, and then, the road to La Crocetta. She was entirely preoccupied with her own feelings, not just with the alarming aversion she felt about returning, but something worse, something more frightening, a sense of doom and foreboding. She gripped her hands together in her lap until they hurt in order to prevent herself from turning upon Giovanni and ordering him, hysterically, to stop the car and let her and Gianni out to return, on foot if necessary, to Siena. She shut her eyes and attempted to count, slowly, to twenty. She was frightening herself. This was panic. What purpose of any kind would be served if she were to panic now?

'Are you unwell, dearest?'

'Only the journey—'

'You must rest when we get you home.'

Isobel nodded, dumbly. Home! Had any house ever felt less homelike to its owners than La Crocetta felt to her? And she was trapped, wasn't she? Trapped in this place and in this smiling, relentless family and the worst of it was that she had, with great determination, walked into this trap, of her own free will. Hadn't she?

The Marchesa was not in evidence at La Crocetta. She had, Donatella said, gone out to supervise the planting of the new apricot trees.

Isobel raised tired eyes. 'What apricot trees?'

'They arrived two days ago. Mamma knew you would worry that they weren't immediately planted.'

'I never ordered any apricot trees!'

Donatella coloured. 'I thought—'

'I haven't ordered anything!' Isobel almost shouted. 'Not for months and months, not a plant nor a stick of furniture nor a rag of clothing!'

'But trees—'

Isobel burst into tears. She stood there in the hall of the house beside the black bust of grandfather Fosco in his absurd golden wreath, and wept and wept. Uncomfortably, Donatella and Giovanni watched her.

'Dearest—'

'Don't touch me.'

'Isobel—'

'Leave me alone!' Isobel shrieked. 'Leave me alone! Don't come near me! I wish I'd never come back, I wish I'd stayed in Florence, I wish I'd never, ever—' she stopped abruptly, as if she couldn't remember what she had been going to say, and then, silently and with a look almost of surprise on her face, fainted on to the floor at their feet.

She stayed in bed for a week, on Dr Roselli's instructions. He had also declared that she was too weak to feed Gianni, and that a wet nurse was to be found, but she had grown almost hysterical again, and the baby was still brought to her, at her insistence. Dr Roselli said she should never have undertaken the journey to Florence, and that she was overwrought and must not be troubled by anything. Isobel, glaring at his heavy, unimaginative old face, wanted to shout at him that didn't he realize that her troubles were all here, inside her own exhausted head?

Giovanni was very solicitous. He longed to know the outcome of Isobel's visit to the bank, but dared not ask. All the furniture that could be returned to its suppliers had gone, but the pink brocade, having been especially made for the bedroom, remained as an almost jeering reminder of all the unwelcome elements in Isobel's life that she appeared to be saddled with. The Marchesa kept an elaborate distance. She sent in posies of flowers and little messes of sweetmeats and fulsome messages with Donatella, but she did not come herself. Isobel, lying helplessly in bed, could hear her moving inexorably about the house and issuing commands in a voice just too low to be overheard.

In the last week of April, Isobel came downstairs. The house was very quiet, as if it was holding its breath to see what kind of mood she was in before it did anything. From the kitchen came the gentle afternoon sounds of Nina and Paolina at work, and the front door stood open, to the soft spring air and the view. The *salone* was empty. The inlaid cabinets and the heraldic carpet had gone, and the purple chairs sat about in a ring on the bare brick floor, looking foolish. Isobel glanced at her escritoire. It too had gone, and the table was back, but without its covering of brocade as if to point out to her how ugly and incongruous a plain deal table, intended for a kitchen, looked in a drawing room.

The table was, inevitably, piled with papers. Automatically, Isobel went over to them, picked up an envelope or two, and put them down again. She would not, she decided, look at any possible superficial problem until she had struck a blow in solving one of the basic ones. She crossed the room to the south-facing view and looked out. Two new flowerbeds had been dug, without her knowledge or consent, precisely across the area where, in more carefree days, she had visualized planting a walk of cypresses leading to a balustraded terrace above the view towards Monte Alba.

'Isobel?'

She turned. Donatella stood in the doorway. She looked both excited and apprehensive.

She said, clearing her throat, 'I'm afraid my mother's enthusiasm—' and then she stopped.

'You mean these flowerbeds?'

'Yes.'

'It doesn't matter.'

Donatella advanced slowly across the room, her face a picture of astonishment. 'It doesn't *matter*?'

'No,' Isobel said.

'Oh, Isobel!'

'It doesn't mean that I'm pleased, or that they will stay there, but it isn't of significance.'

Donatella took Isobel's arm in one hand. In the other she held a letter.

'Oh Isobel, I'm so thankful! How good you are! My mother always means to please you, you know, she's always thinking of ways—'

Isobel shook her arm free so that she could cover her ears with her hands. 'Please don't.'

Donatella looked down. 'No. I'm sorry. I just meant—'

Isobel said, interrupting, 'Is that a letter from the English *capitano*?'

Immediately, Donatella's face filled with eagerness. 'Yes! Yes. It's really a letter for you, in answer to your invitation.'

'Then he's coming?'

Donatella nodded. 'The second week in May, he says. If, of course, that's convenient.'

Isobel smiled. 'Certainly it's convenient.'

Donatella reached up and kissed Isobel's cheek. 'We've all been so worried about you!'

Isobel said tartly, 'Not worried enough, however, to refrain from digging flowerbeds. Donatella—'

'Yes!'

'Where is your mother?'

Donatella looked startled. 'In her room, I believe—'

'Would you fetch her for me? Would you tell her I would be most grateful if she would spare me a few minutes?'

'Yes, I—'

'Don't look so panic-struck! Tell her I shan't keep her long.'

Clutching her letter, Donatella scuttled from the room with the speed of someone used to obeying orders without question. When she had gone, Isobel moved some of the purple chairs out of their circle and rearranged the remaining three so that one was confronting the other two.

'Isobel? You sent for me?'

The Marchesa wore the extraordinary and elaborate silk wrapper in which she was wont to pass her hour of devotion.

'I did, Marchesa. Thank you for coming down.'

'I think, dearest child, that you might have waited just until my special hour—'

'I'm sorry,' Isobel said, 'but I wished to speak to you before Giovanni returns. Would you both sit down?'

The Marchesa seated herself with great dignity, arranging the folds of black and purple silk around herself. Then she motioned Donatella to sit beside her, raised an imperious hand, and announced, 'I'm quite ready.'

Isobel sat down opposite. She folded her hands in her lap. She looked briefly at Donatella, then at the Marchesa, and said, 'Thank you. This won't take long.'

The Marchesa, her eyes fixed on a point somewhere above Isobel's head, gave a small, gracious nod.

'The thing is,' Isobel said in a voice that was almost conversational, 'that I had a most unsatisfactory visit to the bank while I was in Florence.'

The Marchesa did not move, but her gaze hardened.

'It appears, you see, that the trustees of my late mother's estate have made some unwise and speculative investments, and the sum I am to inherit this summer is very much smaller than I had anticipated. As I am sure you are aware, this estate is so far from being in profit, that we – that is, Giovanni and I – cannot possibly regard it as an asset. The only solution for the exigency we now find ourselves in, is to retrench. We must cut down on a great many of our agricultural schemes, and cancel others. I rather fear there can be no more road building. We must also cut down drastically on all domestic expenses, and return to the absolute simplicity which we always intended to be our way of life here. There will only be money in future for the barest essentials. I am afraid, Marchesa, that we can no longer afford to offer you a home. I must ask you to make plans for leaving La Crocetta by the end of May and setting up house elsewhere.'

When she stopped speaking, the room suddenly felt cold. It also felt unnaturally silent. The Marchesa did not move, her gaze was glassy and her face was set.

'Does – does my son know of this *brutal* proposal?'

'I have asked him,' Isobel said, in the same matter-of-fact voice, 'I have asked him over and over again to speak to you, but he has never done anything about it. I've had time – too much time –

upstairs this last week to think about our situation, and I came to the conclusion that I should have to speak to you myself. I have borne a great deal for you, Marchesa, but I will bear no more. This is my house and I now have to plan how I shall achieve a secure future in it for my son. You can't possibly object to any plan that would benefit Gianni.'

'Object!' the Marchesa cried. She rose up, a quivering outraged mass of black and purple frills. 'Object! I have never been so grossly insulted in my entire life! Do you suggest, you bourgeois English miss, that I and my daughter—'

'Oh, not Donatella, necessarily,' Isobel said, hardly caring now what she said or how she said it, 'Donatella hasn't tried to dominate the household or spend my money. Donatella is very welcome to stay, if she chooses.'

'You are a monster! A monster of ingratitude and cruelty! You have no shame, or charity, you have no sense of the honour, the infinite honour—'

'Hush!' Donatella cried suddenly. She had sprung up from the chair where she had been crouching, equally as cowed by Isobel's daring as by her mother's rage and shock, and was holding a hand in the air. 'Listen!'

From outside the closed door of the *salone* came the sounds of some kind of disturbance, running feet and wailing. Isobel sprang up and dashed to the door, flinging it open. Assunta, flying down the stairs, her face distraught, almost knocked Isobel over in her terror.

'Oh Signora, Signora, come at once, come quickly, quickly, the *bambino*, oh dear heaven, the *bambino*!'

Chapter Twenty-three

Patrick Fleming, emerging into the May sunshine outside Siena station, was besieged by cab drivers. When they heard that this tall English signor in the untidy clothes and carrying extraordinary luggage including, apparently, a bag of tools, wished to go out to La Crocetta, they became less enthusiastic. It would be a good fare, certainly, but what hope would there be of picking up a passenger on the return journey? And the track up to the house – the newly-started road appeared to have stopped as suddenly as it had begun – was so bad, ruinously bad . . .

Patrick, used to persuading recalcitrant people in out of the way places to take him where he wanted to go, shrugged, put down his bags – including the one containing his easels and paints – and took a wad of money in grubby folded notes out of the inside pocket of his corduroy jacket. He peeled off a few, laid them on the bonnet of the nearest cab and said laconically, 'For the first man to take me.'

The sight of actual money had the effect it usually did. There was a flurry of brown hands, a blast of shouting and then Patrick's bags were seized by a bow-legged little man, who set off with them at a brisk trot and called for Patrick to follow him. Patrick grinned at the remaining cab drivers.

'Another day, boys.'

He was in extremely good spirits. The weather the last two months in the Veneto had been kind to him, with lengthening days of clear, spring light, and just enough new vegetation out to soften the landscape without blurring its lines. He had meant to spend a week in Florence before coming down to southern Tuscany, but had lingered in Mantua instead, beguiled by the light on the lagoon and by the extraordinary wall paintings in the Ducal Palace which were enough, he considered, to persuade him to paint portraits like his father, if anything was going to. As it was, he had been in Florence only long enough to change trains and was now burdened with all the finished paintings of the last few weeks which he had intended to leave with a friend there. He had also intended to have a haircut, buy a more respectable pair of trousers and call at the Poste Restante for any letters before setting off south. But he hadn't done any of those things; he had simply arrived in Florence on the overnight train from Venice, gulped some breakfast, and caught the next train for Siena. It was really rather brilliant, he told himself, to be arriving the very day he had said he would arrive. Fingering his chin, as he sat in the back of the cab and looked pleasedly at the hills, he wondered if, in addition to the astounding punctuality of his arrival, he really ought to have shaved.

The cab driver was very chatty. He said a great deal about the wonderful things these new Fascists were promising for Italy – 'There will be enforced development of land, Signor! Bad landlords will simply have their estates confiscated!' – and a great deal about the new mayor of Siena, of whom he disapproved, and a great deal about his first grandson, a baby boy he said of such strength and beauty as to amaze all who saw him. Patrick, who was not much interested either in Fascism or in babies, said, 'Yes,' and 'Really?' at intervals, and looked out of the windows and thought in a vague sort of way about Donatella. She remained in his mind as the only person of complete honesty he had met during those terrible war years, an honesty enhanced for him by the fact that she was also so vulnerable. He had written to her because she seemed, in her almost childlike way, to be a fixed spot in a world that otherwise appeared to be falling to pieces. Long after he had left the Villa Calvina and was, with sullen fury at the wastefulness of it all, enduring the mud and slaughter of Northern France, he found that he was almost always soothed by thinking of Donatella in her big pink apron, watching him draw in grave silence while he drew.

That was four years ago. Four years of intermittent letters in her convent handwriting expressed in stiff formal Italian, with tentative phrases of English here and there. They were guarded letters, as if Donatella could never rid herself of the thought that someone – that overbearing mother, presumably – might read them, yet they contained enough for Patrick to gather what had happened to that

200

– in his opinion – supremely self-satisfied household at the Villa Calvina where he had been sent, ill-humoured and reluctant, to convalesce after the Dardanelles campaign.

The high society aunt, it seemed, was dead, and the little stout one who thought she knew all about farming had quarrelled with the toffee-nosed niece about Donatella's brother. Donatella was not given to descriptive writing, but she implied that her brother was the kind of man Patrick would find himself in sympathy with, a man who had elected to drive an ambulance on the Italian Front rather than fight. This choice, Donatella suggested, had been made on principle. Patrick envisaged a high-minded, almost scholarly Italian, with Donatella's long, grave face, who had taken on this rundown estate he was bound for in order to rid it of the *mezzadria*, the rigid system of tiny profit-sharing farms, which choked any path to progress. He also envisaged the toffee-nosed niece, married to such a man. Perhaps he would have softened her, and removed some of the intellectual snobbery that had made her such un-attractive, unsympathetic company for a bunch of decent, ordinary, homesick young English soldiers. She had taken them round the Uffizi gallery, Patrick remembered, with the air of one obliged, out of patriotic duty, to cast pearls before swine. Donatella seemed fond of her, but that, of course, might say more for Donatella's generosity than for Miss Isobel Lindsay's true charm.

The cab was climbing a long shallow ridge, almost treeless, with the earth either side that starved greyish yellow colour in which nothing but weeds and wiry little herbs seem to thrive.

'There!' the driver cried, making a wide gesture across the windscreen. 'There, Monte Alba! There, La Crocetta!'

To the right, a great mountain rose, huge and scarred, and to the left, on an almost equally bleak hillside, a group of stone buildings huddled below a dark patch of woodland. In the valley between the slopes there was an undistinguished river, the white lines of dust tracks, a length of seemingly newly metalled road and a few patches of bright green, presumably crops. There were also, Patrick observed, the most enormous number of boulders. They gave this grim valley an almost prehistoric air.

'Not beautiful,' the driver said. 'Not beautiful. Not like Siena.'

'Not beautiful, maybe, but interesting—'

'Interesting? Interesting! Signor, you must be mad. One hour out here and I would be desperate to go back to Siena!'

The taxi descended the road into the valley. There was no-one to be seen in this great empty landscape, beyond, in the distance, some oxen ploughing and, even further away, a scattering of white blobs that might have been goats. After a mile or so, the taxi came to a great scar in the roadside, and two enormous, but unfinished, stone gateposts beyond which stretched a magnificent driveway, both wider and smoother than the road the taxi was on. The driver turned on to it with an air of deep suspicion. After half a mile, the splendid driveway and the cypresses stopped abruptly, and a stony track took over. The driver grunted, and changed gear.

'This family! They come from Rome, all noise and grandeur and then, pouf—'

'I don't want to hear,' Patrick said. He was growing very interested. This strange, unfriendly landscape, the vast unfinished entrance and driveway all betokened something far more intriguing than the prosperous Tuscan villa amidst its orchards and vines that he had anticipated. This place was primitive, almost biblical. What a vision to take on such a place! What a man this Giovanni Fosco must be! The taxi ground complainingly up the last stretches of the track and stopped outside a large, plain, not particularly friendly looking house. Someone had started the merest beginnings of a garden; there were two random flowerbeds of dug earth, now full of weeds, and a lonely line of espaliered trees in optimistic blossom.

Patrick pulled his bags out of the taxi, dumped them on the ground and gave the driver an extra note because he felt in a humour to. The cab turned slowly, and then began to bump its way down into the valley again, and towards the safety of the Siena road. Patrick stood watching it for a while, and waiting for someone to emerge from the silent house but then, as nothing happened after several minutes, he decided he would go in and make himself known.

The front door stood half open. Inside was a square hall with an ugly staircase rising out of it, and an old man, made of black marble, glaring at him. Patrick looked at his watch.

'Good afternoon!' he called into the silence. No-one came. He looked around him. There were two doors off the hall, both of yellow varnished wood, one shut and one half open, and a passage running back beside the staircase into darkness. Patrick crossed the hall softly to the half open door, and knocked on it. Nobody answered. He put his head in and found a peculiar room furnished like a set for an amateur production of a drawing room comedy, but empty of people. He withdrew his head and went back to the centre of the hall.

'Where are they all?' he said to the black marble head.

He looked upwards. The stairs led up to a galleried landing, shadowy and apparently lit only by a skylight of coloured glass. 'Hideous,' Patrick thought. He cupped his hands round his mouth and called, 'Anybody there?'

There was another silence, then the sound of a door opening and some quick feet came running along the landing.

'I'm here,' Patrick called helpfully. 'Patrick Fleming!'

Donatella's face appeared over the landing balustrade, then her arms and shoulders. She looked horrified. She exclaimed, plainly with dismay, 'Captain Fleming!'

'Yes,' he said, smiling and puzzled. 'Yes. You invited me. Don't you remember? May the twelfth—'

'Oh Captain Fleming,' Donatella said, leaning down to him, 'didn't you get my letter? Didn't you get the letter I sent to Florence?'

'We don't know why he died,' Donatella said. She was seated on one of the purple brocade chairs in the *salone*. Opposite her, on another, Patrick attempted to perch, miserable in both body and mind. 'Dr Roselli doesn't know, nor did the coroner in Siena. There had to be a post-mortem, you see.'

Patrick leaned forward, his elbows on his knees, head bent. 'I'm so terribly sorry,' he said, 'I'd no idea, I mean, I'd never—'

'That's why I wrote to you. I wrote care of the Poste Restante in Florence because I knew you would be in Florence for a week before you came here. I wrote, you see, telling you not to come. Because of little Gianni—'

Patrick groaned.

'Perhaps it was his heart,' Donatella said. She looked so tired her skin was almost transparent, with grape-coloured smudges under her eyes. 'Or did he suffocate? We can't tell. It's agony, Captain Fleming, not knowing. Assunta just found him, in his crib, as if he were asleep—' She gave a little gasp and put her hands up to her face as the tears began to pour down it. 'He was so beautiful, and so good.'

'Yes,' Patrick said. He was appalled with himself. Because of his habitual impulsiveness and carelessness, he hadn't called to collect his letters, and now had, in consequence, blundered in upon this poor family's terrible grief.

'Seven weeks!' Donatella said, 'seven weeks old only!'

Patrick looked down at his hands. 'I'm so sorry. I feel terrible. I should never – you see, I just came straight from the Veneto, I didn't think—'

'No,' Donatella said, 'how could you know?' She took out a handkerchief and blew her nose.

'But now I should go. I must go back to Siena.'

'Yes. Yes, I think so. I'm sorry to seem inhospitable, but you see my mother has collapsed under the tragedy and must be nursed, day and night – I was in her room, you see, when I heard you calling – and – my brother—'

'Of course.'

'He is so angry. He is angry all the time. He cannot accept that it was an accident. He blames Isobel.'

Patrick, half-dazed by this flood of emotion, said stupidly, 'Isobel?'

'My sister-in-law,' Donatella said, drying her eyes, 'Gianni's mother. Poor Isobel. We don't know where she goes every day, Captain Fleming, but she just goes out of the house, all day, every day. She will do nothing Dr Roselli tells her to. My brother is distraught. You understand, distraught about his son, and now, of course, about his wife.'

'Of course.'

'A tragedy is bad enough to bear, but when it is a mystery too—'

Slowly, Patrick stood up. 'I shouldn't have let the taxi go. I'm so sorry, now I'll have to trouble you to find someone—'

'It will be no trouble,' Donatella said. She stood up too, and raised her eyes to Patrick's face. 'Please don't be sorry. It was only a mistake. I – I am sorry too.' She gave a little nervous gesture with one hand, touching her cheek. 'I – I was so looking forward to your coming.'

'Yes,' he said. 'Perhaps another time. Do you ever come to Florence?'

'I don't know. I don't know anything just now. We are all – I don't quite know how to put this – out of our minds.'

He nodded.

'I will send Nina to fetch her father,' Donatella said. 'He will take you back to Siena. Will you wait here? I must, you see, go back to my mother.'

Patrick gave a glance round the room. He said hurriedly, 'May I wait outside? In the fresh air? I feel so badly, being such a trouble to you all, I am horrified by myself.'

'Please,' Donatella said. She put her hand out to him. He took it in his and found it to be as thin and dry as if it were made of paper. 'You will write to me?' she said.

'Of course.'

'When this cloud has passed or, at least, the worst of it—'

'Of course.'

She tried a faint smile. There was something so sad in her eyes, something besides grief, something like longing. His heart smote him.

'I cannot apologize enough. I have never in my life behaved as badly as I have today.'

He raised her hand and kissed it, then she withdrew it, and went quickly out of the room. He followed her, and saw her vanishing down the dark passage towards the back of the house. With a heavy, wretched tread, Patrick crossed the hall, went out of the front door and across the beginnings of the garden to where his luggage lay, as he had left it, in the dust.

Isobel was standing by his luggage. She wore a blue cotton frock with a bedraggled hem, and a straw hat. She was looking down at his luggage with more puzzlement than curiosity. He was filled with a sudden, sharp anxiety about conduct. How did one, even from a full heart, speak to someone who only three weeks ago had lost their baby? He cleared his throat, quite without meaning to. Isobel looked up, and saw him. Patrick stopped a few feet from her.

'I'm – so sorry,' he said, almost strangled with awkwardness, 'I shouldn't be here, I – certainly shouldn't, but I never thought to go to the post office, I never—' He stopped, and then said, idiotically, 'I'm Patrick Fleming.'

'I know,' Isobel said. She held her hand out to him. 'Even though you've altered. I suppose we all have. That was – another world, wasn't it?' She hesitated and then said, almost shyly, 'I'm pleased to see you.'

'No,' Patrick said, gripping her hand too hard in his confusion, 'no, I'm not staying. Your sister-in-law wrote to me, you see, telling me – telling me not to come and I – I never went to the post office. I never got it. I could kill myself, I must seem so insensitive—' he stopped, realized he was almost crushing the life out of Isobel's hand, and dropped it. 'Your sister-in-law has most kindly gone to find someone to take me back to Siena.'

'Oh, she mustn't do that,' Isobel said, 'she was so looking forward to your coming.'

'But I must go, I must, I mean it's quite wrong for me to be here now, all wrong—'

'Why?' Isobel said.

For the first time, he looked at her. He remembered the self-possessed girl in the Uffizi with her perfect teeth and perfect clothes and air of ill-concealed contempt. The teeth were still there, but that was about all there was. Her eyes, which he had not remembered as at all remarkable, seemed to have grown so that they devoured the rest of her face.

'I shouldn't be here,' Patrick said, stammering, 'not now. You shouldn't have a stranger here when you are all – all so full of a private grief.'

'I think,' Isobel said slowly, 'that it would help to have a stranger here. Anyway, you aren't a stranger. Not, at least, to Donatella and to me.'

Patrick felt himself blushing fiercely. It wasn't comfortable, remembering those weeks at the Villa Calvina. He might have had, if one wished to be charitable, a good reason for behaving ungraciously, trying as he then was to come to terms with the death of his brother, as well as too many comrades, on those Turkish beaches, but all the same . . .

'So much has changed,' Isobel said, as if reading his mind, 'hasn't it? Everything, really.' She looked down and her voice faltered. 'You – you must stay, for Donatella.'

He waited, full of apprehension. Consumed with pity as he was for all of them, he wondered if he could cope with this isolated household of grief? Heaven knows, he'd never seemed to show much aptitude, up to now, for delicate sympathy.

'And another thing,' Isobel said. She took off her hat and began to turn it slowly in her hands. 'It would help me, if you were to stay.'

'You? But how—'

'If you could bear to stay, just for a few days,' Isobel said, turning her hat, 'I should be so grateful. Not because of the past, or to make amends for your rudeness to Aunt Sybil, or because of Donatella, but because' – she lifted her gaze to his face – 'because you're English.'

Chapter Twenty-four

Patrick was put to sleep in a room looking out at the woods of scrub oak behind the house. It was a simple room, just as he liked rooms to be, furnished with plain country things except for a most romantic bed with a headboard made of carved wood, darkly gilded and ornamented with cherubs. Patrick peered at it respectfully. An eighteenth-century bed at the latest. Someone in this sad, ugly house – and not the someone who had chosen the purple brocaded chairs in the *salone* – had excellent taste.

He was not at all sure what his role in the household should be. He had no idea how one set about comforting anyone – lord knows, he couldn't even manage to comfort himself – nor of the etiquette of sympathy towards people one scarcely knew. The natural thing to do seemed to be the thing he always found natural to do, and that was to paint. He decided simply to set up his easel and paint this harsh, curious landscape, and hope and pray that at meal times he would be visited by some kindly spirit of inspiration that would instruct him as to what he should say. He unpacked his bags to the extent of tipping their contents on to his bed – shirts, socks, walking boots, books, sketch pads, tobacco tins, shaving things, scraps of paper with messages to himself whose importance he had long forgotten – selected a sketch book, a box of charcoal and a pipe, and went out on to the landing. All the doors round it were shut. Behind one of them, Donatella – whose tired eyes had glowed suddenly at the news that he was to stay – was ministering to her mother who was, she said, prostrated with grief. Patrick couldn't quite visualize what this might mean. His own mother, hearing of her elder son's death from dysentery in a tent on one of the fly-plagued Gallipoli beaches, had simply gone on about her life as if that was the only thing that would keep her sane. There had been no retreating to bed and closed curtains and gently ministering daughters and drama. There had simply been a quiet stoicism that had almost broken Patrick's heart. He looked now, with some contempt, at the Marchesa's bedroom door. Was Donatella, he wondered suddenly, going to spend all his time at La Crocetta closeted in there, docilely soothing and murmuring?

He went downstairs very quietly and out into the garden. He was struck, immediately he set foot outside, by the dominating quality of the mountain to the west. It was a sunny day, a pretty day, but still Monte Alba seemed to glower at him, like an ancient and faintly malign presence, grey and battered against the western sky. He squinted against the sun. It would be interesting to catch the mountain at different times of day, to see if dawn light falling on it made it in any way seem less hostile, gentler. It must be, in its way, magnificent at sunset, a fierce dark silhouette against a glowing sky, ancient and inscrutable.

Patrick walked across the platform of land in front of the house that hung above the view. There were lines of stones here and there, and a few stakes, as if someone had begun on the business of marking out the paths and beds and lines of hedges, and then either lost interest or been interrupted. Come to think of it, the house felt like that too, half-begun or half-finished, with no coherence to it. Patrick was not, himself, much interested in comfort, but he couldn't help thinking that it was odd to find a house with three women in it, which was so strangely comfortless and without charm. It felt as if nobody could decide what to do, or else, Patrick thought, that nobody could agree. He understood that. He had never been very good at agreeing himself, he always seemed to be the one holding a different view. In the past, during his long, painful years of education, schoolmasters had constantly pointed this out.

'Your brother is a credit to his parents,' one enraged headmaster had said to him, 'but you are nothing but a disgrace.'

Patrick hadn't cared. Why should he care? His parents didn't think he was a disgrace; they merely thought, and Patrick agreed with them, that he was different.

At the edge of the rough platform, Patrick found a place beside a clump of broom, sheltered from the gaze of anyone who might be looking from the house, by a boulder. He slung his bag down and stood looking westward, half seeing, half thinking. Isobel had brought him some lunch in the gaunt dining room, a tray of bread and wine and sausage, with a dish of black olives and another containing a white goat's cheese in a little pool of olive oil. She had stayed with him while he ate – he was not given to embarrassment usually, but it was quite difficult to eat with any ease in these circumstances – not saying very much beyond asking him, now and then, about his weeks in the Veneto. He had wanted to ask her what she had meant by saying she would like him to stay because he was English, but somehow he had let the right moment pass. When he had finished eating, Isobel had said she would show him to his room and then perhaps he would like to explore for himself until dinner time?

'Of course,' he said politely.

'My husband is at one of the outlying farms, you see. We are having problems with a new well, the water isn't sweet—'

Patrick nodded.

'And I have things I must attend to—'

He nodded again.

'Nina will bring you anything you want.'

He had no idea who Nina was. He had seen nobody but Isobel and Donatella. It appeared as weird a household as the landscape it sat in, and which he was now, with only part of his mind, gazing at. He sat down on the ground, leaning against the boulder, and pulled his pipe out of his pocket. He yawned. It was warm there, against the rock, under the blue sky and above the quiet valley. He hadn't slept much the night before because the train had been full and his compartment had been shared by a family which included a teething baby. Patrick put his pipe between his teeth, thought a moment, and then took it out again, leaned his head back against the rock behind him, and closed his eyes.

'Good evening,' Giovanni Fosco said.

He stood in front of the fireplace in the *salone*, wearing a waisted suit of elegant cut, made of pale grey flannel. He was, to Patrick's surprise, not in the least like his sister to look at, but extravagantly handsome, with thick dark hair and a carefully cut moustache. He wore no expression of outward grief that Patrick could see, but then his face was so controlled it would have been extremely difficult to detect any emotion simply by looking. It was also extremely difficult to imagine him in countryman's clothes, out on the estate, and his appearance made Patrick, who had very little sartorial consciousness, aware that his own clothes were not only crumpled, but definitely built for informality and comfort. He hadn't been able to find a tie. He knew he possessed one – he remembered seeing it not long ago – but he couldn't think where it had got to. Instead, at the neck of his cleanish but almost never ironed shirt, he had tied a silk handkerchief, dark red with a paisley design in gold and green. It had been a present from his mother.

'I feel rather an intruder,' Patrick said to his host.

'My dear *Capitano—*'

'I'm not really a captain,' Patrick said, interrupting, 'I'm not a regular soldier, you see. It was only a wartime rank.'

'Like my own.'

They looked at one another. Giovanni gave a small smile. This peculiar ramshackle young man appeared to be yet another whim of Isobel's, some sentimental reminder of those days she now appeared to think of as halcyon, at the Villa Calvina. It was typical of Isobel to invite a near-stranger at such a time, and without consulting him. However, Giovanni would give the young man nothing to complain of. He would be treated with superb Fosco courtesy.

'I imagine we shall find much in common to talk about.'

Patrick, who was still quite thrown by Giovanni's appearance and manner being so different from his expectations of them, muttered that he expected that they would, yes. He tried to picture Giovanni inspecting a well, and failed to manage that either. Dressed like that, and wearing a faintly superior expression, Patrick thought Giovanni looked like the classic absentee landlord, forced to spend a few months buried alive in the countryside while longing for the city.

'Ah,' Giovanni said, 'the ladies.' He bowed towards the doorway. Both young women stood there, almost hesitantly, as if waiting for permission to enter. Donatella was still in grey, now ornamented with an apologetic string of jade beads, and Isobel was in dark blue with her hair pulled off her face and fastened at the back of her head with combs.

'I am sorry,' Giovanni said, 'that our guest has spent the afternoon alone. I quite understand, Donatella, that you could not leave our mother, but I cannot imagine, Isobel, what you could find to do that prevented you from exercising a simple hospitable obligation. Mr Fleming is, after all, I gather, here at your invitation.'

Patrick said at once, horrified, 'But I wished to be alone, I didn't mind at all—'

Isobel looked directly at him. Then she looked at her husband. She said clearly, 'Mr Fleming is a painter. He wished to paint.'

'Oh?'

'And I wished to be alone. He quite understood that.'

'Oh?'

A dull flush crept up Isobel's neck. She looked, Patrick thought, like a chided child, her face a visible mixture of misery and defiance. Then she added, 'I did go to find him, actually. To see if he would like company. He was asleep. Out there, on the edge, by the boulder. So I tiptoed away.'

Donatella said, in a rush, as if wishing to defuse the awkward situation, 'Mamma says that as we have a guest, she will come down to dinner.'

Patrick saw Isobel's head jerk up. At the same time, Giovanni murmured, 'My mother bears her grief with true nobility.'

'I – I am so much obliged,' Patrick said desperately, suddenly and violently wishing himself back in the train with his comfortable, ordinary Italian companions and the teething baby, 'but I couldn't allow her, for my sake—'

Giovanni raised a hand. 'It will do her good. It will help her.'

Donatella looked from one to the other. Isobel was standing like a statue.

'Then shall I fetch her?'

Giovanni glanced at his wife as if willing her to utter the proper words of welcome. But Isobel said nothing. Defiance and dislike seemed to swirl in the air between them like smoke.

Giovanni turned to his sister. 'Please do.'

When Donatella had gone, the three of them waited. Giovanni talked about the well and the crops as if putting on a little performance for Patrick's benefit, and Isobel stood silently, not even seeming to listen. After a while, there were the sounds of someone descending the staircase, the swish of skirts, uncertain steps and low voices. Patrick licked his lips. He hunted frenziedly about in his mind for the Italian for 'Please accept my heartfelt condolences on your tragic loss' and then, before he could remember a coherent word of it, the door was flung open and the Marchesa stood there, clad in sweeping black, supported by Donatella as if the weight of her mourning was far too much for her to bear alone.

It was a fearful evening. Dinner had been laid with great formality in the room where Patrick had eaten his bread and sausage, and the Marchesa was ceremoniously escorted to the place of honour at her son's right hand. The food was brought in by a thin, dark young woman Isobel addressed as Assunta and handed round by a little thing, no more than a child, who kept her eyes cast down and gripped the dishes she held with a kind of panic. Conversation was intensely difficult. Giovanni was courteous to Patrick, elaborately solicitous towards his mother, kindly to his sister, and virtually ignored his wife. After the soup and the pasta and a few slices of roast veal, Patrick had decided impetuously that his host was both a fool and a brute, that the Marchesa was certainly mad and probably bad, that Donatella was everything he remembered her as being and that Isobel was the exact opposite. She sat beside him, hardly touching anything on her plate or in her glass, exuding a palpable air of suffering. He could hardly look at her. Isobel Lindsay, that poised and indulged young woman who had stood before Botticelli's 'Primavera' as if wishing to convey that she had far more in common with the painting than with the gauche humanity of the young men in her company, seemed to him utterly changed. It was as plain as if she had spoken out loud that she was quietly bleeding to death inside from a broken heart, and that there was no-one in this place to comfort her. Gulping wine in a sort of fury, Patrick promised himself that he would – since there was nothing he could do for anyone here – leave La Crocetta in the morning.

But in the morning, Isobel asked him to ride with her.

'Only mules, I'm afraid. And' – there was an effort made here – 'the Marchesa has given Donatella permission to sketch with you, this afternoon.'

Patrick shuffled a bit. Isobel said, 'You want to leave us, don't you?'

He put his hands in his pockets, and cleared his throat. 'There's nothing I can do, you see—'

'No, of course not. Nobody expects it. At least, I don't. But I should be so grateful for a morning, just a morning, of speaking English. If, of course, you could bear it.'

He regarded her. He considered the morning ahead. It seemed to him full of pitfalls and probably a fearful strain. But she was so grief-stricken, poor thing, and he really ought to oblige her, if she thought it would be the smallest comfort.

'I'm not much of a hand at eloquence,' Patrick said.

She smiled at him. It was the first smile she had managed since his arrival, and it revived just a fleeting memory of her old confidence.

'No,' Isobel said, 'I remember.'

She took him up a long, rough track, high above the house and the *fattoria* buildings and the wood, to a point on a ridge from which almost the whole estate could be seen. The track was narrow, so that the mules had to follow one another and Patrick had plenty of time to regard Isobel's back, clad in a white linen shirt and breeches, impeccably upright in the saddle, like the true product that she was, of an Edwardian schoolroom. She had again referred to this business of Englishness. 'I should be so grateful,' she'd said, 'for a morning of speaking English.' Perhaps it was lonely, after all, to be marooned somewhere like La Crocetta with no-one of your own nationality within miles? Yet Patrick remembered, couldn't help remembering, Miss Isobel Lindsay's disdain for the English Fiesole. 'Villadom,' she had said scornfully, echoing her aunt.

Ahead of him, Isobel dismounted, pulled the mule's reins over its head and looped them to a bush. Patrick, less gracefully, followed suit.

'This is the place we first came to,' Isobel said, 'when we saw the estate. It was in the winter, and there wasn't a green thing to be seen.'

Patrick glanced at her. Her tone had been completely natural, and he couldn't tell if she was inferring anything by what she had said. He grunted slightly and sat down on a low rock, turning his face to the view.

'When I saw you yesterday,' Isobel said, more warmly, 'asleep by the rock, you reminded me of when I first saw you.' She turned to look at him. 'You'd just arrived at the Villa Calvina and you were utterly exhausted. I remember you leaning against the cab that had brought you up from the station, head back, eyes closed. When you did open them, you just glared at us.'

Patrick said, unable to be anything other than truthful, 'I'm afraid I didn't want to be there.'

Isobel sat down on the ground next to him and put her arms round her knees. 'You made that perfectly plain.'

'I wanted to go home. I wanted to be with my mother, particularly because of my brother's death. And I thought—' he stopped.

'What did you think?'

213

'I thought you were all so spoiled and pampered, so insensitive, living your safe little expatriate lives, talking away about the war without the first idea of what it was like, far more concerned with Latin poetry and Renaissance painting than with men dying wretched deaths because of bungling and—' he stopped himself again and said abruptly, 'Sorry.'

Isobel looked away from him towards the mountain. 'Is that how we seemed? Pampered and insensitive?'

He hesitated and then said, 'Yes.'

There was a little pause and then Isobel said quietly, 'Well, I've been punished for it now.'

Patrick was appalled. He flung himself off the rock and knelt on the ground beside her. 'God, I never meant that! I never meant – I never thought—'

'I know you didn't,' Isobel said, 'but I've thought it. I've thought a lot of things in the last few weeks. It's hard, isn't it, facing yourself, facing the things you are, the things you've done and said; it's all so hard, harder than anything I've ever—' She bit her lip and turned her face to him again and whispered, 'Oh, Mr Fleming, you just can't imagine the waves and waves of *longing* that I have for my baby!'

He stooped over her and clumsily put his arms around her. 'I'm so sorry—'

She didn't relax into his embrace, but she didn't pull away either.

'I can't describe it any other way,' Isobel said, her voice muffled, 'I just ache and long for him all over, with all my mind and body. I lost my mother when I was ten, and Aunt Sybil three years ago and I somehow managed both those losses, in a way, but this one I can't, I can't—'

'Don't try,' Patrick said, 'don't fight it. Don't fight the longing.'

She looked up at him. Their faces were very close.

'Not fight it?'

'No. He'll live in you if you don't fight it. He'll become just a memory, something static, like a cross in a churchyard if you don't let the longing come.'

Isobel closed her eyes and slowly let her head fall against Patrick's chest. He felt the weeping start in her, welling up from the depths of her in great surges. He suddenly didn't feel awkward at all, but very natural, and moved himself a little, to support her better. She wept for a long time, until his shirt front was soaked and she must have been exhausted and all the time he held her, and thought of his mother, and his dead brother whom he had adored, and the grave where his mother would never go in case, she said, her son slipped out of her heart while she was there, and vanished into the tomb.

'My mother says,' Patrick said, after a while, 'that nothing lovely is ever wasted. In the end.'

Isobel, whose sobs were calming, said uncertainly, 'I can't feel that.'

'Not yet.'

'No,' she said, taking her face away from his shirt and fumbling in her breeches pocket for a handkerchief. 'Not yet. If ever. Mr Fleming, what must you think of me?'

He took his arms away so that she could dry her eyes and blow her nose in comfort.

'A great deal more, if you want to know, than I ever have before.'

She looked quickly away from him, so that he couldn't see her expression. Then she got to her feet and said, 'You have been so kind to me. Kinder in a way than anyone has ever been.'

He stood too. 'It's nothing,' he said, 'it's the least I could do. The very least. And I shall like to spend the afternoon drawing with Donatella but – but I think I must leave tomorrow, I think I should go.'

Isobel reached up to take the combs out of her hair, loosened by her grief, and then shook her hair free. Patrick watched her with a detached admiration.

'We mustn't make you stay, Mr Fleming—'

'Patrick.'

She piled her hair up rapidly and thrust the combs fiercely into it. 'Thank you, Patrick. It's selfish to want you to stay, I see that. I promise there won't be any more outbursts. You'll have a calm afternoon with Donatella, she never bursts out, in fact I wish, I *wish*—' Isobel stopped, paused and said in a more collected voice, 'Where will you go next, do you think?'

He untied the reins of Isobel's mule from the bush, and looped them back on to the animals' neck. Without much considering what he said, but conscious that if he was to leave, he must demonstrate that he had a definite destination to go to, he said, almost carelessly, 'To Fontebella, I think.'

'Fontebella?'

'My parents spent their honeymoon there, in 1894. It's north of Florence a bit, in the hills. It's very pretty.'

Isobel looked at him. 'Is it?' she said. Her voice was almost wistful.

215

'It was a painting honeymoon, of course, and they had no money. My father tried to buy the little crumbling fortress there, from the Commune, for thirty pounds. It was all he had with him.'

'Did the mayor refuse?'

'Yes. He wanted fifty.'

'How sad,' Isobel said, as if she meant it. She mounted her mule and turned its head towards the track that led back down the hill. 'You said it was pretty.'

'It is. It's better than pretty, really.'

'Better,' Isobel said, her voice catching, 'than my old valley of the Arno?'

'Not so magnificent. But as lovely in its way.'

'Tell me,' Isobel said.

Patrick clambered aboard his mule and caught up with her. 'Tell you?'

'Yes!' she said, urgently. 'Tell me about Fontebella!'

'Well, it's on a hill, with bell towers and churches, and there's vineyards at the foot of the hill and a river, and the fortress at the top and the main square has a fountain made of three bronze dolphins—'

'Where do you stay? Where do you stay when you go to Fontebella?'

'In the pensione where my parents stayed. It's very small. They used to keep a pig in the courtyard. I liked that, I like pigs—'

Isobel stopped her mule abruptly. She turned in the saddle so that she could look at Patrick. 'Could I stay there?'

He was much startled. 'What?'

'Could I stay there? Could I? Could Donatella and I come with you? Just for a few days, a week, we wouldn't be any trouble, I promise, but could we?' She put one hand on the mule's rump and leaned back on it, as if to emphasize her sudden earnestness. 'Could Donatella and I come with you, to Fontebella?'

216

Chapter Twenty-five

The shutters had horizontal slats of green painted wood and they were fastened across with a bent hook of black iron. Above the shutters was a wooden curtain pole, but no curtains, and either side of the shutters, on the rough, whitewashed wall of the room, hung little painted tin pictures, one of the Virgin and her baby, the other of St Jerome in the desert, with his lion. Before she had got into bed the night before, Isobel had spent a long time looking at St Jerome and his lion. The desert they were in looked so like the valley at La Crocetta, and the man and the lion, companionably side by side with no visible possessions but the saint's bible, looked truly happy to be there.

Isobel, lying in her narrow pensione bed and looking at the lines of sunlight glowing between the slats of the shutters, was, on the contrary, truly happy to be away. It had been a struggle to achieve it, a terrible struggle, with scenes from the Marchesa and worse ones from Giovanni.

'You cannot go! It is absolutely improper in every way! It is unthinkable and I forbid it! Do you hear me? I forbid you to leave La Crocetta!'

Isobel, brushing her hair in front of the hated pink dressing table, had concentrated on keeping her temper by counting the brush-strokes.

'You are supremely selfish,' Giovanni had hissed, prowling back and forth behind her in his dark blue dressing gown. 'You think of no-one but yourself. How can you think of pleasure, of a holiday, at a time like this, with my son scarcely cold in his grave? You are heartless. What of my mother, truly stricken with grief as you haven't the heart to be? Not content with going away yourself, you seek to corrupt Donatella into wishing to go too!'

Isobel had gone on brushing. Thirty-five, thirty-six, thirty-seven. She remembered Donatella's face, her expression of rapture, at the merest suggestion that she might spend a week in Patrick Fleming's company. Forty-one, forty-two, forty-three. Corruption! If it hadn't been for Donatella's undisguised longing, Isobel might have lost her own nerve.

'Answer me!' Giovanni had shouted. 'Answer me!'

'I am not going for a holiday,' Isobel said, brushing on. 'I am going to try to recover, even a little. You have no prerogative on grief, Giovanni.'

'And you have no capacity for it! You are as cold as if you were made of stone!'

'We shall be away for one week,' Isobel said. 'One week only. Assunta will run the house, Paolina and Nina can attend the Marchesa.'

Giovanni had leaned over her shoulder then and brought his fist crashing down on to the glass that covered the dressing table so that all the bottles and brushes clattered together.

'You will not go! You will not! I forbid it.'

Isobel reached sixty, put the brush down and slid sideways off her stool and away from him.

'I am going.'

'I forbid it!'

'You can't, Giovanni. You can't prevent me.'

Then he had crumpled. Fury had given way to tears. He accused her of holding him to ransom because he had no money and it was her pleasure to humiliate him on that account. He said that plainly she had never loved him, that she had married him for his name alone. He said that if he could not order her, could he beg her to stay, instead?

'No,' Isobel had said. She had said it gently, but she still said no. Neither of them had slept after that, stiff and wakeful either side of their grandiose bed.

In the morning, the storm continued unabated. The Marchesa professed to have a migraine; Patrick looked very much like someone who would have sold his soul to be elsewhere; Giovanni demanded interviews with his wife, his sister, the servants; Donatella had looked equally terror-stricken at her mother's fury and at the fear that Isobel might give in. Isobel, lying now on her hard white pillow – what was it stuffed with? Walnuts? Pebbles? – took her arms out from under the sheets and laid her fingers on her eyes. She wouldn't think about it. She wouldn't remember that fearful day of quarrels and accusations which had ended, unbelievably, in she and Donatella and Patrick Fleming sitting in the train bound for Florence, speechless with fatigue and shaky with triumph.

Patrick had been so kind to Donatella. She had never, in the twenty-one years of her life, defied her mother before, and won, and she was wrung out by the effort. Patrick managed to find brandy and coffee and a seat for her by the compartment window which he padded clumsily for her with jerseys pulled at random out of his own luggage. When he had her settled, he sat down beside her and immediately went to sleep, his mouth open and his long legs sprawling across the carriage. Donatella, Isobel thought, revived by her coffee and brandy and secure in her nest of English wool, looked very nearly pretty.

They had spent the night in Florence, at a simple pensione near the station. Isobel paid for it. She insisted, she said, on paying for everything. No, Patrick had declared, he would pay for himself; even painters had their pride. When they got to Fontebella, he said, there would be no nonsense. He would stay where he always stayed; Isobel and Donatella should put up at the Pensione Verdi just off the main square. Isobel, hearing in his voice the firmness of one who must have his freedom, readily agreed.

And now here she was, in the Pensione Verdi, between rough white sheets on a plain wooden bedstead standing on a plain tiled floor. The relief was inexpressible. She took her hands away from her eyes, and pushed herself up into a sitting position. From the street outside came the sound of voices and the smell of coffee. Something close to happiness rose in Isobel, something close to that feeling she had had, waking all those years ago under the painted ceiling of her room at the Villa Calvina, that she was somehow stepping out of shadow – even if only for a moment – into sunshine. She slid a hand under her pillow and drew out the piece of polished coral on its silver ring that Signora Vaccari had given Gianni. She held it tightly. Her eyes filled with tears and she closed them at once.

'Stay with me,' Isobel whispered to the coral, 'oh, stay with me!'

Isobel and Donatella breakfasted under a canopy of vines on the pavement in front of the pensione. The *padrona* brought them bread and coffee and a bowl of thin dark-gold honey which she said came from the Appenines. The sun came down through the vine leaves, warm and welcoming, and several cats emerged from nowhere and waited urgently round their table for crusts. Donatella had brought a sketchbook down to breakfast with her, and a box of pencils, which she laid beside her plate with the quiet purposefulness of someone who has a decided aim for the day.

Isobel said, breaking a chunk of coarse bread into pieces, 'Patrick says he will show us the fortress today.'

Donatella nodded. She had tied a silk scarf Isobel had never seen before, a scarf patterned in rose pink and paler pink, loosely round her neck and it reminded Isobel of the pink apron.

'Donatella.'

'Yes?'

'This is the first time we have been alone together since we swept out those rooms at the Villa Calvina. Isn't it?'

Donatella took a neat swallow of coffee. 'Yes.'

'Will you – talk to me?'

'Talk to you?'

'Yes,' Isobel said, buttering bread, 'yes. Talk to me, really talk. Open your heart. It's such a chance for us, away here!'

Donatella said cautiously, 'What do you want me to open my heart about?'

Isbel leaned forward. It was somehow so easy to say these things on this sunny pavement under the dappling vine leaves, with cats watching and people going past with buckets and bags and baskets of vegetables.

'You know. About you and me and Giovanni and your mother, and – and even little Gianni. And La Crocetta and our life—'

Donatella's hands flew to her face. 'Stop it! Stop it, Isobel! I couldn't ever—'

'Why couldn't you? Why can't you be honest? Why can't you be honest and say, like me, that—' she paused.

'That what?'

'That I hate La Crocetta.'

Donatella frowned. 'What good would that do? What good is there in hating things that must be borne?'

'Why must they be borne? Why shouldn't there be choices?'

Donatella said bitterly, 'When have there ever been choices? You mustn't fool yourself, Isobel. There are duties and obligations and endurances, but for most of us, there aren't choices.'

Isobal pushed her coffee cup away. 'I'm so sorry. I never meant the conversation to be like this. I just wanted us to – to use every minute here for good purpose, like getting closer, being better friends, confiding a little—'

Donatella wasn't listening. She was gazing over Isobel's shoulder down the narrow street towards the main square. Her face had lit up.

'Here comes Patrick,' Donatella said.

He wore an open-necked shirt, and a loose linen jacket, and his curious bony face was full of excitement. Without saying anything, he put his hand in his jacket pocket and pulled out of it an immense iron key which he laid on the table.

'Caramba!'

They gazed at it, fascinated. It was black and old and primitive. 'What is it?'

He was laughing. He put his hands into his thick hair and tousled it a bit more.

'What do you think? The key to the castle!'

'But how did you get it?'

He reached over and picked up a piece of bread and stuffed it into his mouth.

'I went to the mayor's parlour,' he said, chewing, 'and said, I am the son of the English painter, Francis Fleming, and I wish to paint the castle as my father did before me. Eureka! The key. Actually, he asked me if I was a fascist or a socialist and I couldn't remember which it was politic to be so I said socialist and his brow darkened and I said, of course *English* socialist. Whew! Bomb defused!'

Isobel was laughing too. It seemed to her literally years since she had heard anyone talk light-heartedly, even disrespectfully, as Patrick was doing. She glanced at Donatella. Giovanni and the Marchesa were both coming to be believers in fascism. Would Donatella be offended? But Donatella was smiling. She laid her hand almost coquettishly on the key, and looked up at Patrick, eyes shining.

'Can we go? Can we go at once?'

'Of course,' he said, 'what else did you think I'd come for? To make courteous enquiries about whether you'd slept well, and if your beds were dry?'

He led them back into the main square. It had been dusk when they arrived the night before, but now the piazza, oval on the foundations of an ancient Roman amphitheatre, was filled with sunlight and activity. The tall old houses round the rim, ochre and saffron and cream and terracotta, looked down on a morning market clustered round the town fountain, three huge bronze dolphins leaping up together in unison, with shining fins and tails where loving hands had touched them over hundreds of years. Isobel stopped, stunned by the spectacle, the life, the piles of white and green and gold and scarlet, the chatter, the movement.

She seized Donatella's arm. 'Oh look, oh look!'

Donatella nodded.

'I want to cry, I want to—'

'Sh,' Donatella said softly, 'it's because we are so much alone, because we see so little.'

'I know,' Isobel said fiercely, 'I know that, that's what I wanted to talk to you about—'

Donatella lowered her voice. 'Sh. You will embarrass Patrick.'

Isobel glanced up. Patrick was standing a little apart, admiring a basket of fennel bulbs, silky and green-white, with their feathery tops standing separately nearby in an earthenware jug.

'He doesn't look very embarrassable. Why should my enthusiasm embarrass him?'

'It isn't enthusiasm that's embarrassing,' Donatella said, 'it is that you might speak about our troubles.'

'And why shouldn't I? Who else,' Isobel cried, suddenly losing her temper, 'who else should I talk to since you refuse?'

'Don't,' Donatella begged, 'don't. Please don't.' She removed her arm from Isobel's grasp and moved away towards Patrick. Isobel saw him smile down at her, and offer her his arm. She must control herself, really she must. She was alarming Donatella and that was the last thing she wanted to do in this happy sun-filled place, where warmth seemed to lie like a blessing on the bunches of radishes and baskets of eggs, human warmth, of a kind Isobel suddenly felt so hungry for that she thought she might faint. She put her hand into her pocket where the coral lay, and gripped it. Then she followed Patrick and Donatella out of the market square and up the steep, cobbled streets toward the castle.

She didn't really know what she was expecting. The only castle she had ever known at all well had been the Castle of Chillon, on the shores of Lake Geneva, where the famous prisoner had been chained for twenty years and where the merry little Russian boy, Piotr, had done handstands to stop her taking the story too seriously. But this castle was different. It had some similarities, being both a fortress and made of stone, but this stone was warm in the sun, and the town ran right up to the base of the rock on which the building stood, as if to encircle it, embrace it. It had two square towers, facing the town, and battlements, and over the towers and battlements greenery was spilling as if there was a garden up there, a garden high up in the light and air. A steep path climbed in zigzags up one side of the rock, and a stone staircase up another, and both came together in front of a great studded door, guarded by two lions, made of weathered stone with iron rings in their mouths. Yet the chief charm of the place, even beyond its position and its air of sturdy antiquity, was its size. This was a miniature castle, built there on its ledge with its back to the mountain behind it, tiny and impregnable.

They stood in the little square at the foot of the main path and gazed up at it.

'The *fortezza* of Fontebella,' Patrick said. 'You see why my father wanted it. He said he and my mother could have lived there for five hundred pounds a year, including a servant. If he'd succeeded, I might have grown up there. Think of that.'

Donatella said, almost flirting, 'But that might have made you, with these battlements, want to become a soldier!'

There was a tiny pause, then Patrick said curtly, 'No. Nothing would have made me want that.' He looked across at Isobel. She was gazing up at the little fortress with great intensity, as if it were a face whose every feature she meant to remember. He said, more gently, 'Isobel?'

Her glance didn't waver. She said, still gazing, 'How old is it?'

'Very. I should think the most modern bits are fifteenth-century.'

She nodded. She took a little step towards the rock. 'Could we—'

'Go up? Of course. That's why we've come.'

He moved forward, Donatella's arm still firmly held within his. 'Path or steps?'

'Steps,' Donatella said.

Isobel gave them a quick glance. 'I'll climb the path—'

'But it's so steep!' Donatella cried. 'And rough!'

Isobel hesitated. Patrick said, for her, 'I think she doesn't mind. I think she'd like to go up alone. Anyway, I'll have to go at a sedate pace. My lungs aren't, thanks to the Hun, what they were. Will you,' he said, glancing down at Donatella, 'accompany me?'

Isobel gave him a quick glance of gratitude, then she turned away from them both and began to climb the twisting path, hewn out of the rock and tufted with little bright clumps of camomile. Up and up she climbed, towards the waiting lions, while the little town

223

sank below her, towers and spires and tumbled roofs above its shining loop of river. At the top of the path, breathless and panting, she found herself on a neglected square of ancient paving, huge stone slabs across which the medieval owners of the castle must have ridden their horses, with a view before her so lovely it made her gasp.

Patrick and Donatella emerged from the flight of steps at the further side of the paving.

'Look!' Isobel cried, spreading her arms to indicate what lay around them, 'Oh look, oh look!'

'It's about perfect, isn't it? Unchanged since heaven knows when. The landscape of the High Renaissance, the perfect marriage of man and nature.'

Donatella, clinging to Patrick's arm, was laughing at her own breathlessness.

'One hundred and seven steps! It's worse than Giotto's Tower! Who could live here?'

There was a sudden little silence. Patrick glanced at Isobel but she was looking away from him, out across the russet roofs of Fontebella to the country beyond, the river and the patches of cultivation and the yellow-walled farmhouses and the cypress trees, dark and formal, like punctuation marks in a rambling sentence. Patrick put his free hand in his pocket and pulled out the great key.

'Shall we go in?'

'I'll take it!' Donatella cried. She leaned forward, putting her hand possessively on the key for a second time. 'I'll take it! I'll open the door!'

'No,' Patrick said gently, 'no, you won't! And nor shall I.' He quietly withdrew his arm from Donatella's and stepped towards Isobel, holding out the key. 'Isobel should open the door.'

She looked at him. 'Should I?'

He nodded.

'May I go in?' Isobel said. 'May I go in, alone?'

'Yes,' Patrick said, 'yes. You go in first. By yourself.'

Chapter Twenty-six

It was flooded with light. Isobel, expecting darkness and dampness and a smell of mould and neglect, was completely taken aback. She stood, just inside the great door, her hand still on the warm iron of the key, and stared about her with astonishment. The little castle of Fontebella, decayed though it was after three centuries of disuse, was full of sunlight.

Very slowly, Isobel closed the door and moved quietly forward. She was treading, she noticed, on marble, green and white marble squares a foot across, almost obscured under drifts of dust and fine rubble. Above her head was a vaulted ceiling, delicate stone ribs arching from the sides to the centre where they met a grimy but clearly visible carving of three dolphins. On one side of the hall-like room in which she stood was a fireplace, big enough to roast an ox in. On the other side, and ahead of her, stone doorways led apparently straight into sunlight.

She crossed to the one straight ahead, and looked through. There was a courtyard beyond it, a perfect late medieval courtyard, with a stone well-head in the centre and, round two sides, the pillared arches of a loggia with the old pinkish stucco falling away from it in places and revealing the brickwork beneath. There was a wonderful stone staircase on one side, decorated with more carved dolphins at its head and foot, and in the adjacent wall, facing south, a great breach had been made, either by design or accident, so that this sun-filled secret place was also open to the astonishing view. Below the breach, the land fell away much more gently than it did on the rocky front face, and, leaning over, Isobel could see the remains of ancient terraced fields, and a gnarled olive tree or two, tangled up among weeds and a great spreading vine, run wild. Someone who had lived in the castle once had cultivated those fields, laboriously building the little retaining walls, ploughing the earth, pruning the vines in winter, collecting the olives, maybe even keeping some hives of bees down there, on a little green platform Isobel could see by a spur of the castle's stone foundations, clinging to the rock beneath like the fingers of an ancient hand. She could also see the path down to the green platform, overgrown though it was, and she longed to scramble through the breach and follow it, past an old almond tree, and what looked like another stone well-head and – glorious now in the May sunshine – a waterfall of yellow banksia roses, just like the roses that grew so lavishly on the hillsides of Fiesole.

She went back slowly across the courtyard and peered through doorways. The castle was simplicity itself, an enfilade of small square rooms on two sides, each one leading from its neighbour, each one giving a different view over Fontebella, each one floored in stone or marble and ceilinged in wood, some of it carved and painted with stiff, faded flowers. On the upper storey, the pattern was the same, except the floors were wooden and the views ever more breathtaking. The fourth side of the castle lay snugly against the mountain, two rows of dark little rooms which smelled faintly of yeast and sour wine – store-rooms perhaps? – and the roof-top itself, bordered by battlements, had become a cornfield, a cornfield in which poppies were already growing, scarlet amidst the green. There was nothing, up there in the shining light and the ecstatic air, between Isobel and the heavens.

She went back down the stone staircase to the courtyard in a daze. Patrick and Donatella were there, Donatella gazing at the view, Patrick examining the well-head. He straightened up as she descended, and watched her with an expression of grave respectfulness. She crossed to where he was standing and stood regarding him.

'Thank you.'

He shook his head. 'It's nothing, I just thought you might like it.'

'Like it!' Isobel said, wildly. '*Like* it! I – I—'

'Sh,' Patrick said. He leaned forward. 'Don't say it. Don't say what you wish, don't *say* anything. Just think it.'

'Why?' she whispered.

He said, quietly and urgently, 'To *make* it happen.'

She looked round her, slowly and longingly. 'Could it? Could it ever?'

'Sh,' Patrick said again. 'Have you no respect for magic?'

She said, her eyes on the young green corn waving against the battlements above them, 'Why did you let me come in first?'

'Because you needed to. Because it seemed right. That's all.'

'Right,' Isobel said, echoing him, suddenly full of unspeakable gratitude. 'Oh, so right! But how did you know?'

He shrugged. 'I didn't. Or at least, I just felt that it was right, that you should. It was an impulse. I hadn't planned anything.'

Isobel put her hands flat on the warm stone of the well-head. She said slowly, 'I'm not really an impulsive person, but I do feel things strongly and just now, I feel strongly and suddenly.' She looked up at him. 'Perhaps I'm still just overwrought. My – my husband would say that I was.'

Patrick said nothing for a few seconds and then he said almost harshly, 'Why don't you try trusting your own instincts for a change?' He glanced over his shoulder. Donatella had perched herself on a big stone close to the breach in the wall, and had her sketchbook open on her knee. 'She might choose to ignore her instincts,' Patrick said, in the same rough voice, 'but at least, being an Italian, she knows they're there. You won't even look at yours. Why don't you? Why don't you just obey your own longings?'

Isobel straightened her back and looked directly at Patrick.

'Because,' she said, 'I did it once, in defiance of everybody, and it was the greatest mistake I've ever made.'

He leaned towards her. His eyes, she noticed, were grey, clear and light in his strange, strong, bony face.

'That wasn't instinct, Isobel. That was just a rebellion against your upbringing—'

'Patrick!' Donatella called. She made his name sound charming in her Italian voice. 'Patrick! I need some help!'

'Me too,' Isobel said softly.

Patrick was turning away. 'There's no point helping, Isobel, unless you help yourself. Just do what feels, in the depths of you, to be the *right* things to do. For you.' He began to walk away. 'Courage!' he called, as he went. 'Courage!'

Isobel leaned again on her hands, further and further until she could look over the parapet of the well-head down, down to where the surface of the water glimmered like a little coin. And there was her face reflected in it, her tiny face, tens of feet down inside this medieval well, no bigger than a baby's face, a new little face with all the world before it. Courage, Patrick had said, courage and trust your instincts, do what truly feels natural to you. 'Right,' Isobel said to her reflected face, 'right. At least, I'm going to try.'

For the remainder of the week, Isobel went up to the castle every day, collecting the key in the morning from the mayor and returning it to him at sunset. He was very obliging about this, on account of the little rolls of lire notes that Isobel allowed to pass from her hand to his as the key was given over, and he made egregious little jokes about the signora's great interest in antiquity, such a contrast between those dusty old stones and her charming young self.

With the key safely in her pocket, she went into the market and bought herself bread and cheese and fruit and a handful of olives and took this little picnic with her up to the fortress. On two days, Donatella came with her because Patrick had gone off into the countryside to sketch on his own, but the remaining days were her own; long, warm, clear days to explore the castle stone by stone, or simply to lie in a quiet corner, in the sunny silence, and think of Gianni. Often she wept for Gianni, storms of bitter tears, yet even those were, for some reason she couldn't fathom, easier to bear in the castle than anywhere else. The mere stones seemed to comfort her, warm and timeless, so that laying her cheek or hands against them gave her a sense of belonging to life and to history, instead of being, as she had felt so painfully at La Crocetta, some kind of outcast.

The urgency she had felt to talk intimately to Donatella when they arrived had somehow melted away. Whatever had been pent-up in Isobel was now peacefully flowing out of its own accord as she scrambled among the terraces below the castle or wandered through the little rooms, gazing out at the varying views, so lovely that every window seemed like a picture. She felt a strong sense of relief as well as an awakening of something almost happy that she couldn't quite put a name to. She sometimes thought, slightly shyly, that she would have liked to talk to Patrick a little more about these strange, nameless, reassuring things that were happening inside her, but she drew back from that because Patrick was, after all, Donatella's.

Donatella was in love. She had probably, Isobel thought, been quietly so ever since Patrick had arrived, surly and complicated, at the Villa Calvina, and she had kept her love secretly by her all this time, like a little fire to warm her hands at when she was cold. But now, freed from the Marchesa and the narrow confines of her life at La Crocetta, she could bring the fire out of its hiding place and let it blaze up in the air. Isobel watched her with amazement, delight and more than a stab of envy. Donatella laughed, made jokes, ate and drank with enthusiasm and made almost Bacchanalian wreaths of wild flowers for her sunhat. It wasn't envy of her happiness that smote Isobel so much as envy of her choice. Donatella had had the perception – a perception that she, Isobel, had so plainly lacked – to choose a man to be trusted. An odd-looking man, carelessly dressed with no interest in material things and even less in social niceties, but with a heart to be trusted. Isobel was sometimes, alone in her narrow bed in the Pensione Verdi, ashamed as well as envious. She remembered all those dismissive things she had said and thought about Englishmen, naïvely believing that the inhabitants of villadom were true representatives of their nation. She remembered her refusal to believe that any Englishman could have the sensitivity or the passion of an Italian. She remembered her strong indignation at Patrick's inability to be a graceful guest at the Villa Calvina, yet Donatella had understood him even then, had seen that the man had, whatever superficial polish he lacked, a gigantic honesty.

Yet, what did Patrick feel for Donatella in return? He was kindness itself, but he reminded Isobel more of a protective elder brother than a lover. He treated Donatella almost as if she were an invalid, while with Isobel he was uncompromisingly robust, challenging things she said, teasing her, goading her to think for herself. Only once did she protest. They had been talking, over dinner, about the relative freedoms of men and women and Isobel had said despairingly that even if women in England were now free to vote, that didn't change the place of women in society.

'Nonsense,' Patrick said, 'at least, nonsense in your case.'

'Why?' Isobel had said, almost angrily. 'Why nonsense? Society still dictates—'

'No,' Patrick said in English. He leaned across the table. 'Not for you, Isobel. You are one of the lucky ones, you are not like our little friend here. You have economic independence. If, that is, you choose to take it. And don't you ever forget it.'

Donatella said plaintively, 'What are you saying?'

'I'm telling her,' Patrick said, filling their wine glasses in careless, splashing swoops, 'to stop complaining.'

Donatella glanced at her.

'Is – is it selfish to want to be free?'

'No,' Patrick said, taking a gulp of wine, 'it's natural. Birds, beasts, people, we all need to be free in order, at the very least, to be of use to anyone else.'

'It isn't,' Donatella said quietly, 'always easy to be free.'

Patrick looked at her with a glance full of tenderness. 'I know.'

Isobel, raging with several conflicting feelings, said furiously, 'You should have tried it. You should have tried being brought up as I was! You'd have seen what it did to your chances for freedom!'

He looked at her. He looked at her for a long time with a glance that had no tenderness in it at all but which rather seemed to suggest he was seeing again that imperious girl in the Uffizi gallery and that he didn't like what he saw.

'You know what you have to do,' Patrick said at last, again in English. 'You know it. And at least you have the power to do it!' Then he turned to Donatella and asked her, in a quite different tone, in Italian, if she would like an ice cream.

On the journey back to Florence, they were all very silent. Patrick was to leave them there and go on down into Umbria, moving from town to little town on his wandering painting journey that at this moment seemed to Isobel the most idyllic way to live in the world. For her and for Donatella, La Crocetta lay ahead. Donatella would not speak of it, but her unhappiness at parting from Patrick and returning to her old life was written on her face as plainly as if she had uttered the words. Isobel watched her across the railway carriage, her face shuttered and averted, and thought, not for the first time, that she might live with Donatella for a hundred years and never, ever, get to know her any better.

Florence was hot and bright. The visitors were coming again now the war was well and truly over and there was a group of Americans waiting for taxis outside the station in the kind of ultra-fashionable draped and drop-waisted dresses that reminded Isobel suddenly and poignantly of Aunt Sybil. Patrick was fidgeting, plainly longing to be off.

'We are so grateful to you,' Isobel said.

'Please don't be—'

'It was such a wonderful—'

'Don't,' Patrick said, 'don't say anything.' He looked down at Donatella. 'Please write to me.'

She nodded. She looked, suddenly, quite stricken.

Patrick held his hand out to Isobel. 'Goodbye.'

She smiled, with difficulty. 'Goodbye.'

'And good luck,' he said, dropping her hand and then, with a final glance at Donatella, he went loping off towards the city centre, shouldering his bags like a pedlar.

Isobel turned to Donatella. 'Where would you like to go, before we catch the train? Doney's? The gallery?'

Donatella said, almost in a whisper, 'I will come with you. Wherever you go.'

'I'm afraid you can't,' Isobel said. 'I've got an errand to do. Alone.'

Donatella drooped. 'Then I don't mind—'

A sudden exasperation seized Isobel. Donatella had managed such animation for Patrick, and now look at her!

'I shall put you in a taxi for the gallery, then. And I will come and collect you in an hour.'

'What are you going to do?'

'It's private,' Isobel said. 'It's to do with business.' She raised her arm and waved at the nearest taxi, summoning him closer. 'Go and look at pictures and dream,' Isobel said.

She stepped forward and opened the taxi door. Donatella said, out of the blue, 'That was the best week of my life,' and climbed in. She looked at Isobel through the glass, an unfathomable look. Isobel blew her a hurried kiss and began to walk quickly away.

She crossed the Piazza Santa Maria Novella and set out south of it towards the Via Tornabuoni rehearsing half aloud what she was going to say. 'Good morning. My name is Miss Isobel Lindsay, and my aunt—' A woman in a broad brimmed straw hat and long jet earrings gave her a curious glance. 'Good morning,' Isobel began again. 'I wonder if I might speak to the manager? My aunt – oh, a thousand pardons,' Isobel said to an elderly nun in her path, 'I wasn't looking where I was going.' The nun looked at her as if that scarcely needed saying. 'Good morning,' Isobel repeated, pressing onwards, 'I am sorry not to have made an appointment but I wonder if the manager might spare me a moment? You see, my aunt—'

The Via Tornabuoni was crowded and delightful. It gave Isobel the same feeling that the piazza at Fontebella had given her, of activity and human warmth. She walked rapidly past Maquay's Bank, almost fearful that a stray clerk, looking idly out, might see her and rush out full of accusations about the overdraft, and slipped in, like a shadow, to the next door building, the bank of French, Lemon & Co where Aunt Jean had always banked, in mild defiance of Aunt Sybil, and in dutiful obedience to her late husband's habits.

231

It was dark inside, and cool after the streets. Isobel hesitated a little in the banking hall, flanked, just like Maquay's, with clerks behind an immense mahogany counter under weak, green-shaded lamps. She was suddenly full of apprehension, not at what she was about to do, but at what it was going to lead to. Licking her lips, she approached the nearest clerk. He was plainly Italian, and he was writing, laboriously and meticulously, in a ledger as big as a cathedral bible.

'Excuse me—' Isobel said in English.

The clerk looked up, and immediately leapt off his stool. 'Madam!'

'I wonder – I wonder if I might see the manager—'

'You have an appointment, madam?'

'No. No, I'm afraid I haven't. It's rather an impulse, you see. But my aunt has banked here for twenty years. Mrs Arthur Fanshawe.'

The clerk said politely, 'Might I know your business, madam?'

'Oh yes,' Isobel said. She leaned on the mahogany counter. 'I want – I would like, please, to open an account with you. In my name. In my own name. In the name, please, of Miss Isobel Lindsay.'

Chapter Twenty-seven

Giovanni and the Lancia were not waiting at Siena station. The station-master, when questioned, said there had been no sight of the Marchese that day nor had there been a message from him. Was the Marchesa sure he knew of the train's arrival?

'Quite sure,' Isobel said, 'I sent a telegram from Florence.'

She had sent the telegram on purpose, in order to try and make their return as normal as possible after their thunderous departure. The thought of walking back into La Crocetta was bad enough without the additional possibility of walking back into yet another great screaming scene. She said, 'Then we will take a taxi.'

The station-master bowed. He had seen the two young women setting off a week ago in a very distressed state with a young Englishman of very doubtful appearance. Now, here they were, back again, safe and sound. The station-master knew his wife would be disappointed; she had inclined to believe in local rumours of abduction. He opened the door of his office and ushered Isobel out towards the waiting taxis, trying, at the same time, to see if her luggage had acquired any interesting labels that would reveal where she had so mysteriously been.

In the taxi, Isobel turned to look at Donatella. She was already, clearly, adjusting herself to what lay ahead, and her face, so open this last week, was now reverting to its usual shuttered state, the only state in which any face, living with the Marchesa, could hope for any privacy of thought. Isobel hesitated. There was something she had to tell Donatella, indeed ought to tell her, but Donatella's expression wasn't helpful. Isobel looked at her profile, her long, delicate features, her dark eyes and lashes and brows so pronounced against her pale skin. She was so difficult to know, so difficult to help, so difficult in the end – this was hard to admit but it was regrettably becoming true – to love. Yet Isobel felt responsible for her. There was something in Donatella, in her submissiveness and vulnerability, that had always, from their first meeting, reminded Isobel of herself. They had both been, after all, English and Italian, Protestant and Catholic, brought up to be good; good, and obedient.

Isobel took a breath. 'Donatella—'

Donatella turned her head. Her eyes were dreamy. Plainly she had been thinking of Patrick.

'Yes?'

'Donatella, I have a secret to tell you. But it's absolutely imperative that you keep it a secret.'

Donatella nodded. 'Of course.'

'From your mother. From Giovanni. Even from them.'

'Yes.'

'I thought of not telling you, for your own sake, so that you really would be quite innocent of my plans and then, when they were angry, you could honestly say you never knew anything about it. But that isn't fair.'

Donatella looked at Isobel fixedly. The softness of her gaze had hardened a little.

'Who will be angry?'

'Giovanni. And your mother.'

'Why?' Donatella said. Her voice was bursting with curiosity. 'Why? What are you going to do?'

Isobel looked down at her hands. Ever since Gianni died she hadn't worn her engagement ring, a marquise-cut diamond ring, chosen in a jewellers in the Via de' Fossi and paid for – she blushed at the memory of her own deluded naïveté – by herself. What an omen, she thought, twisting her wedding band, the only ring she now wore, which the Marchesa had given Giovanni to give her, with many elaborate speeches about it being an ancient ring of the Foscos. Isobel pulled it gently up her finger, and over the first knuckle, so that she could remind herself of how her hand had looked, before she was married.

'I may not be staying,' Isobel said.

Donatella seized her wrist. 'What do you mean, not staying? Not staying at La Crocetta?'

The taxi bumped suddenly across some potholes, and flung them both together.

'I can't stay!' Isobel cried, struggling to regain her balance.

Donatella shot a look at the back of the taxi driver's head. 'Sh. Quiet. You can't leave, you can't, you are Giovanni's wife—'

'In name only,' Isobel said. She moved a little away from Donatella. 'I don't come first with him, you know I don't. First is the family pride, second is the estate, third is your mother. Don't look at me like that.'

Donatella whispered, 'But I am so shocked! It's the baby, it must be the baby affecting you—'

'No. He was the last unbearable thing, certainly, but no.'

'Isobel! Isobel, what will you do, where will you go?'

The road had reached the top of the pass above La Crocetta and the great mountain was swinging slowly and ominously into view. Isobel said, looking at it with something close to hatred, 'I shall probably buy the little castle.'

'Buy the castle! You cannot, you cannot just leave here and go to lead a new life—'

'Yes, I can,' Isobel said, interrupting her. 'Yes, I can. And I'm telling you in case you want to come with me.'

Donatella gave a little gasp. Her hands flew to her face. For several seconds she simply stared at Isobel and then she said, in a voice of quiet pride, 'Thank you, but I have my own plans.'

Isobel looked out of the window. La Crocetta was visible, plainly visible across the valley.

'I see. Well – I am very pleased for you.'

'You sound so cold!'

Isobel shut her eyes. The sight of the house and the quarter-finished road leading up to it was unbearable.

'I'm not cold. You know that. Giovanni always says I'm cold when he can't get his own way. But you hurt me.'

'Hurt you!'

'Yes,' Isobel said, opening her eyes again. 'Of course you hurt me. I offer you a home as a way of escape and you turn me down flat.'

'Does it not occur to you,' Donatella said, 'that I might want freedom my own way, just as you want yours?'

Isobel said slowly, 'Are you sure you will get it?'

There was a tiny pause. Donatella, her chin slightly lifted, was smiling. The taxi left the road and swept between the two enormous, abandoned gateposts.

'Pretty sure,' she said.

'Welcome back, my dear,' Giovanni said. His voice was very controlled, with the kindly tone in it of a loving father speaking to a recalcitrant daughter. He wore his working clothes and he was studying a long map of the estate spread out on the dining room table. 'I hope you are rested.'

'Yes, thank you,' Isobel said. She wondered if he was going to kiss her. It didn't seem so. He went on tracing some path or boundary with the stem of his pipe.

'Was it a comfortable journey?' Giovanni asked, in the same tone. 'Not too hot?'

'Not at all.'

She noticed that the surface of the table, on which Giovanni's hands rested, was dusty. She looked sharply round the room. Dust lay on the heavy, dark chair backs too and on the sideboard, the pale soft thick dust of the countryside.

'This room's very dusty,' Isobel said loudly.

Giovanni sighed. 'I know. The servants have been so upset by everything, you see. So upset.'

He paused. Isobel watched him. He put his pipe in his mouth with studied nonchalance.

'You see, my dear, first you go, insisting upon taking my sister with you, and then Assunta simply disappears—'

'Assunta? What's happened to Assunta?'

'She left,' Giovanni said, 'two days after you. She has, I imagine, returned to Florence. At least, that's what her note implied.'

Isobel, quite without meaning to, banged her fist down on the table, causing a little puff of dust to rise from the surface.

'What note? What do you mean? What have you done, Giovanni, what did you say to her?'

Giovanni went on elaborately perusing his map.

'She was extremely disrespectful to my mother. I had no option but to reprimand her. She left a note for you but of course I threw it away, it was most improper and completely hysterical. I'm afraid you only have yourself to blame, my dear, rushing off like that, leaving us all. No wonder it upset Assunta.'

'She knew I was coming back!' Isobel cried.

Giovanni looked up. It was the first time he had looked at her since she had entered the room. His expression was quite cold, as if she were no more than an unwelcome stranger.

236

'Oh no,' he said. 'How could she know that? How could any of us know?'

'You sent her away!' Isobel burst out. 'You sent her away, to punish me!'

Giovanni went on looking at her with the same unkind, impersonal gaze, and then, without another word, he dropped his eyes back to the map.

Dinner passed almost in silence. The food was very bad, the pasta overcooked, the meat undercooked, the salad gritty. Both Giovanni and the Marchesa ate with an air of martyrdom. Injury, in fact, hung about them like a mist, mingled with reproach and offence. 'Dear child,' the Marchesa had said to Isobel when she had gone reluctantly up to the over-furnished, under-aired bedroom to announce her return, 'dear child. I hope you are recovered. You find me a broken woman.'

She had offered Isobel an over-powdered cheek. Isobel had obliged, with difficulty. The Marchesa had smelled powerfully, as she always did, of the strong stephanotis cologne she used so lavishly but also of something else, of staleness and a sharp sourness that reminded Isobel abruptly of those long ago travelling breakfasts with Miss Pargeter, when the medicinal properties of brandy, when added to tea, had proved so very efficacious. The Marchesa's toilette table was laden with jars and bottles and silver-backed brushes and little porcelain trays of pins and combs, none of it, to Isobel's eye, quite clean.

'It has been a bitter week,' the Marchesa said, laying a large white hand on the purple and black frills that covered her bosom. 'The defection of my two daughters, the disloyalty of the servants. My health has been ruined.'

Isobel looked at her with contempt. 'You stayed here by your own choice, Marchesa. Nobody compelled you to. You stayed here because you can live at someone else's expense and relish the drama of ruining other people's lives.'

The Marchesa sighed and lifted the hand on her bosom to her brow. 'I pray for you, little Isobel. Day and night I pray for you. This great grief has, I fear, turned your mind.' She twisted slowly round so that she was looking at her own big, heavy, handsome face in the looking glass above the toilette table. 'My poor children, quite in your thrall now. Who is to protect them now from you, if I do not stay to do so?'

A sudden fury seized Isobel so violently that a red haze seemed to blur her vision. This hateful woman, this lying, relentless, monstrous woman. How tempting it was to lean over, pick up that massive silver-backed brush and belabour the Marchesa with it! Isobel closed her eyes. She mustn't do it. She mustn't give anyone in this place the chance to prevent her doing what she now knew she had to do. If she hit the Marchesa, Giovanni would call the police. She opened her eyes again. The red haze had cleared.

Taking a deep breath in an unsuccessful attempt to steady her voice, Isobel said, 'Perhaps we may expect to see you at dinner, Marchesa.'

The Marchesa closed her own eyes, as if the mere mention of food was an insensitivity hardly to be borne.

'If I am sufficiently well. Please, Isobel, go now, and send Donatella to me.'

Donatella had plainly been required to act as lady's maid, for the Marchesa now sat at dinner in black moiré silk with an enormous black and crystal cross suspended from a black velvet choker around her handsome neck. Isobel, pushing her food around her plate, did not even attempt to catch Donatella's eye. What was the point? They had spent a week together, and within an hour of their return, Donatella had slipped back into her mother's thrall as if she had never been away.

'I am sorry,' Giovanni said at intervals, turning his wine glass by the stem in his elegant fingers, 'that Isobel has so little to tell us of her travels. And plainly so little interest in what has happened here in her absence.'

Isobel stayed dumb. She would not be provoked. She tried to close her eyes against what was around her, the dark furniture, the dark Foscos, the darker atmosphere, and see instead, in her mind's eye, the little golden castle with its crown of new green corn, standing there above the town and the river under a sky as blue as a delphinium.

She had half-thought, encouraged by the sarcastic coldness of his manner since her return, that Giovanni would sleep apart from her. Before she went to bed, Isobel went to the kitchen. It was extremely disordered, and two of the farmyard cats, strictly forbidden in the house, were crouched on the table over the remains of the tough and bloody shoulder of veal that they had all tried to wrestle with at dinner. They fled, slinking like rats, as Isobel entered. There was no sign of Paolina. Nina, in a dirty apron, was slowly washing up at the stone sink. She did not want to talk to Isobel, but kept her head bent over the grey cloth in the grey water and muttered her responses to Isobel's questions. She said Paolina was to be married, she was expecting a child and that she, Nina, was going back to work on the farm. She didn't like indoor work, she was lonely without the other women. She refused, point blank, to talk about Assunta.

'I know nothing. She just went. I know nothing.'

There was nothing to be got from her. She was like everything else at La Crocetta; stubborn, suspicious and obdurate. Isobel sighed. Even Nina, even little Nina.

'Good night then, Nina. And please let me find a clean kitchen by the morning.'

Nina said nothing. The cats' heads appeared watchfully around the door leading to the yard. Isobel turned away. It was none of her affair, any more. There was nothing she could do against such massive, relentless opposition. She went back into the hall, past the bust of grandfather Fosco who now wore a white coating of dust on his shining black marble forehead, and climbed the stairs.

There was no Assunta, so Isobel's bedroom was in darkness. No Assunta, so the bed wasn't turned down. The room looked both tawdry and neglected, and when Isobel set her lamp down, it immediately threw up long dark shadows like accusing fingers. Isobel turned the pink brocade bedcover back. The sheets had been smoothed, but they weren't fresh. She considered changing them and decided that she was too tired, and that in any case, she didn't intend to spend more than a night or two in them, at the most. She pulled off the bedspread and piled it roughly in a corner, on the floor. Then she undressed and washed, found a clean cotton nightgown, opened both windows to the warm summer night, and climbed resignedly into bed.

She was tired, very tired, but almost too tired to be sleepy. Her mind roved restlessly around the dusty, untidy house that would soon, if things went on as they were going, be a dirty and neglected house. It was all very quiet. She had no idea if Giovanni and Donatella and the Marchesa had gone to bed, or if they were still sitting, in dignified offendedness, in the *salone*, where she had left them when she went out to the kitchen. She looked up at the gilded crown that held the pink bed curtains above her head, and was seized with a longing for the roughly whitewashed ceiling of her room at the Pensione Verdi, where cracks ran comfortably across like meandering rivers on a map. She put her hand out, to turn off the lamp. At least in darkness, she couldn't see the curtains and the crown, even if she knew that they were there. At that moment, the doorhandle to the bedroom turned. It turned slowly, but not stealthily, and then the door opened to reveal Giovanni in silk pyjamas and his dark blue dressing gown.

'My dear,' he said. He was smiling. 'My dear, I think we should talk.'

Chapter Twenty-eight

Isobel waited. Giovanni closed the door behind him and came towards the bed. He was carrying a cigar. He had never, she thought, smoked cigars before.

She sat up in bed and said, 'Please don't smoke in here.'

He smiled, kindly, as if indulging a little whim of hers. 'As you wish.'

He crossed to the window, and threw the cigar out into the night. Then he came back to the bed, and sat on the edge of it, beside Isobel.

'Isobel.'

She said nothing. This aloof stately politeness was a new manner, adopted, she was sure, for his own ends.

'Isobel, my dear. We must think of a way to end this.'

Hope leaped. 'End it?'

'Yes. End this quarrelling and misunderstanding. It is ruining our family life. It is ruining our happiness.'

Isobel said stonily, 'We have been through all this before. You know what has ruined us. You *know* it.'

'The death of our son—'

'No,' Isobel said fiercely, interrupting him, 'no. Not that.'

Giovanni raised a quelling hand. 'Please do not begin again on childish and discourteous abuse of my mother. That won't help us.'

He looked at Isobel. His beautiful face was, she noticed, softening a little round the jawline. In a desperate attempt to be fair, she tried to remember that same face, years before, on the Santa Trinita

241

Bridge in Florence, but her memory seemed to insist that it wasn't the same face, but a different face altogether.

Isobel said, sadly but clearly, 'Nothing can help us now.'

Giovanni smiled. 'Oh, Isobel. Something can.'

She stared at him. What was he going to suggest? If he said that he was, at last, sending his mother away, what was she to do, hoist at the eleventh hour by her own petard?

'What—'

He leaned forward. His breath smelled of cigar and the rosewater mouthwash he had taken to using, heavy and scented. He took her hand.

'We must have another child, *cara*. My dearest Isobel, think of it! Another little one to heal our hearts and give us back our faith.'

Isobel gave a little squeal and pressed herself back against the pillows. 'How dare you!'

He laughed. He sounded, suddenly, alarmingly like his mother, refusing to be put out, refusing to understand.

'How dare I? Because I am your husband, *carissima*, because we are man and wife, because we have chosen to live our lives here together, with our family. But most of all, because I want to see you happy again. I want my smiling, sweet Isobel back, as she used to be.'

Isobel scrambled hurriedly and awkwardly away from him across the empty side of the great pink bed, and fought her way into her dressing gown.

'No.'

'What do you mean, no?'

'I mean that I don't believe you, I don't trust you and I couldn't bear you to touch me ever again.'

He stood up. The mask of urbane politeness had dropped and his face wore the look of almost abject pleading that Isobel had come to find so distasteful. 'You can't mean this—'

'I do,' Isobel said.

'You can't. It's your grief speaking still, the shock of the baby, it's—'

'No,' Isobel said, 'it's made worse by that, but that isn't the reason. You are the reason, Giovanni, you and your mother and your – your *ruthless* exploitation of me. How can I love and trust a man like you? How can I? Even when we lost Gianni, all you could do was blame me, you never comforted me, you didn't even try. You are selfish and pitiless. At least, that's what you have become. You aren't the Giovanni I fell in love with. He's – he's gone!'

242

He didn't move towards her. Instead, he knelt on the edge of the bed and stretched his hands out towards her in a kind of supplication. 'But you still love me!'

'No,' Isobel said. Her voice was hard and dry. 'No, I don't.'

'Isobel!'

'I did. I loved you for years, all through those battles with my aunts, all through the war—'

'The war!' he cried. 'The war! I kept myself for you, all through the war! All the other officers had women, all the time, whenever they could, but not me, not me, I kept myself for you, only for you, Isobel, my Isobel—'

'Don't,' she said. 'Don't whine. You disgust me.'

He fell forward sobbing, across the rumpled bedclothes.

'You're all talk,' Isobel said, looking down at him without sympathy. 'Just talk. I can't at this moment remember one kind thing you have ever done for me. You only do things for yourself, it's all you know how to do. You've had six years of my life and almost all of my money and you'll go on taking until there's nothing left of me or it. I thought you were a man of vision, a man of passion. But you're not. You're nothing but a sham. A shallow, bullying, greedy sham.'

He raised his face from the blankets, and fumbled in his dressing gown pocket for a handkerchief. He blew his nose. She watched him dispassionately. He said, his voice shaking, 'What are you going to do?'

Isobel put her hands in her dressing gown pockets. 'I shall leave.'

He sat up, with his back to her. He said, his voice thick with reproach, 'I knew you would. My mother—'

'Don't mention her! If you knew I would leave, why didn't you do one single thing to stop me? It would only have taken one act of kindness, one act for my sake rather than your own. I don't believe you. You thought I would stay for ever, your little captive gold mine. Well, you're wrong.'

He said sulkily, 'You can't go. We're married.'

'I can.'

He seized a pillow and held it against him as if it were both a protection and a comfort. 'What will become of me?'

'You can have La Crocetta.'

He whirled round. 'What use is that? With no money?'

'Then sell it,' Isobel said. 'I don't care what you do with it. I leave it to you. I have transferred my bank account so that you cannot touch it any more, but I wouldn't leave you destitute. I wouldn't leave you to starve. I've made arrangements for all this' – she waved her arms in a wide circle as if to indicate not just the bedroom, but the dark, harsh valley beyond – 'to be yours.'

'Please, I beg you to think again, I *beg* you. I will talk to my mother in the morning. I will send a telegram to Assunta, I will—'

'Be quiet,' Isobel said. She moved towards the door. 'What a coward you are. But then, bullies are always cowards underneath.'

'Where are you going?'

'To bed. Somewhere else—'

'No!' he cried, springing up, dropping the pillow. 'Where are you going, when you leave?'

She put her hand on the doorknob. 'Somewhere else. I said so.'

'Tell me!'

'No.'

'Tell me! Tell me!'

'No,' Isobel said. 'I don't belong to you any more. I've taken myself back. I don't have to tell you things.'

Then she opened the door and went out onto the landing, and as she did, the Marchesa's bedroom door closed with an audible sound.

Isobel rapped sharply on the Marchesa's bedroom door. There was no reply, but a line of light was visible from within. She knocked again. Still silence. She turned the doorhandle and went in.

Both the Marchesa and Donatella were sitting upright, still fully dressed, on chairs by a table in the middle of the room on which there was, amidst a disorder of books and gloves and teacups, a decanter of something amber-coloured. A glass of whatever it was stood in front of the Marchesa. Donatella had been crying. She would not look at Isobel, but stared instead at the muddle on the table, her eyelids swollen.

'I think,' Isobel said, 'that I don't need to tell you what has just passed between Giovanni and me. I think you know it all perfectly well, since you were listening.'

'Please leave us,' the Marchesa said.

'I shall. In the morning.'

The Marchesa said, 'You have ruined us. You have broken my son's heart and attempted to corrupt my daughter. You will no doubt now bring bitter shame upon us by demanding a divorce.'

Isobel ignored her.

'When I leave,' she said, speaking directly to Donatella, 'I shall take nothing that isn't specifically mine. I shall take my books and my pictures and *Zia* Sybil's amethysts. The topazes your mother gave me I shall leave here, with my rings. The only thing I cannot take is my cherub bed which I should like, Donatella, to have despatched to Siena station. I will give the station-master further orders about it.'

Donatella didn't move, even by a flicker. Isobel looked at them both, at these two women, who might, if their natures had been only slightly different, have meant so much to her. She said, in a softer voice, 'You aren't the only ones with a broken heart, you know,' and then she went out, closing the door upon them.

She went on down the landing to the bedroom that Patrick had been given, the room where her beloved bed had been banished by the Marchesa. It was airless in there, stuffy and hot, because of both windows and shutters having been firmly closed while the room wasn't used. The bed was unmade. Blankets lay on it in folded squares and the pillows wore nothing but the stout striped ticking covers in which they had arrived from the supplier in Siena.

Isobel lit the lamp and then went across the room to open everything to the night air. The woods behind the house were velvet black in the darkness, dense and still. There were no lights in the *fattoria* – the whole family lived, as their ancestors had lived, by the hours of natural light – and the buildings gleamed pale and blank in the moonlight. It was quite still, warm and windless. Isobel strained her eyes up towards the hillside, desperate suddenly for some sign of life, a bird or a beast, to comfort her, but there was nothing except a cloud of bleached-looking, heavy-headed moths, drawn in by the light to bang about into the glass globe of the lamp.

She went back to the bed, and unfolded the blankets to spread them out smoothly enough to lie on. The sight of those little carved cherubs, so belovedly familiar, all around the bedhead was suddenly deeply disturbing. Isobel put a hand out to touch one and found that her hand was trembling violently. She sat down on the edge of the bed. There was nothing to be afraid of, there was nothing left for either Giovanni or his mother to threaten her with. She must not be melodramatic. She was, as of half an hour ago, free again, free perhaps, as she had never been before, free to live, as she had only ever done so briefly once before in her little apartment in Florence, as her own mistress.

She leaned forward slowly and blew out the lamp. Then she lay down, holding herself tightly against the trembling, on the blankets and the uncovered pillows and looked out, beyond the foot of the bed, to the swathes of silver and grey that the moonlight made outside. So, it had come to this. All these hopes and dreams and struggles and sadnesses, all these quarrels and feuds and terrible pains had come, in the end, to nothing. Isobel, prosperous, well-educated, sensible Isobel, had managed by force of her own will to ruin every relationship she held dear, her aunts, her husband, her father, her mother- and sister-in-law. She had spent most of her fortune on a dream of Arcadia, and failed. The failure lay out there, in the Tuscan moonlight, the empty acres, the half-mended houses, the sullen peasants, the never-started school-room, the only talked-about clinic. She had been a fool, a pig-headed, infatuated, arrogant fool. Her brightest years were gone, her best and brightest years. Exhausted and solitary as she had never been before in her life, Isobel turned on her side, her cheek against the coarse pillow ticking, and simply wept for them.

PART FOUR

Chapter Twenty-nine

Fontebella – 1921

'Forgive me, Signora,' the mayor said. He spread his plump hands out and shrugged his shoulders. 'It is simply not in my power.'

Isobel looked at him, holding on hard to her temper. He was smiling, as he had all those first days when he handed her the key to the castle, but she wasn't at all sure that his smile reached his eyes. He also wore, in the lapel of his jacket, the fascist badge. In the streets of Florence, a week previously, when she had gone, among other things, to look for Assunta, Isobel had seen several gangs of fascists, dressed like militiamen, roaming the streets to the evident terror of the populace. They had made her shudder.

'I am sure the signora understands,' the mayor said, still smiling.

With a supreme effort, Isobel smiled back. 'I don't quite, I must admit. The Commune of Fontebella owns the castle, which it does not use and hasn't the money to repair, yet which it refuses to sell.'

'Signora. Signora, do not use this word refuse. It is not in the power of the Commune, which represents the people of Fontebella, to allow the *fortezza* to pass to a foreigner.'

'I have lived in Italy since I was a child of ten. I am only foreign by birth.'

The mayor shrugged again. 'I think our militia would not like it.' He touched the badge in his lapel.

'Because I am English?'

249

'Because a building of such antiquity and significance should not pass to a born foreigner.'

'Even if I were to repair it and live in it and use local people to work in it and on the land?'

The mayor said nothing. He rubbed his hands slowly together, over and over one another.

'Even if,' Isobel went on, slightly less calmly, 'I were to put money into the town's coffers and employ some of the town's people?'

The mayor sighed. 'Of course things are so much more expensive now—'

'I know that. I have offered you a sum that makes allowance for that.'

An expression of something close to pain crossed the mayor's fat, pale face. 'I can do nothing, Signora.'

Isobel stood up. It was her third meeting with the mayor in three days. Tomorrow she would come again, perhaps with the money in lire notes, packed neatly and irresistibly into an attaché-case.

'Then I will bid you good morning.'

The mayor rose too. He looked at Isobel with real regret. 'You wish for the key again, Signora, the key to the *fortezza*?'

An inspiration seized Isobel. She sighed, picking up her bag and gloves – worn especially for the mayor – with melancholy and deliberate slowness.

'I – think not.'

'Surely the signora wishes as usual—'

'No,' Isobel said, 'no, thank you. There hardly seems any point, any longer. You are adamant. I must accept that. The castle must be left to crumble. The coffers of the Commune must remain empty.'

She walked slowly to the door. The mayor watched her, calculating something, not speaking.

'Goodbye, Signor Moresco, and thank you for your past kindness to me.'

He bowed. Isobel went out of the town hall into the sunlight of the square. The dolphin fountain was playing and the market stall-holders, it now being late morning, were beginning to pack up, dismantling awnings, piling vegetables into baskets, trundling wooden hand barrows over the cobbles. Above the busy scene, high up, higher even than the tallest houses, the castle hung against the mountain, waiting and patient. Isobel looked up at it, biting her lip. She too must be patient. She must not give way to the corrosion of disappointment. She went quickly down among the remains of the market stalls and impulsively bought a whole bucketful of

250

cornflowers from an astounded stall holder who had supposed she was simply going to have to take them home again.

With her arms full of crisp blue flowers, Isobel made her way back to the Pensione Verdi. The proprietors, kind but solely preoccupied with the affairs of Fontebella, had seemed wholly unsurprised to see Isobel back again so soon and scarcely raised an eyebrow when she said that she was now Signora Lindsay, not the Marchesa Fosco. If she paid them – and she did, in advance – she could be the Queen of Tartary for all they cared. They gave her a different room, one with two windows above the vine-shaded pavement terrace.

'A big bed,' Signora Verdi said proudly, indicating the width of the bolster, 'and a table and *two* chairs.'

There were no holy pictures in this room, only a dim, damp-spotted engraving of a rival medieval baron vainly attempting an attack upon Fontebella castle. Isobel had unhooked the engraving and taken it to the window to look long and hard at it. The castle had hardly changed in five hundred years. The studded door was plainly there, and the guardian lions, and the battlements and the path zig-zagging up the rock. In the engraving, a row of archers leaned over the battlements and shot a shower of arrows down into their enemies, some of whom lay about on the rock below, plainly dead with an arrow upright in their chests. Isobel would have liked to do that to the mayor and the Commune of Fontebella – lock herself impregnably into the fortress and shoot arrows down into them, in triumphant defiance.

It had been a difficult few weeks. Leaving La Crocetta had been, in the end, almost an anti-climax. Giovanni had left the house at dawn without a further word to her; the Marchesa had kept to her room and Donatella, although she had made an appearance, to make ritually courteous enquiries about Isobel's breakfast and journey, would unbend no further. Even when Isobel, desperate for some kind of reaction, demanded, 'And who will post your letters to Patrick now?' Donatella merely said, 'I have made arrangements. Other arrangements.' Remembering her enlistment of Chiara at the Villa Calvina, Isobel thought she probably had calmly done just that.

Nobody came to say goodbye. It was as if Isobel had never lived there, had made not the smallest impression upon the ancient suspicious obstinacy of the place. She who had arrived at La Crocetta with trunks of clothes and whole cartloads of furniture and other possessions, left with a single suitcase, three boxes of books, and the two paintings Aunt Sybil had left her wrapped up in a blanket. She was driven down to Siena by Nina's father, a taciturn man who had not addressed a word directly to Isobel since the men had been dismissed after the incident over the schoolroom roof. As the car jolted down the track away from the house, Isobel did not look back, so she didn't see Donatella, standing in front of it and gazing after her. She didn't, in fact, see anything. Until the car had reached the Siena road and climbed up completely away from the valley and the brooding presence of Monte Alba, she did not look out of the window.

Memories of Gianni meant that Isobel had not been able to go back to the Pensione Cipoletti in Florence. Instead, she chose another pensione at random, close to the Duomo, piling her boxes and her bundle of paintings into a narrow dark room looking into an alley off the Via dei Servi. It was a hot room, as well as dark, and the alley was a favourite place for nocturnal dog fights. Florence did not, for some reason, feel very sympathetic. Isobel called on the Vaccaris and found them, though as kind and welcoming as ever, preoccupied with their impending move back to the Veneto. They were returning to the Professor's birthplace, to a village house belonging to one of his brothers. Signora Vaccari would have a garden, and a yard for hens. She held Isobel's hands and said she was too thin and looked tired, and then her eyes filled with tears and she said, 'Oh the poor baby, the poor baby!' and Isobel had not the heart to tell her that she had now left Giovanni and that both her marriage and La Crocetta had been a failure.

'Look after yourself,' the Vaccaris said, waving her goodbye. 'Make sure you rest and eat enough. God will send you other babies.'

Professor Vaccari had written out his new address for her in his cramped scholar's hand, and underneath his favourite passage from Virgil's *Georgics*, '. . . *deum namque ire per omnia* . . .'

> For God, they say, pervades the whole creation,
> Land's and the sea's expanse and the depths of sky.
> Thence flocks and herds and men and all the beasts
> Of the wild derive, each in his hour of birth,
> The subtle breath of life; and surely thither
> All things at last return, dissolved, restored.
> There is no room for death: alive they fly
> To join the stars and mount aloft to Heaven.

Isobel had wanted to embrace him, but had refrained. He smiled at her as he had always smiled, benevolent but ever a little impersonal, his clouding eyes seeing much more than you thought they saw behind his thick spectacles. They were fond of her, the Vaccaris, but she was only a favourite pupil to them, and no more. Their hearts lay where they were now returning, to the village on the banks of the Piave where, almost seventy years ago, a country schoolmaster had noticed in one of his pupils an aptitude and enthusiasm for the ancient tongues.

The visit to Assunta had been even less encouraging. Assunta and her mother and her older sister, who had worked all those years for Signora Vaccari, received Isobel into their dark and formal little parlour in manifest embarrassment. Assunta's mother hospitably produced sweet wine and squares of dry yellow cake flavoured with caraway seeds, but the ice was never broken. Assunta had taken new employment, she said, with a German family, a doctor's family, in Florence. She was starting as a nurserymaid and there were chances of promotion.

'Why did you leave me?' Isobel said, as gently as she could. 'Why did you go as soon as my back was turned?'

Assunta did not look at her nor answer. Her natural boldness of manner seemed to have entirely disappeared. In the end, after Isobel, almost pleading, had repeated her question, Assunta's mother spoke for her and said in a low voice that it had been the *bambino*, the tragedy of the *bambino*, it had broken Assunta's heart, quite broken it. Isobel looked at them all in the gloom, at the dark Italian faces closed against her because they could neither tell her the truth of what had happened at La Crocetta, nor help her further. Isobel, who had been planning to ask Assunta to come with her to Fontebella, rose from her slippery horsehair-covered chair without uttering a word of appeal. There was no point. Assunta had gone away from her, into another life of her own.

Yet the worst aspect of these days in Florence was Aunt Jean's refusal to see Isobel at all. Isobel telephoned the Villa Calvina, but Moody, who answered, could give her no comfort.

'She was awful distressed to hear of the baby,' Moody said, her voice strangled in her conflicting desire to comfort Isobel and obey her employer. 'She took that to heart all right.'

'Then why won't she see me?'

'She says she can bear no more of it.'

'Moody,' Isobel said, closing her eyes in the dark little corner of the lobby where the pensione telephone lived, 'I have done what she wants now. I've admitted that she was right, that I made a dreadful, painful mistake and all I'm trying to do now is to put it right. I think I've paid for my mistake, don't you? I think I've suffered for defying Aunt Jean and thinking I knew my own mind. I want to see her, to tell her she was right and to say I am truly sorry for all the pain I've caused her. Won't she even see me for that?'

There was a pause. Isobel, in her mind's eye, could see Moody's dear, plain Scots face screwed up in misery, as it always was in times of emotional difficulty.

'Please,' Isobel said, 'please try again. Please ask her.'

Then at last, Moody said with infinite sadness, 'I cannot.'

'Just once—'

'She made me promise I'd not mention you again. It's not just you, you see. It's that your Aunt Sybil defied her and left you the money. And you being the apple of her eye.'

'I'm the same person,' Isobel said, 'the same person she brought up. Just sadder and wiser now.'

Moody said, as if Isobel hadn't spoken, 'It's all for Mr Edward's children now. They're to have it all. They're to come out here, in August.'

'The whole family?'

'Yes,' Moody said.

Isobel said, her voice not at all steady, 'Moody, I'm twenty-five tomorrow.'

'Yes, dear. I know that. How could I not know that?'

'That was always the birthday—'

'I know,' Moody said quickly, 'I know. I must run, dear, she's ringing for me—'

'Tell her it was me,' Isobel pleaded, 'please, Moody. Tell her it was me who telephoned. Tell her—'

'Goodbye, dear,' Moody said, and put the telephone down.

Isobel had gone into the cathedral then, in a blind search for comfort; comfort against Aunt Jean's resolute rejection, against the bitter thought of her half-brothers and sister playing possessively in her own childhood places, against Assunta's defection. She had then wandered all that long, hot afternoon alone, through the streets of Florence, through the squares and markets and finally, as if to lay the ghost of youthful optimism, across the river to the Boboli Gardens and up the terraces to the stone seat where Giovanni had proposed to her and she, believing she had found not just someone

254

of her very own, but the right someone, had so joyfully accepted him.

The beginning of her birthday, she scarcely noticed. She went to Maquay's Bank to close her old account there, and to French, Lemon & Co to confirm the opening of her new one. Neither transaction meant anything. 'Isobel Fosco', she signed in one, 'Isobel Lindsay', once more, in the other. She didn't, for some reason, feel particularly like either one of these people, but simply numb. Her names might have been numbers for all they signified an identity for her. After the banks, she had gone to the Uffizi gallery and stared for some time at several paintings she loved, without seeing them. Then she went to Doney's and ate a lemon ice cream and drank a cup of coffee and read reviews in the English newspapers of new novels by D. H. Lawrence and John Galsworthy, and new plays by Bernard Shaw and Somerset Maugham without feeling the smallest desire to read or see any of them. She put the newspapers down, and stared into her empty coffee cup. Nobody knew where she was! Nobody. There was nobody to expect her or depend upon her. She could sit here, at this window table in Doney's, and stare at that coffee cup until the place closed, and it would matter to nobody. Was that what she wanted? Did she want to be so free that in the end she had no significance? Did she intend to let the mistakes she had made wreck all chance of a future? Isobel sat up suddenly and put her shoulders back.

'Certainly not,' she said, out loud.

Two women, eating cake with forks at the next table, turned their hatted heads.

'*Bitte?*' one of them said.

'I beg your pardon,' Isobel said, 'I was merely thinking out loud.'

She got up and walked briskly across the room, and downstairs to street level to pay her bill.

'Ridiculous,' Isobel told herself, 'self-pitying. Melodramatic.'

She pushed several lire notes under the glass screen of the cashier's desk, the same cashier who had taken the money after so many assignations with Giovanni.

'No change,' Isobel said superbly, and swept out into the street.

The Poste Restante that most foreigners used was in the post office situated in the Uffizi courtyard, close to the gallery. Isobel had always been sent in several times a year to check, for the aunts, that no vital but mis-addressed letter had come to rest there instead of being brought up to the Villa Calvina. The aunts had had no faith in the Italian postal system, despite the fact that there had never, in ten years, been either a letter knowingly gone astray, nor a letter for Carruthers or Fanshawe in the locked and varnished cubbyholes of the Poste Restante, with the letters of the alphabet, black on ivory ovals, screwed to the front of each.

Isobel went over to the long bench opposite to the counter where people, hopelessly waiting for news or money orders, often spent listless days. She sat down beside a thin boy reading a German newspaper and, opening her bag, took out a notebook and tore off a page. Balancing the paper unevenly on the side of her handbag, Isobel wrote the place and the date in pencil and then:

Dear Patrick,
I've done it. I've left it all and am on my way back to Fontebella. I am pretty sure I am trusting my instincts and I hope you will be pleased. If I am quite mad, I can't feel it. I hope you will come and see me in the castle. I only own a bed and two pictures, but when I came to Italy, I didn't even own that. I hope your painting is going well and that you are happy.
Yours ever,
Isobel.

She stopped and put the end of the pencil in her mouth, frowning. Then she wrote, as a rapid afterthought, 'Donatella is waiting to hear from you,' and folded the paper into three, tucking the ends in. 'Patrick Fleming Esq,' she wrote on the outside, 'to await arrival.'

The clerk at the counter looked at the note. 'Envelope,' he said. 'I haven't one.'

He sighed. He turned the note over several times and then, sighing again, more heavily, went across to the pigeonhole marked 'F', and unlocked it, dropping the note inside. Isobel, reassured in some way she could not put her finger on, went out into the sunshine. She looked up at the bland blue sky. There were hours of daylight yet, plenty of time, in fact, to get to Fontebella that night, instead of waiting, as she had planned for some obscure reason, for the following morning.

And here she was, five days later, in her room in the Pensione Verdi, with the cornflowers, like captured patches of sky, standing in earthenware jugs borrowed from Signora Verdi. They

256

made the room look domesticated, cared for, and that in its turn made Isobel long for the castle with an abrupt and piercing longing. She pulled one of the hard upright schoolroom chairs, which Signora Verdi had indicated with such pride, out from the table and sat down on it. She looked at the bare white walls and the engraving of the castle and the jugs of blue flowers. She told herself, as severely as she knew how, that as she plainly was not going to get the castle, she must simply think of something else, a villa somewhere, an apartment in one of Fontebella's little old palaces.

There was a knock on the door. Irena, Signora Verdi's skinny little daughter, rattled the handle and called, in her high, squeaky voice, 'Signora! Signora!'

'Come in,' Isobel said.

'A letter!' Irena cried, almost falling into the room. 'A letter for you!'

She skipped across the tiled floor and laid the letter with a flourish in front of Isobel.

'From the mayor, Signora! Look, look, it has on it the arms of Fontebella.'

On the back of the envelope were engraved the three dolphins.

'Thank you, Irena.'

'Open it!' Irena demanded. She fixed her bright dark eyes on Isobel's face. 'Mamma says it must be important.'

Isobel smiled. She slid her finger under the envelope flap and drew out a single sheet of thick white paper.

'What does it say? What does it say?'

'It says, "Madam"!' Isobel said.

'And then? And then?'

'And then,' Isobel said slowly, reading as she spoke, 'and then it says that as I may not, on account of circumstances quite beyond the Commune's control, buy the Fortezza di Fontebella, would I graciously consider the Commune's offer of – of a lease!' Isobel cried, her voice rising almost to a shriek. She leaped up and began to whirl around the room.

'A lease! A lease! They'll let me lease the castle! I can live in the castle! I can, I can!'

Irena regarded her. She was plainly mad. But that was not, after all, in the least surprising because Irena's father had told her that all the English, without exception, were mad. Who but somebody mad would want to live in a dusty old castle with no electricity and no indoor water tap? Irena sidled round

Isobel's dancing, rejoicing figure and skittered back down to the kitchen.

'The mayor says,' Irena announced to her mother, 'that the English signora can live in the castle after all, and she is behaving like a lunatic!'

Chapter Thirty

'My name is Emilia,' the woman said. She stood outside the great door, with a bundle on her head in the country fashion, and a bunch of mimosa in one hand. She was perhaps thirty, stocky and smiling, and the hand that was not holding the mimosa was attempting to restrain a little jumping boy in a blue tunic.

Isobel, in her everyday castle uniform of breeches and a man's shirt, smiled back.

'My name is Emilia,' the woman said again, 'and you are the English *padrona.*'

'Yes,' Isobel said. The little boy wrenched himself free of his mother and skipped up to her. 'And who are you?'

'He is Mario,' Emilia said, 'my son, Mario. I have come' – she paused and held out the pale, fluffy flowers – 'I have come to ask if you need a servant.'

Isobel's smile grew broader. Two weeks in the castle, sleeping on a camp bed lent by Signora Verdi and battling against the dust and the rats, had made her feel she would sell her soul for a servant.

'I went on a pilgrimage,' Emilia said confidently, 'I went to ask Our Lady what I should do, and after that, I dreamed of a rabbit escaping from a snare, so I knew that I should come to you!'

'Did you?' Isobel said, puzzled but delighted. She took the mimosa and sniffed it appreciatively.

'I am a widow,' Emilia said, 'Mario's father died of the influenza. We have seen you in the market place in Fontebella. "See," I said to Mario, "there is the English lady!"'

'English!' Mario cried, hopping up and down.

'I would clean,' Emilia said, 'and cook, and do the marketing. Mario would not be allowed to annoy you.'

Isobel looked down at the merry little face. 'He wouldn't annoy me—'

'It would be nice to live here,' Emilia said. She lifted her hands to her head and swung her bundle easily down. 'We should like it here, in the castle with the English *padrona*, Mario and I.'

'I think,' Isobel said, 'that you had better come in.'

She pushed the door open and led the way into the hall.

'Mother of God!' Emilia said. She looked at the dust and debris that still littered the floor. 'What are you thinking of, *Padrona*, to live in this way?'

'I don't mind it,' Isobel said.

Mario went skipping ahead of them out into the courtyard, singing a rhyme about a boy and a fish and a bridge.

'I would only want fifty lire a month,' Emilia said. 'Fifty lire and our keep.' Her eyes moved with restless longing over the floor again. 'Where are the brooms?'

Isobel laughed. 'Come and see the room where I am living.'

She led the way across the courtyard. Mario had run to the breach in the wall, and was now jumping off the boulder where Donatella had sat, drawing the view below her, and calling for Patrick's help.

'In here,' Isobel said. She led the way through a doorway in the western side of the courtyard, into a room that made her heart lift every time she went into it, even though it was still only furnished with a camp bed, a table and a chair and, on the wide stone windowseat, a row of books flanked at either end by a lemon-scented geranium in a pot. Emilia crossed herself.

'The Madonna sent me to you,' she said. The shock of the room's simplicity had almost turned her pale. 'Where are your carpets? And your curtains?'

'Coming,' Isobel said, 'but first I should get the walls repaired. And the holes in the roof.'

'And where is the kitchen?'

'I'm afraid there isn't one.'

'No kitchen?'

'No. There's a lovely room that ought to be the kitchen—'

'Where have you been cooking?'

'I haven't,' Isobel said. 'I have been down to the town, to eat. Sometimes at the Pensione Verdi, sometimes not.'

Emilia looked at her. She said simply, 'You need me.'

'Yes.'

'And I need you. Mario and I need a home.' She bent and began, with brisk expertise, to straighten Isobel's casually made bed. 'You will see, *Padrona*,' she said, tucking and smoothing, 'you will see that we are intended to come here, Mario and me. Our Lady is not only bountiful, but practical.'

Isobel said, hesitantly and conscious of the neglected dusty rooms everywhere else in the castle, 'I should love you to come. But there is nowhere for you to sleep, you see, nowhere suitable for a child—'

Emilia straightened up. She looked at Isobel and put her hands on her hips.

'By tonight, *Padrona*, there will be.'

By nightfall, Isobel's room had been scrubbed, and so had a second, smaller one on the upper floor, where two truckle beds on wooden wheels, borrowed from Emilia's mother, stood side by side on a temporary carpet of clean sacking. The beds had been brought up by Emilia's father, and her younger brother, Gino. They had also brought up the present of a hard, round yellow cheese, a bottle of wine and a heavy pale-brown loaf studded with olives, packed in a basket under a coarse white cloth. Isobel had tried to make them share at least the wine with her, but they refused. It was all for her. Emilia's father, who had only a few teeth left, said his wife had seen the *padrona* in the market place and declared that she needed fattening up. He then said, smiling, that his brother was an excellent carpenter, and that his son, Gino, knew the ways of bees and pigs and vines. He bowed to Isobel, and said that he and his brother and Gino would present themselves to her, in the morning.

'Are your family simply taking me over?' Isobel asked Emilia.

Emilia had laid out the bread and cheese and wine on Isobel's table, on the cloth that had covered the basket.

'You need us,' Emilia said again.

'Yes, I do, but I also need to make my own decisions.'

Emilia regarded her. She longed for the kitchen to be done, so that she could start to cook properly for the *padrona*, pasta in sauces with clams and cream, meat roasted with herbs, stews with lentils to thicken them and tomatoes and garlic to flavour them and give them colour. In the morning, when *Zio* Ulysse came with his carpenter's tools, they could plan the kitchen together, the cupboards and tables and shelves.

'When we begin to do something that is different to your decision,' Emilia said, 'you tell us and we will stop. But we know Fontebella. We know the people and the customs here, and the earth, what will grow, what won't. My father is a stonemason. Uncle Ulysse is a carpenter. My brother Gino, like my mother's family, loves farming. What more do you need?'

Isobel looked at the table, at the loaf on a wooden board, at the cheese on an improvised mat of green leaves, at the bottle of wine and the earthenware jug of water and the blue and white pottery plate and the greenish goblet she had bought in the market, made of glass full of tiny bubbles. Then she looked round the room, at her neatly made bed and the shining marble floor and the frothy yellow mimosa in a copper can that Gino had found, he said, in a ditch below the breach in the wall. Then she looked at Emilia.

'Nothing,' she said.

She slept that night better than she had slept for months, and although she dreamed of Gianni, it was not in the haunted, wretched way she was so used to, but rather with a sweet resignation. The warm air came in through the open curtained windows, and wafted the scent of the mimosa around the room, and when the dawn broke, and Fontebella began to wake up and open its shutters and bang its pans about in the houses below her rock, Isobel woke to a feeling of well-being that she had supposed she had lost for ever.

She sat up in bed, hugging her knees. Outside her window, the blue Italian summer morning already shone like a blessing, and if she craned her neck a little, she could see the bell tower of the church below her – dedicated to St Zita, patron saint, Emilia had said, of all housemaids – and then, far beyond it across the valley, the other spires, of cypress trees, blue-green in the early sun. She turned her head a little. There on a nail driven into the rough plaster of the wall by her bed hung the coral on a silver ring that Signora Vaccari had given her and which had become her little talisman of Gianni. She blew it a kiss. His baby presence seemed to be with her quite serenely, as it had been all night. Smiling with a combination of sudden relief and optimism, Isobel swung her legs out of bed and put her bare feet down on the smooth, cool marble of the floor.

Outside her door, somebody was already sweeping. Isobel could hear the brisk strokes of a stiff broom on the stones of the courtyard. She could also hear other things, voices and hammering and pouring water. She stood up, pulled on her dressing gown and padded over to the door, a satisfyingly solid studded door, with a

262

great black iron latch, like all the doors in the castle. She opened it a crack and peered out.

'*Padrona*, good morning,' Emilia said, not stopping sweeping. 'It's a beautiful day.'

The courtyard was flooded with sunlight. It was also, Isobel realized, apparently full of people. There was a woman drawing water from the well, and a man with a ladder by the breach in the wall, and another man setting up a sawhorse in the only corner where there was, at the moment, any shade.

'Who are all these people?' Isobel said.

'My sister Lucia has come to help clean today, and there is my father, whom you met yesterday, to repair the wall so that it is safe, and over there is *Zio* Ulysse. He has come to make us a kitchen.'

'I see,' Isobel said faintly.

Emilia deftly swept a pile of grit and debris into a little pyramid, and leaned her broom against the wall.

'And now you must have breakfast. My father has brought a camping stove to make coffee, and Lucia has brought up bread and some of my mother's apricot jam.' She looked at Isobel. 'You need not worry, *Padrona*. We are here to give and not to take.'

Isobel said, 'All these wages—' She remembered, with a pang of recalled panic, all those people at La Crocetta whom she had paid so faithfully and who would, in return, scarcely either work or look at her. She said, rather hesitantly, 'I have not had – a very good experience of employing people. I am determined, Emilia, that I won't again be exploited.'

'You won't be,' Emilia said calmly. 'If you want, I will tell Lucia and my father and Uncle Ulysse to go home at once.'

Isobel thought about this. She looked across at Emilia's father, on his ladder, gently tapping a loose stone out of its moorings, and Lucia – a younger, slimmer version of Emilia – gracefully carrying two heavy buckets of water away from the well. She remembered yesterday's cheese and today's hot coffee and apricot jam.

'No,' she said, 'don't send anyone away. I'll dress now and after breakfast, we will all talk business.'

Emilia's face betrayed no flicker of triumph.

'As you wish, *Padrona*,' she said and went briskly away across the courtyard to fetch the coffee.

Isobel ate her breakfast by the open window in her room. It was excellent. The apricot jam had the kernels of the fruit in it, giving a sweet, nutty taste, and the coffee was brought in a little white china basin with a gold line painted round the rim. Mario carried

263

the bread in, in a little basket. He put it down on the table and then opened his mouth wide, like a fledgling, inviting Isobel to put something in it. Emilia scolded him.

'Don't,' Isobel said, 'don't be cross with him.'

She broke off a piece of bread, spread it with jam and put it into Mario's waiting mouth. His cheeks bulged and his eyes shone. He chewed rapidly.

'More!' he said, swallowing.

'No,' said Emilia.

'One more,' said Isobel.

She spread another piece of bread. Mario craned forward, his eyes fixed on it.

Emilia said gently, 'The signora has no children?'

There was a little pause. Isobel put the second piece of bread into Mario's mouth. 'No.'

Emilia's eyes strayed to the silver ring and the branch of coral hanging on the white wall. Isobel said, seeing her glance, 'I had a baby, Emilia. He died.'

'*Padrona*—'

'It's all right,' Isobel said quickly.

'I would never have asked, *Padrona*, if I'd known, I would never have been so cruel—'

'You aren't cruel. How could you know?'

'Kiss,' Mario said, holding up a sticky, smiling face.

Isobel bent.

'No!' Emilia said, 'Mario, no!'

Isobel kissed him. Emilia swooped down and seized him.

'Impudent child! Wicked boy! *Padrona*, forgive him, forgive us!'

'There is nothing to forgive,' Isobel said. She smiled at Mario. He gave her a wide, beautiful, flirtatious smile in return.

'You see, I noticed, *Padrona*, that you were married,' Emilia said, in a confusion of remorse and curiosity, 'so it was natural to ask—'

Isobel looked down at her left hand. It still bore the gold band symbolizing her marriage to Giovanni. She had left it on, to impress the mayor of Fontebella with her respectability. Now, she gave it a little tug and slid it down her finger.

'I have been married, Emilia,' she said, 'and I've had a child. But now I'm back to where I began, Signorina Isobel Lindsay.'

She laid the wedding ring on the table, beside her coffee bowl.

'*Signora* Lindsay,' Emilia said reprovingly. She began to rub at Mario's face with a corner of her apron. 'I only work, *Padrona*,

264

for signoras. When you have finished, I will send the men to you. Just open the door and call for me. Come now, Mario.'

She opened the door to the courtyard, and went out, and as she did so, Mario blew Isobel a kiss over his mother's shoulder.

Uncle Ulysse said he would build Isobel a range of oak cupboards, with terracotta tiled tops, and a dresser, and two sets of shelves for pans, and a kitchen table sturdy enough to cut up a deer on for a hundred lire plus the cost of the materials. Emilia's father, who was called Giuseppe, said that for the same sum, he would make the breach in the walls safe, and build a flight of stone steps down to the vine terraces, and that he would then turn his attention to the roof, if she so wished him to. Lucia, who was very shy on account of a harelip which both she and her whole family believed to be the mark of the devil in some obscure way, said in a whisper that she would help Emilia until the castle was scrubbed clean. Their brother, Gino, did not appear. He was down among the terraces, Emilia said, looking at the earth and the plants, and when he had finished he would come up and tell the *Padrona* what might be grown there.

'He has green fingers,' Emilia said proudly.

Mario held up his hands. He had been playing with the mud by the well. 'Mine are black,' he said pleasedly.

'Tomatoes, perhaps,' Isobel said, thinking of her future little farm, and smiling at Mario, 'and onions. And maybe fennel, and peaches—'

Emilia nodded. 'And spinach. Gino grows magnificent spinach. And, of course, we should have chickens—'

'And bees—'

'Perhaps a cow?'

'And a dragon,' Mario said.

'He has seen the painting in the church,' Emilia said, 'of the saint killing a dragon. A dragon would not be useful, Mario.'

'No,' Isobel said, laughing, 'no. But charming.'

'A water pipe would be useful.'

'I know.'

'And electric light—'

'Emilia, I have been in the castle two weeks. You have been here *one day*—'

'And already,' Emilia said, picking up the breakfast tray and preparing to carry it out, 'the *Padrona* looks happier.'

Isobel glanced up at her. She was smiling, a simple, open, friendly, uncomplicated smile. Isobel nodded. Before Emilia could move to prevent her, or do anything but give a small horrified cry, Isobel had picked up her wedding ring, which still lay on the table, and flung it out of the open window into the smiling air.

'Yes,' Isobel said, her voice jubilant, 'yes! Yes, I am!'

Chapter Thirty-one

It grew hotter. Isobel, waking soon after dawn, became used to hearing the chink of tools and the murmur of voices as the men arrived for work while the sun was still bearable. At midday, everyone went home and a wonderful sleepy golden silence descended on the castle until the shadows began to lengthen a little, when Giuseppe and Ulysse would reappear in the courtyard, and Gino, and a boy he had found to help him – willing, he said, but very slow – could be seen down among the terraces again, weeding and pruning and repairing the stone walls that held up the little fields.

Gradually, Isobel acquired a *salone* with long cream linen curtains made by a niece of Signora Verdi's, and a tin bath in a temporary bathroom whitewashed by herself, and a set of copper pans to sit in a gleaming row on one of the shelves Ulysse had made. A wood-fuelled stove appeared in the kitchen, terracotta pots of riotous geraniums bloomed in the courtyard and an old cupboard, painted with garlands of flowers poignantly reminiscent of her childhood, was carried into her bedroom, for her clothes. Slowly, holes were mended, windows reglazed, walls repainted and floors polished. An old man, smelling strongly of pigs and alcohol, came up with a canvas quiver of brushes to clean and re-gild the antique patterns on the wooden ceilings, and another one went round the entire castle repairing and oiling the great black iron locks. The mayor of Fontebella made a state visit, with two members of the town Commune, and toured the castle from battlements to courtyard, pronouncing himself well satisfied.

'You are a gracious guardian of our heritage,' he said to Isobel.

Isobel gave a little curtsey. She had put on a dress, especially for his visit, instead of the breeches that were so much more practical for scything down the rooftop cornfield or slapping whitewash on walls.

'I am so glad.'

'Of course, when the castle is in better repair it may well attract a higher rental—'

'Don't try that one on me,' Isobel said, in English, still smiling.

'Excuse me?'

'The rent should go *down*,' Isobel said, in Italian, 'to allow for the improvements I have made.'

'Fascists,' Emilia said, when they had gone. 'You were right to stand up to them.'

She was almost in love with Isobel, because of her kitchen. Isobel had chosen a good room for the kitchen, not a black hole at the back of the castle, but a room with air and light and a beamed ceiling and deep windows looking south towards the town and east across the terraces where Gino worked, with the boy and a donkey. It was a beautiful kitchen. Uncle Ulysse had made beautiful cupboards and the copper pans were beautiful too and so was the polished brick floor and the stove and the adjacent larder with its stone shelves and the battery of knives and spoons and sieves that Isobel had allowed Emilia to choose herself, in the market. In this kitchen, Emilia vowed, she would make meals for a queen, an empress, even if Isobel would not allow her, to her great disappointment, to call her Marchesa.

Isobel was a marchesa, after all. Emilia had discovered this from Signora Verdi, and also that she was an English heiress and that she had had an estate south of Siena. Signora Verdi couldn't say why she had come back to Fontebella, nor why she had returned without the other young lady who had been so very aristocratic with her pale face and her talent for painting. Emilia told Signora Verdi about the dead baby and the wedding ring (which she had subsequently but fruitlessly searched for) thrown out of the window. They shook their heads. It was very mysterious, especially as Isobel hardly dressed like an heiress nor, though generous, spent money like one either.

'But I like her,' Emilia said.

Signora Verdi sucked her teeth. 'The English are so very strange. It's hard to know whether one likes them or not.'

Yet Emilia did like Isobel. It wasn't just the beautiful kitchen, nor the fact that she was teaching Mario his letters and a few words of English, but that she didn't give herself airs. She had dignity but no grandeur, and she carried herself well but not stiffly. Her clothes were hardly wonderful – though Emilia had spotted, in a lilac cashmere coat, the expensive-looking label of a dressmaker in Florence – and she seemed to have no jewellery beyond a set of amethysts in a red morocco case which were kept, very carelessly Emilia thought, in a drawer among Isobel's underclothes. Yet there were signs of past elegance, not only in Isobel's manner and carriage, but in the two lovely old paintings that hung in her bedroom – one of the Annunciation, with a dove flying down in a ray of holiness towards the Virgin Mary with a lily stem in its beak, and one of a Renaissance lady with pale hair drawn back from a high forehead and pearls looped across her brocade bodice – and in the bed. The bed was a marvel to Emilia. It had been brought up from the station on an ox cart borrowed from Gino's last employer, looking like nothing more than an old pile of worm-eaten wood, and then Uncle Ulysse had put it together, piece by piece, and there was a bed, covered in angels! Emilia had never seen anything like it. They were baby angels, *putti*, and they flew round the headboard as if they were guarding the sleeper below. There had been tears in the *padrona*'s eyes when she saw the bed.

Isobel's tears had been partly relief at being reunited with the cherub bed, and partly disappointment. She had searched the pieces of bed, while Uncle Ulysse assembled them with little exclamations of admiration, for a note, even the smallest note, from Donatella. There was nothing, not a single sign of any kind of communication, nor a scrap of ribbon even, or a little drawing. Isobel went over to the stone seat Giuseppe had made at the mouth of the breach in the wall, and sat down on it, looking at, but not seeing, the view. She hadn't realized, until now, how much she had been hoping that Donatella would communicate with her, would give some tiny sign that their shared years together, for all their oddness and lack of spontaneous warmth, had meant something to Donatella too. She had felt guilty at not being able to love Donatella wholeheartedly, but oh! if Donatella had only once taken her part, shown her a mere glimpse of generosity, how freely and loyally Isobel would have loved her!

Isobel had written to her. She had written in very general terms, from the Pensione Verdi, saying that Donatella knew her plans, and if she ever, at any time, wished to join her in them, her welcome was assured. She had signed the letter, 'With my love. Isobel.' Signor

Verdi had agreed to post it for her, on one of his weekly trips into Florence, ostensibly to visit his old aunt who kept a *pasticceria*, but in reality, said all Fontebella, to see a girl who sang in the chorus at the Alhambra Theatre in the Piazza Beccaria. Of course Donatella knew where Isobel was, but Isobel had no doubt at all but that she would keep her whereabouts a secret. It was just that Isobel did not want a letter postmarked Fontebella to arrive at La Crocetta. Her present feeling of security lay partly in her conviction that Giovanni and the Marchesa did not know where she was. Aunt Jean knew, of course. Isobel had written at length to her, telling her story as simply and unemotionally as possible, and giving her new address. There had been no reply. It was hardly surprising, Isobel told herself; it was instead perhaps lucky that she hadn't had the letter returned to her, with 'Unread' written across it in Aunt Jean's decided, old-fashioned hand.

She leaned forward on the stone seat, shading her eyes with her hand. Giuseppe had made a little terrace round the seat, and a flight of steps now led down to the slopes below where Gino could be seen among the vines, painstakingly tying up the wayward fronds. The main pruning, he said, could not be done until January. My vines, Isobel thought, my *podere*. How wonderful it would be to show these things to Aunt Jean, how she would approve of Emilia and Gino and the neat lines of vegetables already showing above the earth, as tidy as the rows of stitching on a sampler. And when they had walked down there among the vines and the bean rows and the clumps of lettuce, and Isobel had asked for advice about wheat and maize and over-wintering bees, they could come up on to the terrace in the sunset and watch the little bats swooping silently in the soft air, and then they could have dinner together, by candlelight with the window open above the darkening town and the smell of the white tobacco flowers floating in from the courtyard. For a second, Isobel closed her eyes. It was twelve, nearly thirteen weeks now, since she had had a meal with anyone else.

She shook herself resolutely. What more could anyone want than this place, this independence, these dear people? She waved down at Gino and he straightened, chest deep in bright green vine leaves, and waved back. He was going to be married, Emilia said, in the autumn, to a girl from over the mountain, an only child whose father had a share in a marble quarry near Carrera. It was a good match, Emilia said proudly, Gino so handsome and hard-working, his bride so well-endowed. Lucky Gino, Isobel thought, waving. Lucky Gino, with so much before him.

'*Padrona! Padrona!*'

Mario was dancing across the cobbles, his blue tunic flapping. '*Padrona*, the gentleman is here!'

'What gentleman?' Isobel said, thinking of the mayor.

'The big one!' Mario stretched his arms out sideways, and then bent, holding his arms horizontally to suggest the enormousness of this person. 'As big as the cupboard!'

Isobel looked up, laughing. Across the courtyard, framed in the stone doorway to the entrance hall, stood Patrick, dressed like a tramp and holding a wide-brimmed hat in his hand.

'Patrick!' Isobel cried.

He lifted his other hand to her. She ran across the courtyard, full of undisguised delight, and threw her arms around his neck.

'Oh, Patrick!'

He held her with his free arm. He was smiling, but almost warily, and his face, though brown, looked very tired.

'Isobel,' he said, 'Isobel. Well done. Well *done*.'

He dropped his arm and gazed about him. 'You've done brilliantly. It looks wonderful. How long—'

'Three months!' Isobel said proudly. 'Three months and nearly a week! Isn't it heaven? Isn't it perfect? Where have you been? Did you get my note? Did you?'

'Of course I did,' Patrick said. 'I got it two months ago.' He moved out into the sunlight, and stood looking at the well-head, its stone newly cleaned, and at the domestic pots of herbs that clustered round it. Then he raised his eyes and looked at Giuseppe's work on the breach and the newly planted geraniums and roses and plumbago in their stone tubs against the walls.

'You've brought it to life,' Patrick said.

Isobel followed him. She said, looking up into his face, 'You don't sound very pleased about it.'

He hesitated. He stepped forward and laid his hat on the rim of the well. Then he said, his back towards Isobel, 'I'm afraid I've rather got something on my mind.'

'Do you want to tell me?'

'Not now,' Patrick said. He turned to look at her over his shoulder. 'It's wonderful here.'

'I know. Are you hungry?'

He smiled. 'Of course. Aren't I always? And dirty and in need of a shave.'

Mario, jigging beside him, caught at his trousers. 'You need a wash!'

271

'Do I, you monkey?'

'His mother says that to him,' Isobel said. 'Doesn't she, Mario? I'll call her to heat some water for you. Patrick—'

'Yes?'

'Will – you be staying? Would you like to stay?'

He looked at her. He looked, she thought, very nearly as wretched as he had looked the first time she saw him, at the Villa Calvina.

'Please.'

She said gently, 'Are you ill?'

He shook his head. 'No. But – but I've done something terrible, something—'

'Sh,' Isobel said, 'it can wait. Until you're clean and fed and rested. Wait here while I tell Emilia. Mario, please amuse the signor. Tell him your English words.'

Patrick looked down at him. 'What do you know?'

Mario threw out his chest and beat it with his little brown fists. 'Everything!' he said.

Isobel hurried across to the kitchen. The postman was there, sitting at the table, his bag of undelivered letters beside him on the floor, docilely shelling peas. This wasn't at all surprising. Most of the Fontebella tradesmen, it seemed, gravitated at some point in the day to Emilia's kitchen and were always put to work. If you didn't work a man, she maintained, he only got into trouble. Emilia herself was draping long pale strands of newly made pasta to dry between two chair backs.

'*Padrona!*'

The postman shuffled to his feet, spilling peas. Isobel motioned to him to sit down.

'Careless!' Emilia said scoldingly, pouncing on him and gathering up the scattered peas.

'We have a guest, Emilia.'

She sprang upright. 'A guest!'

'Yes. An English painter, an artist. He came to convalesce during the war at my aunt's house in Fiesole. He needs a bath, Emilia, and food and we must make up a bed for him.'

Emilia began to fly round the kitchen, seizing the great cauldron in which she heated the water.

'At once! At once!' She whirled round on the postman. 'Go on, you useless lump, get moving! I need ten buckets of water, do you hear me!'

The postman, obedient, shuffled out.

272

'Oh, *Padrona*, if only we had water from a tap!'

'I know—'

'And an electric boiler!'

'I know, I know—'

Emilia lifted the pasta deftly off the chair backs and spread it, out of harm's way, over the ceiling rack for drying clothes. Her eyes were shining.

'A guest, *Padrona*! A guest! Our Lady must have guided me because I bought the most beautiful, plump rabbit this morning, and little new turnips no bigger than an eyeball and a melon that smells like honey!'

She began to sing. Isobel, feeling like singing too, went back into the courtyard.

Patrick was left to splash in the tin bath alone with difficulty. Mario, consumed with curiosity to see if the English signor was as big without his clothes as with them, was dragged away from the keyhole and set to carry bedlinen for his mother up to the room on the first floor which Patrick had been allotted. Isobel knew he would like it. The walls had never been plastered, and the bare stone was clean and rough and pale gold. The ceiling was darkly beamed, and the windows set in the thickness of the castle walls looked west, as her own did, across the picturesque edge of the little town towards the setting sun. There was nothing in the room but a bed, a stool, a chest, a moony old looking-glass framed in dull gold shells Isobel had found in an antique stall in the market, and two blue and white cotton rugs. The main ornament of the room was the view.

Emilia set a table for them in a shady corner of the courtyard. She brought a dish of pasta with peas and cream, a loaf of bread, a blue bowl of peaches and a green jug of white wine. Patrick ate voraciously, tearing pieces off the loaf and cramming them into his mouth in a way that was, Isobel said in mock reproof, a very bad example to Mario. While he ate, he told her that he had been back to London since they met, and had had his first exhibition. It was rather a success, he said. People had come out of curiosity, to see if he had any of his father's talent.

'They found I didn't, of course, but I had a different one. You should have heard the cries of amazement. *The Times* was even kind enough to say I had a robust approach to landscape reminiscent of Turner. Too good of them, I must say.'

Isobel wound pasta on to her fork. 'Did you sell any?'

'Yes.'

She looked at him. 'How many?'

'Thirty-four out of forty-seven.'

'Patrick!'

He grinned at her. 'I groan with money. Three hundred pounds. But what's that to you? A mere bagatelle—'

'No,' Isobel said quickly, flushing.

'But it's the open sesame, isn't it, it's the key—'

'Don't tease me,' Isobel said, 'not about that.'

'Sorry.'

'I often think,' Isobel said, putting her fork down, 'that it's a curse, having money. If I hadn't had money, I couldn't have decided to marry so wrong-headedly, and I wouldn't have become prey to all the Foscos.'

At the mention of the name, Patrick's face suddenly darkened. He threw his fork down, then he stood up abruptly and tramped away towards the terrace, reminding Isobel forcibly of the way he had stood on the terrace at the Villa Calvina, glaring down at Florence.

She got up and followed him. He was standing, slightly hunched, with his hands clenched into fists, in his pockets.

'Patrick?'

He said nothing.

'Patrick,' Isobel said, more firmly. She went closer and put her hand on his arm. 'Whatever it is, I wish you'd tell me. I wish you'd say what's the matter.'

'Not here,' he said, 'not in the castle. Follow me,' and then, ignoring Giuseppe's handsome new flight of steps, he leaped over the breach and began running down towards the *podere*.

274

Chapter Thirty-two

Isobel caught up with him among the first of the olive trees. He had subsided against the trunk of one and then slithered down it until he was sitting on the earth. Isobel, panting slightly, her hair escaping from its combs – Emilia had declared in a shocked voice that Signor Verdi reported that the latest fashion in Florence was to have your hair cut as short as a boy's! – collapsed a yard from him. It was shady under the olive trees and quiet, with the castle looming over them like a benevolent guardian and Gino gone home to his lunch of bread and cheese, moistened with olive oil.

'Well?' Isobel said.

Patrick rearranged himself so that he was leaning back against the tree trunk. He said, his eyes fixed on the blue sky between the grey-green leaves, 'May I tell you the whole story?'

'Of course.'

'When I went to the Poste Restante two months ago,' Patrick said, still gazing at the sky, 'there were two letters. Your little note, and one in an envelope. From Donatella.'

Isobel, who had been breaking a fallen olive twig into little pieces, stopped.

'It was just the same as all her other letters. Friendly, a bit formal, mostly Italian, little snippets of English. There was a sketch of the fountain square here enclosed and a note scribbled on it asking me to advise her about the perspective. She said her mother was a little better, but that Giovanni was worried about the estate and had began to talk of selling it. She never mentioned you. She certainly didn't say that you had gone.'

'She didn't?'

'No. I wouldn't have known, for sure, unless I'd heard from you, even if I might have suspected it. And then' – Patrick paused and took his eyes away from the heavens – 'and then she asked if I would meet her in Florence because she had something to discuss.'

He glanced at Isobel. She had found another twig and was now snapping that, with great concentration, into tiny pieces.

'I wrote you a postcard,' Patrick said. 'I said that I was going to meet Donatella at her request and I hoped to bring her up to you here. Then I forgot to post it. I found it in my pocket a week ago. It was a postcard of the Primavera, for old times' sake. But I think I was meant to forget it.'

'Why?' Isobel said sharply.

'Because I was completely on the wrong track. I thought—' he paused and then said, 'I'll tell you what I thought later. Better to keep telling you what happened. The day after I'd had Donatella's letter, I got a telegram from my father in London, saying that the gallery who were putting on my exhibition wanted to put it on two weeks earlier than planned, so could I return at once, with my whole portfolio. I didn't know whether to telegraph La Crocetta because I bet that old mother has an eye like a hawk, so instead I sent a letter care of the priest in Siena who hears the Marchesa's confession – Lord knows, those must be worth hearing – marked from the Institute of Fine Art in Florence, all as Donatella had instructed me, saying that I couldn't meet her for six weeks because I had to go back to London. I was actually only away for five, and got back here just over a fortnight ago, with three hundred pounds and seven commissions.' He leaned forward and pulled roughly at a clump of weeds. 'There was another letter from Donatella.'

Isobel swept all her little twig pieces into a neat heap and folded her hands in her lap. 'What did it say?'

'It asked me to meet her off the Siena train on a certain day. If I wasn't at the station, she would simply assume I was still in England and would leave another letter. She said she'd take herself to the Bargello Museum, which was where she'd told her mother she'd be. But there was no need for any of that, because I met the train.' He stopped, and leaned forward, wrapping his arms round his knees, and laying his forehead on them so that his voice was muffled. 'She wanted to walk. We walked – it was desperately hot but she insisted – all the way from the station to the Botanical Gardens. She was quite animated, she looked almost – almost—'

'I can't hear you,' Isobel said, sitting as still as a statue.

276

He raised his head. 'She looked almost handsome,' Patrick said. 'Her eyes were shining. We talked about my exhibition and painting and when we got to the gardens we looked at some of the plants there and suddenly she began to talk quite differently, to talk about the future and another kind of life and escaping from La Crocetta, and her mother and – and I realized – oh, my God, Isobel, I was so shaken – I realized that she had come to Florence to ask me to take her away from all that. She was proposing to me. Isobel, she was asking me to marry her.'

Isobel simply stared. She could say nothing.

'And I also realized – and this is what was so terrible – that it had never crossed her mind that I might not accept.'

Isobel said, in a voice that seemed to belong to someone else and which came from a great distance, 'Nor me.'

'What?'

'I thought you would – I thought you loved Donatella, I thought—'

Patrick suddenly lunged forward on to his hands and knees, so that his face was only inches from Isobel. 'I did! I do!'

'Then—'

'But not like that!' Patrick shouted. 'Not like a – a *woman*! Like a child, perhaps, like a sister, like an image of something safe and good and simple but not – not like a man and a woman on equal terms!'

Isobel turned her face away. She was shaking. 'What did you do?'

'I had to tell her, didn't I? I had to tell her, straight out, that I had a profound affection for her, that I would always value her friendship and concern myself with her happiness – *you* know, Isobel! All the dreadful, wicked platitudes that mean nothing, that nobody wants to hear! And all the time she stood and looked at me, getting paler and smaller by the second. I can see her now, standing under some hideous palm thing, looking at me as if I were a murderer. And I could see the hope draining out of her like blood. I wanted to strangle myself, cut my throat, anything! But I couldn't, I couldn't—'

'Couldn't what?'

'I couldn't agree to what she wanted. I couldn't agree to take her away just because I was fond of her and sorry for her!'

Isobel turned back to look at him. She licked her dry lips. 'Beware of pity—'

'Yes!' Patrick shouted. 'Yes! Yes, if that's all there is! Aren't you going to react? Aren't you going to tell me I'm a brute? Are you just going to sit there, like some damned Madonna, and look at me?'

Isobel lifted her hands from her lap and put them over her face. 'You aren't a brute. You're clumsy, but that's different.'

'Take your hands away,' Patrick demanded. 'I want to see your face. Did you know she was in love with me?'

'Yes,' Isobel said, obeying.

He groaned. He flung himself away from her and lay face down on the grass in the dappled shade.

'I walked her back to the station. She wouldn't even let me find her a glass of water. She wouldn't really talk any more. I got frantic. I kept on asking her things, offering her money to get away, or help in finding a place at an art school, and she wouldn't reply, but just kept walking, looking straight ahead of her. All she did say, at the very end, when I was finding her a seat on the train, was that everything was quite plain to her now.'

Isobel said, 'What did she mean?'

Patrick raised his head. 'I don't know. It could have meant anything. That men aren't to be trusted, or that Englishmen aren't, or that I'm not, or that I was simply amusing myself or deliberately trying to deceive her. I don't know, Isobel. All I do know is that I feel cruel and brutal and that I'm the person finally responsible for denying a future and freedom to an innocent girl trapped in a gruesome family and quite unable to exercise her considerable talent. I *am* a murderer.'

Isobel let a little pause fall, and then she said, 'No.'

'What do you mean, no?'

'*I* offered her the chance to come here, with me. She refused me. Because of you, because she preferred a future with you. But you weren't her only chance. Aunt Sybil offered her a chance, years ago, during the war, to break free, but she refused that too, and went back to her mother. I'm afraid,' Isobel said slowly, 'that Donatella might like being a victim.'

'Isobel!'

Isobel turned her head and looked at Patrick. Her gaze was quite clear. 'I think you are admirable to love her. I don't. I tried to, very hard, but I don't any more. In the end, I think, you can only love people who are going to give you some love in return. Loving without return isn't real love, it's just a selfish obsession, a kind of luxurious self-indulgence.'

He stared at her. 'Heavens.'

'She loved you because she knew you were sorry for her, as well as because she could trust you. But—'

'But what?'

'I did think you loved her. I thought she aroused everything protective in you and that you really wanted to make her happy.'

'I thought that too. Or, at least, I didn't *think*. Did I? I didn't really think until she forced me to, I just assumed – this is what I was going to say to you earlier – at some deep not very conscious level, that I could go on playing gallant Sir Galahad around Donatella whenever I felt like it. That she'd be here, looked after by you, and I could—' He stopped and then said harshly, 'I disgust myself.'

Isobel said softly, 'We all do that, at some time or other.'

Patrick stretched out a long arm and reached for Isobel's hand. 'Are you going to divorce Giovanni?'

She bent her head. 'I can't. He's a Catholic. It – it doesn't matter. I'm free here, in a way—'

'But not to marry again.'

'I don't think I want to be married again. It doesn't seem to be something I'm very good at.'

'Isobel—'

'Yes?' she said, gently disengaging her hand.

'Can I stay for a few days?'

'Of course.'

'Even if there's talk, in Fontebella? There's bound to be, somewhere as small as this.'

Isobel got slowly to her feet. 'I don't mind talk. What does it matter?'

Patrick rose too. He stood looking at her, her hand on the trunk of an olive tree, her back straight. He said abruptly, 'Why did you end up in Italy?'

She smiled. 'When my mother died, my father, who was living apart from us, asked me what I would like to do. I was ten, a very sheltered dull little girl of ten. Nobody had ever even asked me to choose a hair ribbon before, let alone where I would like to live. But my father asked me. Would I like to go and live with my mother's parents, whom I feared, or with my father's sisters, whom I didn't know? My grandparents lived in Lancashire, my aunts in Italy. I knew nothing about Italy, but it was, I did know, abroad, and I knew something about abroad. We used to go abroad, my mother and I, to Switzerland when she had one of her nervous collapses, and when I was there, I had a friend, a little Russian boy.

I think he was probably the only friend I had in my childhood, and I loved him in exactly the way I was describing just now, with a heavy, yearning, one-sided love. But he was my *friend*, and something in my mind then associated friendship with abroad. So I came, you see, to Italy.'

He watched her. He watched without smiling, but with an intent gaze and then, when she had finished he said seriously, 'And did you find a friend?'

She looked confused. She reached up and broke off a twig from the branch above her. 'I – I don't know. In a way, yes, because I loved my aunts and my tutor and liked some of the people I played tennis with. I – I think I hoped Donatella would be a friend, you see, that I could rescue her as, in a way, that little Russian boy rescued me. From myself, from being with myself. But perhaps friendship isn't like that, it isn't just a knack or a charm or a twist of fate, it's more a sympathy that's very rare, very hard to find—' She broke off and looked at him. 'Have you got a friend?'

'Yes,' he said, rumpling his hair.

'Oh.'

'Yes,' he said, reaching out again for her hand. 'Yes. And so have you.'

Chapter Thirty-three

Patrick stayed for a week. In the course of it he taught Mario a Gilbert and Sullivan pirate's song, painted a mural on the kitchen wall of a Tuscan landscape that had Emilia speechless with admiration, and talked to Isobel. He told her of his strange, interesting, wandering childhood, and of his adored brother and of his parents' marriage, a union so intense that it had seemed, at times, to have no room in it for children.

'I think that's why my mother was so especially stricken when my brother died. I think she felt she hadn't looked at him enough, noticed and valued him enough. My father is very greedy, you see, he eats up all the emotion round him that he can get, starting with hers.'

He told her of his troubles at school, and all the peculiar, uncomfortable places they had lived in and his parents' staunch defence of his own lack of convention when it offended those in authority. He listened, too. He made Isobel tell him the story of her courtship and marriage, he made her talk to him about Gianni and he made it, almost more importantly than anything, possible for her to admit her disappointment at the failure of her relationship with Giovanni and her pain at the feud between herself and Aunt Jean. Then he said, 'What about *your* family?'

Isobel was weeding between the stones of the courtyard with a broken kitchen knife.

'I haven't really got any.'

'What about your father?'

Isobel sighed. She sat back on her heels and tipped the straw hat off her forehead. 'I don't see him.'

'I know you don't. But don't you write to each other?'

'No. Not really.'

'Why not?'

'I don't know. We never have. He's a nice man but he doesn't like to be bothered, certainly not with emotional things. All the time I was growing up, the aunts wrote and kept him in touch. He's got his own family, you see.'

Patrick, who was sitting on the rim of the well-head, sketching the battlements and the single remaining old tower, outlined against the sky, said, 'But they're your family.'

'No, they're not,' Isobel said stubbornly. 'They're his. He left my mother to marry this Muriel woman and those children are theirs.'

Patrick said nothing for a few moments. Isobel bent forward again and jabbed her knife into the dusty crack between two paving stones.

'If you had been in your father's place,' Patrick said, almost carelessly, his eyes fixed on the battlements, 'would you have stayed with your mother?'

Isobel glared at him. 'What's that got to do with anything?'

'I just wondered about trying to put yourself in your father's place. As a sort of exercise. After all, anybody with half an eye can see that my mother is a nicer person than my father, but that doesn't mean that he doesn't have a point of view, or that we don't have some sympathy for it. Anyway, what about your half-brothers and sister?'

'They're not—'

'They are,' Patrick said, still calmly, even if he was interrupting. 'They are your father's children, so they are your brothers and sister.'

Isobel said nothing. She pulled out a tough little clump of wiry grass and threw it into her trug. 'Aunt Jean is going to give them the Villa Calvina.'

'Where you grew up.'

'Yes.'

Patrick said, 'What are their names?'

'I don't think of them by their names.'

Patrick put his sketchpad down. He climbed off the well so that he could crouch on the stones beside Isobel. She bent her head right down so that he couldn't see her face under her hat brim.

'You're sulking.'

She said nothing. He reached out and tilted her hat brim up. Her face was set.

'Isobel. For perfectly understandable reasons, you tried to be part of an Italian family. It didn't work. Why punish yourself by refusing, on top of all this, to have anything to do with your real family? What are those children's *names*, for God's sake?'

'Angus,' Isobel said.

'And?'

'Robert. And Flora.'

'Angus and Robert and Flora. How old are they?'

'I don't know.'

'Isobel,' Patrick said, 'if you don't stop this, I shall put you over my knee and smack you, in full view of Emilia and Mario and Giuseppe and Ulysse. How old are they?'

'About fourteen, I should think. Or fifteen. And twelve. And maybe nine.'

'Have you got photographs?'

'No.' She looked at him. She didn't look defiant any more, only sad. 'He didn't want me to live with him, you see. He had an excuse because my mother had specified in her will that I wasn't to be brought up by Muriel, but all the same, he didn't want me. He was thankful for the aunts to have me, and they did want me, they really did.'

Patrick reached out again and touched Isobel's cheek. 'It's the next step, you know, really it is.'

'What—'

'Letting go of all the pains and grievances of the past and starting again. Seeing that just because something didn't work in the past isn't a reason for it not working now. You can't live here, Isobel Lindsay, in this magic castle all alone until you are old and grey. It's a perfect landscape, certainly, but landscapes need people in them to come alive. You'll get lonely and turned inward. You'll waste yourself.' He paused and then got stiffly to his feet. 'Enough lecturing. All I can tell you is that if you don't get to know your own family, you're a damned fool.'

Two days later, he left Fontebella. Dressed in the loose, crumpled linen shirt and trousers and jacket in which he had come, and carrying his painting things in an Italian workman's canvas bag, he tramped down the rock on an early August morning, on his way to the station, while Mario wept inconsolably in the kitchen and Isobel tried hard not to imitate him. Two of Patrick's commissions were on the Italian lakes, and another three in Venice. He would be gone a couple of months, and at the end of those, he might go back to England for a while, even, maybe, for the winter. He couldn't decide now, he said and, in any case, he wasn't very good at making plans.

'I know,' Isobel said.

She had got up even earlier than usual to breakfast with him, and was taken aback to find how powerfully she didn't want him to go. She remembered, and not without a pang, saying goodbye to Giovanni in 1915 and feeling that both the beloved and her chance of freedom were going away together, leaving her desolate. This was rather different. She had her freedom now, her hard-won freedom that had left her so battlescarred, and Patrick represented something so very different from Giovanni, something so – Isobel swallowed hard and checked herself. She held out the basket of new bread that Emilia had gone down to collect from the baker shortly after dawn.

'More?'

Patrick shook his head, smiling. Emilia had made him the kind of picnic Italian mothers made for sons going off to seek work in towns ten miles distant from home; a whole salami, a great piece of cheese, a loaf, a handful of dried apricots in a screw of paper, another of olives.

'I shall be eating all the way to Lake Garda.'

He had kissed Isobel goodbye. Standing in the hall of the castle, on the marble squares which now shone with Emilia's attention, he had put his arms around her and held her and kissed her cheeks and her forehead. Then he said, 'Isobel, you do me good,' and went off, whistling, into the sunlight, with his bags and bundles and Gino beside him, to help carry. Isobel and Mario watched from the kitchen window until the tall, untidy, flapping figure had disappeared into the market place and was lost to their view. Then Isobel picked up the sobbing child and went across to the chair by the table and sat down, holding Mario on her knee.

'Sing to me.'

'No!' wailed Mario, pushing his fists in his eyes. 'No, no, no!'

'Sing me your pirate song and then—'

She paused. Mario paused too, in his crying, at the sound of 'and then . . .'

'And then,' said Isobel, 'you shall have a spoonful of jam.'

Mario looked at her. He considered this. Then he gave a huge and shuddering sigh, and opened his mouth. '*It is, it is a glorious*

284

thing,' sang Mario unsteadily in the English he scarcely understood, '*to be a Pirate King!*' and then, remembering Patrick, he burst into tears again, and buried his face in Isobel's neck.

The days that followed seemed unnaturally quiet. There was no shortage of things to be done, as usual, among them planning the roof garden Isobel intended to make where the cornfield had so cheerfully blown behind the battlements, and a second garden on the first terrace of land directly below the breach in the courtyard wall, but the life seemed to have temporarily gone out of the place. She had, she told herself, too much to miss and too much to think about, and too few distractions. She missed speaking English, she missed having a companion while she did the most ordinary things, while she ate meals, she missed Patrick's steady and not uncritical sympathy. She could not divert herself, by talking to him, from thinking about all the issues he had come whirling into the castle with, like an autumn storm full of leaves – Donatella, Giovanni's plans to sell La Crocetta, her father and his family, her future. She had to think about these things, both to come to terms with them and to make decisions. It was not enough, Patrick had made her see, simply to run away, even if that running away had been the right thing to do, the positive thing. 'Don't waste yourself,' he'd said and then, as he was leaving, 'You do me good.'

Oh, and how true that was, the other way about! What confidence he'd given her, in that short week. He never assumed – had never assumed throughout this new friendship of theirs – that she couldn't decide things, that she wasn't, in some way, fit to know what was right for her. His own rambling disordered life, which had no truck with outward polish and social details, was firmly founded on strong principles of loyal, honest, human behaviour. Malice or cruelty, Isobel thought, were as foreign to him as remembering to shave or eat regularly or be punctual or get his clothes pressed. Donatella had seen that. More, Donatella had relied upon it.

Sitting on the stone window seat of her *salone* in the evenings to watch the wonderful, rich, late summer sunsets blaze behind the darkening hills and cypress trees, Isobel could acknowledge to herself now that she had been jealous of Donatella; jealous of her early perception about Patrick, jealous of her quiet hold over him, jealous of his singling out of her. Now Isobel was free of the jealousy – freed by Patrick's honesty – and in retrospect, she was ashamed of it. From a grateful heart, she vowed that she would write to

Donatella. But about what? Was Donatella, after the failure and humiliation of her proposal to Patrick, likely to want to have anything to do with Isobel? 'Everything is quite plain to me now,' Donatella had said to Patrick as her parting shot. Isobel hadn't, at first, known what she could have meant, but now, on reflection, she knew. Donatella, trained all those years, even if only at a subconscious level, by her mother to regard anyone who did not submit to the Fosco family as an enemy, now saw Isobel as one. If Patrick did not want to marry her, it could only be because Isobel was to blame, Isobel who had, as the Marchesa was so fond of saying, destroyed her children.

It was horrible to realize this deeply-believed injustice, but it had to be borne, just as Aunt Jean's refusal to see her had to be borne and also the strangely disquieting news that Giovanni was thinking of selling La Crocetta. Of course, she had given it to him, had even herself, wild with emotion, told him to sell it if he wanted to, but somehow hearing that he was planning to do that, only months after her departure, was disturbing. It not only seemed to underline everything that was weak and lazy and greedy in Giovanni, and thus emphasize Isobel's terrible folly in marrying him, but it also, and this was more painful, seemed to deny, once and for all, the dream they had shared together, young and idealistic, of a model estate whose benefits stretched out to enfold all who came in contact with it. If Giovanni was going to give up the game the minute he couldn't play it with someone else's money, it made their early vision, those heartfelt conversations walking through Florence, or over ices in Doney's, seem not only silly and flimsy, but tawdry.

Patrick had said she had to come to terms with the past, accept it. He had made her feel that the mistakes she'd made in life, or other people's mistakes that had affected her, were not to be lugged about after her like some ball and chain, slowing her down. It was plain that he felt real, deep remorse for allowing Donatella to believe he loved her, but he wasn't going to wear that remorse for ever, like a hair shirt, in order that people should see it, he was instead going to make sure he never, however unconsciously, allowed anyone to delude themselves about his feelings again. She should do the same. She should accept the Foscos' responsibility for the failure of her marriage, instead of being inclined to feel it was all her fault for marrying Giovanni in the first place. She should feel that Aunt Jean had a responsibility to consider giving forgiveness quite as much as she had one to ask for it for causing pain. And as for her father . . . Isobel looked away from the lovely, burning

286

sky and into the soft, dark depths of the *salone*. What of her father? If he had been to blame for leaving her, not wanting her perhaps out of idleness and awkwardness, rather than because of lack of love, was she now to blame for not even trying to understand him? If Ida, all those years ago, had so successfully instilled in Isobel all those habits of guilt and inadequacy, what had she done – or tried to do – to Edward? And what of Ida herself, saddled with her dangerous fortune and parents who wished her never, ever, to grow up?

Isobel got off the windowseat and padded in bare feet across the *salone* to the door to the courtyard. A great moon had swung up already, from the east, a great yellow moon in the dusky blue sky, and by midnight, the light in the courtyard would be almost strong enough to read by. Isobel breathed deeply. The air smelled of the hay Gino had cut that day, and the tobacco flowers, and across the courtyard, the kitchen windows glowed golden in the lamplight and against the light, Isobel could see the little figure of Mario and the larger one of Emilia, companionably eating their supper together. They would be talking, Isobel knew, the tiny child and his mother, because they talked all the time they were together with a great companionableness. Isobel stood looking at them for a long time, her hand on the warm stone of the door lintel, and then, with a sigh she wasn't conscious of giving, withdrew into her room.

She lit her own lamp. Emilia cleaned the lamps meticulously every day as if she could, by emphatic attention to them, silently point out to Isobel what a blessing electricity would be. Isobel knew it would be and she knew she would one day succumb to it, but for the moment she loved her castle softly lit by lamps, and the sight at night time of a lamp being carried up the great stone outdoor staircase to bed, throwing up dancing shadows across its vaulted roof.

She put her lamp down on her desk. It was a real desk, made of rosewood, which Uncle Ulysse's wife's nephew had spotted on a trip to Bergamo, and which he had brought back, with a truckful of piglets for himself, on the off chance that the English *padrona* might like it. She had. It was eighteenth-century with a patina the colour of tea, deep and shining, and tens of little drawers with tiny brass handles. The desk was very neat. Isobel's bills – oh, the unending joy of knowing that there would no longer be a nasty surprise among the bills – lay at one side, clipped together by a clothespeg begged from Emilia, and her receipts beside them. The other side was a neat pile of estimates and, in between, a porcelain hairpin tray, painted with birds of paradise, which Isobel used for pens and pencils. The sight of her desk always pleased Isobel. It was a symbol of her own control over her life.

She opened a drawer and took out a sheet of white writing paper, and then another for a white envelope lined with dark blue tissue. She considered the date. In four days' time, her father and his family would be arriving at the Villa Calvina and would be seeing it with the interested eyes of those to whom it would one day belong. Isobel shook herself. She could only live in one place, and if she had to choose, that place was, without question, Fontebella. She leaned forward and selected a pen and dipped it in a pot of black ink.

'La Fortezza, Fontebella,' she wrote at the top. 'August 5th.'

Then she paused. Two moths flew inside the glass globe of the lamp and began their helpless dance of death inside it. Isobel took a breath.

'Dear Aunt Jean,' she wrote, 'I beg you please, please, not to throw away this letter unanswered. I want to ask you, from the bottom of my heart, to help me heal the rift between us.'

She stopped and put her pen down. She looked at her letter. She had, over the past few years, written a dozen letters that began like this. Slowly and sadly, Isobel picked the sheet of paper up and tore it, across and across, and dropped the pieces on the floor.

Chapter Thirty-four

'I am looking,' a precise male voice said in Anglicized Italian, 'for the Marchesa Fosco.'

Isobel, above the courtyard in the future battlement garden, froze. It was a warm overcast day, quite still, and the voice was as clear as if it were beside her, rather than fifty feet below.

Emilia said something indistinct.

'I believe I have the right address, have I not?' the voice went on. 'This is the Fortezza di Fontebella, the castle?'

'*Si*,' Emilia said.

'Then I am correct, I believe, in asking for the Marchesa Fosco here.'

Emilia burst into rapid speech. There was only her *padrona* here, an English lady called Signora Lindsay, no aristocrats, no Italians . . .

'But the Marchesa Fosco is an Englishwoman,' the voice said, formal still but now with a trace of impatience. 'She is an Englishwoman whose maiden name was Lindsay, and whom I seek.'

Emilia said nothing. There was a space of perhaps ten seconds and then the voice said with more than an edge of command to it, 'I am the British Consul, the British Consul from Florence. Here is my card. Would you please present it to your mistress?'

'*Si*,' Emilia said, defeated. She was probably, Isobel thought, dropping a curtsey. She considered going down, and decided against it as it would reveal she had been able to hear every word. Instead, she watched Emilia running across the courtyard towards the staircase, a scrap of pasteboard shining white in her hand. The British Consul! What had he come for? Panic clutched her. Aunt Jean, could it be that Aunt Jean was ill, or worse, dead? She straightened her shoulders. Emilia, who hated the battlements because she said the height made her dizzy, was scuttling round towards Isobel shielding her eyes from the view with her hand.

'*Padrona! Padrona!*'

Isobel came forward. 'Someone's come—'

'The English Consul! From Florence!' She thrust the calling card at Isobel. 'He asked for the Marchesa Fosco!'

Isobel looked at the card. 'Major Gregory Ramsay,' it said, 'British Consul General. Via Tornabuoni 2-4, Florence. Italy.'

'I will come down.'

'He is so tall!' Emilia said, 'almost as tall as the Signor Fleming! And he has a moustache like little wings!'

Isobel looked down into the courtyard. A man had emerged into it, a tall, thin man in a well-cut, slightly waisted grey flannel suit. He also wore spats, a trim panama hat and carried, in one hand, a pair of pale grey gloves. Isobel looked down at herself. She had on her usual old cord breeches, a faded linen shirt that had once been blue and was now closer to grey, and a gardening apron, its pockets stuffed with rolls of twine and marking pegs. She hadn't put her hair up properly that morning either, but had simply piled it on top of her head and crammed her tattered straw hat on top, to keep it in place.

'Just look at me!' Isobel said to Emilia.

Emilia looked, rather helplessly.

'I can't go down like this!' Isobel peered over the inner battlement wall again at Major Ramsay. 'But I can't keep him waiting either. Better to go down just as I am, I think, even if it does give him a fright. Emilia, will you make coffee and lemonade? I shall take him into the *salone*. What in heaven's name can he have come for?'

Emilia nodded. Mario had strayed out of the kitchen to stare at the stranger, driven by his quite insatiable curiosity, but something about the tall, impeccable, pearl-grey person by the well deterred him from skipping up, as was his cheerful wont, and demanding to know why he was there. Isobel walked swiftly around the battlements and down the staircase. Major Ramsay watched her, incuriously at first, supposing her to be a servant and then with some considerable surprise. He was used, naturally, to expatriate Englishwomen in Italy being suitably interested in their gardens, but he was not used to them being dressed in such a way as to prove that they actually laboured in them.

'Major Ramsay,' Isobel said, coming forward and smiling, with her hand outstretched.

He took her hand and gave a small, stiff bow. 'Marchesa. Forgive an unannounced visit.'

'Perhaps you will come to the *salone*.'

He bowed again. He was very, *very* stiff, Isobel thought, like a toy soldier, with his ramrod back and uncreased clothes. She took off her hat and apron and laid them on the well-head, and then, with a piece of twine from her breeches pocket, tied her hair back at the nape of her neck. He watched her with a mixture of amazement and embarrassment. The contrast between his appearance and hers made her want to laugh. As she led the way across the courtyard, Mario tiptoed stealthily in their wake, his eyes fixed upon the consul. Isobel ushered the major into the *salone*, holding out her hand for his hat and gloves.

'Do please sit down.'

Mario jigged in the doorway, his eyes like saucers. 'Who is this man? What are you saying?'

Isobel bent towards him. 'He's a very important Englishman,' she whispered.

'A *policeman*?'

'No. Not quite. Now, go back to the kitchen like a good boy.' She closed the door gently on Mario's eager face. 'My housekeeper's son. He's as inquisitive as a kitten.'

Major Ramsay gave a small grunt, to indicate that he had heard, but that he had no comment to make. Instead, he said, 'You have found yourself a most unusual dwelling, Marchesa.'

Isobel flinched a little. She laid the hat and gloves carefully on a side table. 'Yes. It's lovely, isn't it? The mayor and Commune agreed to lease it to me.'

'So I believe.'

'Oh?'

'I have been,' Major Ramsay said imperturbably, 'to visit the mayor already this morning. I came up from Florence very early.'

The door opened and Emilia came in with a tall pot of coffee and a pitcher of lemonade. Major Ramsay accepted coffee and Isobel's only armchair. She poured herself a glass of lemonade, and took it over to the window seat.

'As I said,' Major Ramsay said, stirring his coffee, 'I apologize for an unannounced visit. I assure you that it isn't a consular custom to arrive without warning and I only do so today because I was particularly requested to do so.'

'By whom?' Isobel demanded.

'By your husband, Marchesa. He was most anxious that I should speak to you. He felt that you might refuse to see him but that I, being your representative here, might at least be granted a hearing.'

Isobel put her glass down. Her hand shook, and some lemonade flew out inadvertently and splashed over her. Distractedly, she mopped at the spill with the tail of her shirt.

'Why should I not be here if you had telegraphed or written to make an appointment?'

'The Marchese felt,' Major Ramsay said, with less confidence, 'that as you had plainly wished to keep knowledge of your whereabouts from him, you might also decline to see me.'

Isobel lifted her chin. 'And why is it so urgent that you should see me, on my husband's behalf?'

Major Ramsay put his coffee cup down. He sat even taller and straighter in his chair and his face was very grave.

'The Marchese Fosco, Marchesa, has asked me to come to you as intermediary to tell you that he wishes your marriage to be annulled.'

Before she could stop herself, Isobel had gasped. 'Annulled!'

'Yes, Marchesa.'

'Do stop calling me Marchesa! But you cannot simply annul a marriage that took place in church and of which – of which there was a child!'

'It seems that the marriage was not entirely legal, in the eyes of the Catholic Church. There is the difficulty, you see, of your being a Protestant and demonstrating no willingness to convert. How am I to address you, madam, if I may not address you by your proper title?'

'Miss Lindsay.'

'You see,' Major Ramsay went on, more smoothly now and gaining confidence, 'this refusal to use your title, your married name, adds further weight to your husband's wishes. I believe that you are known in this town by the name of Lindsay, that the lease on the *fortezza* is signed in the name of Lindsay, and that you have closed your account with Maquay's Bank and opened another, with French, Lemon & Co, also in the name of Lindsay. None of this indicates, the Marchese feels, much desire to remain associated with either himself or his family, and on these grounds he urges you to agree to an annulment.'

Isobel put her shaking hands in her lap and pressed them hard together. 'How did you discover all these things?'

'Miss Lindsay, there has been no deception, I do assure you. No conspiracy. I believe your sister-in-law had not only your address but a pressing invitation to join you here. Maquay's Bank could hardly deny that you had closed your account and the mayor in this town has cheques in settlement of your lease written upon your new account. I am extremely sorry to distress you. In view of your evident wish to distance yourself from the Fosco family, I had supposed my news might not be unwelcome.'

Isobel looked out of the window. The sky was soft and dove-coloured and the grey light had drained the colour out of the landscape, leaving it merely a series of monochrome shapes. It wasn't the news that was so unwelcome, it was the manner of it, and the implications. It frightened her, for some reason, to feel that Giovanni was asserting the upper hand, and it dismayed her in a way she could have explained to nobody, that he wished to pretend to the world that their marriage had never existed, that he could simply rub it out and turn to a fresh page. That's what to annul meant, didn't it? To reduce to nothing, to abolish, to empty something of its significance. It was horrible, somehow, to think of all those hopes and dreams, all that effort and struggle, all that love, as well as despair, and above all, that beloved baby, being eliminated, as if they had never happened, as if they had never had any value. Isobel felt quite choked by the pain and outrage of what Giovanni was asking.

She took a deep breath and said, not as steadily as she could have wished, 'I do indeed wish to distance myself from the Fosco family, but it is painful and – and wrong, I feel, to have it done in this way. It seems to me that an annulment cruelly invalidates – everything that has happened, good as well as bad.'

Major Ramsay looked, for a fleeting second, as if he sympathized and then he said, with ill-disguised distaste, 'Of course, there is another solution.'

She looked up.

'It is plain, you see, that both you and your husband wish for your freedom. Your husband wishes to take advantage of the new laws to develop agricultural land on State subsidies—'

'*Fascist* laws?'

'Yes, Miss Lindsay. It should not be news to you that your husband is a supporter of Mussolini. The fascist government, as you know, is no lover of foreigners and the grants and subsidies

293

available for an estate such as La Crocetta would be affected to a considerable degree by whether the ownership of the estate was Italian/English, or purely Italian. As I was saying, however, there is another, though less, shall we say, agreeable solution to your dilemma if, of course, you have finally decided that your marriage to the Marchese Fosco is over?'

'Oh, I have—'

'In that case,' Major Ramsay said, putting the tips of his fingers together and staring over them past Isobel at the grey sky, 'your husband suggests that you allow him to divorce you on the grounds first, that your marriage was not fully recognized by the Catholic Church, and second—' he paused, and then said clearly and coldly, 'on the grounds of your relationship with Mr Patrick Fleming.'

Isobel flew up from the windowseat. 'What grounds?'

Major Ramsay's gaze never flickered. 'Adulterous grounds, Miss Lindsay.'

She was aghast. 'But it's lies, lies! I've never – we are simply – Major Ramsay, this is a monstrous fabrication, it's completely untrue!'

He inclined his head. 'The Marchese seemed very certain. I believe he has implicit trust in his sister.'

Isobel stared at him. Donatella! Donatella had gone back to La Crocetta after her afternoon in the Botanical Gardens with Patrick and had . . . Isobel shut her eyes.

'Might I advise you, Miss Lindsay?'

She nodded, hardly hearing him.

'One of the reasons that I was grateful to be asked to come and see you, much though I dislike being the bearer of bad news, is because of our position here. By our, I mean we English. Of course, I am fully aware of how long you have lived in Italy, and thus how well you know the country and its people, but we are, however long we live here, foreigners, and as such both conspicuous and bound to behave both with tact and circumspection. I can't hide from you, I fear, the fact that the Fosco affair is, just now, the talk of Florence. It is extremely unpleasant, especially at a time when Italy's mounting sense of nationalism is not making her feel especially tolerant towards foreigners. Whatever the rights and wrongs of your situation, Miss Lindsay, I am bound to tell you that a scandalous divorce – and how could it be otherwise? – would only add fuel to the flames and make the position of the English community here very difficult indeed.'

Isobel sat down again, on the windowseat. She drew a long,

shuddering breath. What Giovanni was doing, in fact, was not only demanding that their years together be officially as forgotten as if they had never been, but that he should be allowed to step out into his new life, as a landowning loyal follower of Mussolini, his estate financed by the government and his moral reputation without spot or stain. The alternative to agreeing to this lie was to agree to a much worse one. She looked at Major Ramsay.

She said, so quietly that he had to lean forward to catch her words, 'Then I must agree.'

'I am much relieved. I'm afraid that you will be in the hands of those who administer the canon law of the Catholic Church, but I am sure there will be nothing much more involved than a few signatures. The church itself, after all, hardly wishes to advertise either the fact of a mixed marriage, nor its subsequent failure.'

'Major Ramsay—'

'Yes?'

'Why did you go to see the mayor?'

He said carefully, 'In my position, Miss Lindsay, it is extremely important to verify statements that are made about the English community here who are, after all, in my care. The Marchese had supplied me with a great deal of information but, with all due respect, I had to know all the facts for myself. I applied to the mayor, not least for proof of your living here in the castle, but also about Mr Fleming who is, I believe, a familiar figure in the streets of Fontebella. I may say, to be perfectly open with you, that I attempted to call upon your aunt, Mrs Fanshawe, but she was engaged in entertaining a family party.'

Isobel suddenly could not bear having Major Ramsay sitting there a moment longer, uttering his precise and stately sentences, keeping his feelings – if indeed, he had any – well hidden beneath his grey flannel exterior.

She stood up. 'Have you anything further to say to me?'

Major Ramsay rose too. He said, 'Nothing further, Miss Lindsay, except—'

'Except what?'

'It was my impression, Miss Lindsay, speaking to the mayor this morning, that he was a little dismayed by the notion of any impending – shall we say, notoriety?'

'What do you mean?'

Major Ramsay smoothed the twin dark curves of his moustache with a well-kept hand. 'Living up here, you are not perhaps aware of gossip in Fontebella. But not only has news of your husband's wishes filtered up here from Florence, but it was plainly observed by the local people that Mr Fleming was here at the castle as your unchaperoned guest.'

Isobel was almost beyond being outraged. She simply said, sharply, 'And so?'

'The mayor is a loyal and ambitious member of the Fascist party, Miss Lindsay. He is also intensely proud of Fontebella and her reputation. He would, I cannot conceal from you, take steps to terminate the lease on the town's showpiece if he felt that the leaseholder was in any way exploiting Italian hospitality. We are back, you see, to a fierce and growing nationalism that has, as one of its least attractive component parts, a strong xenophobia.'

The room seemed to swim, very slightly, around Isobel. She went, as steadily as she could, across to the side table and picked up the major's hat and gloves. She held them out to him.

'Good morning, Major Ramsay.'

He bowed again. 'I am grateful to you for seeing me, Miss Lindsay.'

She inclined her head. There was, quite simply, nothing more to say – nothing that was at all suitable for the consul's decorous ears. She opened the door to the courtyard and ushered the major out to where Mario stood, brandishing a big wooden spoon like a sword, as if he wished ardently to defend Isobel with it, with all his small, excitable might.

Chapter Thirty-five

Isobel dressed very carefully. She put on a sleeveless summer dress which Emilia's mother had made her, of dark blue lawn patterned with cream chrysanthemums, its handkerchief-pointed hem caught up at one side with a knot of dark blue ribbon. She brushed her hair thoroughly, coiled it up under a cream straw hat acquired especially for the occasion, the brim circled with more dark blue ribbon and a long, plumy ostrich feather which Mario had extravagantly admired. She added cream shoes with Louis heels, cream gloves, pearl earrings and a tiny handbag on a chain. Then she went down to the kitchen.

'How do I look?'

'Beautiful!' cried Mario, jumping up and down and waving a carrot. 'Beautiful, beautiful!'

'Very nice,' Emilia said.

'But do I look respectable?'

'Respectable?'

'Yes. Do I look like an English lady with a very good reputation and high morals?'

'Of course!' Emilia said, much shocked. 'How could I work for a person who was not those things?'

'Thank you,' Isobel said. 'I can hardly remember how to walk in these shoes. Your mother has made my dress beautifully.'

'Of course,' Emilia said reprovingly, 'she is an excellent dress-maker. Very high class.'

Isobel went out into the courtyard. The sun was high and hot. She should have remembered to buy a parasol, to complete her image of a profoundly respectable lady. The courtyard looked beautiful. Only a few warm months, and the fragile blue flowers of plumbago were already climbing up the stone staircase, and the white geraniums by the well-head had spilled over into a waterfall of luxuriant, peppery-smelling bloom. The weeds had gone, the new roses were climbing and climbing, and the pots of herbs, terracotta pots with bas-reliefs of swags of flowers and leaves round their sides, were burgeoning. Isobel had been offered, by yet another relation of Emilia's, the statue of a graceful girl, about five feet high, with a poignantly broken nose and a little harp in her hand. She stood across the courtyard now, her feet almost lost in the fronds of dark green jasmine leaves, silhouetted against one of the dark arched spaces of the loggia. How could I bear to leave this, Isobel thought, how could I even contemplate the thought of being turned out of this for being the kind of person I'm not and never will be, and for something I haven't done?

She went carefully across the courtyard to the terrace, tiptoeing on her unaccustomed heels. The terrace was paved now, round its stone seat, and Giuseppe had discovered from somewhere – he merely grinned when asked exactly where – several yards of lovely worn old stone balustrading which now stood, as if it had stood there for centuries, at the edge of the drop above the new steps down to the *podere*. Isobel leaned her hands on it and looked down. There below her were her vines in their promising rows, her vegetables, her olive grove, her beehive – just where she had imagined it with its straw dome tucked cosily into an angle between two of the castle's ancient buttresses – and the two strips of brown plough where Gino planned to plant wheat and maize. He was talking of a cow next spring and a goat or two. Isobel longed for a cow. She gazed down at the lovely harmony and promise of it all and while she watched, as if to set the seal of perfection upon it all, one of the red-brown hens that Gino kept in the olive grove emerged from among the vines and began, in its decorative, domestic way, to cluck about in the grass directly below Isobel, chestnut feathered and red-combed in the summer green.

'I can't give it up!' Isobel said out loud. 'I can't! I won't!'

The hen looked up towards her, sideways, unable to see her quite, but conscious of the sound of her voice.

'Not this!' Isobel shouted. She looked down directly at the hen. 'Not you!'

*   *   *

She took the shortest cut to the town hall, through the piazza. Several of the stallholders knew her now, and were courteously accustomed to the eccentricity of her clothes, so there was much appreciative murmuring as Isobel, dressed in a frock and hat and gloves, walked among the shining piles of aubergines and peppers and tomatoes, and through – much consternation among the spectators here at the sight of those cream-coloured, Louis-heeled shoes – the distinctly unshining piles of vegetable rubbish on the cobbles. People called out to her, and Isobel smiled and nodded. She paused by the fountain where several women were, as usual, washing eggs and fennel bulbs clean before piling them up for sale, and laid her hand on the tail of her favourite dolphin, favourite because a carelessly flung stone had once, in the course of an ancient riot, struck him on the side of his head, causing a dent beside his mouth which made him look as if he were smiling broadly.

'Please,' Isobel said silently and fervently to the dolphin, 'please, oh please—'

The dolphin went on smiling. A pigeon sat, also apparently smiling, on his head, a carefree pigeon whose lack of anxiety Isobel envied passionately at this moment. She gave them both a last, pleading glance, and walked on towards the town hall.

It was a newish building, perhaps not more than twenty years old, and built, unlike the rest of charming, medieval Fontebella, in the most grandiose and ornate of tastes. It reminded Isobel powerfully and unpleasantly of the equally grandiose pink bedroom the Marchesa had made for her at La Crocetta. Fontebella's old town hall, the Palazzo Vecchio, a beautiful building of tiny russet bricks and with swallow-tailed battlemented towers, was destined to be an art gallery and museum. The Commune had decided that twenty years ago, when they had also decided that they preferred to visualize themselves in a new setting, with a white plastered portico and a façade heavy with columns and statues and bas-relief medallions of past great sons of Fontebella. The new town hall had been built at once, the old one remained locked and barred, its ancient rooms filled only with cobwebs and ghosts, its promised purpose apparently quite forgotten.

Isobel went up the pink marble steps, through the immense, almost imperial door, and into a central hall that resembled a Victorian railway station. A clerk in a dingy black suit – the clerk she had encountered every morning when she had come to collect the key for the castle – sat at a desk at one side peering at piles of dockets and receipts through tiny spectacles. He stood up when

Isobel came in, but his expression did not change. As far as he was concerned, this odd Englishwoman merely represented more paperwork for him, more dockets, more receipts.

'Signor Finzi,' Isobel said, smiling broadly and deliberately, 'good morning!'

Signor Finzi sighed and mumbled.

'Signor Moresco is expecting me.'

Signor Finzi nodded. He had shown, it seemed to him, this persistent signora in and out of the mayor's office in the last few months with the regularity of the cuckoo in the clock his sister had brought him from Switzerland. It was a kind thought of his sister's, but the cuckoo was quietly driving him mad. He thought, sighing, that Signora Lindsay or the Marchesa Fosco, or whatever she was, was shortly about to imitate the cuckoo.

'This way,' he said tiredly.

Isobel followed him obediently, as she had followed him a dozen times before, up the marble and gilded staircase from the main hall, past immense eighteenth-century canvases of allegorical scenes full of pink clouds and limbs and rolling-eyed satyrs, to a first floor gallery along which a hideous imitation Turkey carpet rolled, strident scarlet and blue and green. The mayor's office had double doors and a brass plate a foot square. Signor Finzi put his ear to the door, sighed again, and knocked. Then he opened the right-hand half for Isobel and, with an air of resignation, stood aside for her to enter.

The mayor was not at his desk. He had been standing by the window as Isobel came in, contemplating the activity down in the market and considering how he was going to change things for the people of Fontebella in accordance with these new directives about improved agricultural life – the *bonifica agraria* – that were coming thick and fast from the government. The mayor was anxious to obey these directives, to attract the notice of senior local party officials who might – who knows? one can always daydream – in turn tell other officials, higher and higher up the ladder until his name, Marco Giuseppe Moresco, Mayor of Fontebella, was mentioned warmly to the great Mussolini himself. The mayor revered Mussolini. A huge framed photograph – framed as if it were a painted portrait – of the fascist leader hung here in his office, in the place of honour. The mayor turned as Isobel came in.

'Signora Lindsay. Good morning.' He held out his hand.

Isobel, taking it, thought his smile was not as warm as usual or, at least, not as egregious.

'Signor Moresco.'

He waved her to a chair. It was the chair in which the British Consul General to Florence had sat only a week before. Whatever one felt about the English, Signor Moresco had thought, regarding his visitor, one could only admire their tailoring. He had asked his wife, subsequent to that meeting, to enquire about the price of grey suede gloves.

'I am obliged to you for coming,' the mayor said, seating himself opposite Isobel.

Isobel waited. She put her cream shod feet together and her cream gloved hands together, and tried very hard to be calm.

'I believe, Signora, that you too had a visit from Major Ramsay?'

'I did.'

The mayor looked at her. His little black eyes were not, she thought, twinkling, but rather hard in their expression, hard and decided.

'It is a deeply unfortunate affair, Signora, this scandal that has broken over your marriage.'

Isobel's chin lifted a fraction. 'Not a scandal of my making, Signor Moresco.'

'I know nothing of the history, of course, and do not presume to, but this kind of affair involving a foreigner, Signora, is not good for Italy.'

Isobel said steadily, 'I must repeat, Signor, that the scandal is not of my making. I was legally married. I invested my own fortune in an Italian estate. The reasons for my leaving are not to be publicly known, for my husband's sake as well as for those of privacy and propriety, but they were reasons of unshakable validity. I am, Signor,' said Isobel vehemently, 'a woman of unquestionable principle!'

The mayor sighed. 'There is little that goes on in Fontebella that I do not know, Signora. Who comes, who goes, who stays where. We need not go into detail and thus distress ourselves, but there are elements of, shall we say, irregularity in your life among us here which do nothing, Signora, to help the spirit of pride and dignity that is presently rising among us here in Italy.'

Isobel said stoutly, 'I have done nothing wrong, Signor Moresco, nothing even unorthodox, nothing in fact that you would be dismayed at if your wife and daughter did!'

The mayor was outraged. He rose from his chair. 'Signora!'

'I'm sorry,' Isobel said, 'I'm sorry, I never meant to offend you, but you must believe me. You must believe that whatever horrible

301

rumours are being put about and believed, they are not true. Signor Fleming is a friend and no more. I'll say it again: he is a friend and *no more*. He had nothing whatever to do with my leaving my husband, *nothing*. I have reverted to my maiden name for reasons of mental and financial independence. I have lost a fortune at La Crocetta, Signor Moresco, a *fortune*. I came here because I fell in love with the castle and the place, and for no personal reason other than that. I came here to start a new life *on my own*.'

The mayor sat down again. He seemed to be pondering something. He sat, one fat hand on his knee, the other fingering the watch in his waistcoat pocket for several minutes, and then he said, slowly, 'All the same—'

Isobel leaned forward. 'All the same?'

'Signora Lindsay, I have my town to consider, my people. I have received a formal visit from the British Consul about you, and that has been noticed. The Commune agreed, as you remember, to lease you the *fortezza* for ten years. It is my regrettable duty now to tell you that we must terminate that lease now, at the end of this year. We must ask you, by New Year's day, to have vacated the castle.'

Isobel thought, I'm not hearing him, I'm not, I can't be, I can't be hearing him telling me that because of rumours that have no truth I have to leave the castle, not when I've done so much, not when I love it so, not when I *need* it . . . She closed her eyes briefly and then opened them.

She said, in a voice that shook despite all her efforts, 'Surely the lease is legally binding.'

'Upon you,' the mayor said, 'but because the *fortezza* is still the property of the Commune, not so strictly upon us. Try to see my position, Signora. The castle is, after our fountain, the great feature of Fontebella, a symbol for the people here—'

'Please don't say any more,' Isobel said, 'please don't. I really do not think I can bear it.'

'May I get you a glass of water?'

'No,' she said, rising, 'no thank you. I will simply go out for some air—' She paused. She looked at him. His face seemed to be quivering slightly, and so did his body, and now she came to look at them, so did his chair and the window behind him. It was, suddenly, impossible to be in that room a second longer, let alone to try and think in it.

'Excuse me,' Isobel said confusedly, 'good morning,' and then she turned and almost ran from the room.

Little Irena came out to meet her at the Pensione Verdi. Isobel sank into a chair under the vine canopy and pulled off her gloves.

'I think you're going to faint,' Irena said accusingly.

'No, I'm not. I've just had a bad shock. Be a good girl and bring me some coffee and a glass of water.'

'Why are you wearing a hat? You never wear a hat. I like your shoes. Are those earrings real pearl or are they glass like the ones the pedlar from—'

'Irena,' Isobel said, unpinning her hat with her eyes closed, 'coffee please. And water. And some paper and an envelope.'

'Who are you going to write to?'

Isobel laid her hat on the table in front of her and put her hands over her face.

'Just send me your mother. Go away and send me your mother.'

Signora Verdi came clucking out of the kitchen. Isobel took her hands from her face.

'It's the heat, Signora, this August heat, none of us can stand it!'

Isobel tried to smile. 'Yes, probably—'

Signora Verdi knew all the gossip. 'And of course you have had so many disagreeable shocks—'

'The worst shock,' Isobel said with sudden sharpness, 'is having all these disgusting, untrue rumours believed by people I thought were my friends!'

'Signora, believe me, I never believed one word, I swear upon Our Lady, you may ask Signor Verdi—'

Isobel said tiredly, 'Please just bring me coffee and water and paper, would you? And leave me alone?'

Signora Verdi retreated to the kitchen in silence. Isobel folded her arms on the table and put her head down on them. It would have been a relief to weep, but she was really beyond weeping. She was stunned; hollow-eyed and dry-mouthed and stunned. An ant appeared on the table top an inch from her eyes and she watched it, mindless and mesmerized, as it began a purposeful progress up her hand and arm, faintly tickling her.

Signora Verdi appeared with a tray and set it silently down.

Isobel raised her head, brushing the ant off. 'Thank you.'

'No trouble, Signora.'

Isobel reached out for the glass of water and drank thirstily.

'Would the signora like me to fetch Doctor Belletti?'

'No. No, thank you. I'm really quite well. I just need to write a letter.'

'Of course,' Signora Verdi said, backing away. 'Just call for me if you would like anything.'

Isobel drew the sheet of paper Signora Verdi had brought towards her. It was the same kind of paper on which she had written to Donatella, reiterating her invitation to her to come to Fontebella, thin white paper with, in Gothic script, 'Pensione Verdi, Fontebella' printed across the top, in brown, beside a tiny sketch of the vine-covered terrace. She took a pencil out of her handbag.

Dear Patrick, *she wrote rapidly*, I don't know where you are, and you may not get this for months, but I have to write to somebody because I am in despair. Giovanni and Donatella are in the process of taking their revenge upon me, with a widely circulated series of lies, the chief of which is that I left him because I was having – and am still having – an affair with you. This has brought the British Consul to me with Giovanni's offer of an annulment of our marriage – the hypocrisy of this, Patrick, sends me into a rage whenever I think of it – ostensibly to save me from being sued for divorce on the grounds of my adultery with you, but in reality to leave him sole owner of La Crocetta and thus the recipient of all the grants and subsidies the fascists are handing out to blackguards like him. The other reason, of course, is to avenge himself upon me. But the worst is yet to come. I have to leave the castle. The mayor, whether he believes these revolting falsehoods or not, says he cannot, in these days of rising nationalism, allow a foreigner of even rumoured dubious morality to inhabit the town's most historic and significant building. I am to be gone by the New Year. I don't really know what to write to you, Patrick, I don't even know what I want of you. But you should know what is being said so falsely and wickedly about you, and you should also know that your friend, Isobel, has seldom been so friendless. I shall revive, I know, I always do, but today I write to you from the depths of the blackest pit.

She did not read the letter through, she simply signed it, baldly, 'Isobel'. Then she folded it, and put it into its envelope and addressed it to Patrick at the Poste Restante in Florence.

She went home slowly, through the blazing midday heat. The market was putting itself away as she walked through it and she paused to buy, almost without thinking, a basket of apricots simply because they looked so beautiful, glowing in their nest of vine leaves, as the hen had glowed, earlier that morning, against the

304

green grass. Holding the basket tenderly, Isobel went on up the steep and narrow streets towards the castle, her heart within her as heavy as lead. What, if anything, was she to say to Emilia? And to all her family? Was merry little Mario to be turned out of what had become his home because of Giovanni and Donatella's malice?

The climb up the rock was almost unbearable. Isobel felt as if she were eighty, going step by painful step up the zigzag path, hearing her breath thudding in her ears, and feeling the lawn of her dress begin to cling to her back. At the top she paused, panting, and turned, as she always did, to look down on the tumbled russety roofs and the graceful bell towers of the churches and the loop of gleaming river before the fields and hills began. Usually the sight gladdened her heart; today it smote her like a sharp pain.

She turned and opened the great door into the blessed dim coolness of the entrance hall. Mario was waiting for her, as he so often was, using some sixth sense, like a dog's, of her impending return. He was full of excited importance, jumping round her like a puppy.

'*Padrona! Padrona!*' Mario cried. '*Padrona*, the lady has come!'

Chapter Thirty-six

'I am Muriel,' the lady said.

She was sitting in the only comfortable chair in the *salone*, and she looked quite at home. She was smiling.

'Muriel—'

'Your stepmother,' the lady said. She got up and came over to Isobel. She was shorter than Isobel, and plumper, and her hair was cut short and waved at the sides. 'Your stepmother, Muriel.'

Isobel said, almost in a whisper, 'What are you doing here?'

'I've come to see you, of course,' Muriel said. 'Because of all the horrible stories that Florence is fizzing with. I said to your aunt and your father, "How do you suppose poor Isobel is bearing up with all these things being said about her?" and they would do nothing, so I decided that *I* would. And not before time. Would you give me a kiss?'

Isobel leaned forward slightly. There, before her, was the face from that long ago newspaper, that happy confident face under the curly fringe and the hat with the sticking-up feathers, a bit older, a bit less buoyant, but still the same face.

'Good,' said Muriel, kissing her. 'You look all in.'

Isobel nodded. She didn't seem able to speak.

'I'm sure I've given you a frightful shock,' Muriel said, 'I really should have done it years ago, but your father insisted we wait for the first move from you, so we waited and waited – I'm not blaming you, mind – and then we got out here because Jean suddenly takes it into her head to leave the estate to the children, and I find that you're up to your neck in a beastly scandal and I said to Edward,

306

"Now I'll *bet* there's no-one for that poor child to turn to, true or untrue," and you know what he's like, good as gold unless you ask him to *do* anything, so I thought, "Come on, Muriel, she can't bite you," and I came.'

Isobel said, blurting the word out, 'Untrue.'

'What, dear?'

'Untrue,' Isobel said, suddenly afraid she was going to break down. 'They're untrue. All the stories. They're hideous and untrue and nobody believes me and they're going to ruin me—'

'My dear—'

'They are,' Isobel said, beginning to cry, despite herself, 'they are, they are!'

'Come now,' Muriel said. She moved forward and put her arms round Isobel. 'You cry then,' Muriel said, patting and soothing, 'you have a good cry.'

Isobel put her head down on Muriel's shoulder. She smelled of rose geranium, and the silk crepe of her dress was cool to Isobel's exhausted face. It was terrible, but now she had started crying she couldn't seem to stop, the tears were flooding out of her as they had flooded all over Patrick on the hillside above La Crocetta when he had said to her, of Gianni, 'Just let the longing come!' This was different in that this wasn't grief but it was another kind of despair, and Isobel, fast in the arms of the woman she had refused to meet for over fifteen years, was giving way to it with relief and thankfulness.

It was minutes before she could stop. She finally took her face away from Muriel's shoulder and said, 'I never used to cry, you know. But this year, I can't seem to stop.'

Muriel offered her a handkerchief edged with lace. 'That's hardly much use, but it's better than nothing.'

There was a knock at the door.

'Come!' Isobel called, blowing.

'Excuse me, *Padrona*,' Emilia said, opening the door, 'but may I assume that the signora is staying for lunch?' She took in Isobel's tear-stained face. 'Oh *Padrona*, whatever is the matter, what has upset you so?'

Isobel tried to smile. 'I'm better now, Emilia, thank you.' She looked at Muriel. 'I hope you *will* stay for lunch?'

Muriel nodded. She smiled broadly at Emilia. 'I most certainly will. It's been quite a journey from Fiesole in this heat. Now, we need a respectably-sized handkerchief for your mistress and I would gladly commit murder for a jug of iced water.'

Emilia looked at Isobel, waiting for a translation. The *padrona* might have just finished a storm of weeping, but for all that she looked hardly despairing.

'Some iced water,' Isobel said in Italian, 'and lemonade, please, Emilia. Lunch will certainly be for two.' She hesitated a moment and then she said, with a kind of shy pleasure, 'Emilia, this is my stepmother.'

Emilia laid a table for them in the shady coolness of the loggia. She had made a risotto, and a salad, and brought the apricots Isobel had bought in the market on a glass dish, but still in their nest of green vine leaves. Muriel, looking at the pale wine in the bubbled glasses and then out through the loggia arch at the hot, still courtyard with its flowers and leaves, and the statue and the battlements and the rolling view visible through the breach in the wall opposite, said she thought this was probably as close to paradise as one was allowed on this earth.

'I know,' Isobel said.

'My dear, why sound so lugubrious about it?'

'Because I have to leave. Because of the scandal.'

Muriel put down her forkful of risotto. 'What can you mean?'

'Because a rising sense of Italian patriotism and nationalism under the fascists, the mayor says, makes it impossible for a town like this to tolerate a foreigner of less than impeccable morality occupying its most significant building.'

Muriel thought about this. She ate her forkful of risotto, drank a mouthful of wine and regarded Isobel with a look that, while affectionate, was also speculative.

'My dear—'

'Yes?'

'Are your morals impeccable?'

'What do you mean?'

'*Have* you had an affair with this young painter? I adore his father's work. I'd have given anything, when I was younger and slimmer, to have been painted by Francis Fleming.'

'No,' Isobel said, with emphasis.

'I only ask,' Muriel said slowly, turning her wine glass by its stem, 'because I wish you to know that even if the rumours *had* been true, I'd still have come to your aid, if I could. After all, look at me, veteran of one of the noisiest scandals before the war, and now so stout and respectable! Who am I to throw stones? After all, Isobel, I *was* guilty, the stories about me *were* true. I was a married

308

woman and I wanted another woman's husband. So I took him. As you know.'

Isobel laid her fork down. She gazed at Muriel.

'I was married, quite young, to a bachelor friend of my father's. I was longing to be married. After all, what were girls of my generation to do *but* get married? And Ernest was quite handsome and quite kind and quite rich, and he seemed to find me captivating, and my parents were all for it. I was an only child, like you, and they never could see that I had grown up, so a much older husband was ideal for keeping me, as it were, in the nursery. I didn't dislike Ernest, Isobel, you couldn't dislike anyone so pleasant with such a fair mind, but life with him was stifling. Boring, limited and stifling, cramped by endless little habits and routines and fusses. I met your father at a Royal Academy Summer Exhibition. We were both looking at Sargent's portrait of Lord Ribblesdale. Your father said, "Would you like to bear such a name as Ribblesdale?" and I said, "I'd prefer to be called anything in the world rather than Mrs Ernest Bond," and that was it. Love. Right there in the middle of a Tuesday afternoon in the Royal Academy.' She paused and then she said, 'Would you rather I stopped telling you this?'

Isobel had cupped her chin in her hands. 'No.'

'Because your father had played baccarat with the King when he was Prince of Wales, and shot with him now and then, of course it became a *cause célèbre*. I wish I could say I minded that, that my womanly modesty prevailed, but it didn't. I wanted your father as I had never wanted anything in my life before'—

Isobel closed her eyes, briefly. Oh, Giovanni, oh that passion for Giovanni . . .

—'and, in truth, I was almost exhilarated by the attention. I didn't feel wicked, I just felt elated. Now is the moment for you to say to me, "What about my mother?" '

To her astonishment, Isobel wanted to smile.

'Do you think,' Muriel demanded, 'that she really died of a broken heart?'

'No,' Isobel said. 'You and my father made her bitterly unhappy but she died of pneumonia.'

Muriel took a sip of water. 'I would never consciously make anyone unhappy now, but we are careless and greedy when we are young. I wanted you to come and live with us when your mother died, I begged and pleaded. But we could do nothing, you see, because of your mother's will.'

Isobel said slowly, 'My mother didn't know how to be other than

309

she was. I wasn't the kind of daughter she wanted, but she was stuck with me. As I was with her. I think, now, that we did love one another, in our way.'

'Of course,' Muriel said. She put a hand out to Isobel. It was small and plump, and it wore an emerald and diamond ring much too big for it. 'There are all kinds of ways of loving.'

Isobel took her hand. It was very soft. Isobel's hand, coarsened by her decorating and gardening activities, was far from soft.

'I'm going to deal with Jean, you know,' Muriel said, giving Isobel's hand a little squeeze and gently dropping it.

'Oh—'

'It's ridiculous. She's just being absurdly stubborn now. She won't have you mentioned and there are no photographs of you on the surface, but all the drawers are crammed with pictures and mementoes of you, and if she isn't thinking of you for three-quarters of the day, then I'm a stuffed parrot. Does it distress you that my three should have the Villa Calvina?'

Isobel said uncertainly, 'No—'

'You mean that it does. Heaven knows, I'd mind if I were you. I think we must come to some arrangement. I shall talk to Edward.'

'No,' Isobel said, 'no, don't. I really don't mind, so long as – I don't have to give this up, and as I do have to, I find that I have begun to mind again about the Villa Calvina. But it will pass.'

Muriel rose from her chair and went to lean on the low wall of the loggia. 'I don't,' she said, with her back to Isobel, 'like your mayor's reasons. Even if they were true, I wouldn't like them.' She turned to Isobel. 'All this talk of morality! Hogwash, you know, utter hogwash, if even a fraction of what Edward says about the level of corruption in Italian officialdom is true. I wonder what it is that the mayor is really saying to you?'

'He's very ambitious,' Isobel said, 'he wants to rise in the party. He wants to do things that will make him noticed and I suppose evicting a foreigner who might be a bad influence on local morals might be noticeable.'

Muriel said thoughtfully, 'Quite. But in these matters, these moral matters that always so stink of hypocrisy and self-serving, everyone always has their price.' She looked down at Isobel. Her eyes were bright with something close to mischief. 'Offer him something!'

'What?'

'Offer him something! Offer him something he can't refuse because it will benefit Fontebella, something the fascists would approve of, something for the people!'

'And?' Isobel said, leaning forward.

'Offer him this thing,' Muriel said, clapping her hands together, *'in exchange for the castle.'*

Isobel stared at her.

'Doesn't matter what it costs,' Muriel said, 'does it? You can live here for almost nothing and I'm sure you aren't like your dear papa, behaving as if a lack of limitless money was some kind of mortal illness.'

Isobel rose unsteadily from her chair. 'Muriel. You're wonderful.'

'No, I'm not, I'm merely practical. And I felt—' she paused. She looked at Isobel, and then away from her, up into the vaulted stone ceiling of the loggia. 'I felt I owed you something. At the least, you see, I was not a helpful ingredient to your childhood, nor, I think, to your growing up.'

'But my parents were never happy, not, that is, after the first year or two—'

'No. But I precipitated things. My presence drove your mother to be completely adamant and you to be rigidly loyal first to her and then to her memory. When I have dealt with Jean, will you come and meet my children?'

Isobel smiled. 'Yes—'

'I am delighted. And now, what I would like is to meet every inch of your castle and its grounds.'

In the early evening, Isobel walked Muriel down through the little town to the station. Muriel would catch a train to Florence, where she would then telephone the Villa Calvina and Roberto, who had decided to stay in Aunt Jean's employ after all, and marry Chiara's younger sister, would drive down in the new Bugatti to meet her. Aunt Jean, who had always professed herself violently opposed to such manifestations of progress as electricity, the telephone and the internal combustion engine, had suddenly bought herself a Bugatti.

'She loves it,' Muriel said. 'She would have Roberto sleep with it if she had her way. And if her passion is so much as mentioned, she becomes very indignant and shuts herself away to do the farm accounts.'

'She always did that,' Isobel said, 'whenever she was cross.'

The little train came puffing into the station in a hiss of steam.

'I shall write to you,' Muriel said, 'and you must telegraph me with any news. I shall also set the Florentine tom-toms sounding with news of your innocence and injury.'

She climbed in, her plump legs and neat little feet twinkling up

311

the high metal steps of the carriage. A moment later, her face appeared at the window. 'My dear, I never asked! What are you going to do about Mr Fleming?'

Isobel smiled up at her. 'There's nothing I can do. I wrote to him this morning, but he may not get the letter for months. He's like a wandering minstrel. He's not the kind of man one can *do* anything about.'

The guard in his splendid operetta uniform blew his whistle.

'All the same—' Muriel cried.

The train began to move. Isobel ran alongside it, waving and smiling.

'All the same,' Muriel called again, 'a castle isn't quite enough for happiness, on its own!'

The train hissed again, and squealed and gathered speed. Isobel, running out of platform, slowed down, waving in response to the gloved hand from the carriage window until it was borne away around a curve of the hill and vanished from view.

'If you don't get to know your own family,' Patrick had said to her, 'you're a damned fool.' Looking down the railway line, at the point where the shining track snaked away into the hills, Isobel raised her hand to her lips and blew a grateful kiss.

Chapter Thirty-seven

The weather broke. Thunderclouds, pushed upwards by the hills and mountains to the north, came rolling and booming over Fontebella, grape-coloured and discharging torrents of rain. It remained extremely hot, and the first great drops from the skies fell hissing on to the stones of the castle courtyard like oil poured in a hot pan. In the brief breaks between storms, an eerie quiet fell on the sodden countryside, and plumes of steam rose from the vegetable garden and the vineyard and the olive grove, giving it all a jungly air, so that Isobel, squelching along to inspect for possible damage by the heavy rain, would not have been surprised to meet a monkey swinging through the grapes or a parrot squawking in an olive tree.

At night, when the rain fell in cascades past her window, and the lightning darted into the room and lit up, in a brief flare of light, its rough white walls and deeply coffered ceiling, she lay awake and listened. She heard the rain, running and thudding and trickling, and she imagined it out there in the warm wet darkness, soaking into the grateful earth, sliding down the rocks, washing clean the roofs and gutters of the dusty summertime town. While she listened, she was also thinking. This period of rain was a good time for thinking.

It was, for all its thunderous drama, as if the rain had calmed her. Perhaps she had, along with the mounting heat of late summer, allowed her own emotional temperature to rise to a point where she could no longer even think straight. There was no doubt but that she had been on the point of hysteria the day she had returned

313

from the town hall and found Muriel in the *salone*, smiling and determined in her eau-de-nil crêpe de Chine. She marvelled at that day, at Muriel's courage – almost audacity – in coming to the castle. But Muriel had come in a spirit of true generosity, because she was moved out of real compassion and a strong sense of injustice, to offer help to Isobel, even at the risk of being brusquely rejected. And she had helped. She had believed Isobel and she had restored to her not just a sense of purpose, but a sense of being both valued and loved. Lying in her cherub bed, listening to the rain beating on the castle walls, Isobel smiled wryly. She had always been afraid she might be like Muriel, if she met her. Now she knew. She had been right to be afraid, except that there was no need to be afraid now. Muriel had shown herself, in one short meeting, to be unlike almost anyone else in Isobel's life. Muriel wanted nothing from Isobel except a little affection; she didn't want charm or obedience or money or support or dutiful respect. On the contrary, she wanted to give, she had made that perfectly plain. If Isobel would allow her, Muriel wished to give her love.

She had written to Isobel, two days after her visit. It was an affectionate, cheerful letter, full of praise for the castle and delight at having met Isobel. There had been two opening skirmishes, she reported, in Campaign Aunt Jean, not wholly successful, but not discouraging either. 'I have to find a way of saving her face while she climbs down, if you see what I mean,' she wrote. 'Difficult, but not impossible, and I shan't return to Scotland in September without a resounding victory.' She enclosed a photograph. It was of three children on a rock in a wild moorland landscape. There was a big boy, in a kilt, gripping a thumb stick and glaring at the camera. There was a smaller one, standing by him, wearing knickerbockers and a big tweed cap, and grinning. Sitting at their feet was a girl with her knees drawn up and her arms clasped round them, and a good deal of untidy fairish hair escaping from a cap like her brother's.

'Angus, Robert and Flora,' Muriel wrote, 'taken this spring, at Lindsay, on the moor. Angus and Flora are quite clever but Robert, bless him, is just cheerful.'

Isobel studied the photograph hard. Angus's expression, sturdy to the point of resentfulness, reminded her strongly of how she had often felt, at his age. Robert, beaming under his cap, resembled his father, and Flora, whose expression carried more than a hint of mischief, was strikingly like Aunt Sybil. It gave Isobel a strange sensation, looking at those three faces that bore her own name and

314

had been photographed in a place that bore her name also. There they were, the three of them, flesh and blood Lindsays, as real as she was herself, as full of feelings about themselves and their parents as she had been. And they all belonged together, just as Patrick had said they did, these young Lindsays and Isobel. When she had been only a year older than Flora was now, Isobel reflected, Ida had died. She peered at Flora's tiny photograph face. It was extraordinary to think of herself at that age, extraordinary to think that when she knelt in her long ago London schoolroom gazing at her father's photograph in the newspaper, Flora, her half-sister, waited there in the future, like another dimension to Isobel herself.

She wedged the photograph into the frame of the looking glass in her bedroom. Emilia, burning with curiosity, studied it carefully every time she dusted. No doubt the *padrona* would tell her everything in good time, though she did wish there were some things she would make up her mind about. The chief thing, of course, was the future.

There was no way in which Emilia, her kitchen open to all-comers, could have escaped the gossip about Isobel. At first, she had been much shocked, and had hurried up the mountain behind Fontebella to the little shrine of Our Lady, who had given such guidance to her before. It was just before the rains came, and Emilia had knelt, in the evening light on the stony path before the shrine and explained her problem. The *padrona*, she said, was a good *padrona*, but there were these sinful stories circulating, and, to be honest, Signor Fleming *had* stayed in the castle for a week and he *had* – Emilia had seen it with her own eyes – kissed the *padrona* goodbye in the way you do not kiss someone if they are just a kind acquaintance. Yet Emilia knew, could swear to it, that Signor Fleming had slept in his own bedroom on another floor, even, from the *padrona*'s room, and he had been in it every morning when she had taken him his tea and his shaving water. But there was Mario. He and Emilia would never find a better place to live – two rooms to themselves, that beautiful kitchen – nor such freedom for both of them, but, however wonderful, it was not worth it if Mario was to be, in any way, injured. Mario was her first duty, she told the Virgin, and his moral well-being must come before everything, even his immediate happiness. She had promised her dying husband that.

She looked beseechingly up at the little figure in the shrine. The sun was almost gone behind the western hills and Emilia thought, sniffing the air like the good countrywoman that she was, that

315

she could smell rain on the breeze. She had left Mario in the care of Uncle Ulysse, who was mending a wheelbarrow, and although Uncle Ulysse loved children and was good with Mario, Emilia never liked to be away from him for too long.

'Please, Madonna,' Emilia said, her hands clasped before her, 'tell us whether we should go or stay?'

The sun sank lower, and a rosy light crept across the hills and touched the little figure in the shrine. Emilia kept very still. As she waited, a large and handsome stag beetle climbed the whitewashed roof of the shrine, slowly and ponderously, and when he reached the top, he paused and turned, apparently looking directly at Emilia.

'If he goes on,' Emilia told herself, 'I must go on. If he turns back, I shall stay.'

The beetle remained poised there for some moments, waving his feelers. Then he turned, as if to proceed on his journey, and Emilia caught her breath.

'Please,' she whispered.

He had heard her. He stopped again, considered for a second or two, and then turned himself slowly round and went back the way he had come, into the thyme bushes, behind the shrine.

Emilia let out a gasp of relief. She leaned forward, touching the Virgin's tiny plaster feet, just showing from the hem of her robe, and gabbled a prayer of gratitude. Then she scrambled to her feet and hurried back down the mountain, to find Mario playing at being a pirate with the wheelbarrow as his ship and a copy of the local newspaper, *Popolo di Fontebella*, folded into a cocked hat. Emilia had kissed him, told him he was the darling of her heart and that he should have gnocchi for supper, and had then sped across the darkening courtyard to find Isobel, in the *salone*, and tell her that she, Emilia Buffalini, was going to ignore all scurrilous tales and remain in Isobel's service.

Isobel had not reacted as she had expected. She had been grateful, but she had also seemed surprised that Emilia, of all people, should have believed a syllable of the gossip.

'After all, Emilia, you have been with me all these months. You have seen, with your own eyes, how innocently I live!'

Emilia's joy and relief had become tinged with a little shame. She bent her head and played, rather self-consciously, with the hem of her apron. But then the *padrona* had said something much more startling, something that swept away all her old anxieties in the face of a new and greater one.

'In any case,' Isobel had said, 'it isn't a case of whether just you

316

and Mario go or stay. It's all of us. The mayor has told me I must leave the castle by the end of the year.'

It took Isobel an hour to comfort Emilia. She had got it into her head that she had been in some way, by even slightly believing the stories, responsible for Isobel's coming eviction, and she was consumed by remorse. Isobel had soothed her as best she could, assuring her that all was not yet lost, if only they could think of the right thing to offer the mayor to take his mind off the possible affront to the moral purity of Fontebella. At last, and only when a weary small pirate appeared enquiring plaintively for his gnocchi, Emilia was persuaded to take her apron from her face and return, with as optimistic a heart as possible, to the kitchen. Isobel watched her as she went, Mario holding her hand and brandishing his paper hat, and reflected miserably to herself that she would never again have a situation as perfect as this, the castle, Emilia and Mario and all their smiling family, accepting her as both their mistress and their friend.

It was that night that the rains had begun. Isobel had been woken in the night by the noise, and woke again in the dawn to a very different world, warm and grey-skied and dripping. Gino had been enchanted. Rain now, he said, and then September sunshine for the grapes, would be perfect. The earth below the vines looked dark and succulent, veiled with tiny new weeds, and the grass that Gino had hoped to cut for hay lay flattened and tawny against the earth. It was hard to think that this first vintage of hers, which she had so longed for, would be her last, and the same for the making of the oil from her olive grove. No doubt – she was trying, these long, wet, solitary days, to think as positively as she could – she would have other vines, other olive trees, but that was not just now sufficient consolation for the loss of these vines and these olive trees. She roamed the *podere*, a sack thrown over her head to keep out the wet as Gino did, trying not to tell herself that the castle had realized exactly the Virgilian dream that La Crocetta had failed to do, and that the injustice of having it taken away from her for something she hadn't done was almost more than could be borne.

She acknowledged to herself too, secretly, that it would have been a comfort beyond everything to have heard from Patrick. No doubt he was still on the shores of Lake Garda, painting away and wholly oblivious of the storms, in every sense, that had rocked Fontebella. What a relief it would have been to have had him here, at her side, furiously denying these rumours, publicly defending her innocence

317

and denouncing the Foscos' desire to revenge themselves upon Isobel for removing her person and her bank account from their grasp! And he would be so pleased about Muriel and the prospect of a family reunion and so aghast at the mayor's outrageous demand. Isobel could picture him in the town hall, waving his arms and bellowing at the mayor in his extraordinary Italian, as picturesque and untidy as his clothes. If only . . . She stopped herself. It was no good even thinking 'if only', of Patrick. Patrick, loyal of heart and fierce of feeling, was, if anyone ever was, a free and independent spirit.

On the fourth day, the storms exhausted themselves over Fontebella and rolled slowly away to the south. The sun, obscured by menacing clouds for so long, came out in the afternoon, and the sky cleared miraculously, leaving the day blue and gold and shining. In the early evening – always her favourite time of day – Isobel went across the damp courtyard, its stones thick with wet, scattered geranium petals, and down the steps to the *podere* on what had become a little recent ritual of inspection. The air felt soft and clean, and the swallows had emerged again, swooping like little dark arrows across the dusky sky.

There was no-one in the *podere*. Gino and his boy had gone home and the damp, warm slopes stretched away below Isobel, empty and briefly hers. She went down among the olive tres, laying her hands on the gnarled and twisted old trunks and peering upwards, where the fruit hung, dark and shining among the grey-green leaves. These would soon be picked, Gino said, in the Tuscan fashion, rather than being left until they dropped of their own accord. If you did that, he said, you got an oil that was too fat, too acid. Isobel's olives would be stripped by hand, and put on the great flat trays she had seen at La Crocetta, and taken off on ox-carts to the nearest press, owned by Uncle Ulysse's wife's brother, and as primitive in type, by the sound of things, as the press in the cellar at La Crocetta had been.

Isobel thought of all the work, all the stripping of the olives – Emilia's entire family had declared themselves ready for this – and the grinding and the pressing, day and night, with feverish speed until the exhausting job was done. She thought of other olive groves, those groves spread across the hills all around Fontebella, each one representing the same back-breaking toil, year in, year out, to produce the oil on which the district depended. Then, her hand upon the rough, dark bark of the nearest tree, a thought struck her, a thought so promising that she found she had taken her hand away

318

from the trunk and had flung her arms around the tree instead. She would offer the mayor something for Fontebella, just as Muriel had suggested she should, she would offer him something that he could not turn down because he would have the fury of the people to answer to if he did. She would offer Fontebella its own modern olive press, a co-operative for all the town and its district to use. She would give them Giovanni's dream of white-tiled rooms where electric presses and separators did the work of a hundred weary men and a dozen blindfolded donkeys. She would be the benefactor of Fontebella, she would make it the first town in the area to own such a marvel, she would do for the working country people exactly what she had always hoped and planned to do! And in return, she would say to the mayor, in return, all I want is for you to let me buy the castle.

Chapter Thirty-eight

Florence was like an oven, even by mid-morning. Even on the station concourse, under the shelter of the roof, people were exclaiming to one another fretfully about the heat and fanning themselves with newspapers. The headlines, as far as Isobel could see, proclaimed the discovery of a wonderful tomb in Egypt, the tomb of a boy king called Tutankhamun, buried with fabulous golden treasure. How cool a tomb would be, Isobel thought, stepping out into the smiting heat, how cool and dark and peaceful.

Emilia had made her bring a sunshade. Emilia, bursting with pride at being the servant of Fontebella's new benefactress, was being so solicitous about Isobel just now that she sometimes felt she could hardly breathe. The kitchen fairly seethed with people, all anxious for a glimpse of this English lady who had, overnight, been transformed in the eyes of Fontebella from sinner to saint on account of this wonderful promised gift of a co-operative olive press. It was said that no other town for fifty, even a hundred miles had such a thing. Everyone knew something about it. They knew where it would be sited – a choice of a dozen places – and had nephews or cousins working in the only factory in Milan known to produce these sophisticated miracles, and had been in some ingenious way or other responsible for suggesting to the beleaguered Signora Lindsay that such a thing as an electrically driven olive press was the very thing to appease the mayor and the Commune.

Those who had olive groves already boasted of their future increased productivity; those who hadn't, declared that they had always intended to have one and would start planting immediately. Complete strangers stopped Isobel in the streets and the market square and said congratulatory, grateful things to her. The mayor was seen to bow to her, in public, and offer her a basket of white peaches, grown by his wife. Emilia was ecstatic, and fiercely protective. She allowed Isobel's new admirers to glimpse her from the open kitchen door as she crossed the courtyard in her breeches and straw gardening hat, carrying a trug of twine and tools. Everyone was much amazed. How young she was, how very charming, how strange that she should not be married, how stranger still that she should dress not like a rich and bountiful lady, but like an Italian workman. They left presents for her, a pumpkin, two bantam hens with their feet tied together, a fresh carp from the river wrapped in leaves, a jar of tiny goat's cheeses floating in olive oil. Isobel, charmed and heart-warmed by all this grateful attention as she was, found it made her feel shy. Conscious of eagerly following eyes, she preferred to remain out of sight, gardening and reading and, for a good deal of the time, simply rejoicing, from a full heart, in the knowledge that the castle would soon be hers.

Its purchase, and the great olive press, would, of course, seriously deplete her capital. But she thought Muriel had been right to advise her to regard the possession of the castle as her priority. All else would then fall into place beside it. Muriel had been right about other things besides, very right, particularly about Aunt Jean. If Muriel hadn't been so right, Isobel would not now be walking through Florence in the blue and cream lawn dress she had had made to impress the mayor, under the sunshade Emilia had insisted upon, on her way to the tram stop for Fiesole. Muriel had persuaded Aunt Jean that her children would be quite unable to accept the Villa Calvina unless the rift with Isobel was healed.

'I told her she owed it not so much to my children nor to you,' Muriel had written, 'as to that magnanimity of heart and great benevolence for which she has been known and loved these thirty years along the Florentine hills. I told her she owed it to Sybil's memory and to her husband's, who had, by his own generosity, enabled her to live as she has done, independent and dignified, since his death. She was very indignant with me, I'm afraid, and declined to speak to me throughout one whole evening, but this morning she sent Moody to me with the message that I may as well invite you. Not a graciously expressed victory, my dear Isobel, but beggars can't be choosers.'

Deliberately, Isobel made a detour from the station past the door of the Lungarno Acciaioli that led to Professor Vaccari's old rooms. She looked up the stucco façade of the building to the first floor windows, with their wonderful view of the river at which he had never glanced, and saw that they had been polished and that a row of geraniums in pots stood along the sill where piles of dusty books had once been, in tottering heaps, and that a canary in a cage hung above them. It looked trim and domestic, but Isobel regretted the loss of the dust and the scholarship. 'We have a long way to travel together,' Professor Vaccari had said to her doubtful, stolid eleven-year-old self, 'and we shall pick a great many beautiful flowers along the way.' And weeds as well, as it had turned out, Isobel thought ruefully, though the weeds had been of her own choosing. She raised a hand to her lips, as she had done to Muriel's departing train, and blew a grateful kiss to the memory of Professor Vaccari, scholar, teacher and friend to friendless children. Then she turned away, and, making for the shady side of the narrow streets, walked towards the tram stop.

The gates of the Villa Calvina were open, and newly painted. Beyond it, the steep drive was raked, weed free, and edged with clumps of bright orange French marigolds, a flower Aunt Sybil would never have permitted, declaring them, along with lobelia and begonias, to be fit only for municipal gardens in provincial towns. Isobel started up the slope, her feet crunching on the gravel in the silent heat. They would, of course, expect her to arrive for lunch in a taxi; not even Muriel would have guessed how necessary it was for Isobel to arrive in exactly the way she had always returned from Florence, before the fateful day when she had done so to find the Fosco family paying their respects as newcomers to Fiesole in the *sala degli uccelli*.

At first sight, the terrace seemed empty, and the great striped canvas awnings were pulled out in front of the lower windows of the house, against the sun. The pots along the terrace still contained their citrus trees, but were now interspersed with other pots, full of kaffir lilies, scarlet as blood.

'Jean!' Isobel could hear Aunt Sybil saying, 'have you taken leave of your senses? We are not some dreary dusty little station in rural India, full of dreadful memsahibs! We are in Italy and I will not have such flowers!'

The kaffir lilies made Isobel smile. They seemed to represent, as the French marigolds did, and the excessive neatness of the paths and lawns, Aunt Jean's stubborn love of order. She stood looking down on the great, gaudy red flowers. They were hideous; hideous, yet somehow endearing.

'Hallo,' someone said.

Isobel, startled, looked up. A boy was standing about four feet away, a boy of fourteen or so, dressed in a shirt and shorts, with long dark smears down his clothes and bare legs as if he had been climbing trees.

'Hallo,' Isobel said. She smiled. The boy looked as if he were about to smile, but hadn't quite managed it. 'Are you Angus?'

'Yes,' he said. He stepped forward and held out a hand. 'How do you do.'

They shook hands gravely.

'I am your half-sister.'

'Yes,' he said. 'I know. Mother says you have a castle too, but it doesn't leak as much as ours.'

'It might,' Isobel said, 'I haven't tried it in winter yet. It might leak like a sieve.'

He nodded. The tentative smile shot across his face like lightning and vanished again. 'It's pretty hot here. And there's nowhere to swim. The river's too far.'

'I grew up here,' Isobel said, 'but I wasn't really allowed to swim anywhere. It wasn't thought proper. I didn't swim until I was older than you and taken to the seaside.'

Unexpectedly, he held a hand out to take hers. 'You'd better come and meet the others. Take my hand because we've made a camp and the ground's a bit rough and you've got hopeless shoes on, like Mother wears.'

Isobel put her hand in his, longing to squeeze it. 'I wore them to be polite to Aunt Jean.'

He nodded again. His own feet were bare, and streaked with dried mud. His hand, holding hers firmly, was rough and warm.

'Aunt Jean's a brick,' Angus said, 'giving us all this. But to tell you the truth, I'd rather have Scotland.'

'Wait till you see my castle,' Isobel said, her heart leaping at being able to say it, so possessively.

Angus led her across the lawn behind the terrace and into the wooded slopes behind the house, the tangle of bushes and trees where she had, as a child, played solitary games with imaginary companions. This appealing, solemn boy had no need to imagine companions; he had them for real, a brother and sister, and he was allowed to scramble about freely with bare legs and feet and there was no-one, apparently, to tell him to remember at all times that he was a little lady.

'I'm afraid you'll have to duck,' Angus said, holding aside a curtain of wild clematis creeper. 'Perhaps it would be best if you took off your hat and left it on the grass with that bag and the umbrella thing.'

'At home,' Isobel said, doing what she was told, 'I wear trousers, all the time, because of the garden and the farm.'

Angus looked approving. He took Isobel's hand again, and led her through the creeper curtain, and then over several fallen trees and across several ditches, to a small hot green clearing, where a boy and a girl sat in a primitive shelter made of leafy branches, both dressed as their brother was. They emerged as Angus and Isobel approached and stood before her, smiling and composed without, it seemed, a trace of the shyness she so stupidly felt herself. Angus was plainly the self-appointed master of ceremonies. He indicated his sister.

'This is Flora,' Angus said, still holding Isobel, 'and this is Robert. Flora, you may kiss our sister, but it wouldn't be manly for Robert. You should shake her hand.'

Isobel stooped, bursting with emotion and laughter, over Flora.

'He always talks like this,' Flora said, kissing her as if she had done it all her life, 'you shouldn't take any notice. Robert and I never do. You kiss Robert if you want.'

'May I?' Isobel said to Robert. He was smiling broadly at her, blushing and delighted. She bent and kissed his cheek. He smelled, like his sister, of soap and earth.

'We made you a seat,' Robert said, 'because this is a family camp, you see. Just for Lindsay children. We brought you a cushion because Flora thought you might have to wear a dress and she was right.'

Isobel peered into the shelter. It was hot and dark and smelled of mould. It was also empty, except for four small logs of wood, arranged in a semi-circle. One of the middle logs bore an embroidered cushion Isobel recognized from the chaise longue Aunt Sybil had spent so many hours on, on the loggia. In the centre of the semi-circle was a blue and white towel doing duty as a tablecloth, and on the towel were spread four glasses, a bottle of mineral water and a plate of pink and white marshmallows. A lump rose in Isobel's throat. Four glasses, four logs . . .

'We shall toast those, of course,' Angus said, indicating the marshmallows. 'We rather hoped you would have some matches.'

'I'm so sorry,' Isobel said, her voice shaking, 'I'm so stupid, I never thought to bring any—'

Flora gave her a clear glance. She took her hand. 'It really doesn't matter, you know,' she said encouragingly. 'Really it doesn't. We've done it with sticks before. I'm sure there are plenty of things, apart from lighting fires, that you are jolly good at instead.'

Rubbing sticks together, despite everyone's earnest conviction that it really would work if one persevered, looked doomed to failure as a firelighting method until Isobel remembered that her handbag, though devoid of matches, contained a mirror. Robert was sent back to collect this, from the lawn. Ten minutes later, a spark was encouraged to be a tiny flame and Isobel was solemnly congratulated. She felt she had genuinely achieved something, and hardly noticed that in the energetic business of rubbing and huffing and puffing on all fours, her hair had come down and she had torn her dress and one stocking. The children were solicitous about this, convinced she was in for some kind of nursery ticking-off. Isobel, her face smudged from the fire and her hands and mouth sticky with marshmallow, was too happy to care.

'If anybody scolds me, it will be Moody, and I think, at my age, that she might let me off.'

They nodded. Moody was, in their opinion, a terrible fusspot, pouncing on them constantly with brushes and combs and damp flannels. Muriel never minded about such things; she'd come down hard on you if you were rude and unkind, but she didn't seem to care about unlaced shoes or missing buttons. It looked very much as if this interesting, ready-made elder sister was rather like her.

'Do you think,' Isobel said, standing up and twisting her hair back up into its usual loose knot, 'that we should go into the house? Perhaps, you see, I should let Aunt Jean and' – she paused and then said proudly – 'Father and Muriel know that I'm here.'

'Not yet,' Robert said.

'No,' Flora said.

'She's right,' Angus said regretfully, 'I'm afraid it's only manners, worse luck.'

They collected up the glasses and the empty bottle and the plate and the towel, and stumbled out into the sunlight. All of them were crumpled, all of them had leaves in their hair, and three of them were grubby. Angus stooped gallantly to gather up Isobel's possessions, holding her sunshade over her head like an Indian bearer. Flora wore Isobel's hat, which covered her face as far as her nose.

In stately and ragged procession, the four of them made their way across the lawn to the terrace and up the familiar front steps to the hall.

Once inside, Angus lowered the sunshade. He looked at them all. 'Perhaps we should wash—'

Isobel regarded them. Fifteen years ago, she would never even have considered entering the *sala degli uccelli* without ten minutes of Moody brushing and smoothing and tweaking her into place. But she was not the same Isobel that she had been fifteen years ago; she was a sadder, wiser, more battered Isobel, but she was also an infinitely braver one.

'No,' she said, 'no, I don't think we will wash, just yet. I think we shall go in and see the grown-ups, exactly as we are,' and then she marched forward, leading her little troop.

The furniture in the *sala degli uccelli* was exactly as Aunt Sybil had left it. In her favourite chair, Edward now sat, reading a week-old copy of *The Times*, and opposite him, bursting with merriment, Muriel was pretending to read a catalogue for a fine art sale in Florence, the contents of a palace belonging to an ancient family, fallen on hard times. Between them, as if she were being tactfully imprisoned, and prevented from bolting at the last minute, sat Aunt Jean, upright and stout in her white summer cashmere, peering fiercely through her customary black-rimmed spectacles at a pamphlet on new methods for rearing pigs. She didn't look up as Isobel came in with the children, but looked instead at the pamphlet with increased intensity.

'I'm sorry,' Isobel said loudly, 'that we're all a bit untidy. We've been making a fire, you see, in the woods.'

Edward stood up, crumpling the newspaper onto the floor.

'My darling Isobel,' he said, and held his arms out. Isobel went into them and was soundly kissed. Then she crossed the room to kiss Muriel.

'Now Jean,' Muriel whispered, squeezing her hand.

Isobel stood in front of her aunt. Aunt Jean went on, dedicatedly, reading about the hybridization of pigs.

Isobel stooped. She put her face very close. 'Aunt Jean?'

There was silence.

'Aunt Jean,' Isobel said, 'it's me, Aunt Jean, it's Isobel. Aren't you pleased to see me?'

There was another silence. In it, Isobel stretched out a hand and touched one of the little old hands holding the pig pamphlet.

326

'What I'm pleased about,' Aunt Jean said, suddenly, still not looking up and shaking Isobel's hand off, as if it were a troublesome fly, 'is that at last you've come to your senses! And sense, Isobel Lindsay, is the one good thing you were born with!'

Chapter Thirty-nine

Dusk was falling as the little train climbed up the hills towards Fontebella. In a third class carriage, which was the way she had always preferred to travel, Isobel sat and gazed out at the darkening landscape in a state of near perfect contentment. The afternoon had been spent in a way she had never dared to hope could happen again, pottering round the *podere* at the Villa Calvina with her arm through Aunt Jean's, making gentle conversation about ostensibly agricultural matters though, in reality, about affectionate ones. She had seen again all the old families, had met Roberto's wife and baby, had admired a new hay baler, a promising vintage and a week-old litter of piglets. They had talked of wheat and vines and cheesemaking, and all the time, Aunt Jean's hand lay tucked into Isobel's elbow and gave it, every so often, a little squeeze. When Isobel had kissed her goodbye Aunt Jean announced loudly, as if making a public statement, that when the harvest was over and before the vintage began, she would get Roberto to drive her to Fontebella, in the Bugatti. It would naturally have to be a fine day as the Bugatti was never permitted to be taken out in the rain.

The children had escorted Isobel to the tram stop. Aunt Jean had even offered the precious Bugatti to drive her down to the station, but Isobel preferred the tram. The four of them set out along the white dust road that Isobel could have walked with her eyes closed, and along which she had heard those young country soldier recruits in the war, tramping down to Fiesole and singing their hopeful, patriotic hearts out. She looked at Angus and Robert and uttered a fierce, heartfelt little prayer that such a fate should never overtake them. My brothers, she thought, over and over, her throat constricting, my *brothers*.

Flora held her hand. Flora was everything, Isobel reflected, that Ida would have loved; gay and clever and loving and mischievous. She had Muriel's colouring, and Aunt Sybil's watchful, amused, ironic face. Nobody, as Aunt Jean had pointed out over tea – exactly the same English tea, cucumber sandwiches and Lapsang Souchong, that had appeared every day of Isobel's childhood – had inherited Isobel's bearing or Isobel's teeth.

'They were always,' Aunt Jean had said severely, making everyone laugh, 'your best feature, dear.'

Flora's teeth were charmingly uneven, like Muriel's. Her warmth of heart, so evident in her every word and gesture, was also like Muriel's.

Isobel had had no time alone with Muriel that long and happy day, except for a moment in which Muriel had whispered, 'Any word from Mr Fleming?'

Isobel had shaken her head.

'Never mind,' Muriel had said, smiling, 'there will be other Mr Flemings. Plenty of them!'

Sitting now in the train, dreaming and remembering, Isobel wasn't so sure that Muriel was right. There would probably be other men, but it was unlikely that there would be other Patricks. Of course, Muriel hadn't met him; Muriel simply visualized him as a charming, rather feckless bohemian. He was charming, certainly, in his odd, brusque way, and he was bohemian if that meant someone who dressed like a gipsy, ignored petty social convention and couldn't keep still, but he wasn't feckless. He was, of all people, inclined to take other people seriously, to give them all the freedom he required himself, as well as respect. Apart from Muriel he was, Isobel reflected, the only person in her life who had never asked anything of her, who didn't wish her to fulfil some kind of role in his life that suited him.

She took a deep breath. It was not constructive to think of Patrick. If she thought too much about Patrick, she began to entertain hopes which, try as she might to prevent them, would turn into plans. She had plenty to plan for now, in any case. She had the castle and the olive press and her new-found family and Aunt Jean's impending state visit. It was not only impractical to build castles in the air on top of all these real and happy plans, it was greedy.

The train blew a long announcing blast on its whistle and slowed down for the approach to Fontebella. It was not quite dark, and the town, softly lit by the lamps in its squares and streets and windows, looked like a magical city in a fairy tale, scattered down the hillside. The train clanked over the river bridge and pulled up at the long, low platform where the station master stood, as he always stood, resplendent in his many-buttoned uniform, to greet every train.

Isobel stood up, clutching her possessions, including the little bunch of now wilting wild flowers that Flora had given her, and an extremely crumpled paper bag containing two toffees which Robert had, plainly with much agonizing, thrust into her hand as they parted. They were Scottish toffees, he said, real Scottish toffees and they were his last two. Isobel accepted them gravely and gratefully. One, she thought now, she would give to Mario; the other she would keep as a memento of true, loving generosity.

The station-master held the carriage door open and extended his free hand, gloved in white, to assist Isobel down the steps to the platform.

'Signora Lindsay. I trust you have had a good day.'

His practised Italian eye ran observantly over her torn stocking and untidy hair and the queer little bundle of objects in her arms. Would the English never learn to care about *la bella figura*?

'May I assist you—'

'No, thank you,' Isobel said, clutching the flowers and the toffees even tighter. 'Thank you, but I can manage. I have had an excellent day. I have been to see' – a little proud pause – 'my family.'

'Of course,' the station-master said smoothly, as if one always returned from family visits with torn clothes and one's hands full of rubbish. 'May I summon the taxi, Signora?'

'No thank you,' Isobel said. Her feet were wretched after a day in her unaccustomed shoes, but their wretchedness was overcome by the desire to walk up to the castle as she had done that first sunny morning with Patrick and Donatella, when Patrick had, with his usual sharp intuition, prevented Donatella from going into the castle first.

'Isobel should open the door,' Patrick had said, holding out the key. 'Yes, you should. You go in first. By yourself.'

Isobel closed her eyes for a second and then, conscious that the station-master was watching her for yet more signs of eccentricity he could subsequently report about the town, opened them again. She took off her hat, threaded Flora's drooping flowers through the hat band and replaced it firmly on her head.

'I shall walk,' Isobel said firmly.

'As the gracious signora wishes—'

His mouth shook. Those flowers . . .

'I do wish,' Isobel said and then, with a smile, 'Good night.'

Outside in the little piazza before the station where Fontebella's only taxi waited with its protective rosary swinging from the windshield, the air was warm and sweet. High above, and flickered across by bats, the sky was turning pale blue-green as the light faded. The sounds of Fontebella's evening – mothers calling, the clash of pans, the far-off sounds of someone practising the violin – drifted across the air as timelessly as they had done for four hundred years. Resting her folded parasol on her shoulder like a rifle, Isobel set out alone for home.

She went past the Pensione Verdi, its pavement tables already laid with rough white cloths for the evening, past the town hall where a group of boys lounged smoking on the pink marble steps and past the fountain where the dolphins played on in their streams of water. The market square was almost empty, except for the people sitting on kitchen chairs outside the open doors of their houses, and the cobbles were scattered with bits of rubbish from the stalls that had escaped the broom, leaves and stalks and petals and eggshells. Isobel walked through it all, nodding to the people on their chairs, imagining how she would, soon, bring Angus and Robert and Flora here, and buy them peaches and show them the dolphins.

'I wish—' Isobel said, half-aloud, 'I just wish—'

She looked up, as she always did, approaching the top of the market square, for her first glimpse of the castle, hanging there above the town with its great oil lamp glowing beside the door like a guarding, benevolent eye. How dare I wish, Isobel asked herself, how dare I wish for anything more than what I have had today, and this place, and a good-hearted woman like Emilia waiting for me to come home and remembering to light the lamp? She put a hand up and touched Flora's flowers. Soon Flora would be here. She could tell Emilia about Flora, and Mario too. She could tell Mario that some big boys would be coming to the castle soon, big boys who would allow him to play with them. She would give Mario the toffee, she would . . . She stopped and pressed the backs of her laden hands to her eyes. Stop it, Isobel told herself, stop this snivelling and go *home*.

* * *

331

Mario, for once, wasn't waiting. The lamps were lit all around the courtyard and the herbs in the pots by the well head were giving off their faint, heat-induced, aromatic smells. As she crossed to her rooms, Isobel could see Mario at the kitchen table, wrapped in a big white napkin, spooning something up busily from a bowl. Emilia had her back to Isobel, stirring a pan on the stove.

The lamps had been lit in Isobel's *salone*, too. They cast pools of soft, unsteady light on the few pieces of furniture, the rugs and books and pictures, and on the gleaming polished spaces of the floor. There was a jug of water on a tray, with a spiral of lemon peel in it, and a tumbler beside it and a slice of melon on a plate, under a square of gauze. Dear Emilia. Dear, thoughtful, mothering Emilia.

Isobel took off her shoes and then, raising her tattered skirt hem, unfastened her stockings and rolled them down her legs and off onto the floor. The sensation of bare feet on marble was delicious. She took off her hat too, and her gloves, and shook her hair free. Then she poured herself a glass of water.

There was a knock at the door.

'Signora?'

'Come in,' Isobel said, 'come in, and thank you for everything.'

'I was making the soup,' Emilia said, advancing into the room. 'I was in the middle of chopping, onions and herbs everywhere, when it came! I said to Mario—'

'What came?'

'Why, the telegram!' Emilia said, laying a buff envelope down by the plate of melon. 'I said to Mario, "By our Lady of Heaven, may it not be that the signora's aunt—" '

Isobel said, picking up the envelope, 'My aunt is well, Emilia. I have had a wonderful day with my aunt.'

'Then who can it be? You must open it, Signora. You must indeed. A telegram is an *urgency*, Signora, and this one has been here since this morning.'

Isobel turned it over. There was a smudged stamp on the back, a circle of black and inside the circle, "Post Office. Sirmione." Isobel swallowed. Sirmione. Lake Garda . . . She slid her thumb under the envelope flap, and drew out a small rectangle of cheap cream paper on which strips of a whiter paper had been pasted.

'Is it a death?' Emilia persisted. 'Is it a trouble? What fearful thing has come about that they should send a telegram?'

Isobel, her hands hardly steady, held the telegram towards the light of the nearest lamp.

332

'Horrible,' read the strips of white paper, 'hideous lies saw newspaper shocked and furious coming at once wait for me don't move wait for me evening Tuesday without fail shouldn't have left you coming now wait I beg you Patrick.'

'Signora!' Emilia cried, beside herself with anxiety.

Isobel said, almost in a whisper, 'It isn't anything sad, Emilia. It's – it's Signor Fleming. He's—' she paused and looked up. 'Is today Tuesday?'

'Yes, Signora, today is Tuesday and the festival of the blessed Saint—'

'Then,' Isobel shouted, flinging the telegram into the shadowy spaces of the room, 'he's coming today, tonight, he's on his way, he's – oh Emilia, Emilia, he's coming back!'

Emilia closed her eyes and crossed herself.

'No death, no sickness, no aunt—'

'No! No! Just Patrick!'

'Then I think,' Emilia said recovering herself, 'that it is as well I have made the soup.'

Outside the great door, on the terrace of paving stones between the watching lions, Isobel watched too. She was barefoot still, and her hair, despite Emilia's disapproving cluckings, hung down her back. Below her, under a soft, dark, late summer night sky, Fontebella lay black and secret, with just, here and there, the pink or yellow glow of lamps to mark a street or a square or a window. It was quiet, too, quiet enough to hear the whistle of the last train to come up from Florence for the day, snaking through the hills, as it would do in about twenty minutes' time. Twenty minutes of beautiful, anticipatory happiness here on the warm stones beneath the warm dark sky.

When the train had come and gone, there would be a silence for a time and then, from this vantage point, Isobel would see the lights of the taxi as it threaded its way up the streets, past the Pensione Verdi and the town hall and the fountain, up through the market place and the arch at the top, the lights growing stronger all the time and the growl of the engine louder and closer. And then the taxi would stop, at the foot of the rock, and Patrick would fall out in his usual chaos of bags and boxes and she would say nothing, but just watch him from her eyrie as he shouldered his burdens and climbed the path towards her.

'Wait for me,' the telegram had said, 'don't move wait for me wait I beg you.'

Alone in the lamplit darkness, Isobel laughed aloud. Out of the past, from a hot afternoon in a dusty book-choked room above the slowly sliding Arno, came Professor Vaccari's voice, steady and scholarly and full of love for the words he was reading. 'This is, of course, my dear signorina, late Latin, so we do not look to it for purity of language.'

She could see the twinkle in his eye, smell the rose that Signora Vaccari had given him to put on his desk that day among the cascading clutter of papers.

When the moon's splendour shines in naked heaven,
Stand thou and gaze beneath the open sky.
See how that radiance from her lamp is riven,
And in one splendour foldeth gloriously
Two that have love, and now divided far,
Bound by love's bond, in heart together are.

Two that have love, Isobel told herself exultantly, two bound by love's bond. But not divided far. Not now. Not any more. From several miles away, faint but unmistakable, came the sound of the train's whistle, calling to her, in triumph and reassurance, as it began its slow climb into the hills.